"Oh, Tony,"

"Raoul was n

"Raoul?" Tony stilled his kisses, lifted his head, and gazed toward her face, a face intensely passionate. "Who's he?"

"Oh, nobody."

Tony stroked the side of her thigh. "Your mama never told you not to talk about other guys?" He was too excited to be annoyed . . . yet.

"Oh!" Penelope seemed to snap back to the reality around her. She blinked, then said, "Raoul's not another man. He's, um, he's . . . well, he's a figment of my imagination."

"Uh-huh." Tony didn't feel too impressed by that explanation.

He wanted Penelope to think only of him.

"It's true. He's like a . . . " She waved one hand in a slow circle, as if trying to whisk an explanation out of thin air. " . . . an imaginary lover to keep me from missing things while I've been concentrating on my career."

Such as?"

She sighed and said, "This."

_____

"A treasured find."
Affaire de Coeur

BEDROOM EYES

EYES

HAILEY NORTH

AVON BOOKS  NEW YORK

This is a work of fiction. Names, characters, places, and incidents either
are the product of the author's imagination or are used fictitiously. Any
resemblance to actual events, locales, organizations, or persons, living or
dead, is entirely coincidental and beyond the intent of either the author or
the publisher.

AVON BOOKS, INC.
1350 Avenue of the Americas
New York, New York 10019

Copyright © 1998 by Hailey North
Published by arrangement with the author
Visit our website at http://www.AvonBooks.com
Library of Congress Catalog Card Number: 97-94867
ISBN: 0-380-79895-6

First Avon Books Printing: July 1998

AVON TRADEMARK REG. U.S. PAT. OFF. AND IN OTHER COUNTRIES, MARCA
REGISTRADA, HECHO EN U.S.A.

Printed in the U.S.A.

WCD 10 9 8 7 6 5 4 3 2 1

For my very own Tony-O

With special thanks to the students, faculty,
and staff of Tulane University College
for their patience and support every time I
"take vacation" to write another book.

Chapter 1

Tax attorney Penelope Sue Fields, voted by her senior class most likely to be the first spinster appointed to the Supreme Court, repressed a strong desire to free her plain brown hair from its proper French braid as she stared at the only other occupant of the forty-second-floor express.

She couldn't force her gaze away from the man's smoky dark eyes, half-hidden by hooded lids, eyes that promised passion in a mysterious way that inflamed Penelope's ever-active fantasies. Black slashes of brow added an edge of danger. Smudges beneath the eyes hinted at sleepless nights, nights Penelope just knew must be spent in the most wanton of pleasures.

Wishing the man would turn those eyes in all their glory on her, knowing instead he'd probably continue to stare at the MAXIMUM OCCUPANCY sign, Penelope settled her briefcase, bulging with files, on the floor of the elevator. Men with bedroom eyes never noticed her.

As the elevator sailed downward to the everyday world forty-two floors below, Penelope lost herself in the image of such a man drawing her close, the intense sensuality in those eyes directed solely at her.

1

"Oh, Raoul," she'd whisper, resorting to the imaginary man who always played the leading role in her romantic fantasies. She'd struggle a bit at first, wanting desperately to give in to him, yet fighting the desire all the same. His arms, all male muscle, would tighten around her. The wool of his suit rasped at her breasts, clad only in the silky negligee she'd donned in anticipation of his forbidden nocturnal visit.

Upward edged her chin, his warm fingers guiding her lips inexorably to his. Giving in, she reached one hand around his neck, entwining her fingers in the coal black hair that curled rakishly over the collar of his shirt.

"Oh, Raoul." The only words she could manage were swallowed by his lips, devoured by his tongue. One last time she glanced upward at those remarkable eyes before squeezing her own shut and allowing the wave of passion he'd ignited to crash over her heart.

"Going or staying?"

Penelope ran the tip of her tongue over her lips.

The man with bedroom eyes cleared his throat.

Like an elevator car with a broken cable, Penelope snapped to earth. Her eyes flew open. To her chagrin, the black-haired man looked at her as if she were mildly, if not severely, retarded.

He pointed politely to the open door of the elevator. How long they'd been on the first floor of the office tower Penelope couldn't guess.

Didn't want to, either, or her embarrassment would mount. Gathering her dignity, she hurried forward, sparing neither a word nor a backward glance at the sexy stranger.

When would she learn to control her overactive imagination? Flushed and irritated with herself, Penelope strode in her low-heeled pumps across the marble floor of the Oil Building. As usual, she'd worked late, later than she'd intended, and the crush of workers who staffed the building had long since departed.

She'd agreed to meet David Hinson for drinks at eight at the nearby Hotel Intercontinental, along with some Washington clients. Then they were all having dinner at David's Garden District home.

Her stomach fluttered slightly when she counted the number of times he'd asked her out in the past six weeks, but thoughts of the lawyer caused scarcely a ripple compared to the tumult the complete stranger in the elevator had raised within her.

Therefore, Penelope found it easier to keep her mind within check as she pushed open the glass door that led onto St. Charles Avenue.

The July heat beat at her with the intensity of a wood-burning oven and Penelope shrugged out of her suit jacket. She'd been in New Orleans less than six months, and she could see as clearly as the sky above the Mississippi that she'd have to invest in a new wardrobe. Perhaps, she thought with a whimsical smile, she'd purchase one of the striped seersucker suits she'd seen sprouting like summer pansies in the office.

The suits weren't terribly attractive, especially on women, but Penelope dressed for business, not, she thought ruefully, to catch the eye of men like the guy in the elevator.

Shrugging off that somewhat dismal thought, Penelope slipped her jacket over her arm, then froze. Afraid to look, afraid of what she'd confirm, Penelope slid her gaze to the sidewalk by her feet, patted her shoulder for the familiar comfort of a heavily weighted shoulder strap.

Nothing.

What had happened to her briefcase? She would never leave it in the office.

Then she remembered.

The elevator.

"Puppies, kittens, and cats!" Penelope kicked the sidewalk, then executed an about-face. Her briefcase contained her life, her work, her purse, her—

She gasped and pushed back into the building. Penelope Fields would just die if anyone pawed through her case and found *Love Bites*, her secret cookbook project, the discovery of which would, no doubt, make her the laughingstock of the august firm of LaCour, Richardson, Zeringue, Ray, Wellman and Klees.

Penelope headed straight for the elevator. "Please let it be there," she whispered. She'd give up chocolate for a month if the fates had left it sitting undisturbed. Who'd want a lawyer's briefcase anyway, stuffed with page upon page of paper that paid testimony to the turmoil of people's lives?

The doors to the express elevator stood open. Holding her breath, she peeked inside, picturing exactly the spot where she'd placed it as she'd escaped into her fantasy of the man with bedroom eyes.

Nothing.

All that met her gaze was a coffee stain on the carpet.

If only that man hadn't distracted her. Unreasonably irritated with a man she didn't even know, irritated even more by the knowledge she had herself solely to blame, Penelope whirled around. Someone might have turned it in to Building Security.

Head down, berating herself, Penelope stepped forward.

She sensed someone in her path, too late to keep from barreling into a broad and sturdy chest that didn't even flinch as she hit it in full stride.

Penelope, however, caught off guard, wobbled and might have fallen backward if not for the hand that shot out to steady her, a hand that remained cupped against her lower back.

"Going or staying?" This time the question definitely carried a hint of amusement.

Penelope lifted her head from the wall of chest, clothed respectably in a gray wool suit, blue and white striped shirt, and a tie that—

She squinted, trying to make out what the clearly naked figures on the man's tie were doing, then hastily raised her gaze to meet the stranger's eyes head on. This time she was forewarned. No matter how sensuous an expression she saw on his face, she'd keep her attention planted firmly on planet Earth.

Eyes like dark, loamy earth, a brown so rich it might be black, watched her, a glint in them

Penelope interpreted as mirroring the amusement in his voice. Amusement at her expense.

"I am searching for my briefcase," she said, in a voice designed to remind opposing counsel just who they were up against.

A sweep of warmth, a pressure gentle yet hinting at something much stronger heated her lower back. A matching surge warmed her face. Penelope inched away from him. "Do you mind?"

He grinned, and his eyes glowed even darker.

She turned away. She needed to find Security.

"Don't you want to ask me something before you go?"

What would she ask a man like this? Penelope hesitated. Rough me up? Rip my clothes off and warm my skin with kisses? Tease me. Tickle me. Make me believe reality can be half as good as my fantasies?

She shook her head. Without another glance at him, she moved away.

Footsteps sounded behind her. In a quiet voice, the man said, "Here."

She heard the clunk.

She looked down at the floor, knowing this time she'd find more than a coffee stain.

Her case sat there, but the man had disappeared.

Anthony Olano, better known as Tony-O in his neighborhood, a pocket of New Orleans tucked between Carrollton Avenue and a bend in the Mississippi, eased lower in the seat of his car.

His body moved. His pants did not, snagging

the car's ragged vinyl upholstery. "Shit. My one good suit," he muttered, releasing the threads of the fabric from the rip in the seat. Not that his suit wasn't ruined already, what with the past four hours he'd spent parked outside Hinson's Garden District home, fighting heat, mosquitoes, and a growing desire to abandon his quarry for the sake of taking a leak and grabbing a beer.

Two blocks lakeside of where he'd parked, the streetcar rumbled by. Tony checked his watch. Like the city, the service never stopped. Except of course, for Mardi Gras parades and for the occasional driver foolish enough to turn too sharply into the path of the oldest continuously operating streetcar line in the country.

Anyone who got in the way of that kind of tradition deserved to get his car mangled, Tony figured.

The passing car, the tenth since Tony had begun his vigil, reminded him of the fleeting evening. Much longer and he'd have to pee.

At that moment a figure stepped into the frame of the tall window that opened onto the balcony across the street. Through a sheer curtain, the silhouette of a narrow shouldered man was visible.

And beside the man, a woman.

"Gotcha." 'Bout time, too. His eyes never once straying from the target, Tony hefted his camera fitted with the nighttime telephoto lens.

The window, a typical old New Orleans feature that raised to serve as a passage out to the balcony, scraped upward. The heavy night air didn't even stir the sheer curtain.

Tony took a long look at the man, an even longer look at the woman.

The man he knew well and despised thoroughly. David Hinson was one of those lawyers who gave the whole breed a bad name. Not that Tony wasted much sympathy on lawyers, but ever since his little sister had taken it in her head to go to LSU law school, he'd softened his stance a bit.

But he'd never change his mind about Hinson—despite the fact that if all went according to plan, Hinson would soon be his new employer.

Ironic as it was, Hinson's steady girlfriend, a redheaded court reporter with cleavage that made her a favorite of local judges, had hired the very recently established Olano Investigations to check just why her guy wasn't spending as much time with her as she liked.

Performing his duty to that client, he positioned the camera and began to focus the lens.

The woman on the balcony with Hinson didn't seem his usual fare. Tony had thought that when he'd first studied her in the elevator at the Oil Building, almost believing the girlfriend had her facts confused. No one that pristine should be dating David Hinson, king of the heavy fist.

Even at fifty minutes past midnight, she looked as fresh and perfectly put together as if she'd showered only an hour earlier.

But then, maybe she had, tête-à-tête with Hinson. The other guests had left by cab thirty minutes ago. This woman had been seen now more than a dozen times with Hinson, according to Tony's sniffling client. And Hinson wasn't the kind of guy to keep company merely for stimulating conversation. Any woman hanging around with Hinson had to be putting out. Tony frowned and put his finger on the shutter.

She didn't look the type. Not in that prissy skirt. With her blouse buttoned all the way to the neck. No way to dress for summertime in New Orleans. New in town, or just plain dumb?

Hinson reached for her hand and Tony snapped his first shot. Dumb or not, she was definitely beautiful, he confirmed as he studied her through his lens. The blouse might be fastened as tight as Fort Knox, but the way it clung to her body, rising above a waist he could easily close within his hands, outlining breasts whose fullness was anything but prissy, stirred his interest, exactly the way she'd managed to do earlier when she'd stepped into the Oil Building elevator.

She'd looked just as frosty as she did at this moment, but during that brief contact there'd been moments when her armor had slipped. He'd noticed, all right; but then, he got paid to pay attention.

And he wouldn't have minded paying more attention to the curve of her cheeks. Tony replayed the feel of her under his hand when she'd stumbled into him. Despite her protest, he'd caught a flicker of interest, a hint of passion under that touch-me-not exterior.

Tony shifted in his seat. "You've been alone way too long," he said to himself. To be reacting to a woman who no doubt was as approachable as a mummy in a business suit indicated a serious void in his life.

He needed a woman, a woman as eager to embrace life as he'd once been. But his current situation didn't give him much taste for looking for love.

Sticking to business, Tony took a few more shots. In the few months he'd been running Olano Investigations as a front for his undercover activities, he'd yet to meet one client who didn't claim to want to know the truth.

The adultery business was fairly profitable in Louisiana, where a spouse caught in adultery could be denied alimony. That law accounted for the two wealthy businessmen who'd generously paid him to discover what their wives did to occupy themselves between charity luncheons and visits to beauty salons.

So he gave them what they paid for, but usually he had a feeling they already knew in their guts the truth his pictures would reflect. And it never ceased to amaze him that once faced with that reality, most of them shunted straight into denial.

All in all, not a savory business, and one he'd be glad to be free of.

Hinson, still holding the woman's hand, led her to the edge of the balcony, aiding Tony's view by delivering her into the pool of light cast by a street lamp.

For a woman enjoying a midnight tryst, she looked damn nervous. She smiled, but her eyes remained wary. She laughed softly, but Tony couldn't hear any humor in the sound. He frowned and his frown grew as Hinson pulled her to him, a little roughly for Tony's taste.

Hinson tipped her head back, covered her mouth with his. That ought to rumple her just-pressed look, quiet the phony laughter. For a moment there, he'd felt a link, an instant of empathy and concern, a feeling he'd do well to suppress.

With a shake of his head, Tony lowered his camera and lifted his microphone. This was no time to discover a sentimental streak. He ran a thumb over the cool metal of the supersensitive listening device cradled in his hand. The equipment could pick up moans of passion at well over the distance he'd parked from Hinson's balcony. He held it out his window and hit the record button.

Not the noisy type, Tony decided, watching the woman pull free of the grope. Probably not a screamer. Though you never could tell with those prim and proper females. Her hair, captured in some sort of schoolteacher bun on the back of her head, tumbled free and Tony debated the camera over the microphone. But his client wanted audio. Pictures, she'd said, sniffing and blotting her eyes, wouldn't be enough to convince her.

Even in the darkness, across the distance that separated them, Tony could sense the silky weight of her hair as it slipped over her shoulders. Something about the way it flowed free, shifting all at once, floating down over her shoulders and softening her serious face, told Tony she wore it up because she was afraid of the way the change would affect her image.

He didn't know why he knew that, but he did.

Hinson took her face in his hands, then plunged his fingers into her hair. "Bastard," Tony whispered. A man like Hinson didn't deserve a woman that pure.

Then Tony laughed.

At himself, for thinking such thoughts. What did he know about this chick? His client had hired him for the same reason most of his clients did—to find out whether her man was cheating on her.

Yep. That was the way of the private eye business. Another few weeks hiding in the dark and soon there'd be no way he'd trust a woman. Any woman.

Tony ran one hand through his hair, thinking of his own marriage. Neither one of them had been unfaithful, but he and Kathy hadn't lasted. They'd simply married before either one knew what the hell they wanted out of life.

They'd played house during their senior year in college and for three years after. When he wanted to enroll in the Police Academy, she suggested he owed it to his parents to join the family business. His parents stood behind his decision completely, and Kathy's desire for the path of safety and security rankled Tony.

So he'd thrown himself into being a policeman. His wife had pursued her MBA. Then they'd divorced, as quietly and uneventfully as they'd begun.

At least they hadn't had children.

If any man had been meant to be a cop, it was Tony Olano. Kathy hadn't understood that, but then, neither had the stuffed shirts in the department who wanted him to follow procedure and quit taking so many risks, even though his style, as his superiors called it, had earned him three commendations in as many years. But no guts, no glory, Tony had reasoned.

This attitude got him branded a troublemaker, a reputation that worked against him when he'd been caught accepting an envelope stuffed with hundred-dollar bills from a strip joint operator.

No one stood beside him. No one stopped to question his guilt or innocence, reactions that played straight into the hands of the forces that had engineered the frame-up.

Hinson now had his arm around the woman, speaking to her with an earnest look that made Tony gag. He whistled through his teeth, imagining what sweet nothings he'd pick up on the playback of the recorder. Better to think about that than the holding pattern of his own life.

Still with an arm around her shoulders, Hinson guided the woman back inside. Tony captured the Kodak moment and put away the microphone.

He'd done the job his client had asked him to do. Time to stop for a beer, go home and try to sleep.

As he stowed his equipment and pulled the car away from the curb, the image of the woman's hair spilling over her shoulders echoed in his mind. He might be finished with the assignment, but he didn't feel ready to let go.

He told himself, as he stopped by Parasols in the Irish Channel, that his interest in Hinson's latest was purely professional. When a sleaze-ball like David Hinson spent time with a woman

who looked like a schoolmarm, something had
to be up.

Tony didn't spot anyone he knew in the bar,
so he sat alone, sipping his Budweiser, idly peeling the label free with one thumb and wondering if Hinson too had detected a hint of fire in
the woman's deep blue eyes, a hint that promised some lucky man more pleasure than he'd
ever known.

Tony shook his head, wondering at his flight
of fancy. The woman would no doubt turn out
to be your typical suspect, a lawyer tired of the
daily grind who'd decided it was easier to chase
after Hinson's money and set up housekeeping
in his fancy place in the Garden District. Well,
if this prim one was after marriage with a guy
like Hinson, she'd soon discover she'd be trad-
ing her soul for any diamond that man slipped
on her finger.

He smoothed the label onto the surface of the
bar. Rather than the red, white, and blue of the
label, he saw only the deep blue of the woman's
eyes.

Fingering one of the quarters lying on the bar
with the rest of his change, Tony knew he was
once again about to break the rules. He had no
business dabbling with one of Hinson's women.
Any day now, the undercover operation could
gel and Tony would find himself on the inside
of Hinson's unsavory operations.

Still rolling the quarter in his hand, Tony
made a deal with himself. Heads, he'd find out
for himself what lay beneath her silky surface;
tails, he'd leave her alone.

He spun the coin in the air and slapped it down on the beer label.

George Washington winked at him.

Tony grinned and pushed away the beer he'd barely touched.

Time to go home and get ready for tomorrow.

Chapter 2

The crowd of shoppers in Pottery DeLite had thinned during the time Penelope had been mulling over the choice of placemats and napkins offered by the gourmet cookware store. In her left hand she held the dark blue jacquard weave, in her right a more festive plaid.

Dinner once a week with David Hinson for the past six weeks had been at his invitation each time; that she herself prepare a meal this Saturday had been her suggestion, an idea sparked by the dinner he'd hosted at his home earlier that week. David was an articulate, bright attorney who spoke her language, and the only person she'd seen socially since moving to New Orleans earlier that year.

Besides, Penelope loved to cook. If her mother hadn't railroaded her into law school, she might at this very moment be presiding over the kitchen of a top restaurant.

She fingered the jacquard weave and smiled as she thought of the irascible chef who'd sneaked lessons to her behind her mother's back. Henry—or Henri, as he styled himself—ruled the kitchen of the restaurant where Penelope's mother Margery worked as a waitress, then later as a hostess when her legs swelled and the arthritis in her hands betrayed her.

Over my dead body, her mother had exclaimed, when Penelope had asked to study with Henri. So obedient straight-A student Penelope had sneaked her lessons throughout her high school years.

Yet she'd gone to college, then law school, and on to NYU for a master's in taxation, exactly as her mother had planned. Now her mother was dead and Penelope should have been free.

But freedom, she had been discovering, was an elusive state. With her mother no longer there to shriek in horror, Penelope could have walked out on her life as a lawyer, but a funny thing had happened along the way.

She'd become very good at what she did.

At least she'd had the courage to trade in her childhood home of Chicago for New Orleans. And she'd resurrected her long-ago-envisioned cookbook idea, a project she kept secret from her legal colleagues. No doubt she'd have to publish it under another name.

As she stared at the rich blue cloth, the design wavered and she saw instead the image of an elegant room filled with the movers and shakers of the culinary world. After entering the ballroom, she made her way slowly to the tables reserved for nominees, graciously acknowledging the smiles and waves of well-wishers and hoping against hope she'd finish the night a winner.

When the time came for the master of ceremonies to announce the Best New Chef of the

Year, she waited, one hand clasped against the plunging neckline of her slinky black evening gown. And then she heard the magic words—her name!

She accepted the platinum knife and fork statuette, smiling at the adoring crowd. She thanked Henri; she even thanked her mother. Then she paused. Surely there was someone else to name, someone who'd helped her achieve the pinnacle of her dreams?

Well, hush puppies and hash browns, as long as her imagination was running free, she might as well finish the picture to her complete satisfaction.

She swept her hand to her side. She pictured the sexy stranger from the elevator almost a week ago.

His image danced in her mind. Mysterious, strong, and, strangely enough, also gentle. She inclined her head toward the invisible microphone. The curtains behind her on the stage parted. "For making me what I am today, I'd like to thank . . ."

He moved toward her, as light on his feet as any meringue she'd ever concocted. This time he looked only at her, consuming her with the adoration and admiration shining in his dark eyes.

". . . the man with the bedroom eyes."

She drew him toward her and the audience went wild. Together, a beautiful and glamorous couple, they swept from the stage. Their limo awaited.

"Looks like you dropped this."

Penelope jerked back to reality. Bunnies and

bumpkins! She'd done it again, totally lost touch with her surroundings.

She blinked and cleared the heady dreams from her mind. She glanced at the jacquard weave placemat extended toward her, allowing her gaze to travel up a masculine forearm, covered with a generous dusting of black hair. As she registered the familiar voice, the pulse in her throat raced.

Without continuing her visual journey, Penelope tried to snatch the placemat from the man's hands.

It didn't budge.

"Hey, don't I know you from somewhere?"

Penelope, with great reluctance, lifted her eyes to the stranger's.

He stood there staring at her.

He looked good, more than good, even better than the first time she'd seen him. That day he'd been dressed in the conventional downtown uniform. Today he wore a T-shirt that showed his broad chest to advantage. The white cotton contrasted beautifully with arms tanned a golden bronze. Khaki shorts revealed the kind of well-defined thighs Penelope had known only in her fantasies. Fighting a blush, she said, rather crossly, "You don't know me from Adam."

One brow quirked wickedly. He raked his dark eyes over her and shook his head slowly. "Oh, there's no way I'd mistake you for Adam."

Penelope sensed both her mind and body reacting to the implied compliment. Then she remembered herself. He had to be toying with her. She glanced down at her navy slacks and white linen blouse. Her Saturday shoes were loafers, her navy leather belt a prim and proper choice to match. She was not a woman that men—especially men like this—flirted with.

"I'm sure we've met before."

She tugged again at the placemat. "I'm not Adam or Eve or some woman you met in an airport. So please let go of my purchase."

He grinned and snapped his fingers. "The elevator! You're the woman who forgot your briefcase in the Oil Building."

Penelope nodded, though it hurt her pride to do it. She felt flattered to be remembered, but embarrassed he'd caught her being absentminded. Absentminded! Call it what it was, Penelope, she lectured herself—fantasizing and completely out of touch with reality. And not once but twice. She tugged on the fabric and it gave way.

"You new in town?"

She half-turned, collected three other placemats, stacked them together. Over her shoulder she said, "I'm sorry. I don't talk to strangers."

She saw him grin again, then sketch a salute. "So I'll just have to get to know you," he said, then walked away, whistling.

Frogs and fairy tales! Talk about presumptuous. The man was as annoying as he was attractive.

Besides, if he intended to get to know her, why had he walked away just now? Or had he? Something like an itch overcame her as she battled the desire to turn her head to see whether he'd left the store.

Penelope was made of sterner stuff. She

moved instead in the opposite direction, focusing on a display of napkin rings. Swans in pewter, curling leafwork in brass, fanciful spirals in shaved steel—designs for setting every possible mood filled the oversized basket.

What was it about that man? And what was he doing in Pottery DeLite? She fingered one of the swan rings, willing to bet the man didn't know a paring knife from a pair of poultry shears.

New Orleans wasn't a big city. So what if she had bumped into him a second time? Penelope shrugged, attempting to erase the tiny voice that whispered the meeting was less than coincidental. Twice—okay. But if he popped up again, she'd have to figure out if he meant trouble.

"Oh, dear, could you help me, please?"

Penelope looked around for the high-pitched female voice. No one else stood nearby.

"Yoo-hoo, over here," the voice called again.

The voice came from the basket of napkin rings. Penelope shook her head. A talking napkin ring? Honestly, she had to cure her bad habit of drifting into fantasies. Deciding to buy the jacquard weave placemats and get out of the store swiftly, Penelope turned away from the display.

"Please don't go!" This time the voice shrieked and Penelope detected panic.

Panic? In a basket of napkin rings? She couldn't think of any reason she'd imagine such a thing.

She shook her head, but her curiosity overcame her. Turning back to the display basket, she edged closer.

"That's an angel," said the voice, definitely coming from within the center of the basket.

Maybe she should have gone into therapy, Penelope thought, as she looked into the basket. It worked well for millions of others.

But Penelope had to admit she enjoyed her fantasies, at least most of the time. Right now, though, she might be willing to agree that a bit of professional tinkering was in order.

Perched next to one of the swan rings, clinging to a carved wooden banana, sat a talking figurine in the shape of a woman dressed in a purple and orange caftan, holding on to a thin brownish stick almost the same six inches in height. The design was such that the figure moved fluidly even as it spoke.

"Clever," Penelope said under her breath, wondering how the device worked.

"Not so very," came the reply. "If I were half so clever as I tried to be, I'd never end up in these pickles."

"Pickles?"

The tiny figure shrugged its shoulders and pointed to either side. "Just look where my latest spell has landed me."

The figure beckoned to her and Penelope bent her head toward the basket. The rational part of her mind had begun sending the message loud and clear: This was not a talking mechanical device cleverly fitted with a microchip.

So had Penelope slipped into one of her fantasies without being aware that she'd done so? As a child, she'd learned to escape into daydreams to avoid the drudgery of her life. Now that her circumstances were far more comfortable, Penelope continued the habit, even as she acknowledged that she used it to buffer the lack of emotional involvement with others that marked her life.

Best not to get involved. Unbidden, the voice of her childhood echoed in her mind. Wasn't that what her mother had tried to teach her? *Stick to your path, become the success I never had a chance to be. Don't be led off your course by other people's problems or other people's dreams.*

Penelope sucked in her breath. She'd missed out on so much. Cheerleader tryouts, her senior prom, sorority life.

All because she'd never become involved.

Glancing around, Penelope saw the store remained unchanged. No one stood nearby. She pinched herself and her neurons registered the pain.

So, no, she hadn't lost touch with reality. Speaking in a low voice, she said to the figurine, "So what are you?"

The figure stared at her, head cocked to the side, one lilliputian forefinger tugging lightly on an even tinier earlobe. Raised eyebrows greeted Penelope's blurted question. With a great deal of dignity, the figurine said, "I think perhaps you mean *who* am I. The name is Merlin. Mrs. Maebelle Merlin." She extended a hand and Penelope found herself lifting hers in return. Then she hastily dropped it to her side.

"No need to be afraid," Mrs. Merlin said.

"I'm not afraid," Penelope said, then added, "I'm just not sure of the protocol for this sort of meeting."

"I don't think one worries about protocol in a

life-and-death situation," came the response in a dry voice, followed by a brisk clap of her hands, accomplished without letting go of the dusty brown stick. "Help me out of this basket and we'll take it from there."

We? Penelope wondered at Mrs. Merlin's choice of pronouns. Glancing around, Penelope noticed the sales clerk staring in her direction, but no other shoppers milled about. A check of her watch revealed the store would close in two minutes. She'd all but forgotten the placemats and napkins clutched under one arm. But she needed them for the meal she'd planned for David. She shifted her body so the sales clerk couldn't watch her face and said, "I'm afraid I need to go. I'm expecting company for dinner."

"So you are afraid! And more concerned over protocol than aiding a sister human." Mrs. Merlin sighed and shook her head. "How you could eat dinner knowing I'm stuck in this store overnight, as ravenous as a nutria, is beyond me." The tiny voice rose in pitch. "You should be ashamed of yourself. Even if you're no Good Samaritan, where's your sense of adventure?"

"I—I—" Penelope gaped at Mrs. Merlin. She swiveled her head. The sales clerk had turned the other way. "I do too have a sense of adventure. I just don't use it very often."

"Then brush it off a bit." The tiny woman raised her arms toward Penelope. "Pop me into that purse of yours and get me out of this store."

"But that's shoplifting!"

A sigh much larger than the six-inch-high figurine escaped its lips. "What are you, a lawyer?"

She nodded.

"Well, that's too bad, but let me assure you it's not shoplifting because I'm not for sale. Ergo, no crime."

Penelope smiled despite herself. For all she knew, despite the severe pinch she'd administered to herself, she might be imagining this entire interlude, but something about Mrs. Merlin was impossible to ignore. "Hop on," she said, bending over and opening her palm.

"Pottery DeLite is now closed," the sales clerk's voice rang over the PA system. Penelope almost dropped her passenger on the floor.

"Careful, now."

She lowered Mrs. Merlin and what Penelope nervously thought of as the creature's magic wand into her purse, breaking out in beads of perspiration as she did so. Whatever clever arguments the tiny woman had made, Penelope still felt like she was stealing a napkin ring. Certain she'd be caught, she licked her lips nervously and tried as nonchalantly as possible to walk toward the front of the store.

She'd made it only inches from the door when the sales clerk called out.

"Stop!"

She literally froze. They'd search her and find Mrs. Merlin riding sidecar in her purse. Visions of disgrace filled her mind. Maybe the creature was right and she had no sense of adventure. Slowly Penelope turned to meet her fate.

"Your placemats. I don't believe you've paid for them, miss. I'm just closing the register but if you still want them I'll ring them up." Though she spoke politely, the woman kept looking at her as if she thought she might need to call for help at any moment.

Weak with relief, Penelope giggled. "These silly things?" She held out the placemats. "I've changed my mind." She dropped them on the nearest display and backed from the store.

From within her purse, she heard what was clearly a chuckle.

From his vantage point outside the windowed front of Pottery DeLite, Tony crossed his arms over his chest and marveled at the mix of emotions he experienced watching Penelope Sue Fields as she browsed in the store.

He'd be willing to bet she described herself as conservative, proper, and totally earnest about her professional appearance. Just look at those loafers she had her feet tucked into on this gorgeous July afternoon when most of the people enjoying a day in the French Quarter sported sandals or tennis shoes.

He glanced down at his sandals and smiled. Did she even own a pair?

But the question uppermost in his mind was whether she had any idea how utterly sexy she was inside the protective wrapping she wore.

Tony considered himself something of an expert on women, and prided himself on being able to spot a hot babe a mile away.

Twice now he'd seen her soften and drop the armor when she thought no one was watching her. He'd give his favorite fishing rod to know what had been going through her mind before he'd spoken to her in the store. Her lips had been parted slightly, eyelids lowered, cheeks kissed with a rosy tone—all these signs promised a woman who warmed well to a man's touch. Oh, yeah, despite her icy surface, this one would be hot and slick underneath.

A picture he had no business dwelling on.

Damn!

He uncrossed his arms and jammed his hands in his pockets, as his sense and sensibility returned full force. Just then she turned her back and Tony, caught between tracing the path of her neck with his gaze and reminding himself his interest in this woman was purely related to David Hinson's nefarious activities, almost missed her slick move.

"My, my, my," he murmured, watching her stash an item from the display basket in her purse. "Wouldn't the Bar Association love to know what Penelope Sue does for fun?" He shook his head, registering his own disappointment. He wished now that she'd proven as proper as she appeared.

"Fool." He propelled his body free of the supporting wall where he'd been lounging. He had to keep reminding himself this woman was David Hinson's latest interest. His initial contact might have been incited by a tearful request to check on Hinson's romantic liaisons, but things had gotten much more complicated in the past few days.

He'd delivered the proof of Hinson's dallying to his erstwhile girlfriend. She'd sobbed and called Hinson all sorts of names, then clung to Tony as if he were her only friend in the world. He should have been surprised, but somehow he wasn't when the chick threw her arms around him and begged him to help her drown her sorrows. She'd offered more, but Tony had declined all services. He'd also declined to ease her grief.

People sure were predictable little shits.

And here he was discovering Ms. Prim and Proper Tax Attorney got her jollies by shoplifting. My, my, but what wouldn't the firm of LaCour, Richardson, Zeringue, Ray, Wellman and Klees pay for this nugget of information?

His expression hardened. He observed her as she walked toward the doorway, those boring blue placemats clutched in her hand. To his amazement, she seemed about to brave her way right out the front door when the clerk called to her.

She turned. She dropped the placemats. Twin crimson roses staining her flawless cheeks, she scurried from the store.

"Now, wasn't that clever." Tony heard the disgust in his whisper. Holding the placemats out, pretending to forget she had them, leaving them inside the store—all a clever ploy to distract from whatever she'd lifted and hidden in her purse. What he wouldn't give to still be able to whip out his badge.

He'd bust her. Cuff her. Drag her down to the station.

He stopped in mid-image.

His very next thought had been how he'd enjoy strip-searching her, which of course was ridiculous, as any such search would have been conducted by female officers. Whew, was he out of control or what? The lady was a thief and he still wanted to wrestle her out of that buttoned-to-the-neck blouse.

The strength of his reaction infuriated him. And for that, he wanted to punish her.

Torn between desire and disappointment, Tony pushed out of the mall's side exit just as she stepped into the revolving door. He wouldn't frighten her, but he intended to catch up with her and make sure she went away with Tony Olano imprinted on her mind.

Her startled expression when she saw him standing on the sidewalk pleased him. She fumbled in her purse, then quickly abandoned her search. She stabbed a finger toward his chest and fire danced in her expression, but rather than the scolding lecture he had expected from her body language, she whispered, "Why are you following me?"

Her voice was so soft he had to move nearer, which he did, stepping as close as their bodies could be without actually touching. Around them on the sidewalk the river of tourists parted and flowed around them, but Tony paid them no mind. He looked down on her hair, glossy as silk.

Tony steeled himself. This woman had fooled the clerk in the store, the same way she'd doubtless fooled others. She associated with Hinson; she shoplifted. Some lawyer! Stretching out a hand, he stroked her purse strap where it lay across her shoulder. "Why do you think, Penelope Sue Fields?"

She stiffened, then delivered a quelling glare. If looks could kill, his finger would have shriveled off. "I have no—" Her lips clamped shut on her words. And sure enough, she cast her eyes toward her purse. Tony had seen that look, time and time again—that nervous telling of one's guilt.

He'd seen it in men stopped for a moving violation, whose telltale glances ended in searches that revealed guns, drugs, and, once, a prostitute stashed in the trunk of a businessman's Town Car.

Penelope gave herself away. Tony had wanted to give himself the chance that perhaps he had misinterpreted and she hadn't stolen, but that glance, followed now by a shifting of her stance, of another anxious look toward him, then back to her purse, confirmed his suspicion.

And the darnedest thing about it was the way her cheeks glowed and her blue eyes turned even bluer. "You wear your guilt pretty well," he said roughly.

"Oh, why, thank you." Then she stepped back. "Guilt?"

He tipped a finger toward her purse.

She pulled it closer to her side. "I don't know what you're talking about. Now I have to go, and I do not want you to follow me."

"No?" He drawled the word. "I guess you don't."

"And what's that supposed to mean?"

Tony rubbed the side of his cheek. "You actually enjoy Hinson's company, or does he just buy you nice trinkets?"

If he thought he'd seen fire in her eyes before, it had been only a spark compared to the flames that danced now. "Are you a friend of his?"

"Not as good a friend as you appear to be."

Her fist clenched and Tony found himself wondering whether she'd ever slapped a man.

"What he is to me is none of your business." She turned to go, then swung back to face him. "You *have* been following me, haven't you? Not just today, but for some time. You must have been; otherwise how would you know anything about David Hinson?"

Tony shrugged, gave her his best insolent grin. He wanted her to know he was watching, wanted her to wonder why. He knew she was merely the pawn caught in his and Hinson's sights, but if he could use her to wreak any degree of punishment on Hinson, he'd do it.

Her lips had parted slightly. She was clutching her purse and looking at him with those baby blues as if she'd been born yesterday. Only now he knew better. His shadow fell across her body as he leaned toward her. "Get used to it," he said.

Chapter 3

Penelope had parted her lips to deliver the most quashing retort of her life when she registered a tugging motion coming from within her purse. She clamped her elbow more firmly against the side of her bag and to her dismay heard a definite "Oomph!"

Hoping she hadn't injured her uninvited passenger, Penelope licked her parched lips, so quickly dehydrated by the oppressive heat, then darted a finger under the collar of her blouse in an attempt to cool herself.

What with the humidity added to the heat of this man's intense gaze, Penelope's internal thermostat had risen to the red zone.

In an attempt to dampen at least one source of the heat, she inched away from the dark-eyed man who'd played such a stellar role in her fantasies of recent days. His behavior ought to teach her not to make up stories—look how different he was in real life!

With her free hand, she reached out and tapped on his broad chest, which loomed so close to hers. Mustering a bravado she didn't know she possessed, she said in a tight voice, "Get lost."

His eyes widened. A smile licked across his wide mouth. "Nice touch," he said in a caressing sort of voice, but at least he did retreat a step or so, continuing to watch her in that assessing way he had.

But this time Penelope refused to let his sexy eyes and her attraction to him draw her off course. "If you follow me ever again, I'm calling the police."

His response was a grin that infuriated her.

"You don't think I'll do it?" Penelope's purse began to dance a bit and she wished she'd never, ever gone shopping at Pottery DeLite that day. If she'd stayed home and worked on the stacks of papers stuffed in her briefcase she'd never have run into this annoying man and certainly she'd never have shoplifted a bossy and opinionated six-inch-high mystery woman.

"You're new in town, aren't you?"

"That's the second time you've asked me that question." Penelope broke free from the man's gaze and looked around her. The sidewalk where they stood was near the end of Canal Street, a major thoroughfare that ran from the Mississippi River to parts of the city Penelope had never had time to explore, but one she'd heard ended at the cemeteries, another New Orleans curiosity.

Around them wandered tourists in T-shirts and shorts, many swigging bottled water, just as many sipping those cherry red alcoholic Kool-Aid drinks known as hurricanes in plastic cups. New Orleans, a city of pleasures and passions, wasn't a place she fit into naturally, but it rubbed her the wrong way that she appeared so clearly a square peg.

"The police in this city don't waste much time on complaints like yours," the man said in a deliberate voice, a shadow clouding his eyes. "They have trouble enough getting to the real problems."

"Thanks for the civics lesson, and you're right. You're not a problem. You're merely a pest. Now get lost." She turned on her heel and walked away.

Within the first block, sweat poured off her like the big fountain back home in Grant Park. Even Chicago summers, laden with humidity, hadn't prepared her for the sauna effect of New Orleans. The sidewalk wavered and danced before her eyes. She clutched her purse, harder to manage both from the weight and the antics of Mrs. Merlin jumping about, and wondered if one could faint from heat.

She didn't have to wait long to find out. She suffered another shivery attack of heat so extreme she actually felt an icy cold wash over her body. She would have called out for help, but what with all the talking and walking and not having eaten or drunk any water for more hours than she could remember, she couldn't act quickly enough.

Faintly she heard a "Dear me, we're falling!" from within her shoulder bag as the sidewalk rushed at her face.

Tony hadn't intended to follow her any more that day. The gutsy way she'd told him to get lost had affected him in a way a "Please go away" would not have, gotten to him in a way that sparked a purely male reaction.

Spying once again an edge that belied her proper appearance, he wanted to know more about the lady thief. So when she marched away, he lingered, then shadowed her path up Canal Street.

Which is why he saw her sway, then stumble, in time to dash forward.

Which is why he was there to catch her before her head cracked against the sidewalk like a watermelon in a Fourth of July toss.

She was soft and rounded in all the places that crushed against Tony's arms as he snatched her from what would have been a nasty landing.

And hot. Sweat dotted her face and ran in a bead across her upper lip. With one hand he stroked her damp cheek. She'd yet to open her eyes.

"Damn fool woman," he muttered, reaching under her chin for the top button of her blouse. He'd unfastened the first one and started on the second when her eyelids flickered, then opened.

She stared into his face and Tony saw a vulnerability he'd not noticed before. What was this woman doing consorting with Hinson? Did she simply not recognize the evil that lurked beneath the polished surface?

He slipped his fingers into the placket to undo the third button.

Her hand clamped onto his wrist. Surprisingly strong, pleasingly smooth and soft. Before his mind could explore that thought further, she struggled against him and said in a cross voice, "What do you think you're doing?"

"Cooling you down," he said without letting go of her, then carried her the few steps to the covered bus shelter and deposited her on the bench. Several waiting riders glanced their way, but displayed not a shade of curiosity.

In the French Quarter, the sight of a man carrying a woman wasn't anything to elicit comment.

But for Penelope, Tony would be willing to bet it was a whole new experience. She watched him with wary eyes as he settled her onto the bench, almost as if she expected him to snatch her up again. Her hair, he noted, had loosed itself from the tight knot and sent a damp curl forward on her neck. After what appeared to be a brief inner struggle, she said in a small voice, "It was good of you to keep me from cracking my head on the pavement."

"I'd do the same for any stranger on the street," he said. Good of him? Hardly. He wanted to keep her alive and well to use her to needle Hinson. If she only knew his plans, she'd probably have preferred a crack on the head and a trip to Charity Hospital. Annoyed at the sweet expression stealing over her face, he pushed away from the side of the bus shelter. "I'll find you a cab."

She rose. "I don't need—"

He was back by her side before she sagged to the bench. "Don't need a cab, hmmmm? Don't need any help. Don't need—"

"You." She stuck her lip out. "I don't need you. If you insist, I'll take the cab, but then I want you gone."

He nodded. Let her think she could have her way. There was always tomorrow.

To Penelope's relief, he gave her no argument and stepped away to flag down a cab. Crumpled limply on the bench, surrounded by people who no doubt assumed she was another tourist unable to hold her liquor, Penelope wanted to be anywhere but sitting here. And in her woozy state, she wanted no argument from this man. That could wait until she was strong enough to win.

That thought shot her straight upright. "I am not going to see him again," she said aloud, in a very firm voice.

From her purse, she heard a grouchy-sounding voice saying, "Don't tell him that until he gets the cab. It's getting hotter than Hades here in this purse!"

"Oh!" Penelope opened the top of her purse further and fanned some air in. "Better?"

Mrs. Merlin shook the folds of her caftan, saying, "Mr. Gotho warned me."

Penelope wanted to inquire as to Mr. Gotho's identity, but the man next to her had scooted a few inches away, stared at her, then scooted over even more. Clearly the other people at the bus stop were figuring her for nuts.

Wishing to be home in her cool and uncomplicated apartment, Penelope glanced over at her rescuer-tormentor, wondering how long it would take to get a cab to stop. Then she saw him pull a small phone from the pocket of his shorts. The man must be a Boy Scout.

Perspiration trickled down her neck, pooling beneath her bra and sealing it to her skin in a way that made it even harder for her to breathe. After a furtive glance, she plucked at her shirt, attempting to pull her bra off her overheated skin.

She should have stayed in Chicago.

The thought hit her hard.

"No," she mouthed, and dropped her hand. Better to suffer heatstroke, better to embarrass herself silly fainting in public than to have remained in Chicago.

Here at least she had a chance for a new life.

Her tormentor returned to her side and held out a hand. When she hesitated, he tucked an arm around her shoulders and eased her to her feet.

His touch surprised her. So gentle despite the way he lifted her as if she weighed no more than an empty file folder.

He'd slipped on a pair of dark glasses. Disappointed that he'd hidden those magnetic eyes of his, yet also relieved, Penelope freed herself from his hold before she grew too comfortable. She extended a hand.

He grinned, but took her hand, causing another wave of pleasure at the contact. Fortunately, he let go before she made a fool of herself, jerking his head toward a cab that had pulled curbside.

"The least I can do is thank you," Penelope said.

He grinned again, quirking his brows, and all thoughts of gratitude emptied from her mind. "Oh, you will," he said, and opened the door of the cab.

"Why, you're—you're impossible!" She jumped

into the cab and grabbed the door handle.

He slid the door shut, preventing her from the satisfaction of slamming it.

The cab shot forward.

Penelope turned around in her seat. He stood there, legs spread wide like a sailor claiming the deck of a sailboat, grinning.

Not only was he impossible, Penelope thought, turning to answer the driver's inquiry as to her destination, but she didn't even know his name.

They'd gone about two blocks when Penelope saw her shoulder bag shift and heard a rustling noise.

Mrs. Merlin!

Penelope had been half-hoping she had fantasized the incident in the store and the conversational voice issuing from her purse at the bus stop.

"Do you mind?"

That voice, so strong and insistent despite the tininess of its owner, carried clearly to Penelope's ears. No figment of her fantasy, that!

She glanced at the cab driver, but he appeared engrossed in the sports pages he'd propped next to the steering wheel. Normally Penelope would have taken a cabbie to task for that, but today that transgression scarcely registered with her.

"Shhh," Penelope whispered, leaning over her purse and peering in. The radio, tuned to a jazz station, blared so loudly she didn't think the driver could hear her, but she had no desire to attract his attention.

Mrs. Merlin perched atop Penelope's Coach

wallet, arms on hips, a waspish expression on her face. For the first time, Penelope noticed she wore a tiny pair of reading glasses perched on her nose. Her hair, fiery orange-red streaked with silver, stood in wispy angles out from around her head, revealing ears that winked with red and green stones pinned to their lobes.

"Suffering in silence has never been my style. Don't get me wrong, dear. I appreciate being rescued, but I'll have you know the buses of the Rapid Transit Authority provide a smoother ride than you and that wobbling purse."

"Well, it's not as if I fainted on purpose."

"As hot as it is inside here, I can believe that. I do need some fresh air." Mrs. Merlin looked up, hope in her eyes. "Let me out of here?"

Penelope glanced toward the driver's seat. "I can't do that now."

Mrs. Merlin wagged a minuscule forefinger and Penelope felt as chastised as she had the one time she'd been called into the principal's office in grade school. "Don't ever say anything can't be done."

"But there are some things—"

"How did I get so unlucky as to land in a lawyer's clutches! Always an answering argument." Mrs. Merlin touched her forefingers to her lips, then to her temples. "I promise the goddess of flame and light that if she helps me out of this mess I'll be ever so careful in the future."

Goddess of flame and light? Penelope laughed, a shade hysterically.

"Only the ignorant laugh at the unknown," Mrs. Merlin said softly.

Penelope pressed her lips closed. She stared

into her purse. Slowly she said, "You know, you're absolutely right about that. I apologize."

"Good. Now can I get out of here?"

Penelope exhaled a big breath. Reaching into her purse, she extended two fingers. Mrs. Merlin climbed quite nimbly on, then settled onto the palm of Penelope's hand, still clutching the long brown stick.

Measuring with her eye, Penelope figured the tiny woman stood about as high as a can of soda. She set her on the seat next to her purse, checking to make sure the driver kept his eyes on the sports pages.

Mrs. Merlin fluffed the sides of her caftan and patted at her iridescent hair. "Thank you ever so much. By the way, what's your name, dear?"

"Penelope Fields."

"Ah, Penelope. And what are we weaving today?"

The weaving reference was one Penelope had heard time and time before, as people delighted in asking her whether she'd been named after the Penelope of Greek myth who'd spent years weaving garments while her husband Odysseus was off wandering.

The truth was her mother had been determined from the day of her daughter's birth to make her stand out from the crowd. She simply picked the name because it was uncommon. Realizing she hadn't responded aloud to the woman, Penelope said, "Today I guess I'm weaving some adventure into my life."

Mrs. Merlin smiled. "Chances are that doesn't please you right now, but it might one day. I always like to say things happen for a reason, though I'm bedazzled as to what it was I did wrong this time."

"Wrong?"

Mrs. Merlin worried her lips into a knot and tapped the side of her cheek with her forefinger. "I was working on a spell for Ramona. She's a dear who lives down the street from me, but for all the days in the year the woman doesn't possess a lick of sense. She's gotten herself in trouble with the tax collector and I was only trying to help."

Penelope nodded, but she wondered how Mrs. Merlin could help.

Almost in answer the tiny woman waved a hand airily. "I burn candles," she said, as if that answered every possible question Penelope might have about her.

"Candles."

"Yes." Mrs. Merlin stopped talking, but continued tapping the side of her cheek and began murmuring to herself.

To Penelope's relief, the cab swung onto her block in the Warehouse District. Not only had she shoplifted, fantasized way too much, and made a fool of herself in front of the man with the bedroom eyes, she'd been saddled with a tiny woman who was without a doubt certifiably nuts.

How much simpler her life would be had she gone to the office as she normally did on Saturdays.

The cab halted. Penelope pointed quickly to her purse and with a shake of her head Mrs. Merlin climbed inside. Penelope paid and headed inside the converted cotton warehouse that housed her apartment.

She loved the rich woods and the feeling that time had been captured and rejuvenated with the loving restoration of the old building. Stepping inside always made her glad she'd taken the chance and moved to New Orleans.

And now, stepping inside with Mrs. Merlin muttering under her breath inside her shoulder bag, Penelope smiled and realized she was glad she hadn't gone to the office.

"Sense of adventure, here I come," she said, and punched the elevator call button.

Chapter 4

"Not a bad place," Mrs. Merlin said, peering around from her perch on Penelope's glass and oak coffee table. "A little impersonal, though."

"It serves me nicely," Penelope retorted, caught between annoyance and amusement at this woman who invaded her life, then criticized her decorating style. She'd taken over the apartment as is from an architect leaving in a hurry for an Italian assignment.

"I always think it's the personal touches that add that something certain," Mrs. Merlin said. Then she grasped the stick she'd been dragging around and used it to vault from the table to the floor in one smooth move. There she straightened her caftan, patted her hair, and tucked the stick under one arm.

"What is that thing and how does it work?" Penelope had meant to ask about the stick earlier, but the question had seemed a bit nosy.

"It's an incense stick," Mrs. Merlin said, adjusting her glasses on her nose and fixing Penelope with a look that indicated she found her on the slow side. "It's used to light the candle in the practice of magick, but now that you mention it, I've no idea how it's made. Precious oils and wood pulp, I suppose."

"How do you use it to move like that?"

Mrs. Merlin skipped across the living room, which flowed through a wide archway into the kitchen, then vaulted onto the countertop. "Search me," she said. "But when the goddess provides, I don't question. Nice kitchen," she added, glancing around.

Assuming she wouldn't get a straight answer from her visitor, and leaving her to finish passing judgment on her apartment, Penelope went into the bedroom to exchange her loafers for a comfortably worn pair of house slippers.

Her slippers were under the edge of her bed. As she slipped off her shoes, her mind flashed to the memory of being lifted and carried effortlessly by the man with bedroom eyes. Her feet had floated above the sidewalk as he'd cradled her in his arms.

Penelope knelt beside the bed, reliving the feel of her body crushed against his chest. She sighed, thinking how invincibly strong he was, how heroically he'd rescued her. Even Raoul, her fantasy lover, couldn't have done a better job.

She knew she should tend to the pint-size woman now surveying her kitchen like a broker come to bid, but Penelope, suffering a curiously stirring eruption of sheer physical reactions, couldn't budge.

"Who is that man?" she whispered, idly pulling her slippers on. "Why is he following me?" She rested one hand atop her thigh. Tracing a figure eight with her fingers, she said to herself, "Why does he bother with me?"

She wished with all her being she could answer that question in a way that would bring her pleasure, but she was far too rational, far too honest. He wanted something from her, from Penelope Sue Fields, and it wasn't her feminine allure that attracted him. Perhaps he was in tax trouble? Perhaps he needed a lawyer and didn't know how to ask the bar for a referral? Perhaps he'd mistaken her for someone else?

Surely, Penelope thought, smoothing her hands against her sides and along her slender hips, he did not desire the very thing she suddenly and fiercely wanted him to want.

Her.

Penelope Sue Fields, the last one chosen for softball, the first one picked by the teacher to read her homework.

Penelope Sue Fields, outstanding lawyer, who might one day, if she continued on her current track, set her sights on a federal judgeship.

Federal judgeships were for life.

And so was spinsterhood.

She sighed and turned away from her bed. Best to get back to the moment, back to Mrs. Merlin, however unreal that particular visitor might be. Soon David would arrive, and Penelope had so far neglected to prepare one tidbit of the marvelous dinner she'd imagined only that morning.

That morning, which seemed weeks, even years ago. That morning, when she'd concentrated on the work she'd brought home, then rewarded herself by a late afternoon shopping trip to Pottery DeLite.

"I say," Mrs. Merlin piped up in a voice that carried surprisingly far, "would you happen to have a snack for a hungry woman?"

Hearing her visitor's voice, Penelope hurried from the bedroom. "Honestly," she said. "I'm having trouble believing you're real or I assure you I would have offered you refreshment the minute we walked in the door."

Mrs. Merlin crossed her arms and looked steadily at Penelope. "Do I look like an object of your imagination?"

Thinking of the characters who peopled her fantasy world, Penelope felt a blush rise on her cheeks. "Well . . ." she began.

"Never mind," Mrs. Merlin interrupted. "No need for hypothetical questions. Especially when my hunger is most definitely real. I am craving something shrimp- or crab-based, and perhaps some jambalaya. Yes, jambalaya would be perfect. You do know how to make jambalaya?"

Jambalaya? Escargots she knew. Crepes and other delicacies crowned with sauces ranging from béchamel to hollandaise to béarnaise, oh, yes, all those Penelope knew from heart. But jambalaya?

In the few months she'd been in New Orleans she'd worked so many hours at her new job she'd only had time for one visit to a cook's dream, the Crescent City Farmers' Market. And that took place down the street from her apartment building. As for discovering the mysteries of a roux or an étouffée she'd had not a minute.

But, as Mrs. Merlin had asked her, where was her sense of adventure?

"Jambalaya, absolutely," she said, feeling as much a phony as she had when she'd shoplifted Mrs. Merlin from Pottery DeLite. With a straight face she added, "But I gave away my last batch to the maid. How about some Lean Cuisine?"

Mrs. Merlin made a face, an expression of opinion Penelope had to agree with, but sad to say there were many nights she made do with a frozen entrée. Life as a lawyer didn't lend itself to early evenings with time for leisurely gourmet cooking. Penelope had often wondered how the men and women she worked with professionally managed to maintain any vestige of a personal life. She'd grown used to and sometimes semi-thankful for her state of singledom. At least she didn't have to juggle the impossible with the unattainable.

She plucked two boxes from the freezer, then halted in mid-turn toward the microwave.

David.

She'd completely forgotten about him, about the dinner she'd promised to create. A quick glance at the kitchen clock informed her she had less than two hours before he'd be ringing her intercom buzzer.

"Fritos and frogs," she said, and slapped the Lean Cuisines back into the freezer.

"Does that mean I'm going to bed hungry?" Mrs. Merlin vaulted from the counter to the butcher-block worktable.

"It's all that man's fault." Penelope paced the floor from kitchen to living area and back, thankful for the open layout of her apartment.

One of the appeals of the converted warehouse had been the lofty ceilings and the feeling she couldn't be confined or captured under the weight of a room with walls that crowded and closed in.

"Man?" Mrs. Merlin said, sounding as if she'd far rather talk about food than the masculine gender.

If her eyes had glinted, or if she'd sounded like a neighborhood gossip settling down for a newsy talk session, Penelope might have kept her mouth shut. But there didn't seem any harm in telling her woes to someone who had no connection to Penelope's day-to-day reality.

"Yes, man, as in m-a-n." Suddenly Penelope paused and stared at the tiny woman. "It's very odd," she said, "but I'm talking to you as if you're real and it's hard to realize you're so . . . so . . ."

"Six and one-quarter inches?" Mrs. Merlin didn't sound caustic, but Penelope thought she might have a hard time accepting such a fact.

"That's precise."

Mrs. Merlin sighed. "Well, it just so happens that Ramona's property tax liability was six hundred twenty-five dollars."

"Yes?" Penelope worried her lip and wondered why she'd ever invited David Hinson for dinner.

"Don't you see? Six hundred twenty-five somehow became all mixed up as six and a quarter in height." Penelope didn't see at all. And Penelope hadn't made it to the top of her class in law school by accepting the illogical without argument. "I fail to comprehend how this woman's tax deficit has anything to do with your height."

Off came the spectacles. Lifting an edge of the vivid caftan, Mrs. Merlin began a vigorous polishing job. After a long moment, she looked up. "My dear, how old are you?"

Penelope pulled her pasta machine from a cupboard. "Why?"

"Why?" She popped the glasses back onto the tip of her nose. "Because you've lived long enough to begin learning a few lessons about life."

My, but wasn't Mrs. Merlin bossy! Penelope turned her back and began rooting in her refrigerator. Caesar salad, with her own signature dressing. She'd have to keep the entrée simple or she wouldn't have time to shower and change out of her sticky clothing. David Hinson always appeared impeccably put together and she'd rather send out for pizza than let him see her looking this bedraggled.

Hands full, she deposited the ingredients for pasta from scratch on the counter. "Which lessons?"

Mrs. Merlin held out the fingers of her right hand. She began ticking off, "Fear of adventure, avoidance of facts found squarely in front of your nose, and . . ." She paused and glanced around. "I'd have to add, after looking about this house, that you're avoiding emotional attachments. It just doesn't feel like a home."

Penelope dumped durum flour into the bowl of her pasta machine, along with the eggs and water. "And just how do you make that last deduction?"

Mrs. Merlin pointed to the refrigerator. Penelope collected handcrafted magnets and liked to display them on the refrigerator.

"What's wrong with my refrigerator?"

"Oh, nothing," Mrs. Merlin said, waving a hand as if it were a magic wand. "It's what I don't see that tips me off to what's missing in your life. My fridge, for instance, is cluttered with drawings made by my grandchildren."

Penelope dumped in the water without bothering to measure. Mrs. Merlin's words were passing beyond amusing now, perhaps because they hit their target too accurately.

"Oh, never mind," Mrs. Merlin said. "I'm far too hungry to try to help anyone else. Besides, look what a pickle my last good deed landed me in."

"As soon as I've mixed the pasta I'll whip up some appetizers. By 'good deed,' I suppose you're referring to trying to help your neighbor with her tax problem."

"Exactly."

"Hmmm." Penelope didn't like to be impolite, yet she couldn't help but wonder at the woman's delusions. The thought made her laugh out loud. Wasn't she the one suffering delusions? "I've got to quit imagining things that don't exist," she said under her breath. To Mrs. Merlin she said, "It's much more sensible for someone with a tax problem to consult an attorney such as myself rather than trying to dream up a make-believe solution." There, and let that be a lesson to you and your fantasizing, she told herself. Rather than hiding from life with your imaginary lover Raoul, let yourself go. Let David kiss you the next time he tries.

"You're a tax attorney!" Mrs. Merlin clapped her hands to her forehead.

"I told you I was a lawyer," Penelope said, forcing her mind back to Mrs. Merlin's line of discussion, wondering at the woman's dramatic reaction.

"But a *tax* lawyer! That explains everything!" Mrs. Merlin sat down on a cookbook, chin in hand, and began drawing on her caftan-covered lap with a minute forefinger.

This time Penelope simply waited for an explanation.

"I used verdant and chromium and elixir of violet, but what I must have done wrong was add in the pink. Oh, yes, oh, yes, whatever was I thinking?" She began wringing her hands.

"Whatever are you talking about?" Penelope didn't like the way the tiny hairs on the back of her neck were rising to attention.

"Candle magick." Mrs. Merlin looked up at her as if Penelope were a sweet but not too bright child. "An ancient and positive way of calling on the forces of the universe to aid our journey through space and time."

"Uh-huh." Penelope crossed her arms over her chest, spattering flour on her already soiled blouse. "And I suppose before you burned your last candle you were really a sweet grandmother from Gentilly about, oh . . . five feet four."

"Five feet four and a half. And I am a grandmother." Mrs. Merlin lifted her hands toward the ceiling. "I admit to dabbling in candle magick, but I do have a few things yet to learn."

"You're normally five feet four and a half?" Penelope concentrated on the question of height, trying to ignore the reference to magick.

"And I will be again soon. Quite soon." Mrs. Merlin leaped up. "But I'm afraid that will require some assistance. From you."

Penelope backed away. "Oh, no. Leave me out of this." She selected two salad plates and pasta bowls and carried them to the table. In a firm voice she said, "Shoplifting was more than enough for me. Why, my heart stopped in my chest when that sales clerk caught me in the doorway!" She arranged the dishes and crossed back to the counter.

"Oh, phifil! Like I said, no sense of adventure."

"There's adventure and then there's wrongdoing."

"Granted. But we already decided that I am no more a possession of that store than you are. Ergo—isn't that what you lawyer-types say?—" She peered upward, a sly grin on her face. "you did not shoplift."

Oddly comforted by that logic, Penelope turned back to her interrupted dinner preparations, although the last thing she wanted to do right now was entertain a dinner guest. Charming, attentive, and unquestionably handsome, David had captured her attention by his steady yet respectfully restrained pursuit over the past month and a half. But curiously enough, she felt no excitement at the idea of his coming to her apartment, just as she'd experienced no magic at the dinner party he'd hosted at his home.

Now, if it were the man with the bedroom eyes . . .

"Stop," she said.

"I'm only trying to explain how my spell went awry."

"Oh, not you," Penelope said. "I truly do want to hear how it is you came to be sitting in my kitchen."

"Well, at least you're curious. That's a good precursor for developing a sense of adventure."

Penelope thought of her unchecked fantasies, of how more and more they ran out of control. "I'll have you know I do have a sense of adventure. I just keep it in check."

Mrs. Merlin shook her head. "Better to let it out. Why once upon a time, more years ago than I can count, I used to be a little on the fearful side myself. I tried to do the right things, belong to the PTA and cook spaghetti for the church suppers. But, fortunately for me, my grandmother came to live with us."

"And I suppose your grandmother was a candle magician?"

The small head nodded. "The best there was. My mother lived with us, too, you see, and she strongly objected to my grandmother teaching me anything related to magick.

"There were fourteen of us in a big house off Rampart and Esplanade," Mrs. Merlin continued. "Now, those were the days! Except I was always doing the work for everyone else. But once my grandmother began teaching me magick, I started making everyone else carry their own load. Why should I be washing dishes when I could be learning the spell to cure a pollen allergy, the colors of the candles needed to heal a broken heart, the rainbow blend for financial success?''

"Why indeed?" The fantasy-loving side of Penelope's mind took over as she listened to the tiny woman. Who wouldn't rather heal the sick and weave love spells than do dishes? She pictured the woman life-size, dressed in the flowing caftan, holding court on the broad porch of one of New Orleans' elegant old homes.

Perhaps it would be that magical time between sunset and dusk when the setting sun kissed the clouds with tongues of fire. And even as the flames leaped in the heavens, the flames of Mrs. Merlin's candles would catch hold and lift their entreaties to the mysterious powers she invoked.

"Now, that's an improvement." Mrs. Merlin's voice broke through Penelope's reverie.

She jerked back to the reality of her kitchen.

"Your aura has gone completely blue," Mrs. Merlin pronounced with a satisfied air. "That suits you far, far better than that muddy-colored armor you wear most of the time."

"Blue, schmoo." Penelope turned to finishing the fettucine, then mixed the ingredients for the alfredo sauce she'd decided to serve. She refused to make eye contact with the gremlin magician, refused to acknowledge the woman had observed a difference in Penelope while she'd been off in one of her fantasy trances.

Fantasizing was a bad habit she needed to overcome, a coping technique she'd used during her lonely childhood years and failed to grow out of. She had her feet planted squarely on her kitchen floor and she'd keep them there, thank you.

Mrs. Merlin had taken to muttering again.

Grating fresh Parmesan, Penelope wondered how long her visitor planned to stay and what sort of help she'd require to get her to vacate.

She'd opened her mouth to inquire when the buzzer on the intercom sounded.

"Noodles and napkins!" Penelope shot a glance at the clock. Had she told David seven, not eight?

Mrs. Merlin had stopped talking to herself. "Would that be your man problem?"

"David?" Penelope wiped her hands on a towel. On her way to punch the button to open the building entrance door for David, she said, "No, David's not my man problem."

"Oh?"

Penelope pressed the speaker button. "David?"

Passing traffic muddled his response. With a shrug, she pushed the door release. To Mrs. Merlin she said, "There's this other man. I think of him as the man with bedroom eyes."

"Ahh-ha."

Penelope colored slightly. "I know it's a silly name, but if you could see him, you'd know exactly what inspired the name."

"And what is his given name?"

"Would you believe I don't know?"

Mrs. Merlin didn't look at all surprised.

"Oh, no!" Penelope grabbed the fabric of her slacks in both fists. "Just look at me. I haven't even changed. My hair's a mess." She yanked what hair still remained in the once-tidy French braid loose and her hair spilled over her shoulders.

"If this man cares about you, he won't give a fig what you look like."

"Oh, that's not true," Penelope said. "Men always care what you look like." She thought of the boys who'd ignored her in high school, proper Penelope in her hand-me-down clothes from the church basement bazaar. "Now would you . . ."

Penelope's words dissolved into laughter. "I started to ask you to get the door!"

"I don't see what's so funny about that."

"Oh, I could never explain you to David!" Penelope glanced around, then grasped the cookbook Mrs. Merlin was using as a seat. "I am really sorry about this and I know you're starving, but you'll just have to spend a few hours in the bedroom. Hold on."

Mrs. Merlin clutched her incense stick with one hand, the edge of the cookbook with the other as Penelope carried her from the kitchen. "You clearly have no understanding of southern hospitality. It's a good thing I'm here to help you learn a thing or two about good manners."

"Tomorrow," Penelope said, and set her guest on the bed. She placed the remote control for the bedroom television next to Mrs. Merlin. "I've got cable, but please keep it down," she said, then pulled the door closed behind her.

Chapter 5

The knock on the door sounded before Penelope could prepare herself. The thought of David catching her with her hair a mess, her blouse limp and stained with perspiration and flour, the waistband of her slacks damp, distressed her. Even though he didn't set her heart to pitter-pattering, she had to admit she enjoyed the solicitous attention he paid her. But a man as impeccable as David would no doubt be repelled by the sight of her in this state.

She sighed, then stiffened as the knock sounded again, this time loud and impatient.

"Coming." Well, he deserved whatever shape he found her in, arriving almost an hour early. She gave her head a defiant shake, flounced her hair over her shoulders, and flung open the door.

"How nice . . ." the words of greeting died in her throat.

The man with bedroom eyes lounged in her doorway, managing to tower over her, yet at the same time to convey a lazy, laid-back look she found devastatingly sexy.

". . . you look," he finished her sentence.

Penelope glared crossly. "Did you come here to humiliate me?"

His eyes widened. "Now, what kind of question is that?"

Penelope rolled her eyes and pointed to herself. "Listen to you—telling me I look nice when I'm completely disheveled. What did you come here for?" Her voice rose. "And how did you get in, anyway? This is a security building."

He winked and stepped inside her apartment. "Guess you were expecting someone."

Penelope backed up.

He moved forward. From where he stopped he had a clear view of the dining table, set for two. His eyes darkened. "A man, I'd deduce."

She held her ground.

He scowled. "And apparently your guest is someone you don't mind seeing you *au naturel*— or disheveled, as you put it." He lifted a hand.

Penelope caught her breath. Was he going to touch her? Anticipation warred with indignation. How dare he finagle his way inside her home? How dare he look at her like that? How dare he stop? Then she snapped her mind back on the track of reality. Holding up her hands to block him, she said, "You're doing it again."

"It?" His voice remained casual, but he raked her again with those eyes in a way that stirred Penelope's blood despite her best intentions not to let him get to her.

"Following me," she said.

"Not guilty on that charge." He continued to stare at her from beneath his hooded eyes.

She wasn't sure, but she thought it was her

hair that held his attention. Goodness knew it was a mess. Self-conscious of its disarray, she raised her hands to gather her hair behind her neck.

"Don't," he said.

It wasn't a request. His tone carried no please and thank you; it was a command, pure and simple.

Penelope stared back at him, then dropped her hands slowly to her sides. Her heart picked up speed. She could see her chest rising and falling much more rapidly than could be considered proper. Whatever was she thinking?

Not only did her breathing betray her, but her blood stirred and rose to a pulsing that reached out from her veins to thrum in her legs, her arms, and in secret parts of her body she blushed to acknowledge to herself.

Clearly she'd ceased to think, operating solely on feeling. She shook her head as the still-functioning portion of her brain registered that she'd let a strange man into her apartment.

Crossing her arms over her chest, she said in a normal enough voice, "And why is it that you're not guilty of following me?" As she asked the question she cast a glance toward the bedroom door. If this man proved dangerous, surely Mrs. Merlin would come to her rescue. She might be six inches tall but she could probably punch in 9-1-1 on the bedside phone, which, fortunately for the diminutive Mrs. Merlin, happened to be a speaker phone.

If only she'd fed her! From what she'd seen so far of Mrs. Merlin, Penelope suspected the shrunken magician might be more inclined to help on a full stomach. Penelope knew she herself was always much nicer once fed.

Suddenly she realized he'd followed her look toward the bedroom door. His brows quirked. "Busy day?"

She colored. Well, let him think she had a man stashed in her bedroom. With an attempt at nonchalance, she produced what she hoped passed for a sexy pout and said, "Oh, very."

"I'm relieved to know you're feeling yourself again." He moved toward the door. "And I wasn't following you. Only stopped by to make sure you'd gotten home okay. Didn't want to think you'd passed out from heat again on the front steps." He shrugged a shoulder as if he didn't really care but had felt compelled out of a sense of social responsibility to check up on her. He turned the doorknob, then paused, almost as if waiting for her to say something to invite him to stay.

Not invitation, but irritation better expressed Penelope's reaction. If she wasn't special, she didn't want any consideration from this man. "Thank you very much. As you can see, I'm fine."

His gaze met hers, scorching her with a suggestive look in his dark eyes. "Oh, I can see you're more than fine. You really ought to wear your hair down more often."

Penelope caught a curling strand in her fingers, marveling at the man's brazen audacity, and at her own responsiveness. Why, he created more of a sensation within her than any of her imaginary moments with her dream man Raoul!

He shifted his stance. Gone was the polite person performing a call of obligation. This time he reached out and gathered a handful of hair. "Like a waterfall," he said in a low voice.

Her throat suddenly felt even more parched than it had before she passed out on the sidewalk. She ran her tongue over her lips and swallowed hard.

He dropped his hand. Concern replaced the sensual expression in his eyes. "You're still dehydrated."

She shook her head. It wasn't thirst for water that caused her reaction.

"Come on, let's get you some water." He strode toward the kitchen.

She followed. Reaching into the refrigerator for the bottled water she kept there, she watched him as he sized up her kitchen and opened the cabinet where she kept her glasses, though she couldn't figure out how he'd guessed right the first time.

It was almost as if he could read her thoughts, because he turned, holding out two glasses, smiling. "Closest to the dishwasher," he said.

She found herself smiling back as she filled the glasses. She was surprised, but pleased, that he could find his way around the kitchen, the last thing she would have expected from the man with bedroom eyes.

Scarcely able to believe the stranger in the elevator now stood in her kitchen looking very much at home, Penelope put away the bottled water, then dropped ice cubes into the glasses.

He held out one glass to her, and their fingers touched briefly. Ice and heat collided and she snatched her hand away.

"Penelope?" The voice came from her entranceway, an accusing tone shot like an arrow from the throat of David Hinson.

"David?" Penelope realized the door must have been left ajar. She sucked in a breath, slipped the hand that still tingled from the stranger's touch into the pocket of her slacks and backed toward the refrigerator just as David appeared in the kitchen, cool and immaculate in a tropical-weight wool suit.

"Your door was unlocked. Are you—"

"Downstairs, too?" The man with bedroom eyes drawled his question, his gaze fixed on David in a way that made Penelope extremely nervous.

As he spotted the man with bedroom eyes, David stopped short. "My, my, if it isn't Olano, police department poster boy."

"Hinson," came the wary reply.

Penelope swiveled her head between the two men. David's lip had curled as if he found the other man's presence distasteful.

And the man who only moments earlier had set her senses reeling in his laid-back fashion appeared as steely as an anaconda poised to crush and destroy its prey.

Watching the two men standing there glaring at one another, Penelope experienced a momentary thrill. Then she realized she'd jumped to a very egotistical conclusion. Obviously these two guys knew one another, with no love lost between them. They weren't squaring off over her.

But at least she'd learned the stranger's last name.

To her surprise, David crossed the room and

kissed her on the cheek. Embarrassed at the possessive gesture, Penelope shifted slightly and, thinking to break the tension, said, "So I guess you guys have met."

"From time to time," David said, "but we won't bore you with the details, will we, Olano?"

The other man shrugged and took a long swallow of his water.

"But I didn't know the two of you were friends," David said, staring at Olano with eyes that looked like slits of blue ice.

"Oh, we're not," Penelope said.

"You may as well tell him," Olano said. "Hinson's the kind of guy who wants to know everything that goes on."

David stared at Olano, then back at her. She felt trapped, especially when David put his arm around her shoulder and said, "I thought you were too new in town to have made any friends. Isn't that what you told me?"

He accompanied the question with a smile, but Penelope heard a certain disapproval that she didn't understand. She had said those words to him only a few weeks earlier, but she resented him for assuming she'd had no time to meet anyone other than himself.

Penelope could almost hear Mrs. Merlin chastising her for having no sense of adventure. A spark flamed as she considered the years she'd subsisted on fantasies for emotional fulfillment.

Throwing caution to the wind, she eased from David's grasp and captured Olano's hand. Giving him a gentle squeeze and what she hoped was a coquettish glance, she said, "Well, we're

just now getting to know one another, David,
but I think I've found a great new friend in . . ."
Penelope stumbled momentarily. Hectares and
horses, she didn't even know the man's first
name! "In New Orleans," she finished.

This time it was the man with bedroom eyes
who draped an arm over her shoulders. At his
touch she experienced an electricity completely
absent from David's contact.

He traced the line of her jaw, setting off more
sparks. She smothered a gasp. After all, she'd
started this game; Olano was merely playing
along.

David, annoyance clear in his pale eyes, said,
"Before you get too involved with your new
friend, Penelope, you might want to ask for
character references."

Olano withdrew his arm, leaving her feeling
strangely bare. "Good advice," he said.

" 'Cause dirty cops don't mix too well with
squeaky clean lawyers," David said.

"But they're fine for lawyers with sleaze under their fingernails?" Olano tossed out the challenging words and once again Penelope knew
she was witnessing a running feud between the
two men.

But she'd had enough. "If the two of you
want to argue, you can leave," she said, enjoying her more dominant self. "I've had a rough
day, fainted from heat exhaustion, and the last
thing I want to do is listen to bickering."

David opened his mouth, then snapped it
shut.

Tony, from his stance near the refrigerator,
shot Penelope a mental thumbs-up. She'd stood

up to Hinson and played up to him. Not a bad effort for a woman caught between two strong personalities. Not only did she possess hidden fire, but hidden steel as well.

As if to prove that point, Penelope grasped his elbow and steered him to the door. "Thank you for coming by," she said, once again in that formal tone of hers.

"Anytime you need me," he said, checking to make sure Hinson hadn't stayed in the kitchen, "just call."

Sure enough, Hinson followed, looking every inch the hawk circling its prey.

Almost as soon as he put one foot in front of the other, Penelope dropped her hand from his elbow. She clearly wanted him out, which was just as well. He'd overstayed his welcome, and with a guy like Hinson, that could mean trouble for Penelope. He only wished she'd toss them both out at the same time.

At the door he paused and said to Hinson, "You and I go back a ways, and I want you to know I actually hadn't met Ms. Fields before today, when she fainted at my feet on Canal."

Hinson narrowed his eyes. "No? What a shame." He slipped an arm around her and ruffled her hair. "She's a terrific girl."

Penelope smiled a stiff little smile.

Tony wondered what women saw in the guy. And girl was definitely not the word he'd use to describe Penelope; she was all woman.

A complex woman he'd like to get to know.

"Catch ya later," he said, then halted with one foot out the door. Trained to see and hear the most subtle of indications of something amiss, he'd detected a shifting of the bedroom door. There—again it edged backward, only by a few inches, but enough to alert Tony to the presence of someone behind the door.

Hinson had his hand on the doorknob now, obviously eager to claim time alone with Penelope.

Rather than taking the hint, Tony slouched into his good old boy posture, resting one shoulder against the doorframe, giving himself a moment to analyze the situation.

What if they weren't alone? There could be an intruder, or potentially even more serious, maybe Penelope had another man stashed in the bedroom. She'd hinted at such a thing earlier.

If Hinson found out and lost his temper, it wouldn't be pretty. Penelope didn't look the type, but then, Tony reminded himself, she didn't carry the profile of a petty thief, either.

Shit. Tony hated being the man who tried to do the right thing.

Penelope shifted from foot to foot, glancing from him back to Hinson.

"Before I go," Tony said, straightening his body and checking for the .22 he carried in the leg pocket of his khaki shorts, "I think you should know there's someone else in your apartment."

"No, there's not," Penelope snapped out her response.

Tony raised his brows at her defensive reaction. So she knew.

Hinson stilled the hand he'd been smoothing over Penelope's hair. Tony read the awareness of danger in the other man's body as he shifted onto the balls of his feet and freed his arms. He also, Tony noted, unbuttoned with a swift motion his pretty-boy jacket.

No doubt he carried a piece under that coat.

"Would you mind explaining yourself?"

Even now Hinson had to talk like an overpaid lawyer, Tony thought, then cocked his head toward the bedroom.

"There's no one in my apartment other than the three of us." Penelope hedged backward, moving protectively toward the bedroom door. "And if you don't mind, Mr. Olano, that is one person too many."

"Ooh," Tony said, grinning at Penelope, which only seemed to set her back up more, "Sticks and stones . . ." As he spoke, he loosened the Velcro opening of his shorts pocket.

Hinson shadowed Tony's movement toward the bedroom.

Penelope raised her hands. "Stop." Tony detected a flush to her cheeks and a sparkly light in her eyes he could swear hadn't been there earlier. What was she hiding? How many layers of deception did this lady have built up?

In a lazy voice, Hinson said, "Why, Penelope, what if a burglar has broken in and is hiding in your bedroom? What if there's a desperate character in there waiting for us to leave so he can ravish you and—" He slashed a hand across his throat.

Penelope touched her shapely throat with a hand that trembled slightly. Tony saw the nervous motion and knew she was lying to them.

He exchanged looks with Hinson and nodded. As odd as it was for the two of them, enemies for life, to be acting in accord, they lunged together past Penelope and, with guns drawn, burst through the bedroom door.

Chapter 6

"Guns!" Penelope raced after the two guys. That the man with bedroom eyes wielded a gun didn't surprise her. But David? That was so out of character she couldn't quite grasp that he'd whipped out a gun that looked even bigger and deadlier than the one Olano had produced.

"Are you guys nuts?" Poor Mrs. Merlin! Her heart might stop from fright. It struck Penelope that she'd never be able to explain to the woman's family that they only needed a six-inch coffin, and she bit back a hysterical laugh.

They had the closet and the bathroom door open wide. Olano had gone to his knees beside the bed. David had pulled the drapes and stood checking the windows that led to the balcony.

The cookbook and remote control lay on the bed where Penelope had left them, but no sign of the diminutive Mrs. Merlin existed. Penelope wrinkled her brow and poked the carpet with the toe of her house slipper. Had she imagined the entire incident? Had she gotten so out of control with her fantasy life that she'd created the creature in her mind and projected her into the basket of napkin rings?

Olano had risen from the floor beside her bed and was staring at her with an expression she couldn't decipher. David, too, had turned around and was walking toward her. Penelope backed toward the door of the room. Surely they couldn't get mad at her. They were the ones who had overreacted.

But she might as well not have been in the room. David advanced on Olano, his face gone pale, a dangerous glint in his eye. "Pleased with yourself, Olano? Trying to show off for Penelope, trying to show her what a hot-shot cop you *used* to be?"

Olano, fiddling with his gun, didn't even look up until after he'd slipped the weapon back into his pocket. Then he shot a glance at David. "Forget it," he said.

He turned to her and Penelope realized with a swift shot of clarity she didn't want him to go.

"Better safe than sorry," he said, then sketched a salute and strode out of her apartment.

Out of her life.

David slipped his gun back under his jacket, and Penelope shivered. Walking toward her, he said in a low voice, the harsh tone belying the smile on his face, "Want to tell me how you know Tony Olano?"

So his first name was Tony. Penelope tested the name in her mind. She liked it. And it suited the man with bedroom eyes.

David put his arm around her and drew her down to sit beside him on the bed.

Penelope wondered whether Tony was short for Anthony. Of course it would be. Anthony

Olano. She made a face, thinking it sounded like a mobster sort of name. Maybe that was why he gave off an air of danger, but David had called him an ex-cop.

Pressure on her shoulder, a tiny bit stronger than a squeeze, brought her mind back to her bedroom. Not only was David holding her too tightly for her comfort level, they were sitting on her antique quilt. She tried to edge away, but David held her close to his side.

Tipping her chin up, he gazed steadily into her eyes in a way that made her feel uncomfortable, as if he could read every thought that swirled behind her eyes.

"Olano," he said, not letting go, "is a very dangerous man. Not someone a woman like you, particularly a lawyer, needs to be associating with."

So he was dangerous. Penelope realized with surprise that that trait attracted rather than repulsed her. "What did he do?"

Hinson let go of her chin. She kept her gaze fixed on his face, watching his expression shift and his eyes narrow as he said, "Olano was a cop who just couldn't mind his own business. Always butting in, never following procedure." David gestured around her bedroom. "Look what he did today. Same sort of impulsive behavior. Thinks he's spotted a crime and barges in. Not the sort of cop that makes for true law and order."

Penelope started to comment that David had rushed right into the bedroom alongside Olano, but she held her tongue. David didn't look too open to criticism at the moment.

"And the funny thing is that he got caught with his hand in the cookie jar and was bounced from the force in disgrace."

"What—" Penelope started to ask for specifics, the lawyer in her uncomfortable with such a vague description.

"Forget Olano," David interrupted, putting both his arms around her.

Penelope knew he wanted to kiss her. She'd let him kiss her once before, but kissing while sitting on her bed smacked too much of an invitation she wasn't ready to offer David yet, if at all.

He stroked a hand over her hair. "What happened to that chic French braid?"

She stiffened. Of course he'd noticed how uncharacteristically unkempt she appeared. Pulling her hair into a semblance of order behind her neck, she said, "Fainting is hard on one's looks, you know."

"So I see," David said, reaching for the neckline of her blouse. "Maybe you should slip into something fresher."

She caught his hand with hers. "David . . ."

"Yes?" Twisting his head down to hers, he covered her lips with his. His mouth was hot and demanding and Penelope knew she should respond. But all she could think about was her sweaty armpits. And the gun he had holstered under his jacket.

His tongue broke through the barrier of her lips and Penelope squirmed against him. There must be something wrong with her, a fear she'd carried within her for years. Men who wanted her, she didn't want. Men she wanted never looked twice at her.

She stifled a sigh and tried to force herself to return David's kisses.

He didn't seem to notice her lack of involvement. One hand working on a blouse button, he pushed her back on the bed, his slender body not crushing her so much with weight as with her wild thought that if she didn't make him get off her that very instant, he'd refuse to stop.

She pushed at his shoulders with her hands. He worked one button free, then the one below it, and slid his hand inside toward her breast. She twisted her mouth from his and said, "David, don't. This isn't right. It's not the right time."

He raised up on his hands and stared down at her, breathing hard. Before he could speak, Penelope sniffed and said in alarm, "Do you smell smoke?"

David kept looking at her as if he wanted to ignore the question, ignore her request to stop. Penelope shivered. The smell of smoke grew more definite.

Finally he lifted his body off hers and stood at the edge of the bed. "Something is definitely burning." Then he laughed and added, "Something besides me."

Penelope blushed. Well, it wasn't her fault he'd gotten all worked up. She jumped from the bed and ran toward the kitchen. Had she left something on the stove or in the oven? She didn't think so.

However, flames danced above the stove. "Firecrackers and figs!" She raced for the fire extinguisher she kept under the sink, yanked the pin, and aimed it at the blaze.

David walked slowly into the room behind her.

Penelope already had the fire damped. She tiptoed toward the stove. David moved behind her and looked over her shoulder. Inside the sauté pan atop the stove were the shards of what looked like a heap of toothpicks. And sure enough, the holder where she kept toothpicks handy for testing her baking sat empty.

David looked from the pan to her and back again.

Penelope lifted her hands, all innocence. She certainly hadn't started the fire in the pan.

But she knew who had. And she knew why. That incense stick must serve as more than a pole-vaulting aid.

"David," she said, in a voice she forced into sweetness and light, "would you mind awfully if we rescheduled dinner? I've just had too much excitement today, what with fainting from the heat and that dangerous man following me home, and now this . . . this spontaneous combustion." She didn't add *and what with you throwing yourself on me and not even taking off your gun first!* She wanted him out of her apartment, and apparently so did Mrs. Merlin.

And Penelope wasn't one to ignore help when it came to her aid. What had Mrs. Merlin said earlier? Something about don't question the gifts of the goddess?

"Of course not, Penelope." David adjusted his jacket and shot his cuffs. "You may be right.

This may not be the best time for us. I'll call you tomorrow."

Penelope smiled, relieved he'd taken the rebuff so well.

He leaned over and kissed her on the lips. Again, she didn't feel the way she thought she should. But maybe it was wrong of her to expect to experience shooting stars with every kiss.

Yet in her fantasies she felt so alive she just couldn't believe the feeling didn't exist in reality. Penelope sighed, walked David to the door, and wiggled her fingers good-bye.

She shut it after him, then leaned her back against the door's solid surface, thankful to be alone. Or almost alone. "Thank you, Mrs. Merlin," she called. "You can come out now and I promise you anything you want for dinner."

"Now, that's music to my ears!"

Mrs. Merlin's voice sounded from the kitchen. Penelope ran over and saw her flour canister pushing itself away from the counter wall. From behind it inched Mrs. Merlin, all-purpose incense stick in hand.

The woman said, "Honestly, some men just don't know when to take no for an answer, do they?"

Penelope smiled at her newfound ally. "Thanks for coming to my rescue. But David would have stopped."

Mrs. Merlin snorted. "Honey, when you've been on this earth for as long as I have, maybe you'll get a better grasp of human nature."

Wanting to believe David would have stopped, Penelope didn't argue the point. "How did you manage this diversion?"

Mrs. Merlin patted her incense stick. "Fastest vaulting I've ever done. With this baby I just might set an Olympic record." She winked. "And the toothpicks were just too, too handy."

"Well, thanks, but you might have burned my house down, you know."

"Phifil! Better to take that chance than let that man have you for dinner."

Penelope nodded. "Good point."

"Besides," Mrs. Merlin said, "it's only my candle spells that seem to end up causing trouble."

Penelope started the water to boil for the pasta and whisked together the sauce ingredients she'd prepared earlier. "Oh, you mean like shrinking yourself to six inches tall by mistake?"

"Yep. Only I'm quite certain that if you measured you'd find I'm actually six and a quarter inches." Mrs. Merlin had inched the top off the sugar bowl and stuck a finger in for a taste. "I sure am hungry," she said. Sucking on her finger, and talking around it, she said, "Your Tony wouldn't have forced himself on you."

"How do you—" Penelope looked over from where she stirred the sauce. "He's not 'my Tony.' But how do you know that?"

"His aura was much too violet and he has very old eyes."

"You saw him?"

Mrs. Merlin nodded. "When he looked under the bed."

The spoon stopped in mid-rotation. "He saw you under the bed and didn't say a word?"

"Like I said, he's the kind of man who would've stopped the first time you told him to, no matter how much he wanted to keep going."

Penelope hugged her arms to her sides, unaccountably pleased by Mrs. Merlin's words.

"Besides, I only winked at him."

"Right." Penelope let the whisk slow under her hand. "I'm sure he thought you were some sort of voodoo doll."

Mrs. Merlin smiled a most superior smile. "I suppose that's why he winked back at me."

"He did what?" The whisk quit moving.

"I am awfully hungry." Mrs. Merlin circled a tiny hand over her belly.

Penelope frowned and tried to remember the look on Olano's face when he'd risen from beside the bed, but she drew a blank. She'd been concentrating on the way he rose all in one motion, more graceful than a panther bunched to spring. The man with bedroom eyes moved with the speed and grace of a big cat, and distracted as she was, she hadn't been able to read the expression on his face.

The sauce burbled under her unseeing gaze as she pictured the man with bedroom eyes.

Tony Olano.

She sighed and for a moment forgot that he annoyed her. For a moment he became the man she'd imagined earlier, standing beside her as she accepted the Best New Chef award. She felt the warmth of his touch when he placed his hand in hers, a warmth that traveled up her arm into her heart. She glowed with accomplishment, but most of all with the feelings he ignited in her.

"You're never going to feed me, are you?" Mrs. Merlin dusted her hands together.

Penelope jerked back to her surroundings. "Why do you say that?"

"Just look at that sauce."

"Oh, no!" The once-beautiful alfredo sauce lay scorched and thickened into paste under her perfectly still whisk. Just when would she learn to keep her mind planted firmly on planet Earth?

"I don't suppose you have any oatmeal?"

"Oatmeal with Caesar salad?"

Mrs. Merlin held forth her hands in a begging gesture. "You have salad, I'll have oatmeal."

"Sure." Penelope did have a box of Quaker Instant in her cupboard. Every so often she tried to force herself to eat some, thinking she'd better offset all the rich creams and sauces she loved to devise in the kitchen. So she'd pick up a box with the rest of her groceries, then let it sit at the back of the cupboard until it was so stale she felt compelled to toss it out.

Oatmeal reminded her too much of her childhood.

"And raisins?"

"No raisins." She wrinkled her nose. Her mother had sprinkled raisins on Penelope's morning oatmeal, telling her they made good brain food. Her mother had been so set on Penelope's success, Penelope sometimes thought it was a miracle she'd turned out as well as she had. Most kids, she reflected every so often, would have revolted completely.

"Raisins equal sadness?" Mrs. Merlin spoke softly.

Surprised, Penelope nodded. "You're very perceptive. But I suppose you know that."

Mrs. Merlin laughed, a tinkly sound that brought to mind chimes shifting in the breeze. "Oh, I work hard at what I do. For my grandmother, you see, these skills came so easily." She sighed and sat down on the edge of the napkin holder. "But I have to practice, practice, practice to get things right. And even then—"

"Don't tell me," Penelope said. "Things somehow still get all mixed up."

Mrs. Merlin cupped her chin in her hand. "As soon as you make that oatmeal, we need to talk about how you're going to help me out of this little miscombobulation."

Penelope started to deny any intention to help. But one more look at the determined creature and Penelope knew Mrs. Merlin would brook no protest. And the sooner Mrs. Merlin sprang back to her full size, the sooner she'd be out of Penelope's once-orderly existence.

Even though Olano hadn't said anything, what if he started mulling over the sight of a six-inch-high woman under Penelope's bed? He'd been a cop. No doubt it was in his nature to investigate things that didn't quite add up.

Penelope set some water to boil and found the oatmeal, tucked well back behind bottles of olive oil, balsamic and tarragon vinegars, and her treasured saffron and summer savory.

Mrs. Merlin had taken to muttering to herself again. Penelope smiled despite her misgivings about helping her with the spell it would take to release her. Messing about with magick was totally foreign ground to her. Add to that her firsthand knowledge of Mrs. Merlin's last unsuccessful spell, and Penelope's common sense couldn't help but warn her away. Why, anything might go wrong.

She found a bowl for the oatmeal and a salad plate for herself, then shook some oatmeal into the boiling water and thought about how she'd longed for her life to change for the better.

She'd endured all those years in school with her nose to the grindstone to live out her mother's dreams for her. Now, released by her mother's death, she was free to shape her own dreams.

When the legal recruiter had first contacted her in Chicago, spinning stories of a plum job in an old-line New Orleans law firm, Penelope's silent reaction had been, I can't do that. She couldn't leave a firm where she stood in line for partnership at a record-breaking early age. She couldn't move to a new city, especially not to the South, where she'd never before stepped foot.

Penelope stirred the oatmeal and smiled.

She had done it.

So why turn her back on a little adventure now?

Chapter 7

Sighting the fiery orange ticket on his wind-shield, the infamous calling card of New Orleans' meter maids, Tony swore under his breath, knowing he was far more infuriated by the idea of Hinson holed up alone with Penelope than he was with the "no parking—loading zone" ticket. It also irritated him that he'd had to leave his car around the corner where he had no view of the building entrance.

Tony paused with one hand on the handle of his car door. With the other he crumpled the ticket. He had friends who would deal with the ticket.

Hinson he'd have to handle himself.

He opened the door of his car, tossed the offending orange paper into the backseat, then paused.

"Forget it," he said aloud. "Get in and let Ms. Penelope Sue Fields take care of her own problems." He'd face off with Hinson later, one on one.

He did as he told himself, then reached into the pocket of his T-shirt for his sunglasses. His finger touched a cold round object. He pulled it out along with his glasses, rolling the gold ball of an earring between his fingers.

His fingers warmed, and for a fleeting moment Tony thought he could sense heat from the small piece of jewelry. Then he forced a laugh at the fanciful idea.

The earring had fallen off when he'd kept Penelope from cracking her head on the sidewalk. He'd nabbed it as it had slipped from her ear and had then forgotten about it, though he had intended to return it to her the first time he'd gone to her apartment.

First time? Tony narrowed his eyes, pocketed the earring, and gripped the steering wheel with both hands. "First time" implied he was thinking of going back.

"Forget it," he said again. Then louder, "Forget *her*."

He studied his hands, noticing as any trained observer would the white rims of his knuckles, the fingers tensed much more than the situation called for on the surface.

He'd take the earring back and then he'd leave her alone.

You're not her type anyway. Tony laughed at the idea of a woman like Penelope Fields giving him a second glance. Since the first night he'd spotted her with Hinson, he'd used his professional skills and tools to learn more about her than most men knew after a dozen dates with a woman.

Grew up poor.

Well, they had that in common.

Good student.

Forget that. Tony had managed to graduate

from high school because the teachers didn't want to see his face there when school started the next fall. Not that he wasn't smart, but school bored him and he hated following rules.

Not so Ms. Fields, who'd done college and law school at Northwestern in only six years, then capped it off with an advanced degree in taxation from New York University, her only foray away from Chicago prior to her move to New Orleans.

Tony had joined the Army. There he'd met his match in his CO, a tyrant with a heart of gold who'd bullied Tony into college. Colonel Pridy attended Tony's commencement. That was the first day Tony had ever earned a smile from the old guy.

He wondered who'd attended Penelope's numerous graduations.

Other than her mother.

Tony frowned and jammed his key into the ignition. Instead of starting the engine, he sat and thought of how lonely it must have been growing up the only child of a single parent.

None of Tony's sleuthing had indicated either the identity of or the presence of a father in her life.

Maybe that accounted for her prissiness. He'd bet she'd never played rough and tumble, never gone fishing with her dad or shot baskets with him.

No wonder she hung out with Hinson. The only things a guy like Hinson fished for were compliments.

Hinson.

Tony ripped the key free of the ignition. Why

was he trying to fool himself? Penelope could be in trouble—Hinson couldn't have been pleased to see a man he regarded as a troublemaking fool standing smack-dab in the kitchen of his current love interest. And knowing Hinson, he'd take out his displeasure on that very same love interest.

Hinson's reputation with women gave Tony plenty of concern. Tony remembered one woman who'd staggered into the Second District station in his early days as a patrolman. She claimed to have been beaten by Hinson, but after a few hours in the station, she'd dropped the charges. At the time, Tony hadn't understood the powers at work behind the scenes, but he'd learned quickly when he started to nose about.

He hated men who preyed on women.

"Shit!" Still, going back to check on her didn't mean a thing. He'd do the same for any stranger on the street.

Yeah, sure, any stranger with silky brown hair and a pair of blue eyes so large you could drown in them.

Cursing under his breath, he jumped from the car and bumped straight into a meter maid. Without a word, she slapped another ticket into his hands.

"Not a bad bowl of oatmeal," Mrs. Merlin said, patting her lips with the paper napkin Penelope had cut in fourths.

"Thanks." Penelope smiled. Food had tempered Mrs. Merlin's tongue. "You manage pretty well with that spoon."

"Life consists of a series of adjustments to an

ever-changing reality." Mrs. Merlin ran a finger down the handle of the miniature silver coffee spoon Penelope had dug out for her to use.

"That's an interesting definition."

An impish smile lit Mrs. Merlin's face. "Oh, the interesting part is how we choose to make those adjustments!"

Penelope nodded, thinking of the fantasies that sprang so readily to her mind. In a way, that's how she dealt with life, rather than trying to change her external reality. Her smile faded into a frown.

"Oh, don't go all muddy on me," Mrs. Merlin pleaded, as she licked a last drop of oatmeal off the small spoon, then sat staring at Penelope's salad. "I need all your energies free-flowing while we discuss how to undo this spell."

Before Penelope could respond, the intercom buzzer rang.

"Oh, no!" Penelope glanced across the room in dismay. "Surely David hasn't come back."

"Don't you have any other friends?"

"I've only lived here since February," Penelope said, noting how cross she was sounding once more. "And I arrived after Mardi Gras."

"Oh, that." Mrs. Merlin waved a hand, then used a finger to swipe clean the ramekin Penelope had served the oatmeal in. "As far as I'm concerned, Mardi Gras gets far too much press, and I've lived here all my life. Too much drunkenness and not enough genuine joy."

The buzzer barked once, then twice.

"So why is it so famous, then?" Penelope almost added *Mrs. Know-It-All* to her question, but good manners won out.

"For the same reason McDonald's sells billions of burgers." Mrs. Merlin gave her a so-there look and Penelope could only shake her head.

The buzzer started in, a long, insistent droning noise impossible to ignore.

"Oh, all right!" Penelope stalked to the box on the wall and snapped down the talk button. "Who is it and what do you want?"

A chuckle floated to her ears.

Penelope stiffened. "Is this a joke?"

"Put Hinson on," came the muffled response.

Who would be looking for David at her place? Penelope frowned, feeling as if a private part of her life had been opened to public display. "He's not here. Who is this?"

No answer.

Penelope waited; then, as no further communication came, she shrugged and walked back to the table. Mrs. Merlin was now filching Caesar salad dressing off Penelope's plate with one small finger.

When Penelope caught her, Mrs. Merlin merely grinned and said, "You do have a way with food. Why don't you do the world a favor and leave the law library for the kitchen?"

"I can't believe you said that!" Penelope dropped into her chair and stared at this creature, who, though turning her life topsy turvy, had also brought with her an insight into the world that excited Penelope.

And frightened her, too.

Stimulating a sense of adventure was one

thing, but in one day Penelope had shoplifted, watched two men draw guns inside her apartment, and put out a fire!

She shook her head slowly, then gathered the dishes. "I'm a very good lawyer," she said.

"No doubt." Mrs. Merlin wiped her fingers on her piece of napkin. "Finger bowl?"

Penelope set the dishes in the sink, filled another ramekin with water, and carried it to the table. Mrs. Merlin dipped her fingers into the water, swirling them about in a dainty manner that seemed to contrast oddly with her wild hair and loudly colored caftan. It was almost like watching Phyllis Diller give an etiquette lesson.

At that thought, Penelope smiled broadly.

"Much better," Mrs. Merlin said, nodding toward her. "You can be the best lawyer in the world and not be happy. Why I know of a banker, quite accomplished and successful, who worked her way up in the ranks of management, yet in her heart lived an artist. And you know when she truly claimed her life?"

Penelope shook her head, even though she thought she knew the answer.

"That's right, my dear. After she retired and began creating watercolors and acrylics and stained glass. Then she blossomed."

Mrs. Merlin dried each of her fingers on the edge of the placemat where she sat. "She did good things in both phases of her life, but she did better for herself when she followed her heart."

Penelope blinked. She thought of the half-developed cookbook hidden in her briefcase, of all the recipes she longed to try. She thought of her visions of the Best New Chef ceremony.

"I've been offered a partnership in the firm here," she said slowly. "It's been a goal of mine for a long time."

Mrs. Merlin had removed her spectacles and dipped them in her finger bowl. Waving them about, she said, "Congratulations."

"Doesn't it sound good?"

Mrs. Merlin shrugged. "Good is as good does."

Penelope wrinkled her forehead, trying to parse that particular statement. She wasn't one of those lawyers who hated being a lawyer, she was glad she was good at what she did, but sometimes she couldn't help but wonder what else she might also be good at.

The intercom buzzer blared.

"Maybe you have more friends than you thought."

Penelope shot a glance intended to wither the tiny wit, but Mrs. Merlin paid her no notice. She was drying her glasses on the hem of her caftan. Penelope noticed for the first time that her houseguest wore an intricate silver chain around one ankle. Walking to answer the buzzer, Penelope wished she'd had the nerve to buy one. She found the look exotic and daring and so very unlike Penelope Sue Fields.

Thinking she just might buy one for herself, Penelope said "Yes?" into the speaker, this time in a much sweeter voice.

"Olano," came the reply.

She held her breath. What did he want? Why had he come back? Because he wanted to see her? Because he couldn't help himself? Penelope pictured him drawn to her, unable to resist the temptation of returning for one more glance, one more kiss.

Then she looked at her crumpled blouse, her wrinkled slacks, her hair swirling around her shoulders in an out-of-control mass. Yeah, right.

She sighed and said, "What do you want?"

"Let me come up and I'll tell you."

Penelope shot a glance at Mrs. Merlin, who was listening openly. "Let him in," said her miniature mentor.

"Why?"

"Why not?"

"Because the man is a pain in the ass. He's dangerous, and uppity and annoying and . . . and . . . incredibly sexy!"

Peering over the top of her glasses, Mrs. Merlin said, "Any other reasons?"

"Look at me. I'm a mess! And I'm tired and cranky. Plus I've got at least three hours of work I need to do tonight."

"Live a little. It's Saturday night. I'll entertain your friend while you go shower and slip into something more . . ." Mrs. Merlin tipped her head to the side and studied Penelope, "feminine, something more yielding."

Penelope rolled her eyes. "And what's wrong with what I'm wearing?"

Her only answer was a faint "Phifil!" so Penelope turned back to the intercom.

And shrieked.

Three floors below, the shriek shot out the intercom and Tony grinned. Ms. Starched had just realized she'd had the speaker on during her entire conversation.

He laughed, even though he figured she'd never let him in now. But fortunately, a pleasant-looking couple dressed for a night on the town came out the front door and politely held it open for him.

Ah, security buildings. But as he'd first rung the bell and asked for Hinson and gotten a negative response, Tony figured Penelope was safe for the moment.

That knowledge didn't deter him from making his return visit, though. Crossing the entryway of the elegantly restored warehouse, he found himself wondering what Penelope paid in rent. The building did have a sort of impersonal beauty, but Tony wouldn't for a minute have traded his own uptown shotgun that he'd inherited from his grandparents for the fashionable address, covered parking, and rooftop swimming pool.

Even if he could have afforded it.

Thinking of his bank account, he grimaced and loped up the stairs two at a time. Who would most women choose? Hinson in his thousand-dollar suits or Tony in his khaki shorts?

He took the last three steps in one bound then stopped abruptly when he saw a brunette babe clad in a black miniskirt sashay out of the doorway next to Penelope's apartment. She surveyed Tony with an appraising eye and Tony returned the look, short enough to catch her interest and long enough to confirm her breasts had to be plastic.

"New neighbor?" she asked in a voice that matched her tits.

"Just visiting," Tony said, throwing in a shake of his head and a touch of regret in his voice for good measure, even though his heart wasn't in the game.

"Mmmm," she said, and touched the corner of her lips with a dart of her tongue.

What the heck. He might as well give her a thrill. Sauntering closer, he said, "Maybe next time I'm in town . . ."

She swept her lashes across her upper cheeks, then let them flutter, a gesture that, rather than entrancing Tony, brought to mind the birds downed by his cat Bruno before the cat died of old age.

After her dramatic pause, she sighed and said, "Sure, handsome." She trailed a fingernail across his cheek. "Brenda in 39B."

Then she turned and took her time gliding down the hall toward the elevator. He watched her progress, wondering why women like Brenda had ever interested him.

Knowing exactly what type of woman intrigued him now, Tony turned to Penelope's door, only to hear it slam shut.

"Doing good, Tony-O. Real good," he muttered, wondering whether Penelope would open up again.

"Of all the impossible, egotistical masculine—" Penelope held the palms of her hands against her cheeks. She felt as if she'd been slapped.

Slapped back into reality.

That would teach her to fantasize about men like Tony Olano. Bedroom eyes indeed! He'd practically had his tongue down the throat of that trollop from next door.

Mrs. Merlin made a clucking noise and Penelope turned around slowly, leaning her back against the door. "What is it?"

"I think that's my line."

"He's out there flirting with my neighbor. So what's he doing ringing *my* buzzer?"

A knock sounded at the door, not too loud, not too soft. Penelope winced. The truth was she was embarrassed. He'd caught her eavesdropping on him, waiting to see whether he'd managed to get into the building despite her refusal to let him in. And then to see the way he'd put the moves on that top-heavy brunette only added to her chagrin.

The man certainly hadn't acted that way around her.

"If you let him in," Mrs. Merlin said sensibly enough, "you can find out why he rang your buzzer."

"You're pretty logical for a creature who deals on the outer edges of reality."

Mrs. Merlin shrugged. "The universe follows its own order. I merely tag along."

"Except when you mess up," Penelope mumbled under her breath.

"What an ugly thing to say!" Mrs. Merlin leaped up from the throw pillow Penelope had placed on the dining table for her to use as a chair. She ran to the edge of the table and peered down.

"Don't jump!" Penelope ran across the room.

"Very well." Mrs. Merlin settled down again.

"But it isn't nice to say hurtful things." She sighed. "Even when they're true."

"I'm sorry." Penelope did feel contrite. Mrs. Merlin, despite her frank tongue, seemed like a nice enough person. Certainly an interesting person, far more intriguing than most of the men and women Penelope worked with day in and day out.

The knock at the door grew more insistent.

"I guess I'll let him in."

The woman who'd dropped into her life nodded. "That would be karmic payback for hurting my feelings."

Penelope shook her head, wondering at the new language Mrs. Merlin was teaching her. "I gather that means you think this won't be a pleasant interview."

She blinked her eyes. "Let him in and see."

"What do I do about you?"

Mrs. Merlin waved a hand. "Don't worry about me. I'll sit here and pretend to be a what's-it, a napkin ring."

Penelope started toward the door, then halted. The idea of Mrs. Merlin watching from the table made her nervous. "He's going to see you. He'll think I'm nuts."

"Have a little faith. Open the door."

What did she have to lose? Penelope muttered "I'm coming" for what seemed like the nth time that evening, then opened the door.

Tony Olano fell into the apartment, managing to save himself from a pratfall on his face by extending his arms.

On his knees on Penelope's carpet, he looked

up, managing not even to look embarrassed. "'Bout time," he said.

"Were you listening through the keyhole?"

"Caught me." He grinned and Penelope thought he actually seemed happy to see her.

Then she remembered the way he'd flirted with the brunette only seconds before. Folding her arms across her chest, she said, "Would you care to get up and tell me why you're here, Mr. Olano?"

He rose, echoing that same fluid motion as when he'd stood after checking under her bed for his imagined intruder. "Tony," he said, extending a hand. "My friends call me Tony-O."

Penelope raised her brows. "How nice," she said, not extending her own hand.

Tony glanced down, rubbed his hand on his shorts, then stuck both hands in his pockets. "Well, Ms. Fields, I did return for a reason." He craned his neck and despite Penelope's obvious body language, moved farther into the living area. "But tell me, am I interrupting?"

"Interrupting?"

"You know, Hinson the golden boy. You don't have him stashed in the bedroom?"

Penelope closed her eyes for a moment, then counted to ten. "No, no one is stashed in the bedroom. There's no need to draw your gun and frighten Mrs. Mer—"

"So you do have a guest?" Tony settled onto her loveseat.

"I was referring to my cat," Penelope said, hoping Mrs. Merlin wouldn't get offended. "Her name is Mrs. Mer."

He looked interested. "What kind of cat?"

Penelope knew nothing about cats. She threw a glance toward Mrs. Merlin, who watched the scene with interest from her perch. "Orange," she said.

"Orange. A very rare breed," Tony said. He was rolling something about between his fingers.

"Oh, most." Penelope nodded. "She's a fairly magical cat."

"And does she have the same number of toes as other orange cats?"

Wishing she'd never started down this silly train of conversation, Penelope managed a nod.

"Where did you get her?"

Penelope laughed nervously, thankful he hadn't quizzed her further on the number of toes. If only her mother had let her have pets! But she'd never had a dog or a cat. Once she caught a frog and wanted to keep it, but her mother insisted she let it go in the woods behind the trailer park. *Nasty things*, she'd said, as if that settled everything. She realized Tony was waiting for an answer, so she said, "Oh, she just followed me home one day."

"What an interesting life you lead," Tony said.

Penelope was pretty sure he said that to mock her. That idea put her back up. "Look, why don't you tell me what you want, starting with why you've been following me and ending with when you are going to take your leave?"

"Whew! I bet you're a tough cookie in court."

"If you need a lawyer, call me at my office." He shook his head. Holding out his hand, palm up, he said, "I came to return your earring."

Penelope touched both her ears. Sure enough, her right ear still held the round gold earrings she favored, the first fourteen-karat gold jewelry she'd purchased after she'd finished law school and the financial payoffs were finally coming to fruition. Her left earlobe was bare. "I didn't even realize I'd lost it."

He moved toward her, earring in his outstretched hand. Then he hesitated. Watching her with those dark eyes of his, lids halfway shuttering them in an intense way that made them even more mysterious, he crossed the rest of the way, pausing directly in front of her.

Penelope's breath came faster. Why was it this man could transform from annoying her to tantalizing her in the shimmer of a second?

He lifted his hand and held the earring up to her earlobe. His fingers brushed the side of her jaw, setting her senses aflame. He glanced down into her eyes. "They suit you," he said, then dropped the earring into her hand.

Surprised at the effect his touch had on her, Penelope almost didn't grasp his words. Then what he'd spoken settled on her like the heavy fog of the city's mosquito trucks. *They suit you.* Yes, plain Penelope with her plain boring earrings. The woman next door wouldn't be caught dead in such pedestrian jewelry.

He backed toward the door, watching her in an intense way that seemed at odds with his words. Wrapped in her own thoughts, Penelope followed him to the door. She wished she could think of some cute thing to say, some flirtatious way to let him know she'd like for him to stay, to let him know she wasn't as boring as she appeared. But her tongue might as well have been on strike.

"Later," he said, then disappeared once again from her doorway.

Chapter 8

STEP INSIDE FOR THE POWER OF VOODOO proclaimed a banner hung above the entrance to the Bourbon Street shop Mrs. Merlin had instructed Penelope to visit.

"Don't worry about the schlocky voodoo stuff," she'd told her only that morning over another bowl of oatmeal. "That's for the tourists who think it's some sort of rule that when they visit the French Quarter they have to buy a voodoo doll to go with their daiquiris. The true magick is in the back. Just tell the man behind the back counter I sent you."

Now, hesitating on the sidewalk, feeling pretty much like one of the tourists Mrs. Merlin had derided, Penelope didn't know whether she could go through with the errand.

It was all so unbelievable. Here she was, a lawyer who dealt in the well-defined world of revenue codes and Tax Court decisions, about to purchase supplies for Mrs. Merlin to use in some oddball candle ritual.

But unless she accepted that Mrs. Merlin had been born six inches tall and would go to her grave six inches tall, logic argued for her to go through with whatever it took to help bring her temporary houseguest back to life-size.

The sun beat down on her as she dallied in front of the narrow old townhouse that housed the Bayou Magick Shoppe. The weight of the heat reminded her of the fiasco she'd undergone only yesterday, and she knew she should either enter the shop or seek the shelter of an overhanging balcony.

Still she hesitated, one part of her mind wondering why Mrs. Merlin couldn't simply cast a spell on her own without sending Penelope out for supplies. Another part of her mind drifted to the sidewalk on Canal where she'd fainted in Tony Olano's arms.

The flurry of her tummy, the alarming beating sensations she'd experienced inside her head just before she'd swooned, seemed worth the trade-off of being captured and held close in a pair of arms stronger than any Penelope had envisioned in her fantasies.

She sighed and wondered whether he'd magically appear again, or if he'd given up on following her after she'd fallen so tongue-tied last night. Crickets and Crisco! Any woman half her age could have come up with something flirtatious to say to a living, breathing Tony Olano poised only a few inches from her parted lips.

But not Penelope.

She sighed again. She'd better go in or she would faint. If not from heat, then from frustration with herself.

A skinny young man wearing a denim shirt, with the sleeves torn out, hanging loose over baggy shorts appeared from out of nowhere. Penelope clutched her purse and tried to look un-approachable.

"Hey, lady, I betcha I can tell you where you got them shoes," the man said, rubbing his hands together.

"No way." Penelope couldn't help but object to such an impossible statement. There was no way this unkempt person had even heard of Chicago's Marshall Fields, the store where Penelope had begun shopping once she'd received her first paycheck from the august firm of Pierce, Turner, Steicker, Wagner and Resnick.

"Yessir," he said, and spit out of the side of his mouth. "You pay me a dollar if I'm wrong."

"You've got yourself a deal."

The man studied her shoes, swaggering around her in a broad circle. He put a hand to his chin, then pronounced, "You got them on yo' feet, and yo' feet on Bourbon Street!" The man went off in a peal of laughter and held out his hand. "Now gimme the dollar."

"That's ridiculous," Penelope said, feeling incredibly foolish for getting set up so easily. Nonetheless, she opened her purse and pulled four quarters from her change compartment.

The man pocketed the quarters. "For another five dollars I'll show you around."

"No, thanks."

"What's a matter, you don't like me?" The man sounded more hurt than menacing.

"It's nothing personal, but I'm going into this store and then home."

The man rolled his eyes. "This store? Why you going into this place?"

"That should be obvious."

The man shook his head, a long rolling movement. "You don't want to do that. Go someplace else. Go anywhere but here." The man backed away a step.

At least that had succeeded in discouraging him from continuing to offer his guide services. Penelope settled one foot on the first step.

Walking off, the man called, "You should pay me another dollar for telling you not to go in there, but I ain't gonna wait for it!"

Penelope looked again at the front of the store. It looked hokey, but fairly harmless. Unlike the man who seemed afraid of what lay behind the sagging door, she was more bothered by the silliness of it.

Well, Penelope would take a voodoo practitioner over a street hustler any day.

"Excuse me. We'd like to go in, please."

Penelope turned her head. Next to her on the sidewalk stood a group of five women wearing badges featuring the name of a nationally known tour group.

She hurried into the store, followed by the others, reassured that such normal-looking people visited the shop.

A teenager with purple hair and three crosses dangling from her left ear glanced up and smiled as Penelope entered. "Let me know if I can help you," she said.

Despite the clerk's unorthodox appearance, Penelope sighed in relief at the friendly greeting that had already helped put her at ease. She dug Mrs. Merlin's list out of the pocket of her linen slacks and looked around her.

Poof! went her sense of ease. Glittering glass

eyes stalked her from the dried grass bodies of dozens of dolls. Dressed in multihued fabrics, they were marked with slashes of red paint, but to Penelope, it looked like it might well be blood.

Skulls hung from hooks in the ceiling and sprouted from the walls. Plastic ones made in China, Penelope assured herself, but disconcerting nonetheless. Especially the ones with tufts and patches of hair, setting the impressionable Penelope to imagining how they'd been scalped by doers of evil magick.

Every shelf and counter in the cramped and narrow shop was covered with objects running the gamut from witchcraft to voodoo to tarot cards to the zodiac. And those were only the types of magick Penelope recognized.

A counter ran across the back of the shop. Behind the crowded space sat a man with a long brown ponytail, the brown shot through with strands of silvery gray. Despite the silver and the hippy-style bandanna coiled around his forehead, Penelope thought he was younger than he appeared at first glance, far too young to have experienced the hippy heyday.

He watched her approach, his eyes glittering, producing the same effect on Penelope as did the voodoo dolls that occupied so much of the front part of the shop. But this was the man Mrs. Merlin had described as her mentor in magick and told her she must find.

She swallowed nervously as she stepped toward the counter. Before she could speak, he said in a low voice, "Penelope, I presume?"

She halted. How did this man know her

name? Her skin crawled, then common sense
gained the upper hand. Mrs. Merlin must have
phoned ahead.

Trying to act as if a visit to a magick shop was
a regular part of her routine, she nodded and
said, "Mr. Gotho?"

He returned her nod. "You are on a mission
today?"

"Yes." Penelope glanced around. It couldn't
have been too difficult for him to recognize her,
had Mrs. Merlin called. Unlike the other customers who'd followed her in, she wore no name
tag. Unlike them, she carried no shopping bags
from Café du Monde or Sallie's Pralines or
House of Blues.

He folded his hands atop the counter and regarded her steadily. Slowly, Penelope realized
his eyes weren't at all threatening; they were, in
fact, quite gentle.

"Mrs. Merlin sent me," she said after a gulp.

"Ahh, yes," he said, as if that explained
everything. He rose and lifted the piece of the
counter that blocked the way to what lay beyond. "Won't you come in?"

Penelope glanced around her, then back to the
man's eyes, seeking reassurance. He nodded in
a gentle fashion and she stepped forward. She
couldn't help but think that Richard Speck had
probably nodded just as sweetly to the eight
nurses he'd murdered in Chicago, a story she'd
heard often growing up in that city.

"Do not be afraid," the man said. "Any friend
of Mrs. Merlin's is a friend of ours. Besides"—
he winked and Penelope immediately relaxed—
"if you've met Mrs. Merlin under circumstances

that send you to pay a visit to us, you'll be needing as much assistance as we may be able to offer."

"Does she cause these problems often?" Penelope couldn't help but blurt out the question.

Mr. Gotho nodded. "Mrs. Merlin has a good heart and a true spirit, but she's much too impatient and opinionated to learn the art of candle magick. She simply jumps in, whether she has properly prepared or not."

"Well, I wish she'd have thought through this spell from A to Z." Penelope followed the man through a doorway hung with bells and beads that danced musically against one another as they passed.

"She says she was trying to solve a problem with a tax collector, yet something went wrong with the colors she used and that's why she thinks she ended up with me." She shook her head, then at Mr. Gotho's questioning look she added, "I'm a tax lawyer."

"Ah, I see." He stopped in front of a door, knocked twice, waited, then knocked four times.

The door opened.

Penelope held her breath. No one on Law Review back at Northwestern would believe that she, Penelope Sue Fields, was about to enter the inner sanctum of a voodoo shop. What she wouldn't give to be able to show them a photograph of this moment!

"We must live in the moment, for our souls and not for others," Mr. Gotho said, throwing an unfathomable look over his shoulder as he stepped inside the room, a room empty except for the two of them. So why had he knocked?

The hairs on her arms lifted and swayed. Penelope hesitated in the doorway, trying to assess the meaning of Mr. Gotho's statement.

Mrs. Merlin liked to make similar pronouncements, she realized. As if they were eking out gems of wisdom reserved for the gods—or goddess, as Mrs. Merlin would say—and only shared them in tidbits with mere mortals such as Penelope. Well, really, she didn't need these barely educated men and women to show her the path to wisdom.

Mr. Gotho swung about abruptly, bumping straight into her and practically bruising her nose. He slammed the door shut. "We cannot go further."

"And why not?"

"Something is wrong." He held a finger out, as if testing the currents of the air. "Something has shifted in . . ." He swung around to face her directly. "Something in your aura. It's not clean, not pure."

Guilt shot through Penelope. She stood accused and had no defenses. "I—uh, I was only thinking that you talk as if you know so much, and I can't see why you're so much smarter than I am."

"Ahhh." That seemed to be Mr. Gotho's favorite expression. "Ego."

He stood there, arms crossed against his chest, regarding her steadily.

When he didn't say anything else, Penelope finally asked, "Ego?"

"Your ego stands in the way of your quest for Mrs. Merlin. Until you can put it aside, you will not be able to assist her."

"But that's ridiculous!" Penelope waved in front of Mr. Gotho's face the list Mrs. Merlin had dictated to her. "I have everything that she needs written down here. I only need to purchase the items and I assure you I'll be gone. It's as simple as that."

Mr. Gotho shook his head. "Those without a pure heart may not receive the riches of the inner sanctum of the Bayou Magick Shoppe." He placed a firm hand on her shoulder and spun her about. "Time to go," he said, hustling her through the hall and back across to the other side of the counter.

"When you have cleansed yourself of your ego, you may return. Please tell Mrs. Merlin it is our most sincere wish to assist her, but that you need . . . ah, let us say a bit of work . . . before you may serve as her emissary."

"Well, of all the high-handed—" Penelope swept through the front of the store, nose in the air. She'd rarely been so insulted. Here she'd taken time on her precious day off, on Sunday, the only day of the week she didn't work, work, work, and this man had thrown her out of the store. She had a good mind to storm back in there and tell him what she thought of him.

She looked around her. The glare from the afternoon sun bounced from the sidewalks straight back to her eyes. She needed sunglasses, something she'd have to take care of soon. Even though Chicago summers grew warm, sometimes even unbearably hot, the sun in New Orleans scorched itself into her eyes the way the northern sun never had.

"So you see I was telling ya the truth." The

street hustler popped up, again seemingly out of nowhere. "I can tell you didn't have such a good time in that shop."

Penelope shook her head, feeling dazed and more than a bit ruffled. What would Mrs. Merlin say when Penelope returned empty-handed? And how would she continue to entertain a visitor who demanded almost constant preparation of oatmeal, Penelope's least favorite dish, even lower on her list than meatloaf, her mother's other staple?

"Five dollars, I take you someplace fun," said the man, a hopeful look on his scrawny face.

Penelope shook her head, feeling like a prize-fighter staggering back for another round. "I've got to go back inside," she said. "But thank you."

The man danced away, forming the sign of the cross in front of his chest.

Her heart sinking, Penelope reentered the shop. She walked straight to the front register where the girl with three crosses stood polishing jewelry. Surely this sweet-faced girl would help her to assemble the list. The sooner she got what she needed, the sooner her life could get back to normal.

"Hello," Penelope said, "I have a few things I need."

The girl smiled. "Sure. What can I get for you today?"

Penelope held forth her list.

The girl read it, her face growing grim. Then she smiled, almost too brightly, and said, "I am so sorry, but we don't carry any of these items."

"But that's impossible!" Penelope snatched

the list back. "I was told by a reliable source that this was the only place in the city to buy frog's testicles and horsehair liniment and iguana jelly." She gripped the edge of the counter, restraining her temper.

The girl turned to another customer coming up behind Penelope. "I can take you here," she said.

The camera- and shopping-bag-laden matron pushed her way to the register, elbowing Penelope from front and center. "Good," the shopper said, "I've been looking for these bat's wings for my nephew back home. He said he just had to have them from New Orleans."

"Oh, they're the best," said the salesgirl.

Penelope stood staring at her list, wondering if she was losing her mind. This shop could provide bat's wings but not frog's testicles?

Then she underwent a most horrible thought. Had Mrs. Merlin made her the butt of some joke? Was she up to some magickal mischief while she'd sent Penelope out on a wild goose chase?

Mrs. Merlin was probably laughing into her oatmeal at the idea of Penelope having to ask for something so unbelievably absurd as frog's testicles!

Penelope whirled around and dashed out of the Bayou Magick Shoppe. Running much more quickly than was good for her in the July heat, she jogged toward the side street where she'd parked her car.

She'd start her own fire and hold Mrs. Merlin's feet to it until the wee woman 'fessed up to just what she was about.

About to step into her car, Penelope paused and glanced around her. She told herself she was relieved that the man with bedroom eyes hadn't shown any sign of following her that morning. No doubt after her tongue-tied behavior of the night before he'd loped off after more responsive prey. Like that trollop in 39B.

She squelched a tiny bubble of disappointment. Despite the way he had of annoying her, Tony Olano definitely made her life more interesting.

"Get over him," she muttered, watching as a short fat man in a suit trundled slowly past her on the sidewalk. He looked like a character out of a Dick Tracy comic strip, decidedly a bad guy. Penelope jumped in her car, slammed the door, and locked it.

She'd had enough of troublemakers for one day.

Chapter 9

The instant Tony spotted the man known to both law enforcers and lawbreakers as Rolo Polo tailing Penelope, he knew Squeek had been telling the truth when his old informant had sought him out late the previous evening.

Squeek had found him hours after Tony had left Penelope's apartment—hours after Tony had sworn off using her to get to Hinson. When he'd held the earring to her ear and his finger grazed her cheek, he'd scarcely made contact. Yet that scant touch had socked him squarely in the gut. The vulnerability lurking in those blue eyes of hers haunted him.

Tony had known at that moment he couldn't cause her any more trouble. Not if he wanted to continue facing himself in the mirror.

He hadn't expected the vulnerability. When he'd closed in on her, her eyes appeared more like those of a gator blinded by a night hunter's light than the eyes of a woman about to be kissed.

A damned desirable woman.

Tony shifted his vantage point behind a conveniently unlocked gate to a Bourbon Street townhouse, and pulled his scarred yo-yo, his favorite thinking aid, from a pocket of his shorts.

The funky voodoo shop lay in the residential section of Bourbon, where tourists dwindled to more manageable numbers and locals were glad of the fact. Only an occasional pack of sweating conventioneers decked out in name tags and plastic carryall bags wandered by on the street. The relative quiet gave him time to think about last night.

Last night, when he'd been about to kiss Penelope.

The yo-yo danced to within a hair's breadth of the sidewalk before he called it back. That's how close he'd been to kissing Penelope Sue Fields.

Just to rattle her. Shake her up. Fuss with her prissiness. Yeah, Tony, show her what she's missing by hanging out with a guy like Hinson instead of Tony Olano.

What did Hinson have that Tony didn't? A fat bank account? Fancy suits, lots of them. A law degree. Tony spun the yo-yo harder.

His ego told him she'd been attracted to him. His reason told him she'd been repulsed by his touch.

He checked the storefront of the Bayou Magick Shoppe. Penelope remained inside. Tony had had to hold a hand over his mouth when she'd fallen for the oldest scam on Bourbon Street.

Movement down the street caught his eye and he captured the yo-yo in his palm. A man almost as wide as he was tall, wearing a wrinkled brown suit far too heavy for the heat, turned onto the street. He carried a colorful tourist map and was making quite a fuss over unfolding it and holding it in front of him.

Tony frowned.

Rolo Polo waddled closer, stopping not three feet from the gate that hid Tony. He finished fiddling with the map and stood staring at it, apparently trying to pass for a tourist.

Fat chance. Rolo Polo had the map upside down. Tony shook his head, wondering how a guy like Rolo kept his job as Hinson's boss's number one enforcer.

But then, from his years as a policeman, Tony knew a man didn't have to be smart to be cruel.

The fat man rustled the map, then quickly swapped top for bottom. Tony chuckled under his breath, a sound that died in his throat when he considered Rolo Polo's presence and how it impacted on the reason he'd come in search of Penelope this morning.

When he'd gone out the night before, restless and strangely discontented, Tony had paid a visit to Smokie's on Oak Street, a disreputable bar where cigarette smoke, drunken braggarts, and the siren song of video poker machines provided what passed for ambience.

He'd gone seeking diversion. Looking for trouble is what his ma would have called it. Once inside, he'd exchanged a few hand slaps, winked at Lora and Dawn, the prostitutes Smokie pimped for, then shouldered his way to the bar, where he settled down with a Budweiser.

The beer didn't seem as cold as usual, the TV blared more loudly than he remembered, and the bartender was a new guy who shouted at customers who didn't tip to his satisfaction.

Feeling worse instead of better, Tony threw two bucks on the counter, daring the bartender to yell at him. The guy opened his big mouth the same moment Squeek materialized at Tony's side.

"Where yat, my man?" Squeek, so named for the obnoxious noise he liked to make rubbing his tennis shoes on hard surfaces, raised his hand for a high-five to which Tony complied. High-fiving was a greeting Tony thought pretty silly, but Squeek never failed to greet him that way. A habit, Tony thought, that came from Squeek watching too much television both in and out of prison.

"What's hap'ning?" Tony sat back down, keeping a sharp eye on the streetwise petty crook. Squeek had helped Tony out in the past, and, never one to forget a friend, an enemy, or an informant, Tony had done the same for Squeek.

"Not much. Not much," Squeek said, and licked his lips.

"Give us two Buds," Tony told the bartender, who glared at him, then down at the two dollars, but handed over the beers without giving him any lip.

Squeek's disappeared in three long swallows. Tony replaced it, his senses gloriously alive. With Squeek there were no coincidences. If he'd found Tony, something was up—something Squeek figured was worth a lot to Tony, and by extension, to Squeek.

Halfway through his third beer, Squeek pushed away from where he'd elbowed up to the bar and jumped first forward then backward. His Air Jordans rent the air with the high-pitched rubbing noise he proudly hailed as his namesake.

"Sounding good, Squeek," Tony said, wondering who else in Smokie's was paying attention to Squeek's little ritual. No matter how many times Tony had pointed out to Squeek that his habit of never failing to perform his trademark noisemaker just prior to relaying a hot tip pretty much shot his cover, Squeek still insisted on doing it.

The man grinned and plunked his elbows back onto the bar, a satisfied smile on his face. Peeling the label from his beer, he began talking to the bottle.

Not once did he glance toward Tony. Not once did he check to make sure Tony heard his words through the din of the bar.

But Tony heard.

Loud and clear.

"Your man, you know the one, the pretty boy in the suit who sent you down, he's got some big things planned. Yeah, buddy, big things planned." Squeek rocked closer to his bottle, working a dirty fingernail under the side of the sweating label.

The smoke in the room crawled behind Tony's eyes as he concentrated on what Squeek had to say. The irritation only heightened his sense that something big was afoot.

"Yeah, I heard he be jumping over the broom. Soon, too. But not because his heart says to do it." Squeek cackled. "The old man done told him he has to."

Tony took a long swallow of his beer. He

knew the expression Squeek used referred to a manner of wedding ceremony used by slaves when they'd not been permitted church weddings.

So wedding bells were ringing for Hinson.

His hand clenched on his bottle. And Hinson's boss had ordered the deed be done.

Surely not—

Squeek went on. "Thinking of you, I says to me, Squeek, go find out who the woman is. Tell Tony and maybe Tony can mess with him." He grinned. "You know, mess with him by messing with her. That old devil wouldn't like being the second pig at the trough." He cackled and looked at his empty bottle.

Tony thought about the bills he had left in his pocket. Shit. He hoped some of those singles turned out to be tens. He bought another beer for Squeek and very casually said, "So you got her name for me, right, Squeek? So I can pick something out at the bridal registry."

Squeek slapped his thigh. "You're a funny guy, Tony. But yeah, you right, I got her name. A funny name, though. Not so easy to say."

Tony knew the routine. He knew better than to ask outright what Squeek required as payment in exchange for his information. Squeek had a professional's pride.

Tony's mental replay of the night before was abruptly interrupted when the door to the Bayou Magick Shoppe opened. Tony tore his mind back to the present, watching as Penelope hustled down the steps in quite a huff. Tony wished he'd been a fly on the wall inside the shop, but as he'd been expecting one of Rolo

Polo's flunkies to appear, he'd kept well out of sight.

Rolo Polo peered over the top of his map. Penelope paused on the sidewalk. The same dude who'd taken her for a dollar drifted over. Tony smiled. No way Penelope would let herself be taken for a ride twice. She might be sheltered from reality, but he'd bet she was a quick learner.

Suddenly she turned and reentered the shop.

Tony let his mind drift back to what Squeek had asked of him. Strangely tongue-tied, the informant had danced around his request a bit, then finally blurted it out.

"My woman needs some help."

Tony had narrowed his eyes, figuring Squeek's woman had gotten in trouble with the law. For Squeek, he'd do whatever he could. Never once had Squeek fed him bad information, and that was deserving of a lot. "Shoot. Tell me what the problem is."

Squeek picked at the mess of beer labels on the bar in front of him.

Tony waited. When Squeek didn't say anything, he prompted, "Is she in bad trouble?"

Squeek looked at him with eyes wide with disappointment. "My woman," he said slowly, "don't get in trouble."

"Sorry." Tony hadn't meant it as an insult.

"Me and my woman, we've been together now for five years." Squeek held up four fingers and the thumb of his right hand and nodded solemnly. "A long time, five years."

Tony had to agree with that statement. It was longer than he'd managed to stay married.

"But we got no kids," Squeek said.

Tony heard what Squeek said, but for the life of him he couldn't see how he could help with that problem.

Squeek turned to him then, and grabbed him by the arm. "You promise to find me a doctor who can help my woman and I'll give you Penelope Fields's name right this minute."

His hunch confirmed, Tony said, "You got it, Squeek." He had no idea how to find a fertility doctor, but his ma would know. And knowing his ma, she'd talk the doctor into seeing Mrs. Squeek for free.

Tony forgot about Squeek's problems as Penelope rushed out of the shop again. She'd been in a huff the first time she exited the shop, this time she was livid. Tony raised his brows and pocketed the yo-yo as she slapped one loafer-clad foot in front of the other. Watching her eat up the sidewalk, Tony reconsidered his conclusion that Penelope was a quick learner. For a woman who'd fainted from heat only the day before, she sure hadn't learned that lesson.

Rolo Polo jammed his map into a crumpled wad and took off after her. As soon as he'd moved out of earshot, Tony slipped from behind the gate and, sticking to doorways as much as possible, kept both of them in sight.

Driving through the French Quarter toward her Warehouse District apartment, Penelope gathered steam to fuel her indignation toward Mrs. Merlin. How could she have sent her on a scavenger hunt like that?

Stuck at the red light on Canal, she watched

the stream of people flowing past, among them a contrasting mix of several women, each with a baby stuck on a hip and clutching one child in hand, side by side with geeky guys in white shirts and pocket protectors in town for what had to be a computer convention. Calming slightly, Penelope reconsidered rushing straight home.

She needed facts. Cold, hard, objective information. Only from Mrs. Merlin's lips had she heard of such a thing as candle magick. She pursed her lips in concentration. The blare of a horn behind her jerked her into motion and she swung the car sharply to the right, rather than proceeding straight ahead toward home.

She'd go to the Barnes & Noble in Metairie. She'd read about the gigantic bookstore, but never taken the time to visit. She knew enough about the city to find the freeway and find an exit that would lead her to Veterans Memorial Boulevard, which she understood to be the main drag cutting through the sprawling suburb of Metairie.

Penelope found her way there, getting lost only once, which she reckoned wasn't too bad for someone used to relying on the El in Chicago for her transportation needs.

She knew the second she stepped into the store she could spend the day there, lose complete track of time. Fortifying herself with a cappuccino, she fought off the temptation to wander every lovely book-filled aisle and instead asked directions to the section where she might find books on magick.

Sipping her drink, she took the escalator and

studied the New Age section. Intent on her law and tax studies, Penelope had never strayed into such a section in any of the many bookstores or libraries where she spent so many hours of her life.

Unfamiliar titles and subjects assailed her eyes and she was reminded of the way she'd felt her first day in a law library. So many volumes, so many unknowns. Then she'd been intrigued by the intellectual challenge. And now, facing this odd array, she felt faintly superior, assuming the books were written by nuts who wanted to embrace make-believe rather than accept the rational world in which they dwelled.

Rather than taking charge of their own realities, people retreated into witchcraft, magick, reading auras, chakras—whatever those were—anything that gave them hope for a better world.

Which, now that she thought about it, was absolutely the same thing she did by slipping into her fantasy world. Instead of finding the courage to try to date more, to attempt to meet men, even to do something so bold as to run or answer a personals ad, Penelope had withdrawn.

Her imaginary lover Raoul might occupy her mind, but he was cold comfort on lonely nights, and a poor escort, indeed, for law firm social functions.

Penelope closed her eyes and inhaled the scent of chocolate that sprinkled the foam topping of her cappuccino. Yes, she acknowledged, she needed to make some changes in her life.

Just because she'd followed the path her mother had committed her to didn't mean she couldn't be a lawyer and enjoy the rest of her life more. A lawyer wasn't such a bad thing to be.

Her mother had told her, more times than Penelope could count, "Better a lawyer than a waitress." And even though Penelope sometimes still blamed her now-deceased mother for not letting her carve her own way through life, she had to admit she'd far rather be a partner at LaCour, Richardson, Zeringue, Ray, Wellman and Klees than be pushing coffee across the counter at Barnes & Noble.

Penelope wrinkled her nose, remembering what the ponytailed Mr. Gotho had accused her of. Was it wrong to prefer being a lawyer to being a waitress? Penelope didn't think of that as having too much ego, especially considering she'd far rather have become a chef than a lawyer anyway.

The oddly young but somehow ageless Mr. Gotho had been about to help her, too, Penelope was sure of that, when something she'd done had set him off. It had been right after she'd thought of him and Mrs. Merlin as undereducated. Well, perhaps she was a bit of a snob about that, but she had loved her mother, despite her nagging ways, and her mother had dropped out of high school her senior year, pregnant with Penelope.

That was a story Penelope had heard more times than she ever cared to remember. Just once, filtered in among those stories, Penelope would have liked to have learned something about the man who had fathered her. But on that topic her mother remained constantly silent.

As far as Penelope knew, her conception

might have been immaculate. Living with a single mother who maintained a firm distance from any man, Penelope had often thought it was no surprise she herself had never gotten close to a man.

But she knew it wasn't any fear of repeating her mother's path that held her back. She simply didn't understand how to attract a man.

She stared into her cooling cappuccino, then lifted her eyes to the shelves. She had work to do. Best to concentrate on that.

Spotting a row of books on the art and magick of candle burning, Penelope gathered them in one arm and carried them and her coffee to a deep chair in a reading circle placed near the escalator. Several other customers had settled there, reading everything, Penelope noticed, from *Zen and the Art of Motorcycle Maintenance* to celebrity biographies to comic books.

Penelope wished she'd picked some other, more sensible choices to serve as cover for her reading material. Anyone who glanced over at her selections would assume she was one of those woo-woo weirdos. Why, all the books she'd selected spelled magic with a "k" on the end, as if the word itself carried its own mystical meaning.

Oh, well, she couldn't be any more embarrassed today than she had already been. The very idea of asking out loud for frog's testicles! Coloring slightly, Penelope opened the first book and began to read.

Tony almost lost Penelope leaving the Quarter. She'd surprised him with that sharp swerve onto Canal and her path to the interstate. Old Rolo Polo had clung tight, though, and stopped down the row from her in the parking lot of Barnes & Noble.

Amused by Rolo Polo having to stake out a bookstore, Tony had remained in his car until the fat man had finally turned off his car, and presumably his a/c, then trundled into the store. He'd purchased a cold drink, then retreated to the air-conditioned foyer, where he pulled a throwaway tabloid from the several piles stacked there and propped it in front of his face.

Observing all this from his car, thankful for the broad plate-glass windows that opened the front of the store to easy view, Tony wondered whether Rolo Polo even knew how to read.

Trapped for the moment, Tony had no choice but to wait it out in his car. Rolo Polo guarded the only way in and out of the store. Sooner or later perhaps he'd let down his guard and go in search of the men's room. Then Tony could slip inside.

He hadn't intended to do it, of course, but now he felt a strong urge to see Penelope again. He'd grab some fancy-looking book off the shelf, locate her, then pretend to be deep in the book when she bumped into him.

She'd be impressed. Probably even go out with him. Maybe not to bed. Not on the first date, anyway.

Whoa. Tony ran a hand roughly through his hair. "Get a grip, Tony-O," he said, turning off the ignition and rolling down his windows. It was hot as hell in the parking lot with the sun punishing his car, but he hated to waste the gas to run the a/c.

He reminded himself his only reason for following Penelope to the bookstore was to see where Rolo Polo's interest in her lay. Rolo Polo was a direct path to Hinson and therefore to Hinson's boss, a mobster with ties to both New York and Las Vegas, but a man so clever he rarely showed a hand in any of his undertakings.

Hinson served as lawyer and chief functionary. In the old days he would have been called the *consigliore,* a term made popular in *The Godfather.* But the Louisiana mob types weren't so old-fashioned, and the family Hinson worked for consisted of a peculiarly New Orleans blend of suburban businessmen, French Quarter real estate tycoons, and working-class thugs. Thus Hinson spent a great deal of his time poring over contracts and other legal mumbo-jumbo.

Sweltering in the paved parking lot, Tony wiped a band of sweat from his forehead and prayed for Rolo Polo to take a leak. He and the fat man had too much history behind them for Tony to take the risk of Rolo Polo spotting him.

And since Tony expected any day now that Hinson would be offering him a job on behalf of his boss, it was no time to arouse suspicion. Too much stood at risk.

So he sat in the car and sweated. Within a few more minutes, his shirt clung to him. He hoped Penelope, cool and comfortable inside the store, appreciated his sacrifice.

"Don't kid yourself," he said, fiddling with his radio. A mournful song of love lost and never regained filled his ears and he snapped the radio off.

He wondered what had inspired Penelope to visit both the Bayou Magick Shoppe and Barnes & Noble. She was a studious type, of course, but she'd seemed intent on some purposeful course of action when she'd entered the Bourbon Street shop.

Remembering the odd statue he'd spotted under her bed when checking for intruders, Tony wondered if the respectable lawyer, in addition to masquerading as a shoplifter, also dabbled in the occult. It made as much sense as any explanation he could think of to answer the question why she would have a wild-looking, winking statuette hidden beneath her bed.

Thank God! Rolo Polo had just made a break, no doubt for the bathroom. He hadn't taken his earlier path straight to the beverage counter. Tony was out of his car before Rolo Polo's backside had disappeared into the depths of the store.

Once inside, he frowned, hit by the number of possibilities. The store was huge. Tony wondered how they found enough books to fill it up. His idea of book-buying was picking up the odd western at the corner drugstore, the one that used to be a K&B before they sold out to that eastern outfit.

New Orleans, Tony thought, squinting his eyes and scanning the first bank of bookshelves for sight of Penelope, was changing.

And so was he, he realized, riding up the escalator to check the second floor. Chasing after a woman who hadn't thrown herself at him. His friends wouldn't believe that possible for Tony Olano. They knew him as the guy who collected the Brenda-in-39B's of the world.

Tony knew himself that way, too, which was one reason it was really strange to be in a bookstore chasing after a lawyer who wore her starched blouse buttoned all the way to her neck.

Chapter 10

Candle magick, so it seemed, could produce some fairly powerful results. There were many fine points to consider when practicing the variety of spells, such as type of candle and whether one chose to melt bits and pieces of hair and body clippings into the wax to create a powerful poppet.

Not one mention of frog's testicles, though.

Penelope tucked a foot under her and considered her reading material. The list Mrs. Merlin had sent her shopping with made as much sense as what she read now. Did people really believe this stuff?

She picked up the next book, a paperback that claimed to reveal the best way to learn to see auras. Mrs. Merlin nattered a lot about Penelope's aura. And she'd said something about Tony Olano being too violet to have pressured her the way David had last night.

Only last night.

Penelope touched her hand to the side of her cheek and, skipping the introductory chapters, flipped to the section that discussed violet.

She read of violet as the dominant aura of

people who were intense and on the go. Natural leaders. Visionaries. Sensual as all get-out.

Well, now at last she'd found a statement that matched her objective observations.

Tony Olano *defined* sensual.

Penelope smiled and snuggled more deeply into the comfy chair. She pictured him sitting beside her, both of them deep in a book. He had one arm around her, gently stroking the side of her neck. She leaned into the rocklike shelter of his chest, safe, cozy and infinitely at peace. Rather than the New Age books she had taken off the shelf, in her fantasy she perused a favorite M. F. K. Fisher recently reissued. Visions of menu ideas danced in her head as she turned the pages of the witty and literate work.

And his reading material?

Penelope let her mind drift further into her fantasy. What would the man of her dreams be likely to read?

Hmm. A well-thumbed copy of *War and Peace*? Somerset Maugham? Dickens, perhaps?

She frowned, unable to fully form that piece of her dream world. An image of Tony flipping through a racing sheet flitted into her mind and she stirred, unhappy with the thought.

The book on auras slipped from her lap and landed with a plop on the floor.

Thrust back into her surroundings, she blinked and bent forward to retrieve the book. Before she could curl her fingers around it, a hand, large and powerful and sprinkled with fine black hairs, closed over the paperback.

Her eyes traveled upward, over the now familiar path of toned forearms and biceps boasting of a man at home in a gym.

The cruder the gym the better, Penelope added to her mental inventory, snatching her book from Tony Olano's hold.

He grinned and said, "Come here often?"

Penelope casually shifted the volumes on auras and candles until they all lay face down. "Sure," she said. "You?"

"A regular." He dropped gracefully into the chair that sat at a right angle to Penelope's, stretched out his long legs, and opened the book he carried. He said not another word, apparently lost in his reading material.

Penelope glared at him. It was just like him to show up, then pretend to ignore her. She peeked to see what he was reading but couldn't make out the title.

She picked up her book on auras, holding it so the brightly lettered cover didn't show. After turning a few pages without seeing a word, let alone an aura, she snapped the book closed. Her field of vision had been captured by Olano's tanned and muscled calves and the way he swung his left foot idly back and forth as he read.

Below the khaki walking shorts, his legs had the perfect amount of curly black hair, thick enough to be intriguing but not so dense as to be unattractive. Penelope couldn't help but wonder what his chest looked like. A hint of the same black hair showed above an open button of his short-sleeved shirt.

In another moment she'd be off into one of her fantasies. Trying hard to brake that temptation, Penelope decided to interrupt Tony. If he persisted in following her, he'd have to put up with some idle conversation. Leaning forward slightly and donning what she hoped would pass for an appealing smile, she said, "So, what are you reading?"

He grunted, placed a finger halfway down the left-hand page, then looked up briefly. His eyes seemed darker and more intense than the times she'd seen him before. The circles under his eyes were slightly puffy and more purplish blue today than they'd been yesterday. No doubt he'd found some Brenda-in-39B clone and stayed out all night partying. Penelope sniffed and repeated her question.

He hesitated, glanced around, then answered, "*Social Adjustment of Delinquent Youth Housed in Psycho-Socially Challenged Foster Homes.*" The long title rolled off his tongue as if he were guest lecturing at a conference.

Penelope raised her brows. "Impressive," she murmured. And she was impressed. She had half-expected him to be reading some dumb-jock sports book. Or a mindless western.

He shrugged. His finger still poised on the page, he said, "What about you?"

Now he had her. She wished she could answer with a title half as impressive. "I'm doing some research," she finally said. "In a topic you wouldn't be interested in."

"No?" He shifted forward, drawing his legs closer to his chair. Dark eyes burned into hers, alight with a fire Penelope longed to have the courage to explore. "Try me."

She laughed nervously. "I . . . uh, I'm expecting a houseguest who's into auras and such things, so I'm reading up on them."

He nodded and said, "I thought Tolstoy would be more your cup of tea."

"Oh, but he is! *Anna Karenina* is one of my favorite books ever. But research is necessary." She pointed to his book. "You obviously agree with that statement."

"What?" He looked surprised, then said, "Oh, of course. Like my research into the sociology of juvenile delinquents."

"Are you writing a paper?"

"Right." Tony drummed his fingers on the open book. "Yeah, right, a paper."

"For which journal?"

He frowned, the tempo of his fingers increasing. "I really haven't decided."

Penelope nodded. "It's important to pick the best in the field. Then, if they don't accept it, you can work your way down the list. Don't you find that to be true?"

It was Tony's turn to nod. Which he did, looking as brainy as he knew how. Shit! This woman had him twisted into doing, saying, thinking, and feeling things he'd no business muddling with. Writing a paper for publication? Wouldn't his college professors love that one! Of course, they'd be even more amazed he remembered the name of one of his textbooks, the name that had rolled so easily off his tongue when Penelope had asked him the title of his book.

Penelope must have asked him another question, a question he'd obviously missed. Well, at least she had decided to talk to him. "What was that?" he asked.

A flicker of something akin to annoyance appeared, then dissolved, on her face. The lady wasn't used to having to repeat herself. "I said, what is it that you do, Mr. Olano? Besides following me around the city, that is?"

Her question brought him sharply back to his purpose. He wasn't hanging out in this bluenose bookstore to flirt with a woman who normally wouldn't give him the time of day. He was here on a mission. He quickly checked the floor spread below. Good. Rolo Polo had resumed his post in the foyer.

He brought his gaze back to the woman seated beside him. She waited for his answer, an expectant light in her dusky blue eyes. Her lips were parted the teeniest bit, suggesting breathless anticipation of his answer. Yeah, right, Olano, he told himself wryly. He cast another dark glance, the one he used to such good effect with women like Brenda in 39B, and answered, "Research."

She folded her hands over her book. "Research?"

Tony liked his answer. He grinned. "Yeah, you could call me a professional researcher."

She'd scooted closer to him in her chair. Clearly she was trying to check out his reading material. He edged the book to the far side of his lap. Then she sat back and smiled at him, a genuine, lively, pleased smile. Tony knew, watching her smile at him that way, he'd do whatever it took to win that smile again.

"I think it's lovely that after you left the police force you turned to helping children stay out of trouble."

She spoke softly. "It's nice to meet a man who cares about helping others."

Tony shifted in his chair. He'd been present when Hinson told her Tony had been a cop. God only knew what details he'd filled her head with after Tony had left them alone. No wonder she looked at him most of the time as if he were some sort of criminal leper.

"Many people simply would have spiraled downward," Penelope was saying. "You know, given up under the weight of the disgrace."

Tony saw concern in those big eyes of hers. He took hope. A lot of women liked to rescue the troubled, the downtrodden. He ran a hand roughly through his hair. "You didn't see me a couple of months ago. It was tough. What did you call it? A downward spiral?" He threw in a deep sigh and gazed into her eyes. "I'm afraid you wouldn't have liked me very much at that point in my life."

Penelope caught her book, which had started to slide from her lap. She licked her bottom lip. Tony itched to lean over and let his tongue travel the same path. Nice and slow. She was coming around. Not that he had any business trying to get anywhere with this woman, but he couldn't help himself.

He'd never met anyone like Penelope Sue Fields, and God help him, he wanted to know everything there was to know about her. Lawyer, thief, dabbler in black magic—no matter, he had to find out more. And he wasn't above using her sympathies to achieve his purposes.

"My friends stood by me," he said, reaching over and collecting the piece of notepaper that had fluttered to the ground when her book slipped, "but my wife—" He slashed a hand across his throat.

She swallowed. Lifting one slender hand, she played with a tendril of hair that had come loose from the knot that denied him the pleasurable sight of her hair flowing around her shoulders. "That must have been terrible."

"Better to know it now than later."

"I suppose so," she said. She kept on playing with that hair, then looked down at her book. When she glanced up again, she said, "Your wife. Is she coming back?"

He shook his head. "Nope."

"Wouldn't you take her back?" She sounded curious.

Again, he shook his head. "It's like this," he said. "When you're a cop and you go out on a call and your buddy fails to cover you or back you up, you don't put your ass on the line twice."

She flinched. "When you put it that way, I understand."

Tony suffered a twinge of guilt at describing his ex-wife in such a bad light. Kathy had done the right thing when she'd initiated their divorce, and as a result, they'd parted before they destroyed their friendship. He hoped she wouldn't mind him casting her in such a bad role in order to score points with Penelope, especially since their divorce had occurred long before his set-up dismissal from the force.

Penelope had quit playing with her hair. Her eyes had gone all soft and dreamy. Tony closed his book and leaned forward. He had no business doing this. He ought to leave her alone, but dammit, he wanted to see her loosen that glorious hair, wanted to see her when she wasn't buttoned up tight.

Face it, Olano, he told himself, you want to see her lying in your bed, looking up at you as if you're the most amazing man on the face of the earth.

He swallowed, hard, and opened his mouth to ask her out on a real date.

"Tony-O, what are *you* doing in *here*?" A woman's voice, a voice he'd know anywhere, knifed across the reading area.

Penelope lost her dreamy expression and turned to see who had spoken.

Tony didn't have to look. "Aunt Tootie," he said, rising to greet the aunt who up until thirty seconds ago he'd loved dearly.

"How the heck are you?" His aunt didn't talk, she boomed. She settled a load of books on the table by his and Penelope's chairs and perched her plump body on the edge of the table, waving away Tony's gesture toward his own chair.

Several other readers glanced up. One man put a finger to his lips.

Tony resumed his seat, casting a glance at Penelope.

"I said to myself, that looks like Tony-O, but what in the world would *he* be doing in a bookstore?" She slapped her knee and laughed.

Tony glanced again at Penelope.

His aunt clapped a hand over her mouth. "Oh," she said, then winked at Penelope. "Always did have a big mouth," she said.

"Aunt Tootie, Penelope Fields."

Penelope nodded. "Very pleased to meet you," she said in a voice that would have chipped ice.

Tony groaned. Shit. Just when he'd had her about to melt.

"Just picking up a few cookbooks," his aunt said. "You should come by more often. Come try my new cannelloni. I'm doing a crab and corn one that's to die for." She kissed her fingertips and smacked loudly.

Tony grinned despite himself.

Even Penelope looked less frozen.

"Well, don't make yourself a stranger to the family." She stood up, then bent over to collect her books. "Bring your girl for dinner and we'll tell her what you're really like." She winked again.

Tony stood, kissed her on the cheek, and waved her off.

When he turned back to Penelope, any thaw in her expression had frozen over. She'd gathered her books in her arms.

"So you come here all the time?" She threw him a look designed to wound. "You know what I think? I think you're a liar. A compulsive liar." She snatched the book out of his lap and read aloud, "*The Times Crossword Puzzle Answer Book.*"

Tossing it back, she said, "So much for helping troubled youth." She rose and stood over him. "If I catch you anywhere in my line of vision, Mr. Olano, I'll slap you with a restraining order so fast you won't know what hit you."

Chapter 11

"Front and center, Mrs. Merlin!" Penelope slammed her book purchases down on her dining table, still seething over having fallen for Tony Olano's bogus charms.

"Liar," she muttered, sweeping the room for sight of Mrs. Merlin. She didn't know who infuriated her more—Mrs. Merlin and her frog's testicles or the insufferably egotistical Tony Olano.

Why, she'd actually started to like him as a person, in addition to being superficially attracted to his gorgeous hunk of a body.

Lies. All lies.

Had he spoken the truth once, about anything? She'd known from his first guilty start at the sound of his aunt's voice that the man with bedroom eyes didn't frequent Barnes & Noble. Why, from his aunt's words, Penelope had gotten the impression Olano would rather visit a funeral home than a bookstore.

Where had he ever heard of Tolstoy? Penelope frowned. Maybe he had a sister, an educated sister. She swept into the bedroom, still steaming. She caught sight of her face in the dresser mirror. Anger had stained her cheeks red. Penelope lay her palms over her cheeks and started to count to ten.

When she reached three she pictured Tony rushing in, gun drawn. That fueled her temper, so she had to start over at one. This time she reached five before she remembered how impressed she'd been that he worked with troubled kids.

Hah! She would bet he didn't even have a job.

Penelope dropped her hands and stood staring into the mirror. Forgetting all about counting to ten, she lifted one hand to the side of her cheek and felt again his touch, so gentle for such a powerful man.

Reluctantly this time, she lowered her hand and said to her mirrored self, "Face it, Pen, you're feeling foolish and vulnerable. You were well on your way to melting, well on your way to convincing yourself the man with bedroom eyes was actually interested in you, plain old Penelope Sue."

Turning away from the mirror, she sank onto her bed, unmindful for once of her grandmother's precious antique quilt, which every night she removed, folded, and placed on the cedar trunk at the foot of her bed.

She set her brain to the task she should have performed sooner. But she hadn't wanted to analyze why Tony Olano, ex-cop in disgrace, showed up at her every turn.

Why did Tony Olano keep following her?

The fantasy-loving part of Penelope wanted to believe he found her fascinating, that he wanted to get to know her.

"Oh, right," she said aloud, and plucking a pillow from the pile on her bed, she began to spin it over and over in her hands.

Trained in analytical and logical thinking, she knew she could easily separate fantasy from reality when called upon to do so. She only had to put her mind to the task.

"Fact," she said, turning the pillow more rapidly. "It wasn't until after I dated David that I bumped into Olano." She clutched the pillow to her chest and remembered the way Tony had looked in the elevator the first day she'd seen him.

Smoldering, dark eyes. The crooked angle of his mouth, not quite a smile, but certainly not a sneer. It was, Penelope concluded, a promise of passion. And judging by the way he'd lounged against the wall of the elevator car, lord of all he surveyed, that was a promise on which he could deliver.

Penelope shivered, even though the blood ran hot in her veins. The image in her mind of Tony Olano was so vivid it was tangible. She traced a finger in the air in front of her.

Then she snapped her hand back and sent the pillow spinning once more. That first day, he'd been on her floor in the building where she worked, in the elevator she rode each day to and from the 42nd floor. No accident, that.

A thought crept into her mind and her instinct was to thrust it out immediately. But to face reality squarely, she needed to consider her question.

When had he first begun to follow her?

She couldn't help but glance over her shoulder. Ridiculous to feel nervous. He didn't act dangerous, but one never knew. And even if he was perfectly harmless, just the idea that someone might have been watching her, invading her private moments, observing her in her unguarded ones, both chilled and enraged her.

"Fact the second," she said aloud, returning to her analysis, determined to quit thinking of Tony Olano as the man with bedroom eyes and think of him instead as a possibly dangerous criminal. "There's bad blood between Olano and David."

Thinking of the grim look on Olano's face when he'd answered her question about taking his ex-wife back, Penelope knew he was a man capable of exacting his own form of justice.

"Ergo, he's using me to get back at Hinson. Trying to steal me to get his goat," Penelope muttered, both her ego and her heart deflating at the inevitable conclusion of her line of reasoning.

She tossed the pillow toward the others piled at the head of her bed. "Stupid man," she said, again out loud. "As if David Hinson is even interested in me. To him I'm just another lawyer."

True, he'd kissed her the other night on the balcony of his house and last night tried to do more than give her a peck on the lips. But she didn't feel what she knew she would if he were seeking her out, man to woman. Her fantasies told her so.

And lately Raoul, her fantasy man, had been playing understudy to Tony Olano.

Not once, Penelope mused, had David appeared as the strong man in her fantasies, the man who swept her off her feet. So Olano was wasting his time trying to make Hinson jealous.

She looked down at her lap, covered in sensible navy linen slacks. Her gaze traveled to her feet, clad in elegant but conservative Ferragamo loafers. She slipped her shoes off and wiggled her toes. She pictured her feet encased in the stack-heel monstrosities she'd seen Brenda next door wearing last week.

Penelope smiled. What wouldn't she give to have Tony Olano really dying to have her. More than one person could play "get your goat"! She'd go shopping, and this time it wouldn't be for placemats.

Looking around, she realized she'd sat upon her precious quilt. "Kites and kilowatts!" she cried, and shot off the bed. One more proof that thinking about Tony Olano caused her nothing but trouble.

But her reasoning exercise had helped her to reach a conclusion. Olano would no doubt continue to follow her. He probably laughed at the idea of a temporary restraining order, knowing from his days as a cop how easy it was for an abusive spouse or ex-lover to slip through the cracks of the law even after a court had stepped in.

So, if David did invite her to dinner again, Penelope hoped Olano ate his heart out when he saw just how well she could treat a caring, considerate, polite, and honest man.

She experienced a faint twinge of conscience, thinking that she might be giving David the wrong impression, but Penelope quickly brushed that thought aside. David wasn't seriously interested in her. He'd initially asked her out after a conference concerning a mutual client and they'd talked business over a glass of wine. Most of their conversations concerned law or politics. With David, business clearly came first.

Unlike Olano, Penelope thought, who apparently never bothered going to work.

She turned to leave the room, her mind returning to Mrs. Merlin now that she'd resolved just how to handle Mr. Bedroom Eyes. She paused suddenly at the sound of water dripping and a scuffling noise coming from the bathroom.

Then a voice joined in.

"If you're quite through solving the problems in your love life, perhaps you could come help a friend in need."

"Mrs. Merlin?" Penelope raced across the bedroom toward her bathroom.

"No, it's Mrs. Claus. Who in the stars do you think it is?"

Penelope halted in the doorway, staring at her normally neat bathroom. She liked her things to be in order; too much clutter and confusion made her skin itch under the surface. Penelope knew she'd become that way during her childhood, when her mother was always too tired after her waitress shifts to clean their trailer.

So Penelope had taken care of instilling structure out of chaos.

Chaos certainly described her bathroom.

The bathroom sink had been stoppered; dripping water had filled the bowl and now overflowed one splattering drop at a time onto her tile floor. Her small rack of hand towels lay on its side, the impact having scattered a fine layer of bath salts from a nearby crystal bowl.

But she didn't see Mrs. Merlin.

"In here," the messed-up magician cried.

Penelope looked down, down into the depths of a high-sided silver wastebasket she'd picked up at an estate sale in Chicago.

Staring into the basket at the exasperated face of Mrs. Merlin, Penelope reached with one hand and switched off the dripping faucet. "Well, well," she said.

"That's exactly what this is like," Mrs. Merlin snapped. "It's about time you made it back. How long does it take to run a simple errand?"

Penelope tapped her foot and crossed her arms over her chest. Glaring at her trapped houseguest, she said in a falsely sweet voice, "You call hunting for frog's testicles 'simple'?"

Mrs. Merlin laughed, almost sounding like her normal self. "Oh, that. Now, Penelope, dear, don't hold that little test against me. Help me out of here and I'll explain everything."

"I don't think so."

"But I'm stuck!" Her voice wailed, rising at least two octaves.

Penelope held her fingers to her ears. Lowering them cautiously, she asked, "Where's your magic pole vaulter?" She had trouble believing such a thing existed, but if she accepted Mrs. Merlin's presence, she supposed a magic incense stick was just one more piece of the improbable package.

"When I vaulted onto the sink I lost my grip on it, then I slipped and fell right off the edge into this tomb." Mrs. Merlin patted her face. "And I can't find my glasses, to make things worse. It's a good thing I've kept up my yoga. That fall might have killed a regular old lady."

"I do hope you're all right," Penelope said, looking down to see if she'd crushed the miniature spectacles. She started to get down on her hands and knees to look for them when she remembered how rudely Mr. Gotho had hustled her out of the Bayou Magick Shoppe.

"Tell you what, Mrs. Merlin," she said. "You explain why you sent me off on that wild goose chase and then I'll get you out of this pickle."

Her captive opened her mouth, clearly about to protest, but then snapped her lips shut.

At least this was one negotiation where she had the upper hand, Penelope thought with satisfaction, as she waited for Mrs. Merlin to spill the beans.

The woman, so miniature in size but mammoth in troublemaking skills, took her time settling onto an empty container of face cream Penelope had tossed in the trash that morning. Finally, she said, "I gather you met Mr. Gotho?"

Penelope nodded. "You mean the man who threw me out of that quaint little shop."

"Oh, dear, well, then you obviously didn't pass the test." Mrs. Merlin peered upward, searching for what Penelope could not fathom.

"Explain, please," she said.

"Candle magick is a most delicate art," Mrs. Merlin said. "The ingredients of a powerful candle, the type I need to burn in order to get back to being me, are very sensitive to, um . . . to certain negatives in the universe."

Penelope lifted the stopper to drain the sink. "Negatives such as?"

Mrs. Merlin ticked off on her fingers. "Disordered karma, impurities from the auras of nonbelievers, items handled by those who walk the dark side—do you want to hear more?"

"Might as well hear them all." Not that she countenanced a word the gremlin granny spoke.

"Swollen ego—"

"What does that one mean?" Penelope interrupted. Mr. Gotho had accused her of something bad having to do with her ego right before he'd tossed her out.

Mrs. Merlin's eyes glinted. "So that one catches your interest, eh?"

Penelope shrugged.

"A balanced karma consists of an acceptance of one's qualities, both embracing of the positive and a sincere commitment to improving any negative aspects. Balance requires working on the negative without wallowing about in self-hatred. It also— You sure you want to hear this?"

Penelope nodded.

"Balanced ego also requires accepting one's talents as gifts of the goddess and using them fully without falling prey to hubris."

With a hand towel, Penelope wiped the rim of the sink, then folded it neatly. She wanted to discount the woman's words, but they did make a certain philosophical sense. "I suppose falling prey to hubris is what Mr. Gotho charged me with?"

Mrs. Merlin pursed her lips. "You do act a trifle conceited at times."

"Well, I never!" She dropped the towel she'd just folded.

A chuckle floated up from the wastebasket. "Hit a nerve with that one, didn't I?"

"But I am smart and educated and capable. I went through college in three years. I hold an LLM in tax from NYU. If you say balance implies accepting one's talents, then I say I'm balanced." She swooped down and picked up the towel.

"Do you take every comment so personally?" Mrs. Merlin clucked her tongue.

"Oh." Embarrassed at her own inflated-sounding self-defense, Penelope shut her mouth and set about righting the towel rack that Mrs. Merlin had knocked over in her magical pole-vaulting.

"Ego out of balance comes about from the way we measure ourselves against others, not against ourselves."

Penelope raked the spilled bath salts from the back of the toilet and dumped them into the crystal bowl. "In the shop, I was comparing myself to Mr. Gotho . . ." she paused, sure guilt showing on her face, "and to you, too, Mrs. Merlin, right before Mr. Gotho bounced me out."

"Well, there you have it. Though I can't imagine how you perceive yourself as more talented than I am, but it would put my own ego out of balance to dwell on that thought." She rose and dusted her caftan off, then lifted her arms. "Now will you get me out of this dump?"

Penelope continued collecting the bath crystals. Ignoring the request, she said, "So where do the frog's testicles come in?"

"Oh, that." Mrs. Merlin waved a hand. "I'm afraid I was only having a little fun. I knew if

Mr. Gotho accepted you as pure enough to transport my necessary ingredients, he'd know what to give you."

"Fun? I made a fool of myself and you're still pint-size. So what do we do now? You tell me that and maybe I'll scoop you up out of the trash." She dusted the bath salts from her fingers and stuck her hands on her hips, wondering how her life had gotten so out of balance.

"My, my," Mrs. Merlin said. "We do have a temper, don't we? But it's simple, my dear. We wait for your ego to balance itself."

Chapter 12

So far Squeek hadn't steered him wrong.

Monday evening, Tony watched from a half block away as Hinson's disgustingly flawless Lincoln Town Car pulled to a halt in front of one of New Orleans' best French Quarter restaurants.

Primo's was small and shared not half the national fame of Brennan's or Galatoire's or Arnaud's, but those who prided themselves on eating where the locals ate knew that Primo's was an "in" place for special-occasion dinners and power business luncheons.

Hinson was pulling out all the stops to woo Penelope. Yet something about the setup was off. Tony frowned and studied the shuttered front of Primo's, noting the absence of the valet. Of course! Anyone with half a claim to gourmand status knew Primo's never opened on a Monday.

Hinson had to know that.

He worked for Primo's owner.

Oh, the truth of that ownership was shrouded in dummy corporation upon dummy corporation, but both Hinson and his boss were regulars at Primo's. Goodness knew, the two of them had probably created the sheltering companies that owned Primo's.

Not that Tony had ever eaten inside the hallowed walls of Primo's, but his cousin Leo ran the kitchen. Leo, who was ever-anxious to make peace with the family he'd alienated when he left his position at Olano's Seafood to accept the top seat at Primo's, had filled Tony in on what went on there. And Leo had told him they never opened on Mondays, not even for the owner.

Until tonight, Tony couldn't remember ever seeing one good thing about Leo having gone over to the enemy. But now, when he needed to take a look inside Primo's, he considered it a fat piece of luck that Leo had cared only for creating meals that shone like stars and had wanted nothing to do with family politics.

Finally some movement occurred within the Town Car. The driver's door opened; Hinson stepped out, walked around the car, and opened the passenger door.

Out came Penelope.

"What the hell—" Tony couldn't help himself. What the devil had she done to her hair? And her clothes! The times he'd seen her before, she'd been wearing that stuffy, proper sort of clothing that made him want to kid her a bit about dressing like her mama, but at the same time he'd respected her for it. Professional, it had said. Respect me and keep your distance.

He'd liked that. A heck of a lot better than the come-hither style of the Brenda-in-39B's of this world.

Tonight, though, Penelope dressed like she'd

been cast as the good girl gone bad in a high school play.

Tony swallowed hard and wondered whether Hinson was choking on his own spit. Here he was, driving up in all his glory to a goddamn restaurant that wasn't even open, about to let a woman dressed like a hooker out of his overpriced car.

Tony let out a laugh, wondering if Penelope had dressed to show up Hinson for the ass he was. Then he sobered, quickly, as he wondered whether or not he'd had some sort of influence on her.

She'd caught him flirting with Brenda. Did she think she had to dress like a streetwalker to get his attention? Geez, whatever he'd done to give her that impression, he was sorry, more than sorry.

Then he looked again and couldn't help but notice the way the clingy dress, slit to the thigh, showed off her legs in a way those tidy, prissy trousers had done their best to hide. He licked his lips, and his fingers itched to trace the line of the slit that inched up her leg.

The top of the dress had a low-cut neckline trimmed with ruffles. The ruffles danced and stood out in funny angles that he knew instinctively were caused by the rise and fall of her breasts. Convulsively, he swallowed. He was getting as hard as a live oak and in about two minutes he'd be jumping out of the car and wrestling Hinson to the ground to get a shot at Penelope.

He had to get hold of himself.

He didn't know about Hinson, but Penelope had certainly gotten his attention.

Only one problem, Olano, he told himself as he climbed out of his car and, keeping to the shadows, approached the restaurant. She's not doing this for you, she's doing this for Hinson.

He liked that thought about as much as his stomach liked the smell of andouille sausage after a hard night's drinking, back in his college partying days.

Tony inched closer, not wanting to miss the look on Hinson's face when he discovered the doors to Primo's were locked.

Hinson paused, placed one arm around Penelope's shoulder in a possessive way that set Tony's teeth on edge. She glanced up at him and Tony could have sworn he saw her lashes flutter.

The double doors of Primo's swung open.

"Shit." Tony kicked the side of the stoop where he'd halted, thankful Hinson couldn't see *his* face. As soon as the doors closed, he took off at a lope around the building, cutting down an alleyway that ran between Primo's and the next building, a T-shirt shop hawking every variety of New Orleans souvenir imaginable.

A shop, Tony knew, that Hinson's boss used to launder money.

A shop Tony would love to bust.

One day, he promised himself, one day soon. But tonight, first things first.

The iron gate at the back of the alleyway stood open, the padlock askew. Tony noted the sloppy security, something he expected in a so-called security building like Penelope's but definitely not at Primo's.

It would be just like his cousin Leo to leave a door unlocked and end up getting himself shot. With a shake of his head, Tony closed the gate after him and set up the padlock so a casual passerby would think the gate was shut up tight.

He turned around and rammed into a row of empty trash cans. Three of them tumbled over, clattering on the old brick of the courtyard.

Tony swore under his breath. Penelope had him rattled, and that wasn't something that happened to Anthony Olano. He shook his head like a boxer clearing cobwebs and moved carefully around the other trash cans, piled-up produce boxes, and bins of empty bottles glistening under the light above the kitchen door.

The door stood open to the night, the staff inside no doubt trying to catch any breeze that might waft over from the nearby river. Tony paused in the doorway. Given the restaurant had opened up for Hinson, the kitchen should be well on its way to being heated to steam room temperature, even if they were working on a small scale tonight. Most of the local kitchens weren't air-conditioned, and with the vats of boiling water and massive stovetops all lit at once, sweat was a way of life in the restaurant business.

Before he'd put one foot farther into the room, a short balding man wearing the kitchen uniform of white shirt, black checked pants, and once-white apron appeared at his side.

"Restaurant's closed," he said, blocking Tony's way.

Tony smiled. "Just looking for Leo," he said, "my cuz."

The man didn't budge, but he did yell over his shoulder, "Leo, you got a visitor."

"Not during the soup," came Leo's horrified protest. "Who is it?"

"Tony," Tony called out, loud enough for Leo to hear over the din of clattering pots and pans and the wail of a soprano issuing from the ceiling-mounted speakers.

"Oh, it's only you."

The short man evidently took that as permission for Tony to pass, because he nodded and disappeared back to whatever corner he'd been hanging out in.

Leo kept his kitchen clean. Tony gave his cousin that much credit as he crossed toward the center of the brightly lit, almost antiseptic-looking room. Gleaming pans hung from overhead racks, five or six assistants worked at scattered stations, and in the center of the room in front of a double-wide cooktop counter, Leo reigned supreme.

A baritone joined in with the soprano and Tony winced. Opera and cooking had occupied Leo's attention since their childhood. He and Leo had grown up across the street from one another, their families sharing every holiday at one house or the other, along with a noisy, countless extended family.

At an early age, Leo had begun creating dishes for these occasions; Tony had distinguished himself by planting frogs in his female cousins' blouses and letting off noisy fireworks.

Apparently Leo had finished the most critical

stage of the soup, for he handed his large cooking spoon to an assistant and, arms outstretched, advanced on Tony. He grabbed him in a bear hug and landed a kiss on both cheeks for good measure.

Tony withstood the greeting. He needed Leo's help, and despite the family rift over Leo's decision to go to work for Primo's, he loved his cousin.

When he'd been released from the embrace, Tony said in casual tones, "Hey, cuz, what's cooking?"

"You came to see me to talk about food?" He smiled. "There's hope for you after all, little cousin."

Tony returned the smile. Leo had always had a good two inches and at least twenty pounds on him. "Hey, I thought it was about time I came to see where you're working. Make sure they're treating you okay."

Leo stiffened. Tony knew he'd said the wrong thing.

His cousin flicked a drying drop of milk off his otherwise spotless apron. "The family sent you, I gather?"

Tony shook his head. "No. Absolutely not." Geez, just what he needed—to get his cousin's back up when Tony needed a favor from him.

He placed his hands on his cousin's shoulders. Leo appreciated the dramatic gesture. "I swear to you, Leo Olano, on our grandmother Anna's grave, that I'm here on my own."

Leo returned his gaze, his eyes troubled.

Then, after a very long moment, in which Tony knew he didn't take a single breath, Leo said, "Then sit down and eat. There's no meat on you."

Tony laughed and dropped his hands. He sniffed the air. "What's for dinner?"

Leo raised his hands prayerfully. "Only my best for tonight. To begin, my escarole escargots, followed by cream of artichoke soup—you know, the one Mama invented, only I do it with a shrimp bisque base—"

"Sounds great, Leo," Tony said. His cousin could go on all night about one dish, let alone a complete menu. "So what's the occasion?"

Leo made a face and shrugged, looking more Gaelic than Italian. "A man and a woman. There's no accounting for taste."

Tony smothered a smile and fiddled with a container of oversized cook spoons. "So when did ya'll start opening on Monday nights?"

Leo turned away, moved back to where the assistant stood stirring his artichoke soup. "You disappoint me, Tony," he said, dispatching that assistant and the other young man working nearby on quickly ordered tasks.

With no one else in earshot, he tweaked the remote control, raised the volume on the stereo, and looked Tony straight in the eye.

"So what do you really want from me?"

Tony fingered the tiny, supersensitive transmitter housed in his jeans pocket. Careful, Olano, not too fast, not too slow. "A favor?"

"A favor." Leo shook his head, the picture of dejection. "You couldn't just come visit me, could you? No, that wouldn't be my cousin Tony. A man of purpose, you've always been." Crimson rising on his cheeks, he stirred the soup more quickly. "So what's your purpose tonight?"

"Hey, Leo, I'm a chump." Tony shifted, then stuck his hands in the pockets of his jeans. "You're my cousin and I love you. I shouldn't have stayed away so long. It's just that . . ." he gestured around.

Leo ducked his head. "What you and the others don't understand is that after I work here, I can work anywhere. I can write my own ticket." He thrust out his lower lip.

Tony wondered how many other people had thought that by making their own deal with their own personal devils they'd escape paying the price when called due. Leo was fooling himself. As long as Primo's owner wanted Leo as chef, no other restaurant in the city would offer him a job. But if Leo helped him tonight and Tony eventually won this war of his, Leo would be free.

Another assistant walked up. Leo sent him to the walk-in cooler to collect the escargots.

Tony made a face, wondering how anyone could eat the snails, creatures he routinely picked from his begonias and squashed beneath his feet. Leaning closer, making a show of studying the soup, knowing the short, bald-headed enforcer near the back door would be watching him, he said, "I need you to get this teeny-weeny object onto Hinson's table.

Leo blanched and looked over his shoulder. "I can't get in trouble. You know that."

"Listen to me, Leo. This is important or I wouldn't ask. I would never put you in danger." Fingering the bug, he said, "It's a personal favor, a huge favor, but maybe you could help me out on this one?" Even as he spoke, he checked for some object that could believably be carried to Hinson's table.

He didn't see a thing.

Leo followed his eye, though. "You can't go out there." His hand slowed on the soup spoon.

"No, but you can. The chef-welcoming-the-honored-guest routine, and all that." Leo's spoon stopped.

Tony pointed downward. "Hey, better keep that moving or you'll have artichoke paste and you'll have that to lay at my door, too."

Leo flashed an eye toward the soup, then lowered the heat. With a semblance of a grin, he said, "You owe me more than one spoiled pot of soup. This thing—does it have to stay on the table for the entire meal?"

Tony nodded.

Leo chewed his lip. "Only because you didn't squeal on me when I broke Mrs. Calamusa's window am I doing this for you."

Tony grabbed his cousin and kissed him on both cheeks. Into his ear he said, "Don't use a vase. He'll suspect a switch."

Leo frowned.

But Tony knew Leo loved a good puzzle.

Leo handed his spoon to Tony, then quickly crossed to a cupboard, pulled out a small white item, and returned to check his soup. "It breaks my heart to leave such a tacky object on my beautiful table, but for you I'll do it," he said, flashing a view of the small ceramic container stuffed with packets of artificial sweetener.

"It just so happens the lady ordered iced tea.

Another crime that breaks my heart. At least Hinson, no matter his faults, appreciates fine wine with a great dinner."

Covering the packets with his hammy hand, he flipped the container over, displaying a recessed bottom. "Will this do, cuz?

"You are fucking brilliant, Leo," Tony said, and with a grin, Velcroed the tiny bug into place, grateful for the designer who'd covered it in a white mylar. Even if someone casually turned the container over, the transmitter might escape notice.

Leo stuffed a few more packets of Equal into the ceramic box and barked at an assistant to deliver it and a dish of lemon slices to the lady's side of the table.

Then he grabbed the soup spoon back from Tony and said, "Next time you come to visit, do it because you love me for who I am."

Tony clapped him on the shoulder. For the benefit of the bald-headed guy who'd reappeared, he said loudly, "So I just wanted to tell you myself the happy news. A free man no more."

Leo managed a smile. "I'll dance at your wedding."

"Dance? Hell, you'll be in the kitchen!" Tony shot him a thumbs-up, grinned at the watchdog, and strolled out the door.

Just outside the door, he paused and said to the short guy who'd followed him out, "You oughta check your lock. Sloppy security you guys got here."

Then he walked quickly through the alleyway, anxious to get to his car before Primo's guests of honor got to their escarole escargots.

Chapter 13

The minute the doors of Primo's closed behind her, Penelope regretted her foolish, ridiculous, incredibly immature decision to torment Olano by playing up to David.

Surely what she'd done was far worse than her ego being out of balance!

When David had phoned to ask her to have dinner Monday evening, he'd been so charming, and she'd still been so miffed at Tony, that she'd not only accepted, but she'd left work during the day and purchased a new dress.

Not just a new dress.

A new look.

When she'd told the sales lady at Macy's she needed a special night-out-on-the-town dress, the woman had sized up Penelope's navy suit and selected a deep rose silk sheath with delicate cap sleeves, a dress Penelope would have picked for herself.

Thinking of Brenda in 39B, Penelope had asked the woman to pick an exact opposite style, which was how she came to be standing beside David in a slinky black dress with a low-cut neck camouflaged only by ruffles that danced with every breath she took.

She shivered and rubbed her bare arms.

"Cold?" David asked, taking her by the elbow and leading her across the otherwise empty restaurant to an alcove near the back.

"I'm fine." She smiled at him, her normal serious smile, and this time she left off the fake flutter of her lashes. If Tony couldn't see, what was the point? "But David, there's no one else here."

He stopped in front of a curtained alcove, pulled out the table so she could slip into the semicircular booth. "No, there's not." He looked quite pleased with himself.

Penelope knew she looked shocked. "You didn't pay them to close for the night, did you?" Such a waste of money bothered her.

"Darling Penelope," he said, but lightly, "I'll do whatever it takes to impress you."

"Well, I am stunned."

He sat down beside her. Not too close, she noted with relief. It was beginning to sink in that she'd been completely wrong about David's interest in her. He sure didn't look as if he wanted to spend this evening discussing business.

A waiter approached the table.

"Good evening and welcome to Primo's." He nodded deferentially to David and sketched a bow toward Penelope. She smiled back. Penelope made a point of being nice to waiters and waitresses.

A second waiter appeared, his arms full of a tissue-wrapped bundle. He handed the bundle to the first waiter, then disappeared.

"Ah, the flowers."

The waiter held forth a dozen red roses for

David's inspection. He nodded, accepted them, and in turn presented them to Penelope.

She stared at the baby soft petals of the twelve perfect flowers, twelve perfect flowers the color of blood. "Thank you," she managed, wishing he hadn't made such an extravagant gesture.

The waiter whisked them into a vase he settled on the table. One petal dropped free and floated to the white tablecloth. David frowned and the waiter pinched it off the table.

Penelope felt like she should show more appreciation. Here he was making such a fuss over her. Summoning more enthusiasm than she felt, she said, "They are beautiful, David. I'm overwhelmed."

He lay an arm along the booth, his fingertips just reaching the edge of her bare shoulder. "Good," he said lazily. "Now let's unwind from the day, shall we?" To the waiter, he said, "Bring us a bottle of the 1989 Chateau du France Bordeaux."

"Very good, sir."

"And I'd like an iced tea," Penelope said, knowing full well she was committing a fine dining faux pas. But she needed her wits about her. It didn't take half her IQ to tell her David wasn't planning to discuss law and politics tonight.

"Very good, ma'am."

But David did launch into a business monologue, regaling her with a story of his verbal jousting in court that morning. The familiar language set Penelope at ease and she began to relax, began to forget her dress had a slit that opened her thigh to the wind and a neckline that exposed more cleavage than her mother's old waitress uniform.

She shared a story of a victory she'd won in a Tax Court ruling. David listening intently. She sipped her iced tea, noticing that the waiter poured the wine for two.

She started to ask for sweetener for her tea, but David had launched into a story about the legal recruiting firm that had brought her to New Orleans.

She hadn't realized he was familiar with that agency, but he said something in passing that indicated he knew that was how she'd gotten her job at her firm. She listened as he described a job in New York the recruiter had once tried to get him to take, relaxing despite herself.

Then, as if the waiter had read her mind, packets of sweetener and slices of lemon appeared. Penelope fixed her tea to her taste and smiled at David. Perhaps this dinner wouldn't be so bad after all.

The two of them were having a jolly good time, Tony thought, sucking on a peppermint and scowling. He didn't understand how they could enjoy themselves when all they talked about was law, law, law, but then his little sister always got excited when she told him about law school.

Stretched out in his rackety car listening to the recording equipment he had stashed in his trunk and wired through to a special speaker in his dash, Tony worked the mint around in his mouth, figuring he should be glad Hinson was only talking shop.

Squeek, though, had led him to believe otherwise. Hinson had been ordered to marry and settle down. And Hinson, Tony knew, did what he was told. The runt from the wrong side of the tracks had worked too long and too hard to achieve his version of the good life to risk losing out.

The part of the puzzle Tony didn't understand, though, was why he'd picked Penelope. Having a tax lawyer in the family would come in handy, but that alone wasn't reason enough to single her out. Because she was from out of town? Because—

"Holy Toledo!" Tony sat up so fast he hit his head on the roof of his car. He grabbed his phone and punched in a number.

The waiter removed the crème brûlée dishes. Penelope sighed in appreciation and spoke without thinking. "I'd love to meet the chef. This meal was magnificent!"

"It's as good as done," David said, smiling indulgently. Closing the gap between them, he slid his arm around her shoulders. "Happy?"

Penelope tried not to think about the clear view David had down the neckline of her dress. She thought instead of how if it weren't for Tony Olano she wouldn't be sitting here half-naked. She merely nodded in answer to David's question.

"Glad you moved to New Orleans?"

"Oh, yes." Penelope folded her hands in her lap. "It requires some adjustment, but I like living here."

"Good." David lay his free hand over hers.

His palm was cool. He pried her fingers apart, capturing one hand and bringing it to his lips.

Penelope watched him kiss her hand, almost as if she were watching him kiss another woman. When Tony had merely brushed her cheek, she'd gone hot all over, but now she felt nothing other than a strong desire to escape before the situation grew awkward.

He gazed into her eyes. "Penelope—"

"Perhaps I could go to the kitchen to see the chef."

He tightened his grasp on her hand. "Forget about the chef," he said, not in a mean way, but Penelope heard the annoyance.

"Penelope, I'd like—"

Snatching her hand free, she held a finger against her upper lip. "I think I'm going to sneeze." She wrinkled her nose and willed a sneeze to appear. It was a trick she'd used many times in school when she'd been caught daydreaming by teachers and hadn't known an answer. Rather than admit to it, she'd manufactured the time she needed to return to the reality around her, to figure out the question and come up with the answer.

David produced a beautifully pressed linen handkerchief.

"Oh, thank you," she said, and made a fuss of patting her nose.

A slight twitch appeared in David's right cheek just below his eye. "Penelope"—he accepted the handkerchief she'd folded neatly, then lay a square velvet jewelry box on the table—"I'm trying to ask you to be my wife."

"You're what?"

The twitching intensified. "I don't think it should come as any surprise. We're perfectly suited for one another. You're intelligent, talented, successful." He lifted one shoulder. "We're two peas in a pod."

Penelope blinked. What happened to beautiful, sexy, charming? She was sick of being intelligent, talented, and successful. A murderous feeling rose up within her. She wanted to be wanted for the woman she was, no matter how deeply hidden that woman was, even from her own knowledge.

He popped open the box. Penelope's mouth dropped when she saw the marquise-cut diamond, a gem almost as big as a jawbreaker.

"Like it?"

"It's amazing."

He lifted it from the box and slipped it on her finger.

Her hand almost drooped from the weight. She immediately began to wiggle it off.

"Thank you, David, but I can't—"

"Don't say no." He smiled, which had the effect of spreading the twitch in his cheek. "Perhaps I sprang it on you too soon. Think it over."

"But I don't—"

He held a finger to her lips. "*No* is not a word I like to hear," he said softly.

She swallowed. He obviously wasn't open to discussion, but there was no way she could marry David. Boy, had she messed up. The huge stone winked at her in the light, mocking her.

He slipped it back in place and squeezed her hand. "You could get used to being Mrs. Hinson," he said, tracing a finger in slow circles from the ring, over the back of her hand, and onto her wrist.

Penelope knew a bribe when she saw one.

Gently but firmly she said, "I can't wear this ring."

"I insist."

"Take the goddamn ring!" Tony heard the tension in Hinson's voice. He knew the man was too smart to get too rough with Penelope at this point, but all the same, Tony wanted her out of there. And soon. She could flush it down the toilet when she got home, or pawn it and say she lost it, or mail it back UPS.

It was probably cubic zirconia, anyway. Hinson liked flash, but he liked to spend his money on his own appetites.

Which he'd certainly done this evening. Dinner had gone on and on and on, the extended event driving Tony nuts. He'd munched on the Chee•tos he'd brought to hold him over, his mouth watering as Penelope exclaimed over one dish after another. Leo had done himself proud.

He hoped Hinson would hustle her out rather than fulfill her request to meet the chef. Except for the extra pounds and inches, he and his cousin could have been identical twins. It would be just like Penelope to comment on that resemblance in front of Hinson, and that wasn't something Tony wanted in the forefront of Hinson's mind.

He licked the salty orange crumbs from his fingers and asked Saint Christopher for a bit of help.

A few minutes later, after no further discussion of the ring or the proposal, the two of them emerged from the restaurant. They walked side by side, but at least the creep didn't have his arm around her. Penelope held a bunch of roses in her arms that would have cost a cop a month's salary. Hinson held open the door of the car that had sat in a no-parking zone the entire time, got in, and drove away.

No ticket on his car, Tony couldn't help but note.

Penelope closed the door of her apartment and leaned against it, grateful David hadn't insisted on coming upstairs.

The ring weighted her hand. She tugged it off and stared at it. At least she'd gotten rid of the roses, dropping them on a table in the entrance area of her building. Someone would find them, take them, and maybe even appreciate them.

"Eventful evening?" Mrs. Merlin sat cross-legged on the sofa, curiously looking at her hostess while keeping one eye on the portable television Penelope had positioned on the coffee table.

She answered with a shaky laugh, crossing to the sofa and holding out the ring. "Just look at this diamond! And he absolutely insists he won't take no for an answer. It's almost scary."

"Hmmm." Mrs. Merlin used the remote to switch off the TV. She tapped on the stone with the end of her magic incense wand, then shook her head. "Men," she said with a sniff. "Some of them you just can't trust."

"What do you mean?"

"Are you familiar with the expression, 'All that glitters is not gold'?"

"Oh." Penelope stared again at the ring. "How do you know it's not a real diamond?"

"No fire."

"No wonder he insisted I take it with me even though I said I wouldn't marry him."

"Oh, cubic zirconia is still pricey. And that's a pretty good fake."

"Gee, thanks for that." Penelope dropped her head back on the sofa. "At least dinner was delicious. The most marvelous appetizer, escargots wrapped in escarole and served with a sauce of—"

"Stop!"

Penelope clapped a hand to her mouth. "I'm so sorry. How rude of me, when you're living on oatmeal."

"I like oatmeal."

"It's a good thing." Penelope laughed. "Come on, I'll make you a dish."

In a flash, Mrs. Merlin vaulted off the couch. It amazed Penelope how she managed to zip around using her stick. She traveled in leaps and bounds, literally, into the kitchen and landed on the counter. Straightening her skirt, she said, "I think you're ready to call on Mr. Gotho again."

"Am I?"

She nodded, smiling as Penelope mixed oatmeal into the water.

"Why now and not before?"

"When you found out the ring wasn't real, you didn't take it personally."

Unaccountably pleased, Penelope stirred the oatmeal. Mrs. Merlin did make a strange kind of sense.

"Maybe you should run over there now, dear,

while your ego is properly aligned."

"Tonight?"

Mrs. Merlin nodded. "But finish my oatmeal first and change your clothes. Go to the Quarter dressed like that and you'll likely be mistaken for a hooker."

"Mrs. Merlin!" Penelope flicked the burner off and filled a small dish with oatmeal. "The lady at Macy's assured me this was a perfectly respectable dress."

"So who are you trying to convince? You or me?"

Penelope thrust her hands on her hips. The neckline ruffles swayed. "Oh, forget it. I'm just not made to look sexy."

Still on the counter, Mrs. Merlin dug into the oatmeal with her demitasse spoon. "Not true. You're just wearing the wrong dress. How much did that cost? I bet that woman worked on commission."

Penelope laughed. "An arm and a leg, and I did it just to torment that rascal of an ex-cop, and Hinson defeated my entire plan by taking me to a restaurant where the guy couldn't see or hear me."

Mrs. Merlin's eyes twinkled. "Oh, he seems like a determined fellow."

"David and I were the only diners. He had them open the entire restaurant just for us."

"Why does he want to marry you?"

Penelope had headed into the bedroom, but she turned back at Mrs. Merlin's question. Dropping into a kitchen chair, she said slowly, "That is a very good question."

*   *   *

Tony saw Penelope delivered to the door of her apartment and watched Hinson drive away. Torn between a raging desire to find some excuse to see Penelope and the instinct that tonight Hinson would do something violent, he followed Hinson.

Another member of Tony's undercover detail was already tailing him, but Tony wanted to be in on the chase.

No man with Hinson's ego could take a rejection and not explode in some fashion. That he'd remained under control with Penelope spoke volumes to Tony. That meant he *needed* Penelope to marry him.

The call he'd made earlier had confirmed what he'd suspected. The law firm Penelope had joined represented the other party in a long-contested multimillion-dollar lawsuit that Hinson's boss had been waging both in and out of state and federal court.

None of the wiretaps in place on Hinson or any of his boss's several offices had disclosed any clue as to Hinson's interest in Penelope. He'd kept completely mum. Hinson's boss was on tape making one reference to how marrying settled down a man, but the comment had been made in passing.

Or so Tony had thought until Squeek gave him the word from the streets.

Hinson must have told one of his favorite whores that he was tying the knot, no doubt, which is how the news had filtered to Squeek.

To visit one of those whores was no doubt where Hinson was headed at the moment, as he swung out of the Warehouse District and drove speedily toward the seedy end of Tulane Avenue. That bleak street, lined with hole-in-the-wall bars, run-down motels, and abandoned buildings no one would spend the time or money to repair, served as backdrop for many a prostitute.

Tony stopped at a red light, keeping Hinson in sight but making sure at least another car separated them. He hated to see how sad this stretch of the city looked, and nighttime showed it to better advantage than the harsh light of day.

He alone of all his family had remained in the city. Everyone else had migrated to the suburbs. Too dangerous, too full of minorities, too crowded, too expensive. He'd heard all the reasons, but he stayed behind, keeping up the shotgun house his grandparents had built in uptown New Orleans more than ninety years ago.

Ahead, Hinson pulled his Lincoln to the curb. Tony watched as a young girl in a tight white dress slunk from the shadows and approached the fancy car.

"Bastard," he said, and reached for his radio.

It crackled to life before he could send a message out for backup to create a diversion that would send Hinson scurrying off like a cockroach into the night. Hinson wasn't to be arrested before he'd offered Tony a post, no matter what he did on his personal time, but Tony would be damned before he'd let him beat up a girl who looked no more than fifteen.

"Your favorite lady lawyer's going for a drive," said the voice over the radio.

"Roger." Tony swung into a U-turn, sent the

message he needed to send, and left Hinson and the girl's fate in the hands of the uniformed law.

Where in the hell was Penelope going at eleven o'clock on a Monday night? To the office? Nah, not even Penelope Sue Fields qualified as that extreme a workaholic.

And even though his undercover assignment required him to track Hinson, and he knew Penelope wasn't headed toward Hinson, he couldn't stop himself from choosing to follow her.

He had to know what she was doing.

"Face it, Olano," he said, "you're obsessed with the woman. Not healthy. Not a good thing at all."

On Canal nearing the turn toward the area where she lived, Tony slowed and tried to talk himself into returning to Hinson. Instead, he checked with the man he had tailing her, another private investigator whom he'd hired earlier that day under the auspices of Olano Investigations to help him keep an eye on Penelope when duty required him to be otherwise occupied. After what Squeek had told him, he had to protect her, without her or anyone else knowing he was doing so.

Tony got her location, headed into the French Quarter, and, ignoring the NO LEFT TURN sign, veered onto the streets of the Vieux Carré.

Penelope hugged her arms to her chest and hurried up the dark street. The lower end of Bourbon Street where the Bayou Magick Shoppe was located was residential, as different as night and day from the stretch where tourists traditionally came to drink, gawk, and act out in ways they never would have thought of doing back home in Iowa.

She'd had to park four blocks from the shop. Most of the house fronts were shuttered from the street. Warnings about muggings raced through her mind and she wondered why she'd agreed to chase after Mrs. Merlin's stupid magic supplies in the middle of the night. And a work night, too!

Then she reached one house where lights blazed, a dinner party in full swing. Several young men sat on the stoop, drinking wine and chatting. For a moment she felt safer, and her spirits rose.

She crossed to the next block and the feeling vanished. Walking up the steps to the door of the Bayou Magick Shoppe, Penelope couldn't banish the feeling that someone watched her. Probably Mr. Gotho, she tried to convince herself, as she rang the bell and waited anxiously for him to come to the door of the shop, a shop clearly closed for the night.

Her mood was darkened by her concern over something David had said at dinner. In her mind, she'd been working it over and over, the way she did when a popcorn hull got stuck in a tooth. Pretty soon her mind grew frustrated and she tried to let go of the worrisome thought that Hinson was more than he appeared on the surface.

More what? She shivered and rang the bell again. More dangerous?

Don't be ridiculous, she told herself. He's a

lawyer, same as you. Maybe he has some bad clients, but he also has good clients.

But how did he know which legal recruiting firm had found her the job in New Orleans?

Behind her she heard shuffling footsteps. Penelope whirled around.

An old man walking his dog glanced up at her.

"Evening," he said. The dog lifted his leg against the metal post of the RESIDENTIAL PARKING ONLY sign. Penelope smiled weakly and turned back to bang on the door.

"Come on," she said, wanting nothing more than to be in her bed safe and sound. She should have insisted on bringing Mrs. Merlin along with her, though she would have been good for nothing more than moral support.

But at this moment, with the wind picking up and the street darker than ever with the clouds covering the moon, moral support was exactly what she needed.

Mrs. Merlin continued to insist this mission had to be accomplished alone.

Penelope was beginning to get the feeling Mrs. Merlin pretty much made up her magick rules as her mood suited her. On the other hand, the kindly woman wouldn't knowingly have sent her on a risky errand.

Of course, she probably hadn't been on the lower end of Bourbon Street after dark for half a century.

She heard a lock scrape on the other side of the door. Another echoing slap of footsteps accompanied the noise. For a fleeting instant, Penelope wondered whether Tony was the source of her sensation of being followed.

The door creaked open and she discarded the idea. This time of night, he'd probably bedded down with his babe of the moment.

Mr. Gotho wore jogging shorts and an LSU T-shirt. With his inscrutable gaze, he studied Penelope as she stood framed in the door.

Her imagination had dressed him in a crimson dressing gown, pipe in hand, nightcap on his head. She didn't know why; despite his silvery brown hair, he didn't look too many years her senior. It was his eyes that looked as if they'd lived for at least a century.

Watching him watch her, though, she decided not to comment either on his wardrobe or his age. She wanted to pass whatever test he'd summoned for her, get the goods, and get home.

"Come in, Penelope," he said in that low voice of his that sounded so mysterious.

She stepped inside the shop.

He shut the door behind her.

And locked it.

Penelope decided she'd lost her sense of adventure before it had a chance to blossom. "Uh . . ."

"Do not be afraid. You are safer in here than you are on the street. There is"—Mr. Gotho inclined his head sideways, as if listening—"evil out there. But there is also good."

Yeah, right. Oops. Penelope told her mind to behave itself. How did one keep one's ego in line?

Mr. Gotho smiled. "To wonder is to begin to understand."

Could he read her mind? Penelope wanted to ask him, but she felt silly doing so.

"It's okay to ask me whatever you wish," Mr. Gotho said, walking to the back of the shop. He lifted the counter gate and waited for her to follow him. "I don't read minds. But I do interpret expressions."

Penelope laughed nervously. "And everything I think shows on my face, I guess?"

"Oh, I wouldn't say that." He paused beside the door where he'd been when he'd tossed her out the other day. The other day? Only the day before. Penelope couldn't quite grasp that her life seemed to be changing with such lightning speed.

Certainly since she'd met Mrs. Merlin everything had been topsy-turvy.

And since you met Tony Olano, she reminded herself.

Tony? Tony is only a bossy, arrogant, troublemaking ex-cop who got himself thrown off the police force. Why should his existence make me feel as if my life has changed?

"Do you wish to go on?"

Mr. Gotho's voice broke into her thoughts. Penelope blinked and stared at the snarling purple tiger on the front of his golden T-shirt. "Sorry," she said, "I forget myself sometimes."

"Of course," he said, and opened the door.

Once inside the storeroom, Penelope stared at the rows of shelves covered with bottles, boxes and bags of all sorts, shapes, and sizes. Candles in a rainbow of colors lined one side of the room.

"Your list?" Mr. Gotho held out a hand.

"List?" Penelope knew her face fell. Mrs. Merlin had said she wouldn't need a list. Then she smiled. Mr. Gotho was only testing her. "I only need what is necessary," she said.

"Very good." Her personal shopper in the realm of magick moved about the small storeroom, a gentle smile tugging at his lips as he pulled various items off the shelves and put them onto the tiny round table in the center of the room.

The candles were arranged by color, starting with white, then gray, then black along one wall. Another shelf held candles in varying shades of red. As she looked around, Mr. Gotho selected one of the cherry-red candles and placed it on the table.

"What a wonderful color," Penelope said, reaching out to stroke the candle.

"It carries strength of heart," Mr. Gotho said. "This candle is for you."

"Me?" Penelope stilled her hand where it touched the smooth, waxy side of the candle. "These supplies are for Mrs. Merlin, not for me."

Mr. Gotho smiled. "Perhaps."

"I do like this color," she said. "It feels right."

"It is you, as you can see."

She let go reluctantly and stepped back as Mr. Gotho started to pack the candles and other items into a shopping bag.

"Mrs. Merlin may fall short when it comes to patience, but she is an excellent teacher," Mr. Gotho said. "If you listen to her, you will learn from her."

"Learn? You mean to do my own spells?" The

very idea was incredible. Penelope, as much as she lived in her fantasy world, was very much a believer in the rational and logical.

"You never know what you're capable of until you reach for the stars, my dear," Mr. Gotho said, handing her the bag.

She accepted the weighted shopping bag. "How much do I owe you?" It was a good thing she'd brought her checkbook. It looked as if Mrs. Merlin's supplies could add up to a large sum.

He shook his head. "Mrs. Merlin will pay me later."

"You're sure?" Penelope reached for her shoulder purse. "I really don't mind taking care of it."

"That's not necessary." He opened the storeroom door, held it open for her, then followed her back up the hallway to the front of the store.

Penelope paused at the door. "You believe in all this, don't you?" She didn't ask in a skeptical way; she really wanted to understand this enigmatic man.

He cocked his head to one side, a finger to his chin. "I believe in what is possible," he said. "And I think you do, too. Go quietly into the night and seek the forces of good."

"Thank you, Mr. Gotho," she said, surprisgly touched by his words. She nodded and slipped out the door.

She heard the bolt shut behind her. Squaring her shoulders, she started walking down the now deserted street.

The four blocks to her car seemed like a mile, but she felt safer now, somehow protected by the peace she'd absorbed during her visit with Mr. Gotho.

That was why when she heard the footsteps behind her, she ignored them at first.

Only your imagination, she told herself.

But when she speeded up, so did they.

Chapter 14

If she walked just a little faster, she'd reach her car ahead of whoever stalked her in the darkness.

Penelope forced herself to concentrate on putting one foot in front of the other as she worked her car keys out of her pocket and into her hand. With a sweaty palm, she grasped the bag Mr. Gotho had given her. Whatever happened, she had to hang on to that.

The steps kept pace behind her. If only she had the courage to turn around, she might find that they belonged to yet another innocent old man walking a dog.

But Penelope knew better.

Fear drove her on.

She turned the corner to the sidestreet where she'd parked her car.

Right at the corner.

The blacktop of the street glared back at her, empty under the streetlight.

She glanced over her shoulder. Her fears materialized in the shape of a young man, one hand thrust into the pocket of a windbreaker.

She swallowed, gathered her breath to scream.

A car pulled up beside her, the front passenger door hanging open.

"Get in," called a low voice.

She froze.

"For Pete's sake, it's me."

Penelope started to laugh. Then she bolted toward the car as the youth who'd been following her ran in the opposite direction.

"I've never been so glad to see anyone in my life," Penelope said to Tony Olano, sliding into the car and locking the door behind her.

He grinned. "Just call me a knight in shining armor."

Her teeth chattered. "I knew someone was following me, but I didn't have the nerve to turn around."

"Just as well," he said, squealing rubber as he roared into a left-hand turn in front of an oncoming cab. As the car steadied into a slightly more moderate pace, he turned toward her, a grim look on his face. "Now, do you want to tell me what the hell you were doing on this end of Bourbon Street at this time of night?"

Penelope bristled. "That's none of your business."

He slammed on the brakes. "Want to get out and walk?"

"I certainly will." She grabbed the door handle.

He yanked the wheel, sliding the car to the curb. "Forget it," he said. "I'm not letting you out on this street. Jesus," he said, running his hands through his hair, "do you know how much trouble you are?"

"No, I do not." Penelope swung around in the

seat. "I didn't ask to be rescued, so just take me home—now, if you please. I need to call the police and report my car was stolen."

"Your car is probably locked up tight in the impound lot 'cause you parked too close to the corner. Forget about that. You didn't ask to be mugged, either, but that's what was about to happen to you. Do you have any idea how frightened you would have been then?" Tony reached over, and before she knew what had happened, he had his arms around her, pulling her close to him.

She caught her breath in her throat, half-sob, half-laugh. "Oh, Tony," she said, snuggling against him, wondering how he'd happened along when he had, but too thankful to question the timing. She'd started to shake, and he ran his hands up and down her arms.

"There, there," he said in a low voice, "you're okay, you're with me. Tony-O is here to take care of you, so don't you worry."

She nestled her head against his chest, wondering if she'd ever felt so safe.

He stroked her hair, murmuring silly words about brave Penelope taking on the world.

For the longest time, she lay wrapped in a security she'd never known existed. Then she struggled to sit up, to regain her sanity.

"I—"

"Shhh," he said, and lowered his lips to hers.

She lost all notion of reality, sanity, order, and discipline as his mouth claimed hers. With a gasp of surprise, she opened her lips and his tongue accepted the unconscious invitation to explore her mouth. Greedily so, as he plunged deeper, circling the roof of her mouth, causing her to cry out in an ecstasy she'd never known.

"Oh, my," she whispered, and snuggled even closer to his chest. One arm crept around his waist, claiming a path above his belt in a way that felt completely right and natural to her.

Tony leaned into her, his hands on her hair, her back, her breasts, stroking, teasing, finding their way to the most responsive parts of her body. It was as if he knew what would make her cry out, what would make tears sparkle in her lashes.

She moaned, responding to his lips still hot on her mouth. He lifted his head slightly, so that his lips barely brushed hers. She raised her hands, shyly, only knowing she wanted his lips back on hers.

He grinned and placed her hands on the back of his head. "Pull me down, sweetheart. Tell me what you want."

Her eyes widened. Then she did exactly what he'd suggested.

This time he moaned as he plunged his tongue inside her mouth. Abruptly, he stopped and pulled back, holding her at arm's length. "You're shivering," he said softly.

She nodded, realizing she'd been trembling since she'd first heard the ominous footsteps behind her in the darkness.

"I know just the thing to make you feel better." He let go of her and pulled the car into traffic.

Penelope felt like telling him he was already making her feel better, but shyness held her tongue. Hugging her arms around herself, she said, "And what does Dr. Olano have in mind?"

"A true New Orleans remedy—café au lait and beignets at Café du Monde. Have you been there?"

She shook her head, thinking she ought to quit working so much and see more of the city she now called home.

"Going to Café du Monde, especially at night, is a local tradition." He smiled. "I used to date a girl in high school whose mom would only let her go out with me if we were on a double date to Café du Monde. That's how safe you'll feel there." He winked.

Penelope couldn't help but smile. She wondered if the girl's mom had ever considered just how devastatingly charming Tony Olano must have been between home and the café and how little time they must have spent sipping coffee.

She pictured him in high school, same great body, same killer eyes. He must have been the heartthrob of every teenage girl, the very opposite of her own secondary school experience. Penelope sighed and touched her fingertips to her lips.

"Do you have any idea how beautiful you are when you go all dreamy-eyed like that?" Tony had stopped the car and turned toward her.

Penelope started to blush. "No," she said frankly. "I don't think of myself as beautiful."

"And they tell me how smart you're supposed to be," he murmured, reaching over and loosening the knot of her hair. "How about we get our coffee and beignets, then I teach you just how beautiful you are?"

Speechless, unable to believe the man with

bedroom eyes was saying those words to her, Penelope managed a nod. Looking out the window, away from Tony's intense gaze, she saw by the name emblazoned on a green and white awning that they'd parked by their destination.

Tony opened the door for her. Despite the late hour, the sidewalk activity was going strong. From across the street came the drivers' cries advertising buggies for hire. "Bugg—ee! Bugg—ee!" An unblinking mime commanded the nearby entrance to the sidewalk café, hat held forth for tips. Almost half of the many tables were occupied and waiters hustled about.

Penelope smiled up at Tony. "This is fun," she said.

He draped an arm around her shoulders and led her to a table. As she sat down, Penelope realized she'd stopped shaking.

Tony took the seat beside her, his thigh brushing hers in a way she found both exciting and comforting. He pointed to a battered aluminum napkin holder. "The menu."

She bent her head to read the choices plastered on the side of the napkin holder. Her hair swung forward. Shifting her hand, she reached to tuck the wayward strands behind her ear, but Tony was faster.

He gently brushed her hair from her face. "Like silk," he said, then in a quick change of tone he added, "I recommend two orders of beignets."

She nodded, not hungry for food, but definitely starved for every minute she could have with this man. When he wasn't annoying her, he made her feel like a princess. A sexy, desirable princess.

A waiter approached, a stack of thick white saucers lodged under one arm. "Take your order," he said in rapid-fire, heavily accented English.

"Two café au laits and two orders of beignets," Tony said.

Penelope decided she'd better keep her thoughts firmly on food and far away from her other appetites. "What is a beignet?" she said, stumbling over the word as she tried to imitate Tony's pronunciation that sounded like bin-yeah.

"A donut coated in powdered sugar. And café au lait is coffee made with steamed milk."

"New Orleans has its own version of so many things," Penelope said. "In any other city, they'd simply say donut and coffee with steamed milk."

"And it wouldn't taste nearly as good," Tony said. He reached over and stroked the back of her hand lightly. "Everything's better in New Orleans," he murmured.

Penelope was saved from trying to come up with an appropriate response by the waiter delivering steaming cups and saucers piled with what looked like mounds of powdered sugar. "Wow," she said.

Tony selected a beignet from the stack and lifted it toward her. "Take a bite."

She did and her mouth smiled at the succulent blend of sweet fried dough and the luscious coating of sugar.

Tony lowered the beignet to the saucer, then

leaned closer. With his thumb, he patted her upper lip and showed her how much sugar decorated her face from only one bite.

"Messy but delicious," she said.

Tony raised his thumb to his mouth and slowly licked the sugar he'd taken from her lips. "Definitely delicious," he said, his eyes darkening in a way that signaled he wasn't describing only the sweet treat.

Watching him lick his finger in such a sensuous manner played funny tricks on Penelope's insides. She took another bite of the pastry. Tony sipped his coffee, watching her as if he wanted her for dessert.

Feeling braver and more desirable than she could recall ever experiencing, Penelope dabbled her forefinger in a pile of sugar on the saucer and lifted it to Tony's lips.

His eyes widened and he smiled, a look both gentle and wicked, as he accepted her offering. He circled her wrist with one hand and oh so slowly worked her finger in and out of his lips. All the while he held her gaze in his.

When he finished, he leaned closer and whispered, "Let's take our café au lait to go."

Shivering again, this time from the sensations Tony had created within her, Penelope nodded. He corralled the waiter, dumped the liquid from the thick crockery mugs into paper cups, then piled some dollar bills on the table and rose.

Penelope followed him out to the car, excited by the way she trembled with anticipation. Tony handed her into the car and walked around to the driver's side. She saw him whisk a paper off the windshield, crumple it, and toss it into the backseat as he got into the car.

He drove quickly and they didn't talk. Penelope sipped her coffee. Within ten minutes, they were clear of the French Quarter traffic and only blocks from her apartment building. Suddenly Penelope realized she'd forgotten about Mrs. Merlin's presence. She couldn't invite Tony up with a chaperone!

She choked on her coffee and he glanced over quickly.

"Are you okay?"

She nodded. Donkeys and dumbbells! Should she say something? Or maybe he'd simply drive them to his place. She finished her café au lait in one quick gulp.

The radio barked.

Tony slapped at it with one hand.

Penelope looked from Tony to the radio and back.

"It's nothing," he said, then the radio blared again. "Nuts," he said, and grabbed the microphone. He radioed in.

Penelope gazed over at him, curious, but too far gone with passion to worry about anything other than where the two of them would end up.

"I've gotta take you home," he said. "Gotta work."

"Oh," she said, relieved to learn he hadn't been planning to.

He stopped at a light, then reached over and pulled her close. "If it weren't for work," he said, "nothing would keep me from finishing what we just started."

She blushed, then found the nerve to whisper, "Me neither."

They roared the next few blocks through the Warehouse District. Tony said abruptly, "Have dinner with me tomorrow night?"

"Dinner?"

"Yeah, you know, in a noisy restaurant full of happy people? The place Primo's chef used to work."

"You did follow me tonight, didn't you?"

"Is the Pope Catholic?" He grinned and shot through a light more red than yellow.

"You're impossible."

"Thanks. Seven?" He paused, keeping an eye on her, obviously assessing her reaction. "Great seafood. Right on the lake."

She pursed her lips, placed one finger against them, feeling his kiss once more. Did he want to see her again or was he being polite? Whatever the answer, she lectured herself, she shouldn't run away from adventure, even if she ended up with a heartache. "All right," she whispered.

"Cheer up, we may not have slugs wrapped in grass, but I predict you'll like it even better."

"You really did follow me, didn't you?"

"Into the kitchen," he said, squealing to a stop in front of her apartment building. Leaning over, he thrust her door wide. "Forgive me for not seeing you up?"

She was surprised, but nodded. "Busy night for the unemployed?"

He grinned in answer; then, suddenly looking much more serious, he called her name as she stepped from the car.

"Yes?" She wet her bottom lip and turned toward the man with bedroom eyes, the man who'd turned her world upside down.

"Don't ever marry a man who doesn't make you feel like you do right this minute."

Eyes wide, Penelope feathered the tip of her little finger over her lips and backed inside her door. It wasn't until she was on her way up in the elevator that she regained her senses enough to worry about her missing car.

Rushing into her apartment, Penelope almost stepped on Mrs. Merlin. The tiny woman lay flat in the center of the living room on the rectangular Persian carpet Penelope had picked up for a song at a flea market. Her arms and legs were spread loosely from the side of her body, her eyes closed.

Was she dead?

Penelope set down the bag from the Bayou Magick Shoppe and knelt on the floor. With relief, she saw Mrs. Merlin's chest slowly rise and fall.

Just as well her miniature houseguest wasn't paying attention. Tiptoeing into the bedroom, Penelope hugged her arms to her sides, savoring the taste of Tony's lips on hers.

Who would have thought he could make her feel so . . . oh, so magical, like a hot air balloon sailing toward the moon? Arms circling an imaginary dance partner, she swayed toward her bed, then dropped down, her hands pressed to the insides of her thighs.

I'm trembling, she realized. Well, it wasn't every night a woman had her car disappear, escaped a mugging, then got kissed by the man with bedroom eyes.

The trembling in her legs increased as she relived him saying to her in his low, rough voice, "Tell me what you want." Ooh, the power of that suggestion!

Despite her hours of fantasy life with her mystery man Raoul, Penelope had never once envisioned the incredibly intoxicating concept of a man holding her close and uttering such a phrase in her ears.

She heard a rustling noise in the other room, just in time to keep herself from curling up on her bed and going off into a long, long, fantasy about what might have happened between her and Tony Olano had he not had to whisk off to work.

Then she frowned.

She'd never seen any evidence that he even had a job.

So where was he going?

Penelope dragged herself off the bed, her energy drained by the notion that Tony had misused her, and badly. He'd kissed her, dumped her at her door, then run off to somewhere more exciting. Or someone, more than likely.

A tear welled in her eye and she commanded it to evaporate.

"Penelope?" Mrs. Merlin called her name from the living room and Penelope forced herself to move. He'd only been using her. How could she even have thought that he wanted her, desired her, couldn't live without seeing her again?

She shook her head, trying to rattle some

sense back into her brain. Then she sighed and went to see what Mrs. Merlin had been doing playing dead.

The woman sat cross-legged on the floor. Looking amazingly refreshed, Mrs. Merlin surveyed Penelope from her position in the living room. "You have the materials, don't you?"

Penelope nodded. She sat on the sofa, then pointed to the shopping bag. "Everything you need."

Mrs. Merlin made a slight *tch-tch* noise.

"What?" Penelope spoke more sharply than she'd intended, but she was just so darned depressed. Tony Olano would kiss anything in a skirt. Why had she even let herself feel special?

"My, my," murmured Mrs. Merlin. "Maybe you should try some creative visualization of your own."

"What's that?"

Mrs. Merlin stretched her hands over her head, then bent forward, rolling into a pose that resembled a bedbug. When her head resurfaced, she said as she rose from the carpet, "One of the steps in candle magick is to prepare oneself with creative visualization."

"Planning the outcome?"

"Very good. But then you already know you're smart, don't you?"

"What's wrong with that?" Penelope wanted to be cross with Tony, but since he wasn't there, she took it out on her houseguest.

Mrs. Merlin regarded her steadily. "Why don't you tell me what's happened to you since you left Mr. Gotho with this bag of goodies?"

"What do you mean?"

"Your aura is very, very clouded. Mr. Gotho never would have entrusted these supplies with you if you'd been in that state in his shop."

Penelope made a face, then caught herself. Mrs. Merlin had been right before about the question of her ego. Perhaps she truly could see something different about Penelope. Certainly Penelope would never be the same, not since that kiss, and not since reality had set back in.

"Oh, Mrs. Merlin," she said, tucking her feet under her on the couch, "maybe you have a spell to help *me*. I mean, what do you do when you want someone to want you, only he doesn't really want you, he's just toying with you?"

"Hmmm."

"Or at least I'm pretty sure he is."

"I take it you're not referring to the pretty boy who gave you the ring."

"Him?" Penelope waved a dismissive hand. "I'll send that thing back via messenger. Maybe I'll insure it, maybe I won't. No, I'm talking about . . ." she paused and felt herself blush, "I'm talking about Tony."

"Olano?"

Penelope nodded.

"Well, thank the stars," Mrs. Merlin said, hopping from foot to foot. "I thought you'd never wake up and smell the coffee."

"What do you mean?" Penelope dropped her feet to the floor and leaned forward, anxious to hear what Mrs. Merlin had to say.

"That's for me to know and you to find out."

Penelope lunged toward the shopping bag and held it high. "Still want my help?"

"Feisty creature, aren't you? Very well, put

the bag down and I'll tell you what I mean."
Mrs. Merlin climbed onto her incense stick
launcher and the next thing Penelope knew, the
miniature magician was settling next to her on
the couch, folding the skirts of her brightly colored caftan around her calves.

"Do you think he likes me?" Penelope
couldn't help the question from slipping out.

"Do you?"

Penelope laughed. "You would have made a
good lawyer, Mrs. Merlin."

"Too many of them as it is. No offense," she
added quickly. "But do you like him?"

"Sometimes yes and sometimes no."

"Well, that's a start."

"Sometimes he drives me nuts, then others
he's so . . . so . . ."

"Irresistible?"

Penelope nodded. "And cocky."

"Charming?"

"And overbearing."

"Sexy?"

"Most definitely!" Penelope made a noise that
was half-sigh, half-moan.

Mrs. Merlin chuckled. "All right, so he's the
man for you. But somehow you're not con-
vinced he thinks you're the woman for him.
What's the problem?"

"Problem?" Penelope hated the squeaky way
her voice rose. "Why would a man who could
have any woman on the street, in the entire city,
want me?"

"Oh, now, that is a problem. Could you tip
that bag over, dear, and let me look in it while
we chat?"

"Oh, of course." Penelope spilled the contents, but gently, onto the sofa. No telling what Mr. Gotho had put in there. The only thing she was sure they wouldn't find was frog's testicles.

Mrs. Merlin walked up to the cherry-red candle that stood as high as her breastbone. "Have you ever been with a man?"

"You mean . . . ?"

She nodded and walked in a circle around the candle.

"Um . . . well, no, not exactly."

"So, you have doubts about your sexuality?"

"Do you mean about whether I'm attracted to men?" Again, her voice squeaked and Penelope blushed, thankful that had never happened to her in the courtroom.

"Or whether they're attracted to you."

"Oh, that. I don't think much about it," she lied.

Mrs. Merlin stroked the side of the cherry-red candle. "But you're thinking now about whether Tony Olano is attracted to you?"

Penelope nodded. She couldn't lie about that.

"Did Mr. Gotho mention anything about this candle when he included it in the supplies?"

Penelope thought back, but with all the excitement she'd undergone, she couldn't remember what he'd told her about the candle. She shook her head.

"I want you to lie on the floor, exactly as you found me lying," Mrs. Merlin said, suddenly sounding very, very bossy. "And don't ask 'Now?' in that little voice of yours. Do it."

Penelope stared at her. She thought of objecting, reminding Mrs. Merlin of the heavy schedule she had the next day, starting off with an important breakfast meeting at eight o'clock at the Windsor Court.

One more glance at the tiny woman and Penelope held her tongue. Obediently, she slipped off the sofa and onto the floor, stretching out as she'd seen Mrs. Merlin do earlier.

Goodness only knew, none of this stuff made sense, but she might as well give it a shot. Wanting Tony Olano to want her as badly as she wanted him, she'd almost sell her soul, let alone light a candle, to accomplish that goal.

Attempting to pick up the prostitute had been a predictable move on Hinson's part. His next move had been much more diabolical, Tony thought, his stomach roiling as he watched from the sidelines as a rookie street patrolman roped off the bloody crime scene on the other side of town from where Hinson had headed for his rendezvous with some unlucky hooker.

They hadn't killed Squeek, but he'd be in Charity Hospital for a good long while by the looks of him. Tony dropped his head to his hands and cursed himself.

He wanted to drop to the sidewalk and throw up the dinner he hadn't eaten, but he stood rock-still, forcing himself to watch as the paramedics strapped Squeek to the stretcher and lifted him into the waiting ambulance.

And you thought you were clever, he mocked himself. And careful. You aren't worth silt from the river, Olano. Fear, genuine fear, pricked a line across his scalp as he thought of what Hinson's men had done to his informant.

Because, of course, he thought of Penelope. And what they'd do to her if she didn't agree to marry Hinson. They'd handpicked her, brought her to New Orleans, wanted her working for them, set up so she wouldn't testify against the man she'd married. And as a bonus, no doubt her law firm would have to resign from the huge case opposing Hinson's boss.

The siren wailed and Tony wanted to howl along with it. Nothing he'd found indicated Penelope knew anything about Hinson; nothing indicated she was in with them in their dirty money schemes, their drug rings, their automobile chop-shop operations, their legitimate businesses dressed up to hide their ill-gotten gains.

She'd shoplifted, true.

But a momentary impulse didn't equal criminal intentions.

Or did it hint at what lay under the iceberg and he wanted to blind himself to that possibility?

Especially after that kiss.

Talk about heat bubbling under the surface. Tony took in a sharp breath and felt her again in his arms, her lips opening under his hungry kiss.

More officers than either usual or necessary milled about the crime scene. Squeek had worked for lots of them, not just Tony, and they'd all be wondering who he'd taken the hit for.

Tony knew.

And he was pretty sure someone else walking around the dark alley lit only by the lights from the officers' cars knew, too. Someone who worked for two bosses, someone who'd veered over the line of duty into the gutter of corruption.

And whoever that was knew about Penelope, might even know Tony had kissed her. In this game, everyone was following everyone else.

Dammit, Olano, you've gotta leave her alone, he argued with himself.

I can't.

Got to.

Just one date.

Date? Are you kidding. You don't want a date. You want her in your bed.

Well, that's part of a date. Dinner first, then bed.

And what'll Hinson do if he finds you jumping the bones of his intended?

Dinner only?

Maybe.

Nope. No way.

He tugged his hands through his hair.

In the morning, he'd leave a message with her secretary that something had come up. She'd figure him for the playboy he had been, but no longer wanted to be.

Chapter 15

Reluctantly at first, battling her mental objections, Penelope followed Mrs. Merlin's instructions for the process she called creative visualization. The first step, hissing and chuffing and blowing out air from deep in her belly to expel what Mrs. Merlin described as negative energies, left Penelope feeling extremely foolish and wondering how she'd stay awake during her important breakfast meeting the next morning.

But as Mrs. Merlin, in a voice much more soothing than her usual caustic commentary, guided her to choose a safe place within herself where she could return again and again when life closed in around her, she quit fighting and eased into the experience.

It wasn't too different from her tendency to escape straight into her fantasies in the midst of her day-to-day routine.

Letting her mind drift free at last from the anchor of self-consciousness, Penelope saw the image of a riverbank in her mind. Mrs. Merlin instructed her to find a place of peace, and as the vision swam full-blown into her mind, she knew instinctively this place of peace was one she'd visited many times before.

She walked along the bank, beside the murmuring stream just past sunset. That was the same hour of the evening she'd escaped from the trailer park during her childhood, running off to the creek that bordered the property, the creek that hinted of a cosmos that lay beyond the borders of her world.

Her mother worked a split shift so each afternoon she could return home to supervise Penelope's homework, something that Penelope resented at the time, but later, when her academic scholarships provided the escape route she craved, she came to appreciate. But as soon as her mother returned to work for the evening dinner rush, Penelope would hightail it out the door, eager to breathe in the night air and talk to the stars that came out one by one.

Even now, as she walked the riverbank in her mind, the feeling of peace crept over her. Frogs croaked, crickets chirruped, and the birds in the trees called good evening.

From a far distance, she heard Mrs. Merlin speaking in a soothing voice. "You may return to this place at will. It is your home away from the world, it is your cocoon in which you may visualize the outcomes of your life. It is the place you will come to visit before you practice your candle magick."

Penelope heard Mrs. Merlin's words. She'd immersed herself so completely in her place of peace she'd left her other reality behind, so utterly she didn't object to Mrs. Merlin's reference to her practicing candle magick.

Something she normally would have protested as highly unlikely.

But this evening nothing felt as it normally did.

She'd been asked to marry a man.

She'd been kissed by another.

Penelope stirred and feathered her thumb across her mouth.

Mrs. Merlin guided her out of the visualization and back into the living room.

"Well?" asked the wee woman, sitting forward, hands on her knees.

"Interesting," Penelope said.

Mrs. Merlin shook her head. "You're a tough nut to crack, Penelope. Yet you've got the eyes of a seer, if you'd only free yourself to use them."

Penelope stretched her arms over her head, feeling surprisingly energetic for someone who'd worked all day, dined at leisure, gone on a mysterious errand, been chased by a mugger, and been rescued by a Lothario. She sighed and sat up. "What's next?"

Mrs. Merlin's eyes twinkled. "I can see why you did so well in school."

"How do you know that?"

"I don't have to have been the valedictorian to be good at deductive reasoning, you know."

"Right. Sorry. I was good at school and if I hadn't been, goodness knows what my mother would have done to me."

"Perhaps loved you for the good person you are?"

Penelope sighed and rose from the floor. "I

hope so, but I honestly don't know the answer to that question."

"And she's gone beyond and you can't ask her?"

Penelope nodded. "You sure you don't have some sort of advanced degree in that deductive reasoning?"

Mrs. Merlin smiled and bounded off the sofa. "Bring the goodies Mr. Gotho gave you to the dining table."

Penelope obeyed, thinking again of the cherry-red candle. As she did so, the image of Tony kissing her, urging her to tell him what she wanted, claimed her mind.

"It's okay to use the magick for yourself, you know," Mrs. Merlin said from the tabletop, watching Penelope carefully.

"I wouldn't want to be selfish."

The woman shrugged. "Whyever not? As long as it's not directly harmful to someone else, that is. We humans spend a lot of words and time denying our desires to be selfish, when what is selfish is essentially the purest form of energy in the universe."

Penelope sat down on the edge of a chair next to Mrs. Merlin. "What do you mean?" she asked, thinking she did know what Mrs. Merlin meant, but that she couldn't quite embrace the philosophy.

"Well," Mrs. Merlin said, folding back the sleeves of her caftan, "let's take you and Tony Olano, for example."

"For example," Penelope murmured, blushing.

"You're obviously attracted to him. He's attracted to you. Yet you seem to think he's not interested in you, the Penelope Sue Fields you define as your true self."

Penelope frowned, concentrating on Mrs. Merlin's words. "Well, I don't see him as wanting me, Penelope the Nerd, Penelope the Vir—" She bit her tongue, embarrassed that she'd almost repeated this personal confession.

Mrs. Merlin didn't seem to mind at all. "You think if he knows the real you he won't like you at all. Though, if I were to place a bet, and I am a betting woman—oh, I do love a trip to the casino!—I'd say something's happened between the two of you that gives you hope."

"How do you know so much?"

Mrs. Merlin chuckled. "I don't; I just guess really, really well."

"I'll say."

"Anyway, my point is there's nothing at all wrong with using candle magick to achieve your self-oriented wishes." Mrs. Merlin winked. "There, do you like that term better? You want to use that cherry-red candle to summon desire, affection, even love from Tony Olano; there's no harm, only good, that can come of it."

Penelope laughed, hearing the nervousness in her voice. Wow, was she tempted to do just as Mrs. Merlin suggested. What harm could it do? After all, it was a ritual whose total effect would be to make her feel a little bit better. As long as she didn't end up feeling completely foolish, that is.

"My only warning, as I said, has to do with wishing for yourself something that will bring harm to another," Mrs. Merlin said, breaking

into Penelope's thoughts. "This you should not
do. It's very bad karma. But I think Tony Olano
would welcome your spell," she finished with a
mischievous grin.

Penelope nodded, then returned to the business at hand. "First, let's take care of you, Mrs.
Merlin. Which of these things do you need?"
With her question, Penelope began the first of
two trips to ferry the magickal supplies from the
couch to the tabletop.

"Ah!" Mrs. Merlin rubbed her hands together
and walked right over to a black feather almost
her size. "Raven," she murmured, then turned
to a waxy white pillar candle that had rolled
onto its side. "Will you stand this up?"

Reaching for the candle, Penelope paused
with her hand in midair. She couldn't say why,
but she didn't feel right touching that candle.
The cherry-red hadn't affected her that way at
all.

"It's a powerful one," Mrs. Merlin said, "so
all the more reason to set it upright."

Penelope nodded and turned the candle on its
bottom. It was an inch higher than Mrs. Merlin.
"How are you going to do anything with
these?"

"Ever heard of Merlin's assistant?" The
woman laughed and pushed her glasses farther
down her nose. "We start with this mirror and
some sand, both of which I see Mr. Gotho has
thoughtfully provided, and if you have something that smacks of those infernal tax people,
that would help a lot."

Penelope wrinkled her nose. She did have
some tax papers in her briefcase, but she hesi-

tated to offer them to the altar. She could just see them catching on fire from the candle flame. She yawned and tried to think what she could use. Yawning again, she said, "Couldn't we do this tomorrow?"

"Do you think I like oatmeal that much?" Mrs. Merlin threw that retort over her shoulder as she walked around the rectangular mirror, scattering sand from a baggie over its surface.

"How selfish of me." Penelope went in search of her briefcase. Of course Mrs. Merlin wanted to get back to her normal size as soon as possible. One sleep-deprived night shouldn't be too much for Penelope to contribute. She'd come to enjoy Mrs. Merlin's company and she had to admit she'd been learning a few things from her, too, but Mrs. Merlin clearly needed to set her life back to rights.

Penelope opened her briefcase and pulled out the file she'd brought with her in preparation for the next morning's business breakfast. Inside was a copy of an Internal Revenue Service Opinion Letter issued to her firm's prospective client, a ruling that if not reversed would result in a significant fiscal blow to the man's company. Penelope had been mulling over the ruling and trying to come up with a supportable argument against it, but so far she hadn't found such a basis, something she knew the senior partner meeting her and the client in the morning had been counting on.

Since it was a photocopy of the original and the original was safe in her office, Penelope pulled it out, folded it so the letterhead showed and not the client's name, then carried it over to Mrs. Merlin.

About to place it on the table, Penelope said, "Hey, wasn't your original problem with the property tax collector, not the IRS?"

"Tax-schmax. What's the difference? They're both a bother."

"If you're sure . . ."

"It's merely a representation." Mrs. Merlin pointed toward the candle. "Put that right in the center of the altar."

With a vague feeling that she might regret her actions in the morning, Penelope did as instructed. Grunting a bit, Mrs. Merlin nudged three objects alongside the white candle, almost as if marking compass points. To the right went the black feather, to the left she lugged an ice-blue marble Mr. Gotho had included; at the bottom she located a Moon Pie, an object that immediately piqued Penelope's curiosity.

She pointed to the Moon Pie. "What is that for?"

Mrs. Merlin shot her a half-smile, half-frown. "It's Mr. Gotho's sense of humor. See, when you build an altar, you represent the North, East, West and South, which correspond to Earth, Air, Water, and Fire. Mr. Gotho likes to use the Moon Pie to symbolize South."

"I take it he's not from here." Penelope spoke the words dryly. Already several people at her new firm had used that same phrase when referring to her. It was said partly as condemnation, partly as absolution. Being from somewhere else was grounds for forgiveness of ignorance of local customs and traditions.

Mrs. Merlin arched her brows, all the while studying her altar and muttering, "North, North, he didn't send anything to represent Earth. Most perturbing, really!"

"Can't you just pick something yourself?" Penelope found herself interested in Mrs. Merlin's machinations, but she desperately wanted to go to bed. Once there, she wanted to hug to herself the physical and emotional memory of Tony's lips on hers, then drift to sleep, a smile on her face.

"Guess I can." Mrs. Merlin placed her hands on her hips, then swung to face Penelope. She stared at her, then said, "Give me an earring."

"Why?"

"Lawyers. You guys question everything. You said use something, I picked your earring. Now give it to me."

"No need to get testy." Penelope pulled the back of the gold ball from her ear, the same earring Tony had returned to her the other evening. As her hand passed her cheek, she relived Tony's touch. As fleeting as it had been, it had shaken her in a way David's proposal hadn't even begun to emulate.

And tomorrow night, she'd be having dinner with him! New Orleans truly was a magical city. Smiling now, she placed the earring on the spot Mrs. Merlin indicated, the rounded gold ball just touching the cherry-red candle.

The copy of the IRS Opinion Letter lay within the area formed by the four objects representing the compass points. Penelope stared at it, thinking she'd lost her mind. Rather than assisting with this spell, she would have been better served poring over code sections and case law at her office, trying to find a way to salvage the position of the company whose president she'd be meeting for breakfast in less than eight hours. Plus, she remembered with a start, with her car either stolen or towed, she'd have to take a cab in the morning.

Mrs. Merlin held forth her magick incense stick. "Please clear your mind, enter your place of peace, then when you are ready, go to the stove and light this with the flame from the burner."

Penelope accepted the incense stick, attempted to banish all thoughts of something so mundane as a missing automobile, took a deep breath, then crossed the floor and flicked on the gas burner. She'd had a real estate firm locate an apartment for her back in February before she'd moved from the ice and snow of Chicago to the warmth of a New Orleans spring. Her one requirement: a gas stove. No decent cook could endure electric burners.

Coddling the flame on the stick, she walked back toward Mrs. Merlin. The miniature magician stood before her altar, her eyes closed, her arms lifted toward the candle. Without knowing why, Penelope knew she should light the powerful white candle without interrupting whatever meditative state Mrs. Merlin had entered.

Bending forward, she brought the flame of the incense stick to the wick of the candle.

It sputtered, caught, died out.

Frustrated, she joined the two again, then again. Just when she'd considered going in search of the matches she'd picked up from the table at Primo's, the wick caught, almost a fiber at a time, then blossomed into life.

She caught her breath and stared into the candle's flame.

For the first time in her life, she studied the light of the candle, saw the intense blue at the center of the flame, watched as it danced in a slow, almost sensual circular motion, then blew repeatedly toward the North, or head, of the altar that Mrs. Merlin had created.

Practically hypnotized, Penelope stared, losing herself in the dancing fire of the waxy white candle, giving herself over to a beauty and a power she'd never before recognized.

Mrs. Merlin seemed to do the same, staring now with her eyes opened wide, her tiny spectacles pushed up atop her carroty hair.

She murmured phrases under her breath, paused, then murmured again, gazing into the flame.

She blinked.

And vanished.

To Penelope's astonishment, the letter she'd placed on the altar disappeared along with her miniature houseguest. Not burned, not singed, not blown off the table by a puff of air; simply no longer there.

Unnerved by what she'd just witnessed, Penelope stared at the spot where Mrs. Merlin had been only a moment earlier. The white candle flickered and danced, bobbing in a circular motion, glowing more orange than blue. Then it suddenly sputtered and died as its wick drowned in the molten wax surrounding it.

Without knowing she was going to do so, Penelope lifted the still-glowing incense stick.

Gazing at the unlit cherry-red candle, she heard Mrs. Merlin telling her it was okay to be selfish.

Penelope licked her lips, then mated the glowing tip of the incense stick with the wick of the cherry-red candle. As she did, she called to mind her place of peace.

In her mind she walked along the riverbank, passing by a tree. To her delight, Tony lazed just beneath the spreading branches of the tree, kicked back on a blanket. With a happier smile in his eyes than she had seen in actual life, he patted the spot next to him.

Penelope blinked. The flame swayed, slow and sensuous. Following it with her eyes, listening to the wispy sighs of the candle's song, Penelope forgot to worry about whether she was supposed to light that candle without Mrs. Merlin being present.

For several minutes she remained entranced with the beauty of the candle and the tender feelings the aromatic scent aroused in her. Penelope began to understand Mrs. Merlin's fascination with the art of candle magick.

The flame shot higher, then dipped.

With a shake of her head, Penelope drew back. She walked a few steps away from the table and studied it, seeing this time the clutter, the jumble, and the melting candle wax she'd have to clean.

With a sigh, she smothered the flame of the cherry-red candle and started to gather the items Mr. Gotho had sent. The apartment was too, too quiet. Imagining Mrs. Merlin lecturing or asking to be fed, Penelope smiled and decided to leave the magick items exactly as Mrs. Merlin had placed them for at least a day. Who knew? Perhaps she needed the altar to guide her safely to wherever it was her spell had carried her.

Home.

That's where she'd wanted to go and Penelope hoped she'd accomplished her desire, and that the next morning when the irascible magician awakened it would be in her own bed, all five feet four and a half inches of her.

Wandering around her apartment, reviewing the events of the remarkable day, Penelope found herself wishing she had a cat or a bird or even a hamster. Before tonight she'd never noticed how empty her apartment seemed.

Before Mrs. Merlin had entered her life, Penelope had been so busy working, working, working, she'd really only stopped in long enough to sleep, shower, and change one suit for another.

Only one annoyance clouded her mind, and that was the realization that she'd have to get up extra early to swing by the office to pick up another copy of the IRS Opinion Letter. What Mrs. Merlin had done with it, she had no idea. Penelope only hoped that in some way the original spell had also been successful, and that Mrs. Merlin's dotty neighbor had been freed from the tax collector's clutches.

But there was no way Penelope could appear at the meeting with the senior partner and the prospective client without a copy of the letter—and even more importantly, some suggestion to solve the man's corporation's tax dilemma.

Frustrated with herself for not having concentrated on it earlier, Penelope set her alarm for five a.m. and prepared for bed.

Instead of mulling over the various exceptions she might argue to the ruling, she let her mind drift as she slipped between the sheets.

Tony's lips, warm, questing, yet tender and succoring, tugged at her mouth.

His arms, so strong and powerful, hugged her to him.

Penelope wriggled and clutched a pillow to her breast. "Oh, my," she murmured, feeling the weight of him as he'd crushed her to the car seat, claiming her.

She ran her tongue over her lips and sighed. All thoughts of Raoul, her former fantasy man, had vanished as completely as Mrs. Merlin had disappeared from her dining table.

Raoul could not compete with the reality of Tony Olano.

Penelope's breasts pushed upward, her back arching against the desire consuming her. Caught unawares by the out-of-control passion, she hovered between embarrassment and absolute rapture.

Finally, a smile on her face, Penelope urged herself to sleep, reassuring her rational mind she'd feel sane in the morning, and in almost the same moment promising the part of her mind that thrived on fantasies that she would dance with Tony in her dreams.

Chapter 16

Penelope dreamed she overslept for her breakfast meeting. Tossing and turning, she watched in dismay as Hubert Humphrey Klees, most senior of the firm's senior partners, dressed her down in front of the entire wait staff of the Windsor Court's Grill Room, including her mother, who burst into tears at her daughter's downfall. The client, of course, had already stormed off, bouncing away on a version of Mrs. Merlin's magick pole-vaulting stick.

She came to wakefulness with a start, pushing her hair from her face and breathing rapidly. Thank goodness it had only been a nightmare. Penelope prided herself on never oversleeping. Each morning when her alarm sounded, she rolled out of bed without dawdling.

Her alarm . . .

It hadn't gone off.

Penelope grabbed her bedside clock. The digital numbers blinked rapidly. Sometime during the night, her power had failed.

She literally sprang from the bed to the dresser to check her watch. Staring at the dial, she clutched her tummy. She had fifteen minutes to make it to the Grill Room or the expression "dreams come true" would take on a whole new meaning for Penelope Sue Fields.

There'd be no time to pick up another copy of the Opinion Letter. She called a cab while she twisted her hair into a knot; jumped into her stockings and suit while reviewing the client's profile in her mind; grabbed shoes, purse, and briefcase; and made it to the ground floor just as the cabbie blew the horn.

She arrived at the stroke of eight to find Hubert already settled at a window table with the patrician Fitzsimmons. The prospective client wore a flinty expression that looked as if it had the effusive Hubert unnerved. Everyone liked Hubert—his charm had won him as many clients as his sharp legal mind—but Fitzsimmons appeared to be a tough nut to crack.

Her heart sinking, Penelope followed the maître d' across the lush carpet. Having dressed in such a rush, she felt a need to tug at her skirt, smooth her jacket, check to see whether she had on a pair of shoes that matched.

Resisting the temptation, she approached the table, hand extended to Clarke Fitzsimmons, president and majority shareholder of a company worth a quarter of a million in billable hours per year.

"Ms. Fields," Hubert said, rising slightly and glancing at his watch.

She smiled. She must have overdone the expression, because Hubert blinked twice before he introduced her to Fitzsimmons. But it was Hubert who'd criticized her only last month, telling her she needed to loosen up a bit, not always approach a client meeting with her briefcase open and her calculator in hand. "Give 'em a good time," he'd urged, practically ordering her to act more sociably.

Penelope knew how to handle herself when she dealt with law and facts and figures. But she didn't play golf or tennis or understand the art of chitchat over cocktails. Even one drink sent her off into the giggles, a most inappropriate behavior for a lawyer seeking to impress a client.

So Penelope stuck to business.

She held out her hand to Clarke Fitzsimmons, the same wide smile appearing on her face. "Mr. Fitzsimmons, what an honor to finally meet you."

Surprise flicked across his high-cheeked face. Frosty blue eyes, remarkably similar to the blue marble Mrs. Merlin had placed on last night's altar, regarded her steadily. Then he half-rose from his seat and leaned over to pull out her chair.

"Thank you," he said, settling back and lifting his menu.

Whew! Penelope risked a glance at Hubert, who'd taken to gnawing on the inside of his right cheek, a sure sign he knew they were in trouble with Fitzsimmons. He wanted to reel in this client badly. Hubert's brother had recently been appointed to a federal judgeship. Firm gossip said the two had always been competitive and Penelope figured he wanted this coup to balance out his brother's achievement.

Sensing the tension mounting, Penelope almost started chewing on her own cheek. Instead, she surprised herself by reaching over and touching Fitzsimmons on the fine wool covering his forearm. "I am simply dying to hear about your new yacht."

Hubert blanched.

Fitzsimmons put down his menu. His face defrosted by about three degrees. "Oh, you know about *Melodee*?"

"Oh, yes." She removed her hand from his sleeve, ever so slowly. "I adore boating. Don't you, Hubert?" Penelope didn't know where her words were coming from; her voice, all sugary and slow, didn't even sound like her own.

Her secretary, bless her soul, had scoured the Internet for every fact she could find about Fitzsimmons and come up with the gem that he was crazy over yachting and had just slipped his latest man-sized toy into the waters off Hilton Head.

Hubert nodded.

Fitzsimmons launched into an animated description of the love of his life. Every so often Penelope nodded, swinging her knee gently under the table, leaning forward, looking entranced.

The waiter came by and Hubert waved him off.

Finally, Fitzsimmons wound down. Fingering his menu, he bestowed a slight smile on Penelope.

Hubert quit chewing on his cheek.

Tony didn't have any cousins in the kitchen of the Grill Room. Even if he had, the keepers of New Orleans' only five-star hotel wouldn't have let him in, even at the employee entrance.

He'd been up all night and the stubble on his cheeks gave him the air of someone who slept on the streets, rather than a man sworn to preserve and protect their safety.

He practically had slept on the streets last night. Hinson had been summoned to a rare in-person meeting with his boss, which is why Tony had dropped Penelope at the door of her building and raced off.

Exactly at midnight, Hinson had stepped from a cab in front of the Mid-City all night grocery and restaurant where his boss liked to conduct business.

It never failed to occur to Tony as he passed by the location that its similarity to Olano's Seafood at the Lakefront was startling. He considered it one of the more poignant ironies of his life that several generations earlier, before any of his forebears had come to America, the trunk of his family tree had split. One branch had followed the path of corruption, the other had clung to the sweat and toil of the restaurant business.

And so it remained to this day.

Except for Tony, who pursued the fallen element with a vengeance even his own family didn't understand.

Last evening he'd parked his car on a quiet side street, then made his way on foot to the surveillance van housed in a car repair shop across the street from the twenty-four-hour grocery.

The night owls of the neighborhood loitered in front of the store, many with bottles of beer dressed up in brown bag finery. The store stuck to the right side of the law, at least on the surface, careful to check ID to weed out any minors foolish enough to think they could buy a beer at this corner market.

Inside the van, Steve and Roy, two members of the hand-picked federal task force surveillance team, were tossing dice at the small worktable behind the front seats. Despite their casual attitudes, the two had earphones tight to their ears and Tony knew both were listening carefully. Recording equipment lining the sides of the cargo van whirred quietly.

Tony nodded at the men and picked up an earphone. All he heard at the moment was the sound of dishes clattering. He cocked a brow. "So what did I miss?"

One guy laughed. "A pretty good joke. It seems the old man personally picked out a wife for Hinson, some favor he promised an old friend in Chicago to look after his daughter born on the wrong side of the bedspread."

Tony tensed. Forcing a casualness he didn't feel, he said, "Keeping it in the family, huh?"

"I guess. Not that the girl knows who her father is. Anyway, the joke is—" he slapped his knee then paused to cast the dice, "the real joke is Hinson's asking what he did to be punished. Seems the girl's colder than a nectar snowball."

In one swift motion, Tony knocked the guy's chair out from under him. The dice and cup clattered to the floor.

Both officers stared at Tony as if he'd gone nuts.

Which he had.

From the floor of the van the other officer

said, rubbing his jaw, "I take it you've gotten to know the bride-to-be."

Tony nodded, then offered the guy a hand up. "Sorry, Steve. No hard feelings, I hope."

Steve shook his head and righted the chair. Staring curiously at Tony, he said slowly, "Even Boy Scouts who play with fire can get burned."

The other officer pointed to his earphones. "Knock it off, guys. Take a listen to this."

"All right, so I'll marry her." Hinson.

"I'll dance at your wedding." His boss.

"That'll take her firm out of action. So when that's done, for good service, what about an annulment?" Hinson, ending with a nervous chuckle.

Tony clenched his fists. He'd been right about the law firm. With Penelope compromised, the firm would no doubt pull out of representation of the other side in the biggest legal battle the old man had fought to date. The client might even give in.

In a simpler world, Penelope only had to tell Hinson her heart wasn't engaged and he'd go away, his tail between his legs. But this twist about her unknown father could have an unexpected impact on her decision.

"One more thing." Hinson's boss.

"Yes, sir." Hinson, not having lost his manners completely.

"You lift one finger, even your pinkie, against this girl, and I'll have your throat."

Tony nodded, pleased to hear proof the old man wasn't totally bad.

"I'll take care of my needs elsewhere." Hinson.

"Mmmmph." Disapproval clear.

"You like what I did to that fool with those noisy tennis shoes?"

"You gotta talk like you have a big mouth all the time? They teach you that at Harvard?" The old man rumbled, then the conversation died out, replaced by the scraping of a fork on china.

Steve lowered his earphones. "Got him on assault, at a minimum."

Tony nodded, pleased by Hinson's slip, but saddened at the thought of Squeek bandaged and doped, lying in a crowded ward at Charity Hospital, his wife at home, even further away from her dream of carrying Squeek's child. He'd stopped in to see him, but Squeek hadn't recognized him.

Tony had stayed in the van two more hours. Inside the store the men played chess. Nothing else of much interest had happened and Tony considered leaving the listening to Steve and Roy when Hinson called, "Check."

The move must have boosted his chutzpah, because he asked in his silkiest voice, "So who is my future father-in-law?"

Tony and the other two men jerked to attention, Tony for personal as well as professional reasons.

"He doesn't acknowledge her. To do that would be to break his wife's heart."

"But he keeps an eye out for her?"

Snake, Tony thought. Hinson was fishing to see what was in the deal for him.

"All I will say is she comes by her legal mind through her father. He's Chicago's best, and if ever I need advice and you're not around, he's the man I would call. So if you try hard, you'll figure it out. But"—the old man's voice shifted to that of a father warning his child—"when a man doesn't want to be found, it's better to leave him alone."

"Hmmm." Hinson.

"We're your family here and we'll be that for your wife, too. Bring her to dinner. The missus will teach her how to cook."

"She knows. Fancy stuff, too."

"Imagine that. Never met a lady lawyer who could cook. So count yourself lucky and quit whining into your wine about tying the knot." A grunt of satisfaction sounded. "Would you look at that—just captured your queen."

Tony glanced over at the two other guys. Steve and Roy were good men—honest, smart, considered incorruptible. That's why they'd been assigned to this post and entrusted with the truth behind Tony's staged dismissal from the force. He knew Roy better and instinctively trusted him in a way he didn't Steve, but chalked that up to personality differences.

He sensed them studying him now, an added measure of alertness revealing their speculation. How far gone was Tony Olano over Penelope Sue Fields? Tony watched them watching him, cursing himself for losing his temper and knocking Steve to the ground, and wondering whether they'd guessed the identity of Penelope's father from the clues the old man had given Hinson.

Chicago's best. The man the boss would call.

Reginald Vincelli—had to be.

Steve and Roy exchanged glances. Roy said,

"Better to let Hinson have her, Tony. There are millions of other fish in the sea."

Tony shrugged. "Yeah, you're right. Just swimming around waiting for me to hook 'em with my rod."

The guys had laughed with him and the moment of tension passed.

To himself he had said, "But there's only one Penelope Sue Fields."

Now, loitering on the sidewalk just outside the Windsor Court's driveway as Penelope appeared sandwiched between two suited types, he repeated that line to himself.

It made no sense, his fascination with this woman. Tony had tried to argue himself out of being interested, tried to deny the attraction. She said something to the silver-haired man and he gave her a pleased look.

They shook hands. For once Penelope didn't have her blouse buttoned all the way to her chin. He squinted, surprised that he couldn't even see the top of her blouse today.

Her lips curved into the most appealing smile and her cheeks were rosier than usual this morning, her eyes shining. Tony checked out the two men from head to toe but couldn't see anything so special about them that they'd make Penelope look so happy.

Perhaps it had been his kiss.

He sure wanted to think so.

"Move along there, no loitering," a pimply-faced man in a hotel uniform called to Tony from the bricked drive. Tony ignored him, waiting to see whether Penelope left on her own.

A Cadillac pulled up, driven by a chauffeur.

The man opened the passenger door for Mr. Silverhead.

The valet delivered the next car, which the other man claimed. Penelope got into the passenger seat and the two drove off.

"If you don't leave, I'll call the police."

Very funny. Tony shrugged and ambled off.

Like it or not, he had a telephone call to make.

"I have to give it to you, Penelope, you had Fitzsimmons eating out of your hand." Hubert spoke more warmly than he ever had to her. He also looked at her more closely from his seat behind the wheel.

Penelope glowed from his praise.

"I like your new style." He winked, then said in a more serious tone, "I don't know what you've come up with on his tax situation, but I trust you to solve it. Now that he's signing with us, you're going to be one very busy lady lawyer."

At one time in her career, Penelope might have corrected Hubert, asking him to delete *lady* in front of *lawyer*. But today she simply smiled and said, "I like to be busy." Some leopards never changed their spots; as long as she got the credit and the work, she'd overlook his old-fashioned ways.

But what did he mean about her new look? She wore the same type of outfit every day, the conservative uniform that suited her so well. She shrugged off the comment and listened as Hubert added, "We were certainly fortunate to steal you away from Pierce, Turner."

Her Chicago firm. Something niggled at the

back of her mind as she recalled David commenting on the legal recruiting firm. "How did you locate me, Hubert?"

His brow wrinkled. "Well, that's an odd thing. We'd pretty much settled on another lawyer when Greif"—who was one of the "of counsel" lawyers rarely seen in the office—"called and said we ought to talk to you through this recruiting firm. Said not to call you directly."

"That's odd. I certainly wasn't looking for a new job."

Hubert chuckled and pulled into the Oil Building garage. "Then I guess we just got lucky."

They were riding in the express elevator, the same car where Penelope had first laid eyes on Tony, when Penelope asked, "Is Greif friends with David Hinson?"

Hubert made a sound of disgust. "Hinson? I should hope not. How do you know that snake?"

She blanched but said casually enough, "I met him several weeks ago at a pretrial conference."

"Well, I hope your relationship doesn't go beyond meet and greet. You're not"—he looked at her with fatherly concern—"considering getting involved with him, are you?"

Penelope thought of the giant-sized engagement ring she had to return. "No," she said faintly.

"Good. It would be quite sticky for our firm if you were to see much of him."

"Oh?"

"He's opposing counsel for the XYZ Shipping case."

Penelope's eyes widened. She knew that case was worth millions to the firm. She'd done some tangential work on it, all tax-related, and Hubert had already indicated she would be getting more involved.

Feeling weighted in complications, no longer buoyed by her successful wooing of Clarke Fitzsimmons, Penelope excused herself and trudged into her office.

She'd thought there was something odd about Hinson knowing details about her recruitment she'd never mentioned. She turned that kernel over in her mind, only to be interrupted by her secretary, who whisked in behind her and shut the door.

"Look at you," she said.

"What?" Penelope tried never to be cross with Jewel, but sometimes her assistant's good spirits rubbed her the wrong way.

"A new look usually means a new man."

"What new look?" First Hubert had said that, and now Jewel. Penelope settled her briefcase and purse. As far as the new man, last night's kiss had given her hope, but the way Tony had rushed off had plummeted those hopes almost immediately.

At least they were to have dinner tonight.

That thought cheered her. She played along with Jewel, who really was the world's best assistant. "I don't know what you mean about a new look, but you earned lunch at Commander's for coming up with that scoop about Fitzsimmon's yacht."

"Oooh, you remembered to use it."

Penelope half-laughed. "Frankly, I couldn't

think of anything else. I haven't come up with one decent argument for his IRS problem. I lost my copy of the letter, overslept and had to wing it at breakfast."

"Definitely a new man."

"Would you stop?" Penelope sat down at her desk. "Any calls?"

"Several on your voice mail, and one other." Jewel handed her a pink message slip. "No name, just this note."

CAN'T DO DINNER.

Penelope crumpled the paper. That was that. He'd kissed her, found her uninspiring, and was blowing her off.

Jewel watched, head cocked to the side. "Bad news, huh?"

Penelope nodded, then pulled the Fitzsimmons papers out of her briefcase. "I've got a lot of work to do anyway." She refused to let Tony Olano's rejection get to her. The man could jump off a short pier as far as she was concerned. She didn't care if she ever saw the man with bedroom eyes ever again. All he did was drive her nuts.

The pencil she had picked up snapped in two.

Jewel shook her head. "Don't let it hold you down long. With that new look, you can get any man you want." With those fine words, her secretary whisked out of the office.

Her curiosity overcoming her, Penelope rose and walked to the mirror over an antique bookcase. Peering in, she studied herself for any sign of change.

Her blue eyes might glow a shade bluer than they had the day before, her brown hair, thrust so quickly into its knot, had slipped into a much looser chignon than usual. A stray tendril of hair curled around one cheek.

She stood on tiptoe to check the neckline of her blouse. Perhaps in her rush to dress she'd forgotten to fasten the top button or two.

Penelope stared into the mirror, at the image of a woman who looked exactly like her.

But the woman looking back at her in the mirror was dressed in a way Penelope would never. The delicate silver chain and initial "P" pendant she always wore tucked discreetly beneath her clothing winked at her. Worse, the lacy cups of her bra peeked past the lapels of her suit.

Penelope stared at the woman, a female so unlike Penelope Sue Fields.

She had *forgotten* her blouse.

Rather than the wave of humiliation and embarrassment she had expected to wash over her as she regarded this sexy woman so unfamiliar to herself, she experienced curiosity and daring. If the lack of a blouse did this much for her, what would happen if she let her hair down at the same time?

Raising her hands slowly, Penelope grasped the pins holding her chignon and let her hair spill over her shoulders. She fluffed it with her fingertips and blew a kiss toward the mirror.

Gazing at this new self, Penelope sensed a rush of power. "Hah," she said aloud. "Tony Olano, just see what you're missing."

Chapter 17

A few moments later, as reality set in with a shock wave, Penelope dropped into her desk chair, one hand pressed against the chain around her otherwise very bare throat. Not only had she made a fool of herself flirting with Clarke Fitzsimmons, she'd appeared in public half-dressed!

And now, faced with that fact, her first reaction had been to try to look like a complete sexpot in order to catch Tony Olano.

Whatever had happened to her common sense?

Mrs. Merlin, Penelope thought, wielding her letter opener and tapping it against one hand, had a lot to answer for. Before the day Mrs. Merlin had entered Penelope's life, all had proceeded in an orderly fashion.

Since Saturday . . . Penelope shook her head, unable to finish the sentence.

"I can't believe you're blaming that sweet little woman for your own actions," she said aloud. "You're the one who's let the man with bedroom eyes turn your life upside down. Mrs. Merlin only happened along at the same time."

Glancing toward the door, Penelope reassured herself Jewel had shut it behind her. She didn't need anyone to overhear her, compounding her embarrassment further. Even now she was sure her outrageous behavior at breakfast must be the talk of the office.

With a sigh she turned to her file on Fitzsimmons. Time to look at that Opinion Letter again; she had all night to mope about Olano.

She placed the letter in the center of her desk, but instead of focusing on the black and white text, she found herself wondering what Mrs. Merlin was doing this morning.

Was she at home, sitting on her front porch sipping coffee with chicory, eating anything besides oatmeal? Or had something gone awry, as things often did with the miniature magician's spells, and Mrs. Merlin was even now caught up in a new adventure?

Penelope stared at the letter then at the rest of her desk piled neatly with work waiting to be done. She fingered the Fitzsimmons file and made a mental note to have Jewel make another copy of the Opinion Letter for her to take home.

She opened her Day-Timer and powered on her computer.

But her mind returned, again and again, to the message slip she'd crumpled. Bending down, she found it on the plush carpet beneath her desk and slowly unfolded it. CAN'T DO DINNER.

The unspoken message was clear. He might as well have added, "Tonight or any other night."

Penelope sighed, then something inside her

toughened. Who the heck did he think he was, brushing her off that easily?

The old Penelope would have buckled, would have stayed at work late, not surprised by the rejection, expecting it, assuming she deserved it.

She straightened her shoulders and glanced down. The lacy edges of her bra shifted against her skin, revealing even more of the undergarment.

Never in her life had she done such a thing! To have forgotten her blouse was to have paraded naked in the streets.

So let an insufferable egotist like Tony Olano stand her up for dinner. She'd show him!

Not that she had any idea exactly how she'd do that, but she had a sense growing within her, like a flame taking shape from a pile of kindling, that she'd sure figure something out.

A soft knock sounded at her office door.

Burying the turmoil within, Penelope called, "Come in."

Jewel pushed open the door, most of her hidden behind a bouquet of pinkish yellow longstem roses.

Penelope's heart leaped, then settled hollowly. Any man who canceled dinner didn't send flowers.

Did he?

"So, is this Mr. Right?" Jewel carried the vase to Penelope's desk and settled it beside the framed picture of Penelope's mother. The other junior partners at LaCour, Richardson, Zeringue, Ray, Wellman and Klees had photos of children, dogs, cats, fishing trips, and Mardi Gras costumes littering their desks. Penelope had one picture, that of her mother, taken at her law school graduation.

Staring at the roses, Penelope shook her head.

"You know, for someone who claims to work twenty-four hours a day, you sure are developing a horde of admirers." Jewel settled the vase.

"What do you mean?" Penelope reached for the florist's card in her assistant's hand as she asked the question.

" 'Can't do dinner'—that implies a date was planned. And somehow my instincts—purely female, you understand—tell me that these flowers didn't come from the same guy."

That interpretation intrigued Penelope. "Why do you say that?" She flicked open the envelope containing the card.

"The wording. 'Can't do dinner'—now, that's a real he-man sort of message. Prissy pink roses, these have got to be from a different sort of man."

"Hmmm. What sort of flowers would the first guy send?"

Jewel tipped her head to one side. Her braided hair swayed softly, giving off a melodic tinkling as the fasteners swayed one against the other. "I don't think he would. Flowers would die far too soon to suit him."

Penelope stared at the note: I'LL DIE IF YOU DON'T SAY YES. Glancing quickly at the half-dozen roses in the vase, she shivered. They might as well have been blood red.

"Ooh, an evil admirer." Jewel folded her arms, clearly settling in for a complete confessional.

Penelope laughed. How glad she was she'd hired Jewel, despite the warnings of the three-piece-suited mannequin who ran the law firm's personnel office. True, she was irreverent, had quite a mouth on her, and always spoke her mind. But her research, typing, and people skills surpassed that of any other assistant Penelope had seen strolling down the halls of the firm.

Not only that, Jewel was the closest thing Penelope had found to a friend in this exotic but somewhat overwhelming new city.

"He may be," Penelope said slowly, thinking of her earlier conversation with Hubert. "You know a lot of people in this city." Her assistant had worked in various law firms, as well as at federal court. "Can you tell me anything about a lawyer named David Hinson?"

She thought she'd asked the question in a casual enough fashion, but the drop of Jewel's jaw told Penelope she hadn't fooled her one bit.

"Tell me no," Jewel said, sinking into one of the two leather armchairs in front of Penelope's desk. "Tell me these roses aren't from David Hinson."

Penelope nodded, wondering whether her old law school mentor would criticize her for fraternizing with the help at the firm. Always keep your business to yourself, Mrs. Rosen had said, time and time again, to the charges she'd been sending out to the shark-infested waters of some of the nation's top law firms.

"Whew!" Jewel glanced over her shoulder.

"The door's shut," Penelope said, "so cough up whatever it is I ought to know."

"Well, I know you're new to the city," Jewel

began slowly, pleating the lap of her skirt, "but it doesn't take long before you figure out there are certain forces at work here."

"And Hinson is allied with one of those forces?"

Jewel nodded. "Bad blood, Penelope, very bad blood. Not only does he do all the legal work for the guy everybody who's anybody knows is the old geezer who controls the New Orleans mob element, he's a creep. And I mean big time."

"We're talking about David Hinson?" Penelope studied her secretary closely. "About six-foot-two, blond hair, blue eyes—"

"Yep." Jewel nodded. "For fun he beats up his girlfriends, or prostitutes, whoever he happens to find at the right moment."

"I can't believe we're talking about the same man." Could she be such a bad judge of character?

"Ever seen that twitch below his right eye?"

Penelope froze. "Twitch?"

Jewel nodded. "Comes out when he doesn't get his way. Then—bam! Watch out!"

Penelope pictured him at Primo's, awaiting her answer as he held out the gaudy ring.

When she'd hesitated, the twitch had been very much in evidence.

"How do you know so much about him?" She had to ask. Jewel always seemed to know the skinny on everyone, but Penelope had never figured out her sources. Actually, Penelope had never questioned her fallibility before today. But now she felt she had to know.

Jewel shrugged. "My brother's a cop. My

great-niece is a prostitute. Go figure."

Penelope shivered. "So you know of what you speak."

"Fancy way to say it, but yeah, my dope's straight."

Penelope considered the information. A thought spiraled up within her, and she decided to risk the question. "And Tony Olano, ever heard of him?"

Again her assistant nodded. "Who hasn't?"

Penelope wanted to scream. Did she have to prompt, or was that all she was going to get?

"Stay away from him, too," Jewel said, rising from the chair. "Not for the same reason as Hinson, of course, but that guy breaks even the toughest hearts. And he got into trouble for taking a bribe." She shook her head. "I always thought that was too fishy to be true. Had to be someone's idea of revenge. Whatever happened there I don't know for sure, but I do know Mr. Love 'Em and Leave 'Em Olano would eat you up and spit you out. But he is gorgeous. Those eyes!"

Ah, yes, those eyes. "Thanks for the scoop, and the advice."

Jewel rose. "Anytime," she said. "Anything else?"

"Hmmm. Why don't you take these roses out to the reception desk?" Penelope tore the card into bits even smaller than what she'd done to the message slip.

Lifting the vase, Jewel said, "And I know there's no need to mention where these came from."

Penelope smiled. "Thanks."

With one hand, her assistant saluted and backed from the office, flowers in tow.

Penelope twirled around in her chair, then reached for her phone.

Chewing on the stub of a pencil, she dialed information.

"New Orleans. Primo's," she said.

Mrs. Merlin was discovering that being short and flat was a hundred times worse than only being six and a quarter inches tall and her usual round self.

Five times now she'd called out for help, but either no one could hear her or the heartless souls inhabiting what looked like a very stuffy sort of library would not deviate from their schedules to involve themselves with her plight.

From what she could figure out, she'd become a one-dimensional human bookmark. She could see in one direction and as far as her line of sight extended there were books lined neatly on shelves in a pretty classy-looking room done in dark wood. Men and women wandered in, collected a book or two, then either disappeared or sat down at one of two tables.

Whatever their particular progression, they uniformly ignored her.

Mrs. Merlin sighed and remembered Mr. Gotho warning her that she hadn't traveled far enough down the path of enlightenment to attempt the type of magick she so wished to conduct. He'd lectured her as to the inappropriateness of candle magick for her overwhelming desire to help out in other people's lives.

Of course, Mrs. Merlin recollected with what

would have been a sniff if her nose hadn't been as flat as the rest of her, he hadn't used the word *desire*. He'd called her a busybody who didn't know when to leave well enough alone. Mr. Gotho believed strongly that people should handle their own affairs, something Mrs. Merlin had learned by observation of human nature was quite impossible for many.

He'd even suggested that she consider college with a major in social work.

Mrs. Merlin had laughed at the very idea!

Why, before she could go to college, she'd have to finish high school.

A door opened and Mrs. Merlin tried to wiggle. "Over here," she called, but even to her ears the words seemed to disappear in a puff of air.

If only she'd stuck to a simpler spell last night. But no, she'd been determined not only to put her body back to rights, but also to throw in a smidgen of help for Penelope, who'd been so kind as to rescue her from that basket of napkin rings.

If only Penelope were here now!

Mrs. Merlin wriggled and tried to edge herself higher between the pages of the book, to no avail. Only her neck and head showed. She'd have to hope that someone walked straight up to the shelf where she'd been stranded or she might live out the rest of her days as a bookmark.

She sighed, thinking how she'd grown tired of oatmeal. Why, she'd never complain about eating the same thing ever again, not when she faced sure starvation, inch by inch.

Footsteps muffled by the thick carpeting approached. Miraculously, they stopped in front of Mrs. Merlin, but far enough to her other side she couldn't see the person. That made her nervous because not everyone would handle a summons by a human bookmark as neatly as Penelope had fielded her plea only last weekend.

She was about to call out again when she found herself—within the book she marked, of course—lifted and carried through the air. Thank the stars! She blinked and held her breath as the book dropped to the table with a teeny thud.

"Ouch! Be a little bit careful, why can't you?" Mrs. Merlin couldn't help herself. Her tongue got her into trouble a lot, but her bones were a bit too brittle to be bounced around, particularly when they'd already been flattened.

"Mrs. Merlin?"

When Mrs. Merlin heard Penelope's voice, she promised the goddess, the stars, and Mr. Gotho she'd never misuse candle magick ever again. Aloud, she said, "Who do I look like? Yul Brynner?"

Penelope laughed and opened the heavy book.

"Ah." Taking a long breath, the first decent one in hours, Mrs. Merlin blinked, then blinked again. All she could see was black type dancing before her eyes above the glossy wood of the table. "You might turn me over," she said.

"I might."

Oh-oh. Mrs. Merlin detected a note of grim determination, bordering on a ruthlessness she'd not gotten from the lawyer before. Most of the time Penelope struck Mrs. Merlin as a little girl playing dress-up, but that voice belonged to a woman made of sterner stuff.

What else had last night's spell wrought?

"Do you want something from me?" Mrs. Merlin asked the question in a cautious tone.

"The truth. Did you throw in any bonus in your spell?"

"Whatever do you mean?" Even to Mrs. Merlin's ears, her own voice sounded less than innocent.

Penelope must have leaned over the table, because her voice sounded right behind Mrs. Merlin's flattened head. "I overslept, I practically flirted—flirted!—with my client at breakfast, and to top it off, I came to work without a blouse on under my suit."

"Well . . ."

"The truth."

She found herself flipped over, about as elegantly as one would flip a flounder. Staring into Penelope's blazing eyes, Mrs. Merlin couldn't help but smile. The girl looked much better with a fire lit within her. "I did scrape just a bit of that cherry-red candle into my own flame."

"And?"

Mrs. Merlin shrugged one squared-off shoulder. "I was only trying to help you get in touch with your passionate self, stimulate a few chakras, show you what you've been missing."

"Gee, thanks." Penelope pointed to Mrs. Merlin. "Please don't take this wrong, but it looks as if you're the one who needs help."

Her finger strayed to the page facing where Mrs. Merlin lay. "Hey, look at this," she said, sounding pretty excited. "I thought I knew every exception to this rule by heart, but . . ."

Penelope wheeled around. "I've got to tell Hubert. I think I've found the solution to Fitzsimmon's tax problem!"

"You can't leave me here!"

"Oh, right."

Mrs. Merlin found herself shut into the book again, this time with only the top thatch of her hair poking free. She mumbled and moaned and thankfully Penelope had the presence of mind to raise her so at least her neck and face were free.

"Sorry, I just got carried away," Penelope said as she walked rapidly down the hall. "I had this vague idea to recheck the exceptions, which is why I pulled this particular volume off the shelf, and then, voilà! Problem solved, almost magically."

Mrs. Merlin felt Penelope stop dead in her tracks. Aha! About time the smarty-pants lawyer learned a lesson about magick.

"Did you hear what I just said?" Penelope said in a low voice.

"Yep."

"You didn't—no, what you did last night had to do with passion, not taxation."

"Oh?" Mrs. Merlin couldn't keep from sounding pretty superior. "Think again."

Penelope lowered the book and stared into Mrs. Merlin's face, or rather the representation of her face. "You had me put the Opinion Letter on the altar."

"Morning, Penelope."

"G-good morning, Mr. LaCour, Mr. Richardson."

"Talking to ourself, are we? Guess that breakfast with old Clarke must have been a tough one?"

Mrs. Merlin couldn't tell who was speaking. She heard two different male voices and assumed they had to be bigwigs because Penelope flipped the book over so Mrs. Merlin stared down at the floor. Penelope also stammered a bit as she responded.

Then the men passed on by and Mrs. Merlin found herself flipped face up again.

"Nah," Penelope said, "I would've thought to recheck the exceptions whether you threw in a spell or not. It's simply coincidence."

Mrs. Merlin kept silent. It tickled her to listen to Penelope fight to maintain her rational order. She wondered how she'd explain forgetting to wear a blouse.

"And rushing about, getting ready in such a hurry. Why, anyone could have forgotten to put a blouse on."

Mrs. Merlin uttered a flat chuckle. "Anyone, maybe, but not Penelope Fields."

The lawyer hesitated, gazing down at Mrs. Merlin. A smile flitted across her lips and she began to laugh softly. "Well, you're right about that. So I guess I owe you and your magick thanks twice over."

Mrs. Merlin attempted a wink. "From a friend, once will do."

Penelope smiled, turned the corner, entered an office, shut the door behind her, and deposited the book on a desk. She opened the pages and Mrs. Merlin breathed yet another sigh of relief.

"Well," Mrs. Merlin said brightly, "now that I've solved your little tax problem, how about a wee bit of help with my predicament?"

The menu at Olano's Seafood House didn't feature escargots, nor did it flaunt any low-cal, heart-friendly specials.

It was seafood the way generations of New Orleanians loved their seafood: fried, raw, boiled, and grilled, in quantities guaranteed to stuff even the hungriest diner's belly while tantalizing the taste buds.

Tony had grown up here, done every chore, from taking out the trash to blending the spices used in Olano's Crab Boil, now packaged in gift boxes and sold to tourists in shops all over the city.

There was even an 800 number now, where people could call and order their seafood shipped by air. Tony's oldest sister ran that part of the business from her house, where she had three children under age five keeping her busy when the phone wasn't ringing.

Olano's had come a long way from the turn of the century when his immigrant grandparents had staked out a small patch of land at the lakefront and began making their living fishing. Later, as the population grew, they began serving meals out of their home kitchen.

Standing next to one of the cauldrons used to boil crabs, Tony called to his brother Chris, "What are you using these days? Red dye number two?"

Chris lumbered over and peered into the pot. "Maybe I tossed in a little extra paprika, that's all. Since when did you become a food critic anyway?"

Tony shrugged. Even though he hadn't wanted to continue in the family business, he did have a knack for food.

"Hey, you haven't changed your mind, have you?" Chris spooned a sample from the boil, blew on it, then stuck a finger into it to check out the blend.

"Nah."

"Your business coming along?" Chris reached for a bag of lemons. "Make yourself useful. Add a few of these and cut that down a bit. Least you haven't lost your touch."

Tony grinned and set to work on the lemons. The steam from the boiling pots had clamped his shirt to his back, reminding him that even the longest of stakeouts in summertime New Orleans was cooler than a night in a restaurant kitchen.

Before Chris returned to the worktable where he'd been supervising one of his own sons battering catfish, he said, "You need any money, you let me know."

"Sure, sure." Tony couldn't meet his brother's eyes, but not for the reason Chris assumed. The thing Tony hated the most about his current investigation was putting his family through his supposed disgrace.

"Hey, Uncle Tony," called one of the busboys running back into the kitchen with a pan of plates covered in fish bones, shrimp tails, and smears of tartar and cocktail sauce.

Tony waved at another of his nephews. Of his two sisters and three brothers, he was the only one to have been divorced, the only one who hadn't yet produced an Olano grandchild.

He gazed at the lemon in his hand.

"You guys oughta see the babe at the bar." Chris's oldest son swaggered into the kitchen, drying his hands on a bar towel. He'd been barbacking this summer, and to the seventeen-year-old the gruntwork was nothing compared to the satisfaction of getting to check out what he called "the babes."

"This one's different," Chris, Jr., said. "Hey, Uncle Tony, you ought to take a look. All dressed up like she's on her way to church, but if you look real close, you can tell she's just pretending to be snooty."

"Oh, yeah, and how can you tell that?" Tony quit staring at the lemon and sliced it neatly in two. Now wasn't the time to figure out his personal life. He had his assignment and everything else had to wait.

Even Penelope. But after he'd held her last night, and kissed her, Tony had known he didn't want to wait.

He wanted Penelope.

Now and forever.

Chris, Jr., leaned closer to Tony and wiggled his brows. "You can see her bra 'cause she's not wearing a blouse."

"Is that right?" Tony thought his nephew was probably exaggerating for effect. Olano's was the kind of restaurant where families brought children of all ages. The long bar served as a watering hole for many of the regulars, but also doubled as a resting place for many diners waiting for their names to be called. The bartenders served as much iced tea as they did beer.

"She's all alone, too." Chris, Jr., punched Tony playfully in the ribs. "Maybe you should take my place. You can sure get an eyeful!"

"Yeah, go ahead," Chris's father chimed in. "You've been moping around. Go catch yourself a woman. Maybe you can retire—" he bit off his words. "Sorry."

"Hey, no problem." Tony wiped the knife and rinsed the lemon juice from the counter where he'd been working. "Come on, Chris, I'll check out this babe, but from the other side of the bar."

"As a customer?" The disgust in Chris's voice was evident.

Tony grinned. "Come on, you can watch your uncle in action."

Chris slapped his hand in a high-five and the two moved out into the entryway of the restaurant. Chris headed to his post behind the bar and Tony slipped down the hall to the restroom to clean up a bit. His heart wasn't in the chase, especially on this evening when he'd intended to be having dinner with Penelope, but he couldn't bring himself to disappoint his nephew.

Chapter 18

Fortunately for Penelope, Jewel knew immediately what to do when she learned Penelope's car had disappeared from a French Quarter street. Just as Tony had surmised, her car had been towed for a parking violation.

By the time Penelope was ready to leave the office, with Mrs. Merlin safely stashed in one of the books she carried home, Jewel had located her car at the city impound lot.

Not only had Jewel found it, but she'd made a few phone calls and the $97 towing ticket had disappeared. Penelope accepted the help and the ride from Jewel to reclaim her car in a lot huddled beneath a freeway overpass.

Seated once again behind the wheel of her car, Penelope waved good-bye to her assistant, then said, "So I guess it's back to my place, Mrs. Merlin."

Her answer was a drifting sigh from where the squished grandmother lay atop Penelope's briefcase in the passenger seat.

"Come, now, I'm sure we can figure something out," Penelope said.

"This time you'll have to do the entire spell,"

Mrs. Merlin said in a voice full of doom.

"Well . . ." Penelope bit her lip. She'd been about to say she didn't see how she could do a worse job than Mrs. Merlin had, but that smacked of ego. And ego, she knew, would get her into a pickle.

"Go ahead, say it. I've made a mess of things again. Maybe you should just take me to Mr. Gotho and let me throw myself on his mercies."

Two days ago, Penelope would have zipped the car around and headed straight to the Bayou Magick Shoppe, more than ready to hand over the responsibility. Today, though, she pressed on through the traffic, intent on getting back to her apartment.

"Oh, I'll see if I can't help you."

In record time, she made it to her place, whisked her déjà vu houseguest up the elevator, and settled her on the dining table near last night's altar, portable TV at the ready.

Then, despite Mrs. Merlin's protests, Penelope whisked into her bedroom to freshen up, and to strap herself into the ridiculously high heels she'd worn the night before.

Knowing the woman would howl upon hearing she had to wait until Penelope performed a particular mission of her own, she paused only for a moment to tell Mrs. Merlin she'd be back soon, hoping the woman wouldn't notice her shoes.

"Soon?" The woman's eyes opened wider. She swayed slightly forward and back. "What about me?"

Penelope couldn't help her mischievous answer. "You did say it was all right to be selfish.

And I'm not hurting you because I know while I'm gone you're going to come up with exactly the perfect spell to undo this pickle."

"Smarty-pants lawyer," Mrs. Merlin muttered, and closed her eyes.

Now, sitting in the parking lot of Olano's Seafood House, a lot overflowing with far more cars than she had pictured, Penelope felt none too daring.

Lights streamed from the sprawling wood-framed building, reflecting off the waters of Lake Pontchartrain lapping at the edges of the homey structure.

Olano's was situated literally on the lakefront.

More cars meant far more people than she'd expected to encounter.

Wondering whether her nerve would fail her, wondering why walking into a friendly-looking restaurant all alone should bother her—Penelope Sue Fields, who'd grown up in the shadows of the restaurant business—still she hesitated.

The chef at Primo's, who to Penelope's surprise turned out to be Tony's cousin, had assured her in a friendly way that if Tony had invited her to a place at the lakefront that he described as far better than Primo's, he could only mean Olano's, the family business, and the place he had last been chef.

He'd also hinted that Tony could use a good woman in his life, and urged her to drop by Olano's. Tony might not be there, but someone in the family would make sure he got the message that a gorgeous woman had been there looking for him.

At that point in the conversation, Penelope had interrupted to inquire how Leo could assume the woman in question—herself—was beautiful.

She'd almost been able to hear the man's shrug over the phone. Then he'd said, "Tony wouldn't have asked you out otherwise."

Penelope had hated to admit to herself just how much that remark thrilled her. She'd thanked Leo, both for the compliment and the advice, then gone in search of the tax code provision niggling at the back of her mind.

Which, of course, is where she'd bumped into Mrs. Merlin again.

Penelope experienced a twinge of guilt thinking how she'd rushed off in chase of a man who was no doubt a cad, while Mrs. Merlin couldn't even enjoy a dish of oatmeal. But this twinge she quickly crushed.

She'd questioned Mrs. Merlin about the wisdom of mixing the IRS letter in with her own return spell and had been brushed off. So Mrs. Merlin would have to wait. Penelope wiggled her feet, staring at her heels, the only change she'd made to her day's wardrobe.

No, she hadn't put on a blouse.

Penelope blushed and pushed open the car door. It had worked for her earlier; perhaps it would again.

Though, she reminded herself sternly, her only goal in going to Olano's was the vague hope that she'd run into Tony and torment him with what he'd missed.

No way would she actually fall for the guy ever again.

Or kiss him!

She ran her tongue over her lower lip, stepped from the car, and stumbled over a very fat cat.

"Eee-rarrhh!" The cat let go a meow loud enough to wake the dead.

"Sorry," Penelope said, adding, "Nice kitty." She knew less than nothing about cats, but she saw no reason to offend one.

She glanced around the parking area and realized several dozen cats shared the grounds with this one. They milled about, many of them eating from cartons placed on the ground. One large orange cat jumped on the hood of her car and sat there on its haunches, staring at her.

"Almost daring me to ask you to move, aren't you?" Penelope said to the cat, deciding she admired the look of determination on the feline's face. Maybe she would get a cat. She wondered whether Mrs. Merlin would be offended if she named the cat after her, then laughed at the idea. She ought to be thinking how she was going to get Mrs. Merlin back to her house in Gentilly and out of her apartment, rather than daydreaming about owning a pet.

For that matter, she'd be better off at home poring over her notes on the Fitzsimmons file than here picking her way among cats and abandoned Styrofoam cartons on her way to an assignation designed to punish a man who had intended to give her the brush-off.

But she'd promised herself to sit at the bar, make sure the bartender knew her name, then flirt outrageously with the first man she could get to respond. According to his cousin Leo, Tony would be sure to hear about her visit.

Despite her inner commentary, she stepped forward. One somewhat wobbly step at a time, Penelope crossed the swaying wooden bridge than led from the parking lot to the porch of the restaurant. Quite a few people sat on benches there, obviously waiting for tables. Well, Penelope didn't need a table. She only needed to take a seat at the bar.

She swallowed nervously and thanked a big-bellied man who exited, holding the door open for her.

To her relief, she spotted a long bar just inside the door, covering the right wall of the waiting area. It was actually fairly impressive, especially the floor-to-ceiling carved mahogany piece behind the bar featuring lifelike mermaids and dolphins.

She spotted an empty seat at the bar and advanced on it, wishing she'd worn her sensible loafers rather than these silly heels that caused her to teeter like a drunken sailor.

A pleasant-faced woman with a child on her lap made room for her. Almost at once the young man behind the bar asked her what she wanted to drink.

Penelope glanced longingly at the sweating glass of iced tea at the place next to her, then said, "Wine, please."

The bartender stared at her. "Any preference?"

She had definite preferences as to cooking wines, but at a bar, Penelope was pretty much at a loss. However, this ignorance didn't suit the siren image she'd determined to adopt. So she took a breath and rattled off the French Bordeaux David had selected at Primo's.

The bartender slapped his thigh. "Hey, Chris, we got any '89 Chateau du France Bordeaux?" He laughed. "Got a comedienne here."

Penelope smiled weakly, then said, "Whatever you have that's red."

"That's more like it." The man slapped a small glass onto the bar and poured from a jug. "We stick to the basics at Olano's," he said. "You've never been here before, have you?"

She shook her head. "No, but it seems nice."

He nodded. "That'll be three twenty-five, or are you running a tab?"

Yet to lift the wineglass, Penelope waved a hand. "Tab."

He drifted off to serve another customer and Penelope glanced around. Behind her people were coming and going in a steady stream from the dining room. Aromas that made her mouth water filled the air. Compared to this place, Primo's had been a pristine sanitarium where food appeared mysteriously in elegant dishes.

Here, Penelope got the feeling she was right in the midst of a celebration of eating. Swinging doors to the side of the bar led to the kitchen. What she wouldn't give to pop in there and take a lesson or two!

Of course, she'd felt the same way about Primo's, but the difference in the atmosphere intrigued her. It was the difference between rich kids dressed in velvet and told not to get dirty before Christmas dinner versus children running riot out-of-doors during a family gathering before they plopped down on picnic benches to wolf hot dogs.

The woman seated next to her slipped off the stool and headed for the dining room.

"This seat free?"

Penelope stiffened. She'd know that voice anywhere. She swallowed, forcing herself to relax. Turning her head toward his voice, she said in a slow drawl, "For you, big guy."

"You!"

Penelope was positive the shock in his voice couldn't be faked. Had he not even glanced at her before throwing out his pickup line? My, my, but did this man need to learn a lesson or two.

She widened her eyes, crossed one leg at the knee, beginning a slow kick in what she hoped was a seductive rhythm, and toyed with the stem of her wineglass. Penelope found herself hoping Mrs. Merlin had thrown a spell or two extra into last night's ceremony. What she wouldn't give to be the sexiest vixen alive and leave this man panting for more.

He'd taken the barstool, turning toward her in an assuming way. His knees, bare and marvelously dusted with those fine black hairs, brushed her leg.

She stopped her leg in mid-swing. "Were you expecting someone else?"

Tony shook his head, attempting to sort out his scrambled brain. What was Penelope doing here at Olano's? Hadn't she gotten the message he couldn't keep their date? And hey, he'd never told her where he'd planned to take her.

She watched him with those big blue eyes, and he figured he ought to come out with some sort of answer. Retreating to the lazy grin and detached voice that worked so well for him with the opposite sex, he leaned forward on one elbow and said, "No one near as lovely as you."

Her fingers tightened on the wineglass, then relaxed. Tony hid a smile. Penelope was way out of her element. That she'd tracked him down gave him a start, but also quite a thrill.

Tonight, he thought, would be far more interesting than he'd resigned himself to. Not that he could let things get out of hand, of course. He had to keep the danger to Penelope uppermost in his mind.

Which was damn hard to do when he could see straight down her lawyer suit to the lacy edges of her bra. Tony swallowed. What had she done? Taken off her blouse in the parking lot and sashayed in here half-naked?

She swirled her wine, then gulped at it. She made a face as she sat the glass down carefully on the bar.

"Bad vintage?"

She shrugged. Her suit jacket slipped a bit, exposing the top of her shoulder and highlighting the scalloped lace of her bra even more. Her foot set to swinging again and Tony leaned a bit closer, both to admire the view and to see whether he could rattle her just a bit.

"How was your day at the office?"

She looked surprised at his question. "Interesting," she said. "Very good, actually."

"Oh?"

She furrowed her brow slightly. "I solved a problem, a tough one, and I brought in a new—" She stopped abruptly.

"Go on," he said in a low voice, playing with

the edge of the napkin that lay under her wine-glass.

"Do you really want to hear this?"

"Please." And the darnedest thing was he really did want to know everything there was to know about Penelope Sue Fields, beginning with what she'd eaten for breakfast, and ending with why she'd appeared at his family's restaurant.

She sat up straighter.

Tony registered his disappointment as his view of her cleavage shifted.

"I brought in a new client today. Quite a coup, actually." She sounded surprised.

"You mean you don't do that sort of thing all the time?"

"Now you're making fun of me. I've done it before, but not in quite this way."

"Oh?"

She swigged another gulp of wine.

Taking a look at her reddening cheeks, Tony signaled his nephew Charles and mouthed, "Two iced teas."

She stopped talking. Pointedly, she stared at his hand playing with her napkin. "I'm not good at flirting. I shouldn't tell you that, when that's what I'm trying to do here tonight, but the amazing thing was this morning at breakfast I did not say one intelligent thing and the client loved me."

"Is that right?" Tony wondered whether Penelope had gone to a convent school. What in the hell did she think motivated men? Sure, figures and profits had to be considered, but did she think any man could ignore his gut reaction to a beautiful woman?

And she was beautiful, even though Tony had pretty much figured out Penelope had no idea of that fact.

Perhaps, Tony thought—taking in her wide-eyed innocence as she attempted to look very much the siren and succeeded in looking exactly like a sweet-souled woman who knew only how to be herself, which was exactly what he wanted her to be—that lack of knowledge only magnified her charms.

"So," Penelope was saying, sipping on her wine, "it was quite an interesting day. Except"— she sighed—"for Mrs. Merlin's problem, that is."

"Is she okay?" Tony remembered her mentioning her cat's name as Mrs. Mer, but perhaps he'd misheard.

Penelope shook her head slowly. Then she drained her wine, looking at the empty glass with an expression of surprise. After a quick grimace, she chased the wine with a long swallow of the iced tea Chris, Jr., had delivered.

"I'm afraid she's . . . flattened."

"I am sorry," he said, and meaning it. "Poor kitty."

"Kitty?" She sounded confused, then her eyes widened and she clapped a hand over her mouth. She lifted the empty wineglass and studied it, as if searching for an answer. "I really am not a drinker, you know."

He nodded, having already figured that one out, and leaned closer. What other tidbits would she reveal after one glass of Olano's house red?

"Is that why you came here tonight? To drink?"

"Of course not." Her eyes sparked. "I'm on a mission."

"Ah, a mission."

Penelope smiled in an arch way Tony had not seen before. "A mission to torment you, Mr. Olano."

"So is that why you left your blouse in the car?"

She jerked back. "I did no such thing!" She blushed slightly, then said, "Behold the new Penelope. I went to work this way. Except for the shoes."

Tony eyed the frilly edging of her bra. "No wonder your client signed on."

"I would never use sex as a substitute for competent lawyering." She practically bristled.

"So why'd you dress like that?" As much as Tony enjoyed the sight of the plunging neckline, he hated the idea of any other man sharing the view. Other than a delicate silver chain and pendant, nothing broke the view between her chin and her cleavage.

She drank some tea. Looking down at her lap, she mumbled, "I forgot it." Then she fastened her gaze on his and said, "Gosh darn, I'm a failure at flirting."

She sounded so mournful he couldn't even laugh. She had absolutely no idea how adorable she looked, sitting there on the barstool all prim and proper, wishing she could fulfill some image she carried in her mind of the perfect flirtatious female. And all the while, Tony had to keep reminding himself he'd promised he'd have nothing else to do with Penelope—for the moment.

For her own sake.

Trying for a light tone, he said, "Let me be the judge of your flirting." Then he reached for her hand, ignoring the bells and whistles sounding in his brain. Right now he was thinking with an entirely different portion of his anatomy.

His heart, amazingly so.

He shook his head, realizing the truth of that thought. He started to speak, to tell her he was sorry, so very sorry, for canceling their dinner date, even though he'd done so to protect her from Hinson's jealousy, but just then his nephew bounded up behind the bar.

"Hey, Tony-O!"

Tony froze, then reluctantly released her hand.

Chris, Jr., leaned halfway over the bar and said with a wink, "So, how's it going?" Then he cocked his head toward Penelope in a gesture that couldn't have been less subtle than an announcement on the loudspeaker.

Then, addressing Penelope, Chris, Jr., said, "So has he gotten to first base with you yet?"

Tony shook his head and covered his face with one hand. Doomed—he might as well admit it. Trying to get anywhere with Penelope here in ground zero of the family business had to have been the thinking of a madman. He had to get her out of here, away from interruptions, however well-intended, by members of his very extended family.

Then Penelope smiled at Chris, Jr.

That was all the encouragement the

seventeenyear-old needed. He dropped his elbows on the bar and gazed at her. "Did Uncle Tony tell you what great eyes you have?"

Just wait till he got hold of his nephew!

Penelope also shook her head, then whispered, "No, he didn't."

Well, that did it. That took the cake! Just when would he have had time to clasp her gently by the shoulders, gaze into her face, and whisper that her eyes were the most beautiful blue he'd ever seen, bluer than any bluebell, bluer than indigo, bluer than any sad song ever belted out by a bluesman . . .

Chris, Jr., kept on going, plowing ahead, digging himself into deeper and deeper doo-doo as far as his uncle was concerned. "Well, did Uncle Tony tell you what great . . ." the seventeen-year-old's point of focus drifted lower, far lower than Penelope's blue eyes. He licked his lips.

Tony interrupted his nephew's waking wet dream. "I think it's time you cleaned the beer cooler."

Chris grinned. "Yeah, right, Uncle Tony. Remember me in your will, won'tcha?" Then he pried himself off the bar and ambled toward the beer cooler.

He was a good kid, one Tony's brother could be proud of. But right now Tony could have done without the coaching from the sidelines.

Penelope's blue eyes had been drilling into him for enough time now that he couldn't return her gaze without either excusing himself for not asking her out, or giving in to weakness and spending the rest of the night with her. Compromising with his conscience, he settled on asking her, "How about a walk outside?"

Penelope fingered the side of her tea glass, capturing the drops of moisture the way he wanted to capture her lips. Tony had to force himself not to edge off the barstool while he waited for her answer. He figured he had something going in his favor: Most women faced with a canceled dinner date wouldn't come around looking for the weasel. So just maybe she was at least interested.

"Sure," she said, in a voice that carried just a hint of anxiousness.

Wanting her not to worry, wanting her only to want to be with him, Tony slid off the stool, then guided her gently through the throng of waiting diners, anxious to be alone with Penelope.

"This way," Tony said, guiding her off the porch, onto a side path that led to a footbridge that arched over the waterway joining the marina to Lake Pontchartrain. Reluctant to let loose of Penelope's arm, he maintained the contact as they stepped from light to darkness.

In the shadows that rose up beside the restaurant, he hesitated, then said, "I'm glad you came looking for me."

She turned to face him and in the light streaming out from the restaurant windows, he could see her eyes shining. "Me, too," she said. "Though I did it for different reasons, I'm glad I came out here."

"So you like me a little better now?" He said it half-jokingly, but he wanted to know.

She nodded, then almost in slow motion raised one hand to his right cheek. "Yes, I do," she whispered, barely grazing his face with her touch. "And I like your family."

"They're a good bunch," he said, taking her hand and leading her along the path to the marina and lakefront area surrounding his family's restaurant. He knew every square inch of the place, having played hide and go seek there years before taking his high school dates to the darkest pockets for midnight kisses.

Now, leading Penelope toward the footbridge, he moved forward carefully, sensing with every step that he'd started down a course he'd either regret like hell or fall to the ground over in thanks.

"Do you have any idea how appealing your innocence is?" Tony asked her, when he could corral his thoughts into words. "You're practically trying to seduce me and yet you're so incredibly naive. . . ."

"I am?" She puckered up and wrinkled her brow in that way of hers that drove Tony over the edge.

"Oh, yes," he said, tracing the outline of her full lips with the pad of his thumb.

She leaned backward, just a bit, against the railing of the bridgework, and he regretted causing her to pull away.

"It's okay," he said, "I won't throw myself on you."

"Oh," she said, and the disappointment came through loud and clear.

Pleased, Tony said, "Unless you want me to, of course." He inched closer, wedging one leg around hers, pulling her close by clasping her around her waist.

She looked up into his eyes.

Her lashes fluttered.

"Do I scare you?" he asked in a low voice.

"Mmm," she said, sounding breathless.

"I'll take that as a no," he said, and, leaning into her, closed his lips on hers.

"Mmmmmmmm," she murmured, curling into his embrace.

He smiled, his lips moving against hers. What a babe. What an incredible, impossibly innocent woman he'd stumbled across, yet an innocent so accomplished she managed to make him feel like a stumblebum half the time.

Forcing that thought from his mind, he kissed her more fiercely. She moaned and tangled her fingers in the hair at the back of his head. He caught his breath and plunged his tongue deeper into her mouth. The more he kissed, the more tightly she clung to him, until the tables were practically turned and he felt like crying out for mercy.

But of course he didn't.

He kissed her back. He raced his hands up and down the back of her trembling body, a wonderfully soft body wedged against his own aching body.

A horn split the night.

She jumped and pulled away. "What was that?"

Tony opened his arms, hoping like heck she'd race right back into the safety he offered. "A boat going out into the lake."

"Ohhh . . ." She seemed to consider his answer, shifting from foot to foot, nibbling on her bottom lip.

"It's okay," he said. "It's a noise you get used to at the lakefront."

"Oh," she said, gazing at his arms.

He opened them wider, and to his relief and delight, she stepped back into the space of his arms.

"Tony?"

"Yes?" He didn't care what she said. He had her in his arms, for better or for worse, Hinson be damned, for this one night.

"You're nice," she said.

Those words almost undid him. All he'd been thinking about was wooing her back to his place, ripping her clothes off, and having his way with her. He could taste her, envision her writhing beneath him, dancing in the candle-light burning beside his bed.

But nice? How in the hell did that comment equate to the wild visions he had of thrashing about in the sheets with her?

Tony nuzzled his lips against her neck, unwilling to let go, to come to grips with what she had to offer in reality, versus his own fantasies.

"Want to go to my place?" he heard himself asking, about to kick himself. Of course she'd say no. This was Penelope Sue Fields, rising attorney, star counsel, straight-A student. Why would she go to Tony Olano's house?

She stilled, then her body went almost slack. He started to laugh, offer up a joke about his request, but somehow he found he couldn't do it. She meant too much to him.

He sighed, realizing he was doomed.

What an idiot, he thought, and began to pull away.

"I'd love to," she said softly.

"You'd what?"

"I'd love to see your place," she said.

"Hot dog." Tony hugged her close, then, one arm around her shoulders, hustled her off the bridge and toward the parking lot.

Then he stopped, rock-still.

"Is something wrong?" Penelope sounded anxious as she asked the question.

"No, I just remembered we can't go to my place." Was he out of his mind? He knew for a fact Hinson had a man watching his house.

"Oh." Her disappointment showed clearly.

He put his arm around her. "Don't worry, I'll think of something else. It's just that . . ." Tony racked his brain for some excuse, "I've, uh, had the place fumigated. Termites. Very bad in New Orleans."

"Oh," she said again.

She didn't invite him over, which was just as well. Everyone was watching her building. Still, Tony thought, she might have offered.

"We could . . ." her voice trailed off, then strengthened. "We could go to my place, but that houseguest I mentioned has arrived."

It was Tony's turn to utter an "oh." Placing a kiss on her lips, he said, "Never fear. I have the solution." He opened the door to his twelve-year-old Plymouth as suavely as he'd seen Hinson sweep open the door of his brand new Town Car in front of Primo's.

Penelope smiled at him and Tony knew he had to have tonight with her. He wanted Penelope, in his arms, in his heart, and in his life.

Chapter 19

Penelope didn't know where Tony was taking them. But, driving along the darkened streets, so near to him she could feel his heart beating, Penelope didn't care.

She trusted him.

She did wish she hadn't told that silly fib about Mrs. Merlin being the name of her cat.

After Tony's sympathetic reaction to the news of Mrs. Merlin's flattened state, he'd no doubt think she was nuts if she launched into the tale of the six-inch magick practitioner.

And now, driving through the night together, the last thing Penelope wanted was any reason for Tony to reject her.

In the occasional illumination from street lamps, she studied Tony's face, especially the darkly brooding eyes that had so captivated her from the first moment she'd seen him in the Oil Building elevator.

Tonight the dark fire in his eyes burned even more intensely. Penelope, however, thought maybe she was reading that intensity into his gaze due to her own incredible thrill at having him look at her as if he wanted her and only her.

Just then he glanced over and found her watching him. A slight upward curve to his lips, he said in a deep, low voice, "Like what you see?"

She nodded.

"Good." Reaching over, he took her hand and started circling his thumb against her palm.

She sighed.

"Like that?"

She nodded again.

In a low voice, he said, "I want you to like everything we're going to do tonight."

Penelope shivered and clutched his hand, then reminded herself she wasn't turning back. No matter what bridge she was about to cross, no matter the irrevocable consequences, she wanted to give herself to him, if only for one night.

For so many years she'd been the perfect example of goal-driven virtue.

Tonight, she'd live for the moment.

When she'd moved to New Orleans, she'd promised herself she'd begin to live life in a way she'd avoided for far too long. Tonight she wanted to turn a corner; from the tips of her toes to the edges of her hair, she wanted to feel alive, wanted, desired.

A radio sounded and he slowly withdrew his hand from hers and lifted his radio microphone.

Immediately missing the connection, she shifted toward him, needing to bridge the gap between their bodies. She kicked off her heels, then pulled her legs onto the seat. Feeling bold and daring, she stroked the side of his rock-hard thigh with her toes, wondering where within herself she'd found the courage to do such a thing.

He smiled and let the radio dangle from its cord. His hand drifted in a teasing feathery path from the tips of her toes, along the length of her calf, behind her knee, and along her thigh, where her skirt had inched up dramatically.

Penelope sighed and instinctively tilted her body more openly toward his exploring hand.

She thought she heard him utter a noise somewhere between a growl and a sigh.

She smiled.

She might grow to like this flirting stuff.

She sure hoped Tony liked the way she did it, too. From that sound he'd just made, she couldn't tell, and she was too shy to ask.

"Penelope?"

She shifted toward him, thankful for the darkness that hid her expression. She didn't want him to see just how consumed with longing she suddenly felt. "Yes?" she managed the question in a languid tone, trying to sound like a woman accustomed to running her toes over a man's thigh.

"How'd you find me tonight?"

"Good detective work, I guess." Remembering suddenly the cherry-red candle she had burned late last night, she added, "And a little bit of magick."

"Threw a spell on me, did you?"

He kept on stroking her leg, making it almost impossible to answer. And since there was the teeniest chance she'd done exactly that, Penelope couldn't think of anything to say.

Just then Tony pulled off the road and the car

bumped along a gravel lane before stopping in front of a small house with a sprawling porch that extended on pilings over the water. "Here we are."

Penelope shifted around, scrambling for her shoes. Before she got both of them on, Tony had whipped around to her side of the car, opened the door, and held the right shoe out. "For you, Cinderella," he said, a provocative smile curving his lips.

Feeling a lot like she'd fallen into one of her own fantasies, Penelope slipped her foot into the shoe as he held it for her. Then he took her by the hand and led her from the car and up a path that crunched underfoot as they walked on it.

From underneath a flower pot, Tony produced a key that glinted in the moonlight. "Thankfully my brother is a creature of habit," he said, inserting the key in the door.

"Should we? I mean, will he mind?"

Tony chuckled. "Not Chris. He'd be happy to know someone was getting good use out of the place."

Penelope hesitated. "So no one lives here?"

Tony had the door unlocked. "It's a camp, a summer place, but Chris is so busy at the restaurant he rarely gets out here. We used to come here as kids, everybody, the cousins, aunts, uncles, you name it, and run wild."

"Wild?"

"Oh, the usual, swim, fish, pull the girls' pigtails." He turned and caught her hand back in his. "That was my favorite," he said, staring down at her face with those incredible dark eyes of his. Penelope noted extra circles under his eyes and wondered with a tug of tenderness whether he had trouble sleeping at night.

Then she forgot all about that as he pushed open the door and said, "After you, Cinderella."

She told herself to move forward, to enter this strange house that belonged to someone else, with a man she scarcely knew. She sent the message from her brain to her foot, but somehow it seemed to get all tangled up.

Tony must have sensed it, because he simply picked her up in his arms and carried her inside the house.

"Oh, my," she said, her words muffled in his thick hair curling over his shirt collar. She wondered for the most fleeting of moments if Cinderella had experienced this incredible mix of anticipation and trepidation as she stepped into the glittering golden coach on her way to the ball.

Tony settled her gently on the floor. Dim light glinted in the room through gaps in the window coverings.

He closed the door behind them.

Turned the key in the lock.

And took her in his arms.

His lips moved like velvet over silk as he caressed and nibbled at her mouth. She sighed and nestled even more closely against his chest. He stroked the back of her neck with one thumb and as she uttered a tiny moan at the magic of his kiss, his tongue eased between her lips and danced in rhythm with the raging beat of her pulse.

She moved in unison with Tony as he half-waltzed, half-circled his way across the darkened room. In the rush of his kisses, Penelope scarcely noticed when her head settled against a nest of pillows. Then, his arms still encircling her, Tony lay atop her.

A tiny note of warning, a last echo of common sense, began to sound in her head.

Then Tony slipped his hand under her jacket, beneath the lacy cup of her bra, and the warning drowned in the wave of pleasure that swept over her.

Tony was pretty sure he'd lucked out and gone off to heaven. The touch of Penelope's skin under his hand, the curve of her breast, the rise of her excited nipple, all combined to assure him that no matter what else happened in his life, he had to have this woman as his tonight.

Any questions, hesitations, or reservations had long since fled his mind.

He freed the buttons of her jacket, shrugging it from her body as she wriggled and sighed beneath him in a way that was fast driving him over the edge. For a fairly prissy woman in fussy suits with her hair slicked back, Penelope warmed up faster than a cup of soup in a microwave.

Sure enough, the only thing she wore under that jacket was her bra, a concoction of lace and satin that barely covered her full breasts.

She lay with her head thrown back on a sea of pillows. His hand on one breast, he turned his attention to the other with his tongue, palming the nipple through the lace of her bra.

She squirmed and he let go long enough to unbutton his shorts and reach for his zipper.

Between kisses, he said, "For someone so incredibly starchy, you are the most passionate woman I've ever known."

Her eyes flickered wide and the most adorable smile curved on her lips. "Really?"

The innocent way she asked the question undid Tony. Working on her skirt, he shed it along with her pantyhose. The scrap of satin that passed for panties he left in place, excited by the sexy outline of the white silky fabric and the wisps of hair that curled around one edge, beckoning him inward.

Tony groaned, choking in a ragged breath.

She lay beneath him, the picture of female perfection, her breasts under the lacy bra rising and lowering rapidly, offering herself to him with every breath she took.

Of course he accepted the offering, after first tugging off his shirt and tossing it somewhere on the floor along with the rest of their clothing.

She had the most incredibly awed look on her face. It tugged at his conscience as he lowered his mouth to suckle on her breast, first warming the tightened nipple through the barrier of the fabric, then edging back the lace playfully with one finger.

She gasped and raised her hands to the back of his neck. Murmuring jumbled words Tony couldn't quite make out, she curled her hands in his hair and kissed the top of his head.

She was more than ready.

Tony eased one hand beneath her back, making quick work of the catch of her bra. He skimmed it off her body and tossed it over his shoulder.

This time not even a wisp of fabric lay between him and her ripe breasts. He circled first one nipple, then the other before edging off the couch and patting his hand around the side table until he found what he sought.

With a click, the soft light of a table lamp cast a glow in which Penelope basked. Staring up at him, she looked completely open, totally vulnerable, utterly beautiful.

"You don't mind the light?"

She smiled. Tracing the shape of his lips with her little finger, she said, "All the better to see you."

"Ah, Penelope," he whispered, tracing a line from her lips down her throat, around the silver pendant engraved with the letter P between her breasts, over ribs that showed clearly against her skin, in a slow circle around her navel, then lower, past the scrap of satin that barely covered the part of her he didn't think he could wait much longer to explore and lay claim to.

She lay with her head thrown back, an almost drugged expression on her face. She whispered in response, "Tony, you're making me feel things I never knew existed."

He couldn't help but smile before he lowered his lips. With his teeth, he tugged at the edge of the satin panty, then traced a path of demanding kisses where satin teased the edge of her thigh.

She quivered violently and he kissed the same path on the other thigh, reveling in her excited reaction.

"I want you to feel everything I do tonight in a way you've never felt before," he said.

"Don't worry about that," she half-whispered, half-murmured.

Satisfied, he kissed her thigh, then the damp center of her panties. He'd been ready for her for so long now he thought he'd probably explode, like a balloon released with too much helium, but he willed himself to wait.

He wanted to show Penelope just how good she could feel with Tony Olano.

Not yet freeing her of panties, he stroked her with mouth and tongue. She writhed under him, calling his name. God, but she was hot. He eased his tongue under the edge of the satin, tasting her, teasing her, promising her more pleasure to come.

"Oh, Tony," she cried out, "Raoul was never like this."

"Raoul?" Tony stilled his kisses, lifted his head, and gazed toward her face, a face intensely passionate, intensely concentrated on the pleasure he'd been giving her. Dragging the name out into three syllables, he said, "Raoul? Who's he?"

"Oh, nobody," she said, opening her eyes and looking rather sheepishly at him.

Tony stroked the side of her thigh. "Your mama never told you not to talk about other guys?" He was too excited to be annoyed ... yet.

"Raoul's not just another guy."

"Oh, no?" Tony edged up on his elbows. "Then who the hell is he?"

"Oh!" Penelope seemed to snap back to the reality around her. She blinked, then said, "Oh, Tony, Raoul's not another man. He's, um, he's ... well, he's a figment of my imagination."

"Uh-huh." Tony didn't feel too impressed by

that explanation. She might have started off the reference to this mystery man with a less-than-favorable comparison, but Tony wasn't into any compare-and-contrast point systems.

He wanted Penelope to think only of him.

Penelope pushed up on the pillows. "It's true. Raoul's an invention of my imagination. He's like a . . ." she waved one hand in a slow circle, as if trying to whisk an explanation out of thin air, "an imaginary lover to keep me from missing all the things I've not had a chance to experience while I've been concentrating on my career."

"Such as?" Tony wanted to stop talking and get back to business. The way he'd been kissing and pleasuring Penelope had him so excited he couldn't stand this interruption. But neither could he stand her thinking of another guy.

She giggled, a bit nervously. Tony stroked her beautifully flat stomach, then edged his hand higher, past her ribs, until he captured first one breast, then the other. She sighed and said, "This."

He followed his hands with his lips, leaning over her, claiming her, tasting her. When he could force himself to pause, he lifted his mouth and said, "You mean this, for instance?"

She nodded.

He returned his lips to hers, to the warmth and excitement of her mouth, her tongue responding to the dancing inquiry of his own.

Then his tongue slowed as the messages she'd been sending him filtered through the haze of desire ruling his mind. *An imaginary lover. To make up for what she'd never experienced.* He added up her words, plus what she hadn't said, to what her almost-surprised reactions to his love-making signaled.

Lifting off her, he said, very slowly, and very clearly, "Penelope, are you a virgin?"

No answer came; she said nothing.

Beneath his embrace, she ceased her wriggling and soft moaning.

He groaned and sat up. "Shit," he muttered, tugging at his hair, ready to explode.

"What's so bad about being a virgin?" She, too, sat up, and glared at him, crossing her arms over her bare breasts.

"Nothing." He pulled away from her, yanking at his shorts, tugging them up around his less-than-willing-to-give-in-to-reason body. He hated the way she'd closed in immediately, like a flower shocked by too much heat, when before she'd been so open to him. "It's just that I can't simply plunge ahead. It's not right."

Her chin quivered. "You don't want me, do you?"

"Don't want you?" He caught her hand, brought it to his body, showing her quite clearly how much he wanted her. He stared into her eyes.

She returned his look, quite steadily, though a wash of color mounted on her cheeks.

"I can't do it this way. It's not right, when you've waited this long, to give yourself away on a one-night stand." He hated putting it that way, but he knew Penelope would wake up in the morning despising herself.

Who was Tony Olano to her, other than a guy in the wrong place at the right time? He tugged at her hand, pulling her delicious body from the couch. "And don't tell anyone I stopped, for pete's sake, or I'll lose my reputation."

"Great," she muttered, letting him slip her bra back on. "My one big chance and you're worried about your reputation."

He handed her her skirt, intent on dressing her, refusing to give in to the desire raging within him, desire he could see she'd do nothing to derail.

It was probably just as well that a different type of fire sparked in her eyes. She snatched her clothing from him, rose from the couch, and turned her back on him as she yanked her clothes on.

Good. Better for her to be angry at him than hate herself in the morning. Still, he couldn't believe he, Tony Olano, was now about to deliver this ready, willing, and wanting woman back to her car, follow her home, and tuck her into bed.

Alone.

Since when had he grown a conscience?

"My reputation," he finally answered when she turned to face him, her suit jacket buttoned securely, "is the least of my worries."

"I guess you're worried whether I'll still respect you in the morning," she said in a cross voice.

He couldn't blame her for sounding upset; hell, as worked up as he was, she had to be pretty crazed with need right now, too. He placed his hands on her shoulders and gazed into her eyes—eyes passion had darkened to cobalt.

"As a matter of fact," he said, trying for lightness, "I do care about that."

Then he marched her out of the house before she could wear down his unexpected spurt of conscience.

Chapter 20

Penelope had sat frozen as Tony slipped her bra onto her arms, then reached around to the back to fasten the clasp. Her skin burned where his fingers touched it, but not even that heat thawed her mood.

His touch had, however, jerked her back to her senses and she'd snatched the rest of her clothing from his hand, not meeting his gaze, whipping into her nylons and suit.

A volatile blend of humiliation and pride ruled her as Tony now propelled her out the door and into his car. She'd started to argue with him. At twenty-nine, she was certainly old enough to know her own mind. If she chose to have sex with him, what did it matter to him whether she'd never done it before?

But the words he'd used had stopped her cold.

One-night stand.

Forgetting she'd gone off to Olano's telling herself that's exactly what she sought, Penelope hugged her humiliation to her chest. Even as her skin still tingled from the touch of Tony's lips and hands and mouth, her ego reeled.

She shouldn't have let herself hope, not even for a second, that she could have meant anything more than that to a man so obviously worldly-wise and experienced.

When they reached the restaurant parking lot, Tony took her hand. Against her own better judgment, she let him clasp it softly in his, registering with a rush of emotion how good his touch felt.

Gazing into her eyes, he said, "I want you to remember I stopped because I care about you. Not the opposite, not for any silly reason you've got racing through your head." He brushed his lips across her knuckles. "You're a sexy, desirable woman and if things were different, we'd still be back there on that couch."

He sounded so sincere. Penelope softened slightly. Then he tipped her chin gently and feathered a kiss across her lips. She sighed. Could she believe him?

His lips moving slowly from her mouth to her ear, he whispered, "When I can, I'd like to see you again."

She didn't answer. She didn't know what to say. Her body, awakened to sensuous pleasures and turbulent sensations she hadn't even known enough about to include in her fantasy life, trembled and quivered and cried out for more of Tony Olano. Her mind, however, counseled caution.

She thought of the articles she devoured in silly women's magazines, ridiculing them even as she wished she had more in common with the stories she found there than with the dry fodder of her legal journals.

Such articles always advised women against appearing overly anxious. Only last week she'd read one entitled, "Let Him Chase You—And You'll Both Be Glad when You Finally Let Him Catch You."

Taking a deep breath, Penelope slipped free of Tony's embrace and opened the car door. She turned back toward him, traced the line of his lips, her heart beating faster than was probably healthy. Feeling like a pauper risking her last dollar on a lottery ticket, she forced a casual tone to her voice and said, "Call me when you think you can handle me, big guy."

Then she whisked out of his car and into hers.

Watching her dash to her car, Tony whistled, his mood a mixture of admiration and extreme frustration. He admired her for playing it cool. And once he had Hinson out of the picture, he knew just how he intended to deal with his frustration.

"And just where have you been?" Her bookmark-sized self still propped up on the dining table, Mrs. Merlin glared at Penelope. "And my, if you don't look like the alligator that ate the egret."

Penelope touched a hand to her cheek. "I'm that transparent?"

"Yeah, yeah, yeah. But so what? You may be transparent, but I'm translucent. And it's past the prime time for the spell to work, so I do wish you'd stop dawdling and get down to business. I need every ounce of magick I can make tonight to bring myself out of this sorry state, and messing up on the timing of the heavens won't help."

Penelope halted in her path across her living room, pretty much oblivious to the scolding words. Instead, she thought of Tony saying she'd cast a spell on him. She kicked off her shoes and, despite Mrs. Merlin's impatience, paused to select some mood music for the CD player.

Along with Mrs. Merlin, last night's magick altar still occupied the table. Remembering the magician's instructions about the importance of centering oneself before performing candle magick, Penelope dropped to the floor on her Oriental carpet and stretched out. If she, Penelope Sue Fields, who lived her life immersed in the black letter of tax law, was going to perform a supernatural ritual, she planned to do so by the book.

She eased first one arm, then the other over her head and began to form the image of her place of peace in her mind. Sounds of water lapping at the riverbank filtered into her consciousness, only to be rudely interrupted.

"We don't have time for that."

"What?" Penelope raised her head, not feeling at all like moving. After the fire Tony had stoked in her, she needed some time to return to her usual self. And lying there on the floor, the lilting strains of the music filling the room, she wanted to be left alone to relive the incredibly sweet and passionate sensations Tony had created within her.

"Up. Up." Mrs. Merlin waved her one-dimensional body forward, then back, like a stalk of wheat. "You're my only hope."

Penelope rose slowly to her feet. She sure

hoped she'd centered herself sufficiently to assist Mrs. Merlin, so she could get the job done and then be free to snuggle under the covers and dream of Tony.

"By the way, that man of yours called earlier. Three times."

"He did?" She couldn't keep the hope out of her voice.

"Yes. I didn't know how to use that newfangled speaker phone, but I heard every word on your answering machine."

"What did he say?"

"Well, the last time, he said he knew you were going to accept his proposal, so he was going forward with wedding plans."

"He what!" Of course Mrs. Merlin wasn't referring to Tony. "Of all the nerve."

"He said even though you didn't have family to notify, he had lots of business associates and needed to spread the news."

Penelope stormed over to the table, hands on her hips.

"Hey, don't kill the messenger," Mrs. Merlin said.

"Sorry, but what a creep. And he seemed so pleasant in the beginning."

"Those are the ones to watch out for," Mrs. Merlin said. "I say find a man with a few rough edges, then sit back and watch as he tries to smooth them off to win you." Unbelievably, she winked. "Ready to help me now?"

Penelope nodded, turning Mrs. Merlin's words over in her mind. "As much as I want to help you, are you sure we shouldn't call Mr. Gotho or someone else?"

"Hah!" Mrs. Merlin waved her body again. "Forget Gotho. He told me only last month, and I quote, 'Don't come running to me for help the next time you get yourself into a fix. I've rescued you for the last time.'"

That news sure didn't bolster Penelope's confidence. "So what went wrong that time?"

"Is it the lawyer in you that makes you ask all these questions?"

"Search me." Hiding a smile, Penelope lifted the incense stick from its place on the altar, carried it to the stove, and lit it from the flame of the gas burner. Mrs. Merlin had impressed on her that matches, manifestations of brimstone and sulfur, brought bad karma to all that was magickal.

Penelope wasn't sure why a gas burner made much of a difference, but as she had prior to last night's spell, she went along with Mrs. Merlin's point of view. The woman was, after all, a guest in Penelope's home, and though she might have wreaked havoc on her ordered life, she'd also brought a refreshing sense of adventure along with it.

The white candle from last night's spell occupied the center of the altar. Penelope eyed the cherry-red candle, the one Mrs. Merlin had described as representing the essence of love and desire.

Without meaning to, she reached out and stroked the smooth side of the pillar-style candle. "What happens if we light both candles at the same time?" she asked, trying to sound as if she were merely gathering information in a disinterested fashion.

"Candle magick is a matter of personal sensitivity. If your instincts prompt you to add a second candle, it's the right thing to do." Mrs. Merlin recited the words as if reading from an instruction book, but Penelope noticed the flattened magician eyed the cherry-red candle with a half-smile on her face as she answered the question.

Before she could change her mind, Penelope lifted the cherry-red candle and with one swift gesture placed it in the center of the altar, wedged against the side of the white candle. Then she lit the two wicks using the still-flaming incense stick.

"Place me in front of the flame," Mrs. Merlin commanded in an excited voice. "But be careful, not too close."

Quelling her anxiety, Penelope scooted the bookmark shape of Mrs. Merlin in front of the white candle. Her anxiety came from both conscious and unconscious sources. The good student in her couldn't help but remember that only yesterday Mrs. Merlin had emphasized repeatedly the importance of the place of peace, the importance of one visiting this place prior to embarking on any practice of candle magick.

Yet tonight Mrs. Merlin had hurried her onward.

Penelope swallowed, unable to contain her nervousness. Staring at Mrs. Merlin, she said, "But what do I do? How do I help with a spell I don't understand, let alone believe in? Last night you did everything and I just watched." As she spoke, she jostled the cherry-red candle and a blob of wax splashed on the back of her hand.

"Ouch!" Penelope raised her hand to her mouth, about to cool the burn with her breath. Then she paused, staring down at the shape the wax formed on her hand.

"You're dreaming," she said aloud, her voice held to a low whisper.

"No, you're not," she answered herself. "You're perfectly sane and aware of your surroundings.

"But then why," she asked herself, " am I seeing the shape of a cat in this blob of wax?"

Mrs. Merlin chimed in with, "Sure looks like a cat to me."

Penelope shrugged. "It's only my overactive imagination that makes me see a cat." Besides, she had cats on her mind because of the misunderstanding Tony had about Mrs. Merlin being a cat. That was the only reason she was interpreting the blotch on her hand as the shape of a cat, back arched, mouth wide and spitting.

"If you're finished with your attempt to rationalize the language of magick, can we get on with this spell? It's getting hot next to these candles."

Trying not to stare at the shape of the cat, Penelope nodded. She ought to scrape the wax off, but it didn't feel as if it had burned her skin. It was curiously cool.

Mrs. Merlin had begun muttering under her breath. Her voice rose and she said, "Now, concentrate on the flame. Picture me whole. Picture me round and tall and scarfing down some of that pasta you cooked the other night. Picture me eating anything but oatmeal."

"I thought you liked oatmeal." Penelope murmured the words, intent on the hypnotic effect of the flame combined with the fantasy images that filled her mind.

Tony dominated her mind, replacing her make-believe world, rendering it obsolete. No longer could she remember her years of fantasizing over Raoul, the once-perfect romantic hero of her mind. Now only Tony would do for her.

In her senses, he held her in his arms, claiming her, making her his woman. She pictured him possessing her in the most intimate way, and as she saw them joined together, she stroked the base of the cherry-red candle, heedless of the heat seeping through the wax.

She must have moaned, because Mrs. Merlin said in that caustic voice of hers, "I didn't know magick excited you so much."

Penelope blushed. "I'm just trying to get involved in the process." Involved with Tony was what she wanted, involved to the point where he wouldn't whisk her out of his arms and out of his house the next time they lay together. Her eyes following the two flickering yellow-white-blue flames, she hoped there would be a next time.

Mrs. Merlin rippled slightly, then the movement grew stronger. "Involvement," she said, her voice rising and falling as her flattened body swayed, "requires setting aside your fears, opening your heart to whatever may come of the process. Magick is a lot like love in that respect."

"My heart is open," Penelope whispered, thinking of the expression on Tony's face after she'd confirmed the truth of her dire lack of sexual experience. He'd been shocked, true, but she'd seen a dawning of something close to admiration, too. Thinking back on that, Penelope realized he had stopped out of respect and concern for her.

And those feelings gave her hope—hope that Tony hadn't thought of her as a one-night stand.

The flame of the cherry-red candle leaped higher then danced itself in a circling arc around the wick.

Mrs. Merlin smiled and called out, "To the moon and the stars and the goddess above . . ."

The words were quite musical. Enjoying the flow of the moment, Penelope swayed along with the dancing candle flame.

"Chant," Mrs. Merlin commanded. "Last night I said the spell to myself, but tonight you must repeat it after me. I'm afraid I may not have enough substance to summon the necessary powers."

Penelope repeated the phrase, not quite as musically, but the effect pleased her. She'd long forgotten to feel self-conscious or ridiculous. Somehow Mrs. Merlin's ritual felt exactly like what she should be doing on this amazing night.

"We offer these flames. . . ."

Penelope closed her eyes halfway and, without knowing why, reached out and placed her fingertips on the squared-off form of her unusual new friend before repeating, "We offer these flames. . . ."

"We ask that the stars form the path, the moon light the way, and the goddess grant this wish. . . ." Mrs. Merlin's eyes had closed. The flattened body quivered and swayed, then sagged beneath Penelope's hand, giving her the oddest sensation that she'd just experienced Mrs. Merlin's essence departing the bookmark-shaped self.

Yet the voice of Mrs. Merlin came again, as she murmured, "Hear this wish to make me whole again."

The flames leaped, then sputtered, then dissolved into twin spirals of dark gray smoke.

Mrs. Merlin's eyes flew open. "Merciful mergatroids!"

"What's happened?"

"Nothing. And nothing's going to tonight." Mrs. Merlin's mouth quivered. "And I am so hungry."

"Can't we try it again?" Penelope did feel badly for Mrs. Merlin. "Maybe the air conditioner came on and blew out the candles."

"I'm afraid that's only wishful thinking," Mrs. Merlin said. "I may make a mistake here or there with candle magick, but I understand when the stars are telling me I blew it."

"Oh," Penelope said, feeling guilty. If she'd gotten home earlier, perhaps the spell would have worked.

"And there's no need to blame yourself," Mrs. Merlin said, as if she'd read Penelope's mind. "Everything happens for a reason." She sighed. "Let's just go to sleep and try this again tomorrow night. At eleven-eleven, sharp."

Penelope settled the flattened Mrs. Merlin onto a cushion, and after one last look at the cherry-red candle, she turned out the lights and tiptoed to her bedroom.

Empty lots in Tony's Riverbend neighborhood ran to weeds accented by empty beer bottles, discarded hubcaps and tires, and the occasional used condom.

The corner lot on Tony's block, however, sported no weeds and no trash. Where it backed up against the Southern Pacific rail crossing, a thickly grown hedge of oleander separated it from the passing trains. The kids in the neighborhood took turns trimming the grass around the edges of the lot.

It was the center of the lot that held their real interest, where Tony had created a basketball court. A cousin in the construction business kept the court smoothly paved and the lighting operational. Another cousin had planted the oleanders and seeded the grass.

He had to hand it to his family: They might have all moved to the suburbs but, when he went to them for help in improving their old neighborhood, they pulled through.

It was Tony, though, who four years ago had replaced the hoop net stolen only one week after he and the kids had opened up the court. The neighborhood banded together, found the wise guy who'd nabbed it, and the kids administered a well-deserved thrashing.

No one had stolen a net since.

The court closed at eleven, when curfew sent

the youths of the neighborhood home. It was way past that time when Tony rose from his bed in frustration, grabbed a basketball, and went out to shoot a few hoops by the light of the street lamp.

Most of the neighborhood stayed home behind locked doors this time of night, barricaded against crime. Tony hated the crime that ravaged his city, too, but unlike so many others, he'd sworn to do something about the problem. As a police officer, and as a neighbor, he tried to make a difference.

The ball tucked under his arm, he let himself out of his house and walked to the corner lot. There he raced, dribbling the ball the length of the half-court, leaped, spun, and dunked the ball.

The movement released some of his pent-up energy. He knew he'd done the right thing for Penelope, stopping when he had earlier that evening. The only problem was, his body didn't agree with his mind.

What an incredibly wonderful surprise she'd been—soft and curvy and responsive—a secret delight hidden under that "don't touch me, don't even look twice" exterior! He'd sensed that hidden passion since the first time he'd seen her, but what a joy to confirm his hunch.

Pacing back to the free throw mark, Tony snapped the ball against the court a whole lot harder than necessary. Bending at the knees, poised for the shot, he pictured her beneath him, her breasts full, nipples puckered and glistening from the strokes of his tongue.

He let go of the ball and it slammed the edge

of the rim and shot off at a wild angle, rolling toward the street.

"Nuts." He had to quit thinking of Penelope. Remembering only made him want her more. And he couldn't have her.

"Not yet, anyway," he said aloud, then jogged after the ball.

A dark-colored car with tinted windows turned the corner, moving at a snail's pace.

Instantly on alert, Tony slowed his approach toward the curb. His instincts prompted him to reach for his gun.

Of course he didn't have it.

They'd made him turn in his official weapon the day he'd been stripped of his uniform, his badge, his public honor.

He'd bought another one the very next day, from a helpful youth on a dark backstreet near the riverfront. Only twenty-five dollars and no waiting period. Not traceable, either.

But tonight, caught up in thoughts of Penelope, he'd left it in his house.

The car stopped opposite where he stood. The back window rolled smoothly downward.

Whistling softly, Tony bent to retrieve the basketball.

"Move nice and slow and you won't get hurt," said a voice from the backseat.

Tony rolled the ball onto his foot and with a quick movement, vaulted it into his hands. Spinning it, he said, "Nice of you to visit, Rolo Polo."

"Shut up and get in."

Okay, so the fat guy didn't want to converse casually. Tony took note of that as the door opened. One of Rolo's regulars stepped out. As he was hustled into the car, Tony's main thought was thankfulness he hadn't brought Penelope to his place.

He turned his head toward the man occupying the other side of the backseat. "You're up late, Hinson."

The lawyer smiled, a tight-lipped expression, and the skin close to his right eye twitched. "Never too late for a little business, is it, Tony, my boy?"

Evil, Tony reflected as he studied Hinson, wore many faces. During his years on the force, he'd seen the mask of the dumb joker who thought cruelty amusing. He'd witnessed evil sparked by impotent frustration and fueled by the rage of domestic disputes. He'd served as spectator to the aftermath of far more shootings than he cared to remember, most of them the result of drug deals gone sour.

Drugs, to a large extent, controlled by Hinson's boss.

They rode only a short ways from the basketball court, bumping over the railroad tracks and shooting off the gravel and oyster-shell road that crossed over the levee. The whistle of a tug sounded its alert as it pushed a string of barges by on the river. Tony caught the glimmer of lights in the distance as he looked past Hinson, focusing himself to play this moment exactly as it had to be played.

Inside the car the only sounds were those of Rolo Polo chewing on his unlit cigar. The flunky who'd hustled Tony into the car stepped outside when they ground to a halt on the top of the levee access road.

The tick in Hinson's cheek spasmed. Tony considered that a good sign. The more tension Hinson experienced, the more quickly he would crack.

"So," Hinson said, breaking the silence, "you must be running a little short of cash after a few months off work."

Tony shrugged. "I'm picking up a few jobs here and there."

"Is that right?" Hinson smiled thinly and shifted his hand. The diamond ring on his pinky glinted. "I've been authorized to inform you that if you were to apply for reinstatement to the police department, you would more than likely receive a favorable reception."

Tony knew better than to seem too eager. "Yeah, they'd take me back to do what? Walk the streets of some housing project? Shuffle papers behind a desk?"

Hinson picked a speck of lint from his trousers. "You'll go back with full pardon, apologies, and champagne all around, from the chief down to the janitor. A promotion, too."

Tony raised his brows, wondering just how high Hinson's boss had reached into the department. Apparently farther up than any of them had detected. "Your boss has friends in high places."

"Don't worry your head over who they are. We're not paying you to think. We're paying you to run the details, protect the goods, and deliver when someone needs a little extralegal aid." Hinson smiled at his own play on words.

Tony rolled the basketball over his thighs, appearing to be deep in thought. At last, he said, as if the words were being dragged from his throat, "And what would I owe?"

Again Hinson smiled. "We'd let you know."

"Open-ended?" Tony spun the ball. "What kind of a deal is that?"

"You want to get your own lawyer, go ahead."

Tony pictured the only lawyer he wanted, but forced Penelope's image from his mind. "I do need my job back," he said slowly, "but I need more than that."

Hinson raised his brows.

Tony thought he heard Rolo Polo make a rude noise.

"Cash." Tony pointed to Hinson's ring. "You understand the value of money. I could use a new car. Maybe some new clothes."

Hinson steepled his fingers. "And when you're given a job to do, you'll do it?"

Tony shrugged. "Hey, I've got no love for a department that kicked me out in disgrace. I never took money from anyone, but where were the powers that be when I needed backup?" He narrowed his eyes. "I'll laugh at them all the way to the bank."

"*If* we pay you."

"No money, no deal."

Rolo Polo bit down hard on his cigar and half-turned. "Mr. Hinson don't like to be told no."

"True, Rolo, true," Hinson said in a tight voice.

"Besides, whatcha got to lose?" The fat man reached over the seat and jerked Tony's chin up. "Look at you, living in that slum, surrounded by all those blacks. You oughta get a life. Do a good job and the money will come later. Then you'll get those new clothes, a decent car, some Cuban cigars." He rolled his cigar in his teeth and winked. "And working for us you can afford any woman you want."

Tony let his interest show in his eyes. "Any woman?"

Hinson's cheek twitched more rapidly. "Rolo, when I need your assistance, I'll ask for it. Perhaps you don't understand your position, Olano. Once you've made it known you're willing to come to work for my boss, you no longer call the shots. No, not even a hothead like you."

Tony thought of how he'd heard Hinson over the wiretap asking the old man if he could get an annulment after he'd married Penelope. Hinson was sure trying to call the shots in the organization and if he didn't watch out, he'd land in a shark tank someplace.

Hinson glanced out the window, then back at Tony. "I've never liked you and if I were in charge you wouldn't be getting this chance. But as long as you're going to work for us, you may as well keep from embarrassing the outfit."

The lawyer pulled out a money clip and tossed a wad of bills toward Tony. "You'll get a call regarding your reinstatement hearing within two weeks. Go back repentant. Then keep your nose clean. When we need something, you'll hear from us."

Tony nodded, then leaned over and chucked Hinson on the shoulder. "Always knew you were a stick," he said, then collected the bills and stuffed them into the pocket of his basketball shorts.

Rolo turned back around. He pulled his cigar from between his teeth and said, "Remember, Olano, there ain't no annulments in this marriage."

"Very well spoken, Rolo," Hinson said dryly. He cracked his window, said something to the man outside, who reentered the car, staring at Tony with eyes as mean as a snake roused from slumber. "Now shut up and drive."

"S'okay, boss."

Tony nodded once, then again. Taking a deep breath, he said, "So I'm in."

Hinson inclined his chin, the prince deigning to recognize his subject.

"A dirty cop is still a cop, you know," Tony murmured.

"No need to justify yourself to me," Hinson said. Then staring straight at Tony, he added, "as long as you're not screwing with me."

Tony held his hands up.

"Or with anything that's mine," Hinson added.

"Yeah, the boss is getting married," Rolo Polo threw over his shoulder as the car crunched over the oyster-shell road, then bumped back over the railroad tracks.

"Should I offer my congratulations?" Tony kept his voice light, showing only a vague curiosity. Or so he hoped.

Hinson laughed. "Your first job can be to dance at my wedding. You can even dance with the bride. It'll look good to have a nice showing by the men in blue. And you'll be a commander, so that'll make the old man happy."

"A commander?" Tony wanted to ask about

the bride, but this news took him completely by surprise. "I'm getting that much of a promotion?"

Hinson shrugged. "The boss always wanted a son." His eye twitched furiously.

Watching the lawyer's face, Tony suddenly understood a piece of Hinson he'd overlooked. Hinson the orphan coveted the role of son. But he'd never be more than the lawyer, the mouthpiece, the front man, despite the fact that he provided much of the brains behind the operation.

With Tony's recruitment, Hinson stood to lose even more stature. Even more reason never to turn his back on the guy.

"So who's the lucky woman?" Tony said.

Rolo laughed, a nasty sound that made Tony's skin crawl. The laugh, of course, said exactly what Tony was thinking: No bride of Hinson's could be considered lucky. He tensed, knowing he could not react to the name he was about to hear.

"I do believe she's a friend of yours," Hinson said, his voice as sickening as an oil slick spreading over an unspoiled bayou. "The lawyer you rescued the other day."

Tony refused to say her name. He didn't want to hear it in this context. "Yeah?"

"She's not my first choice, but it's what the boss wants." He picked another speck of lint off his suit trousers. "He'll want you to marry, too, so you might as well get used to the idea."

"What about all those women my new money was going to buy for me?" Tony couldn't keep the sarcasm from his voice.

Rolo Polo snickered.

Hinson raised his brows. "What's marriage got to do with that? I've learned that lesson from associating with you Italian men, whom I must congratulate on ordering the universe nicely."

"And what order is that?"

"Let's just say you'd never let a wife get in the way of a mistress."

Remembering he was supposed to be one of the guys, Tony slapped the side of the basketball and laughed heartily. "You've got that right," he said, noticing Rolo had driven around his block several times now. "So when's the wedding?"

Hinson shrugged. "Whenever it can be arranged."

"I supposed your intended is thrilled?"

Rolo Polo laughed again. "She's a little slow in figuring out the boss don't like to be told no."

"You've got a big mouth tonight," Hinson said, the twitch working overtime.

Rolo quit laughing.

"She's delighted," Hinson said. "Get out, Olano, and keep doing what you're doing until you hear from me again."

"Oh, yeah, you know I will," Tony said, sliding across the seat after the strongman got out of the car.

He bounced the ball up his sidewalk, hoping Mrs. Sanderson next door didn't mind the noise too much. As he walked, he whistled, knowing the occupants of the car kept him in their sights.

Chapter 21

The morning after the failed candle spell, Mrs. Merlin was so grouchy Penelope was guiltily grateful to escape to the office. She experienced a flash of insight into why someone would become a workaholic rather than face a difficult situation at home, something she hoped she wouldn't do to a family of her own.

Of course, the way her life was going, she'd never have to worry about that. No one, other than a man she didn't love, wanted to marry her.

And the man she wanted to want her, the man she wanted to devour her, initiate her into the mysterious pleasures of lovemaking, had developed a most ill-timed conscience.

Penelope rode the elevator upward to her office, conscious of her keen sense of frustration— with herself, with Mrs. Merlin's failed spell, with Tony Olano for doing the right thing.

She squeezed her eyes tight and wished she could be like Dorothy in the Wizard of Oz. If she could have anything she wanted in the entire world right this minute, it would be Tony Olano holding her close and murmuring sweet nothings in her ear. Impishly, she clicked her heels together three times.

All she got for her imaginative trouble was a glare from a stern-faced woman standing opposite her in the elevator. Probably a spinster, Penelope thought, then could have bit her mental tongue. Look who's talking, she chided herself, stepping out of the elevator and into her workday.

When Tony's call came three hours later, Penelope should have been surprised, but somehow, staring at the receiver clutched in her hand, she decided no other result could have transpired.

She wanted Tony.

He wanted her.

If only for the moment, she would give herself to him.

Accepting his invitation to lunch, Penelope knew instinctively she was agreeing to more than the sharing of a meal. Even though the address he'd given her was clearly that of a restaurant in a historic small hotel she'd noticed several times before, Penelope couldn't help but feel she'd consented to something much more personal, much more momentous than lunch when she'd agreed to meet Tony.

Business, he'd explained, kept him from coming to the office to collect her.

No doubt the same business that had sent him on his way after their interlude at Café du Monde, but Penelope swallowed her pride at that thought.

She hurried out of her office a little after eleven, unusually early for someone of her work credo. Pausing by Jewel's desk, she said, "I'll probably be back late from lunch." Jewel glanced up, smiled, and said, "Can't do dinner, but can do lunch?"

Penelope blushed, thereby giving her secretary all the data she needed to confirm her conclusion. Jewel saluted and said, "No need to hurry back on my account. I've got work to last me till five."

Penelope nodded and said, "Of course, I won't be that late."

"Right," Jewel said, and wiggled her fingers as Penelope passed by.

Riding down in the elevator, Penelope wondered what it would be like to take a three- or four-hour lunch. She rarely broke from work at all, choosing to spoon down a carton of yogurt or a cup of soup while she studied her legal problem of the moment.

She knew the others in her firm thought her a dull, bookish sort of woman, but she derived no pleasure in going out for lunches with people she didn't know, and didn't know how to get acquainted with. It wasn't that she was stuffy, she'd pointed out to Jewel, she simply didn't speak any language other than law.

Or cooking, but somehow she never figured how to share that with her co-workers.

So she ate alone.

But not today.

The weather had cooled slightly, bringing with it a sense of relief and a sprightly spring to Penelope's step. She covered the several blocks to the address Tony had given her, deviating between nervous anxiety and a reckless sense of abandonment.

Whatever the day brought, she decided as she pushed open the door of the Hotel Fleur de Lis, she would embrace.

After a restless night capped off by a nightmare in which he walked Penelope down the aisle and gave her away to Hinson, Tony awoke knowing he had to see Penelope.

See her?

Hell, he wanted to make love to her, wanted to claim her in a way that would make it impossible for her to even think of another man. As he showered, he told himself to forget it. Going undercover as an employee of Hinson's meant he couldn't see her at all. As he slapped lather on his face and stroked the razor across his night's beard, he stared into the mirror and recognized the eyes of a man who would not be denied.

Just once, he promised himself.

He poured milk on his cornflakes and argued that he wasn't being totally selfish. He was sure that Penelope, despite the way she bristled at him every now and then, wanted him as much as he wanted her. Why, she'd gotten angry when he'd held back the other night at Chris's cottage.

He rinsed his bowl and spoon and stared at the portable phone lying on the counter. He'd never met a woman like Penelope Sue Fields. And despite all the women he'd dated, he'd never wanted a woman the way he wanted her.

Face it, Olano, you've got it bad, he told himself.

He knew as soon as he began planning where to take her there was no turning back. Both his place and hers were out. Just any old hotel room wouldn't do. Not for Penelope, not for their first time together.

He drummed his fingers on the counter and thought about who he knew well enough to ask a favor of. Tony rolled over a few possibilities in his mind, then suddenly thought of Lucien, who'd retired from the force last year, grumbling that his wife was going to turn him into a sissy running an old place she'd inherited where all the rooms were prettied up for honeymooners.

Tony found his phone book and studied the entries under both bed and breakfast and hotels. He knew Lucien's place was somewhere in the Central Business District. Whistling under his breath, he thought of Penelope naked and open beneath him, her hair wild against the pillows. He sucked in his breath and decided to try the Hotel Fleur De Lis. That sounded romantic. If that wasn't Lucien's, he'd keep calling till he found him.

He'd gotten lucky on the first call, with Lucien promising him his nicest suite, and even luckier when Penelope had agreed without hesitation to meet him for lunch. Fortunately, Lucien's small hotel also housed a decent restaurant, so he'd been able to innocently suggest lunch.

A meal that could be delivered to his room, Lucien had assured him.

Having set the stage, Tony took himself off to

check in at the supersecret site of the undercover task force operation. If he didn't work, he'd go nuts waiting to meet Penelope.

Penelope arrived early. Peering into the dining room of the Hotel Fleur de Lis, she saw no one else had yet been seated for lunch. Embarrassed at her anxious behavior, she shifted from foot to foot and began to back away. She'd pop into the coffee place down the corner and wait until the agreed-upon time.

She turned around and bumped straight into Tony. The touch of his hand on her shoulder as he reached out to steady her shot pleasurable shivers of anticipation through her.

"I'm early," they both said at the same time, then laughed.

"Thanks for meeting me," Tony said.

He smiled into her eyes in a way that made Penelope wish she had the nerve to suggest they skip lunch and feast on one another. Instead, she nodded and said, "Thanks for asking me."

Another couple came in and from the rear of the dining room a silver-haired man in a crisp white shirt and black pants entered through a swinging door and hurried forward. He waved in Tony's direction and led the other diners to a table by the window before heading back. Penelope couldn't have sworn to it, but she thought the man also winked at Tony.

"A friend of yours?" Then she thought about his family in the restaurant business. "Or a relative?"

"A friend," Tony said as the man approached.

"So this is the woman!" He took her by the

shoulders and kissed her on both cheeks. "Very pleased to meet you."

"Uh, Lucien . . ." Tony began.

"Only the best for you today, my dear," Lucien said, with another wink at Tony. "Any woman who sends Tony into such a spin must be the special one."

Penelope glanced at Tony, expecting to find him writhing in embarrassment. Instead, she found him gazing at her as if he were studying a Renoir.

"Very special, Lucien. Meet Penelope Fields."

"It's good to meet you," Penelope finally managed to say as the older man looked her over as closely as he probably did the fish he purchased for his restaurant.

"It's good to see Tony at last has developed a sense of taste," Lucien pronounced. "Just call the front desk when you want your lunch sent up."

Penelope wasn't sure she'd heard that right. She shot a glance at Tony, who did look embarrassed now.

Four businessmen came in and Lucien waved and led them to their seats.

"I . . . uh . . . I thought we'd have lunch in a private room," Tony said.

"That would be an adventure," Penelope said, wondering if this was another New Orleans custom or if what Tony had actually booked was a hotel room.

He held out his hand and Penelope sighed as he closed his strong fingers around hers. They strolled from the dining area down a hallway that opened to a courtyard in the center of the building.

A fountain splashed amid a jungle of leafy plants, most of them tropical ones Penelope didn't recognize. Tony paused under the archway. "You know, I didn't really ask you to lunch," he said.

Penelope's heart leaped. Gazing into his eyes, she said, "I would have been disappointed if you had."

He laughed and pulled her to him. Tipping her chin up, he kissed her lightly on the lips. Then, with a noise like a growl, he deepened the kiss.

Penelope pressed against him, willing her body to merge with his. Breathless, she answered the demands of his lips, his questing tongue. When he broke away, she cried out softly.

"Don't worry, darling," he said, leading across the courtyard to a stairway almost hidden by a banana tree, "that was only an appetizer."

With those tantalizing words, Tony ushered her up the stairs, produced a key, and swung open the door at the top of the stairs.

Feeling incredibly daring, Penelope crossed the threshold. "What a lovely room," she said, taking in the sitting room done in rosewood and chintz. A love seat faced a fireplace and a table for two sat by a window that opened out onto the balcony at the top of the stairs.

Tony walked in behind her and shut the door. "I'm glad you like it," he said, and held out his arms.

She stepped into his embrace and lifted her

lips for his kiss. Snuggling against him, she slipped her hands around the back of his neck and curled her fingers into his hair.

He pulled her more closely against him and Penelope felt a rush of power as she felt the proof of how excited Tony was. Arching her body, she offered herself to him, an offer he clearly accepted, as, still kissing her, he led them in dancelike steps across the sitting room and down a hallway.

Sanity returned slowly to Penelope as she realized they were only steps from the bedroom. Tony must have sensed that she was beginning to hesitate. Lifting his lips from hers, he said, "You know you can tell me to stop at any time." His voice husky, he said, "Though you know I don't want to. And this time I won't, unless you request it."

Her breath came faster. His eyes were dark pools she would gladly throw herself into, even if it meant drowning. She touched her tongue to her lips, tender from his kisses. "I want you, Tony Olano. Today. Now." To herself, she added, And forever.

He answered her by picking her up and cradling her in his arms, the way he'd done the day she fainted. She kept her eyes fixed on his face, watching the emotions playing there. She saw passion, she recognized desire, and though it might be her own foolish imagination taking over, she thought she detected something stronger, something closer to caring and affection, evidence that to Tony she meant more than just a one-night stand.

The bedroom of the suite was even more impressive than the sitting room. Tony set her down beside a second fireplace next to a four-poster bed. He pointed to the opposite side of the room and Penelope saw why. A huge square spa-type tub occupied the space between the bedroom and the bathroom, designed to encourage indulgence and intimacy.

"Oh, my," Penelope whispered.

Tony encircled her waist and pulled her back against him. "What do you say," he said, nibbling on her ear and working the buttons on her blouse at the same time, "we feast on one another, then play in the tub?"

Penelope swallowed. There was no point in losing her sense of adventure now. Tony kissed the back of her neck and freed her hair.

The expression *carpe diem* flitted across her mind. Seize the day, indeed! Slowly she turned so they were standing face-to-face. She traced the path of his mouth with her little finger, then, in slow motion, unfastened the rest of the buttons of her blouse as Tony watched appreciatively. In a sultry voice she never imagined she'd hear from her own mouth, she said, "What do you say we play in the tub first?"

"Whatever you say." Tony slipped her jacket from her arms and her blouse came off with it. She kicked off her sensible pumps then worked off his shirt and jacket as they moved together toward the tub. He turned the faucets on, then shimmied her free of her skirt and pantyhose.

Wearing only her underwear, Penelope stood shyly in front of Tony. Still half-dressed, Tony scooped her up in his arms and sat on the edge of the bed, holding her. "Repeat after me," he whispered. "I, Penelope . . ."

"What are we doing?"

"Shh, trust me," Tony said. "I, Penelope . . ."

With a smile, she said, "I, Penelope . . ."

". . . am the most beautiful woman . . ."

". . . am the most beautiful—stop, Tony! Mrs. Merlin is already lecturing me over my ego."

"You have a talking cat? Never mind. Just try the words and see how they feel." He freed the catch of her bra and nuzzled his lips to her breasts.

". . . I am the most beautiful woman . . ." Penelope caught her breath as Tony suckled her nipple. She parted her lips, and her breath finally released itself in a gaspy moan.

"Oh, yeah," Tony whispered, "the most beautiful woman in the world."

". . . in the world," Penelope repeated as Tony lowered her to the bed, stripped off the rest of his clothing, and managed to make her panties disappear all in what seemed like one smooth motion.

The water spilling into the tub nearby provided accompaniment as Tony's kisses made her body sing. Penelope gasped and flung her hands above her head as Tony stoked a path of fire in her body with his kisses. His tongue, warm and wet and greedy, was everywhere. On her breasts, her nipples, her throat, her eyelids. Then, as the passion built within her, he moved lower, to the heat between her legs.

"Tony!" she cried out as he kissed the inside of her thighs, then traced a path closer and closer to the most intimate spot of her body.

"Yes, my lucky penny?" He lifted his head and gazed at her with eyes dark and stormy with desire. With the palm of his hand, he covered her mound and trailed a gentle finger beneath the curly hair to part her inner lips. Teasing, probing, stroking, he created the sweetest and yet in some ways the most frightening sensations she'd ever experienced.

She called his name again. He paused. In a serious voice, he said, "If you change your mind, you only have to tell me."

"Oh, no," she said in a breathless voice. "Don't stop. Not now! I feel as if I'm about to lose total control of my senses and you know"— she heard the wonder in her own voice—"that's truly a beautiful thing."

He smiled and lowered his mouth to where his hand had been. She trembled with desire as his mouth imitated his fingers.

Tony slowly trailed off his kisses, then slid onto the bed alongside her and took her in his arms. "Perhaps we'll leave that adventure for another day," he murmured.

"Whatever you say," she said, caught between a desire for him to continue kissing her in exactly the way he had been, and the need to answer the insistent hunger claiming her body.

"I don't usually carry condoms to lunch," Tony said, nibbling on her ear, then reaching down to the floor where he'd dropped his trousers, "but I knew today we had to be together." He laid a packet on the bed beside them. Lifting up on one arm, he said, "Something came over me today, Penelope, and no matter what, I had to be with you. God forgive me if I'm doing the wrong thing."

She smiled up at him, reveling in being wanted by the man she craved. "It's the right thing," she said softly.

"Yes!" Tony ripped open the condom packet and worked it on himself. Penelope must have stared, because Tony grinned and lifted her hand to assist him. Feeling very bold, she watched their joined hands, trying not to think how he would ever fit inside her.

The protection in place, Tony eased over her. "You know it can hurt a little at first, but I promise you I'll make that up to you. In a hundred ways, a thousand ways."

She nodded and wrapped her arms around him.

He moved slowly, entering her only enough that she felt the size of him.

She widened her eyes. "Oh, my," she said.

Tony lowered his head, captured her lips, and began to move in a slow and sensuous dance in, then out a bit, then more deeply into her body.

Penelope cried out against his lips and arched her back, urging him inward. He accepted the invitation, entering her in a swift movement that registered momentarily as pain, then quickly transformed to more marvelous sensations as he thrust in and out, creating spirals of pleasure that she gave herself up to.

As their joined bodies moved as one, Penelope lost all sense of time and place. She knew only Tony, his mouth on hers, his hands caressing her face, her hair, her breasts as he brought her ever so slowly but surely to a peak of passion.

"Tony," she cried out, amazed at the shimmering waves overtaking her body and seeming to flow out from some magical place within her.

He thrust more quickly, his eyes closed now, his hands around her shoulders in a fierce grip. Faster and faster he moved, and then as his body shuddered, he called out her name and dropped to the bed beside her.

"Sweet, sweet, Penelope," he murmured, cradling her against his chest. "Did I hurt you?"

She smiled and snuggled more closely. "You gave me only pleasure," she said.

Her senses returning somewhat to normal, Penelope realized the water still gushed into the tub. She turned her head lazily to look, just in time to see the water lapping at the edge of the huge tub. "Tony, the water!"

He dashed for the spigots and stopped the water before it spilled over the sides. Then he walked back to the bed, gazed down at her, and said, "How about a bubble bath?"

An hour later, Penelope lay on her side on the bed, sated from their second lovemaking. Tony had just slipped off the bed and was collecting their clothing. Turning to him, she smiled and said, "Thank you for the most wonderful lunch I've ever had."

He winked, and started pulling on his clothes. "Sorry to eat and run, but duty calls."

"Oh," Penelope said, sitting up. Something about the abrupt way he was dressing made her nervous. "We haven't eaten yet."

"No time. I'll tell Lucien to send something up for you."

"I don't want to eat by myself." Penelope rose from the bed, feeling very naked. She found her underwear and she, too, began dressing. "Not in a room this romantic."

"Romantic?" Tony shrugged into his jacket. "Hey, babe, it was a nooner. That's all. Nothing more. Nothing less."

He couldn't have wounded her more harshly had he tried. Penelope jerked her head as if she'd been slapped. Not even a one-night stand, simply a nooner. She turned her back on him and struggled into her clothing, tears welling in her eyes, tears she refused to let him see.

"Penelope—"

"Don't say another word. Not one word!" Penelope grabbed her jacket and her purse and, without looking at Tony, stormed to the sitting room, out the door, and down the steps.

Halfway to the front entrance, she heard Tony behind her. Lucien stopped him and she heard the older man say, "Tony-O, tell me you didn't mess this one up."

She didn't wait to hear his response. Instead, she hurried back to the office and threw herself into work, unable to meet the questions and concern she saw in Jewel's eyes.

Precisely at eleven minutes after eleven, Penelope rose from the rug on her living room floor, stretched, then crossed to the table where the altar lay waiting. She'd informed Mrs. Merlin earlier that she was taking no chances and had allowed almost an hour to find her place of peace.

After the day's roller-coaster ride in which she'd gone from the heights of passion to the depths of rejection, Penelope didn't trust the spell to work without extra time to cleanse the hurt from her mind.

Mrs. Merlin studied her from her post on the altar. "You've been awfully quiet tonight. Before I go, I want you to know that if you want something badly enough, you can usually get it."

Penelope gazed into the eyes of the woman who'd become her friend, seeking wisdom she knew she herself lacked. With a faint shrug, she took the incense stick, lit it at the stove, and hesitated before touching it to the wick.

"When it comes to love, don't both people have to want the same thing?"

"What makes you think that's not the case?"

Penelope tossed her head back. "I don't have to look up *rejection* in the dictionary in order to define it."

"Don't go all egotistical on me before you do this spell." Mrs. Merlin sighed. "I'm too hungry to remain a bookmark any longer."

"I'm so sorry," Penelope said. "It's selfish of me to be thinking of my problems when you're in this condition. And you said it's only okay to be selfish if it doesn't harm anyone else."

"True."

Penelope let her hand hover between the dancing flame of the white candle and the silent wick of the cherry-red candle. She took a deep breath, then lit it, too. She wanted Tony, and she knew in her heart he wanted her, too. She might be an innocent, but she didn't believe he'd only been toying with her affections when they'd made love. Perhaps he was afraid. Whatever his reasons, she'd win him back.

"You're doing better," Mrs. Merlin said. "Your aura just sparked with white energy."

Penelope smiled. "Good. Let's do this spell."

They repeated the words they had uttered to no effect the evening before. Mrs. Merlin swayed, almost in time to the dancing of the white candle's flame.

Without warning, the bookmark shape of her new friend burst into flames. The last sight Penelope had of Mrs. Merlin and her altar of candles was fire arcing from the figure of Mrs. Merlin to the white candle, then burning down the wick of the cherry-red candle.

Then Penelope felt herself hurtled back, back, back through darkness, a darkness ever so gradually illuminated by pinpricks of distant stars and the faint glow of a moon on the rise.

"Well, thank the stars," Mrs. Merlin said, opening her eyes to find herself standing in her very own kitchen in her very own house in her very own corner of the city.

She moved her arms, her legs, swiveled her neck, checked her height against the edge of her kitchen sink. Her hip came right to where it should and she smiled in relief. She had to hand it to Penelope. For all her desire to stick to the rational and logical, the lady lawyer had come through on the all-important spell necessary to give Mrs. Merlin back her shape.

"Not only my pudgy body," Mrs. Merlin murmured, "my life!"

Glancing around the room, she saw that most everything remained exactly as she'd left it. Her neighbor Ramona knew better than to disturb an altar with a spell in progress, but she had kindly washed up the cups they'd used for tea before Mrs. Merlin had undertaken her well-intentioned magick to rid her neighbor of that pesky tax collector.

Her cat's food and water bowl had been filled, fairly recently, too, Mrs. Merlin concluded, judging by the untouched state of the dry food favored by her orange tom. She bustled out of the kitchen toward the front of the house, calling his name.

Having outlived three husbands, Mrs. Merlin got quite a kick out of having added the "Mr." to her cat's name, whom she'd named "M" due to the pronounced white M shape defining the area above and between his golden yellow eyes.

Her neighbors thought her daft, but then, they always had.

"Here, Mr. M," she called, "be a good kitty and welcome me home. My, but I've had such adventures. And made a new friend, too." She'd have to call Penelope up and invite her over for a cup of tea.

That reminded Mrs. Merlin of the grumblings of her empty tummy and she forgot all about finding Mr. M as she hustled back to the kitchen and foraged in the freezer for some jambalaya she'd put up only last week.

She set it to thaw in the microwave, then went to change her dress. She'd worn the same caftan for more days than she cared to count. Tossing it to the floor of her bedroom, Mrs. Merlin stretched her arms over her head, slipped into fresh underthings, and selected her very favorite caftan from her closet.

Purple, she thought, suited her best. She ran a brush over her bright hair, thinking it was about time to try another one of those rinses. She might be a grandmother, but she didn't have to look like one.

Pleased with herself, happy to be home, she called again for Mr. M. When she still got no response, she figured he was sulking. He did that when she left him alone in the house for more than a day. Mr. M liked nothing better than to be the center of her world; second to that, he used to love to do battle with every cat in the neighborhood, but once he'd come to live with her, she'd put an end to that.

He lived inside, safe from the dangers of the streets.

She heard the microwave beep and headed back to the kitchen. As she passed by the table where she'd erected the altar for her neighbor, a silvery glint caught her eye.

She paused, struck by something she'd never considered during her stay at Penelope's. Mrs. Merlin rarely used the kitchen table for the practice of candle magick. She'd done so that ill-fated morning partly out of laziness, as she was so comfortable drinking tea and chatting.

Then, at Penelope's, she'd again used what Penelope called her dining table—the only table in the apartment. Mrs. Merlin frowned and bent for a closer look at the metallic reflection that had caught her eye.

What she saw caused her to clasp her hand to her throat.

"Poor Mr. M," she said, staring at the silver ID tag attached to the purple collar he always wore. The collar lay wound around the base of the candle she'd used for Ramona's spell. Stuck to the collar was the thick black hair belonging to Tony Olano she'd added to the altar back at Penelope's apartment in an effort to help the woman who'd assisted her. And even more ominous, Penelope's shoes sat next to the hair. Mrs. Merlin stared at that and nervously licked her lips. That hair had followed her home, her cat was missing, and the goddess only knew what might have happened to Penelope.

The tag, engraved with RETURN TO MRS. MERLIN plus her phone number, had been meant to protect him, but now here it was and her kitty was the stars only knew where.

Had he been shrunk? Or flattened? Or worse?

Then the thought hit her full force and she forgot all about her jambalaya.

There were no coincidences in candle magick. Mr. Gotho had told her that over and over again. She could see the wise but bothersome man shaking his head over this mix-up. Because mix-up it no doubt was, a confabulation that no doubt had resulted in trouble for the very woman who'd helped Mrs. Merlin find her way home.

Sinking to a chair, Mrs. Merlin fingered the tag on her cat's collar, knowing in her heart that wherever she found Mr. M, she'd find Penelope and Tony Olano, too.

"Oh, dear," she said. "What a muddle. I just hope they haven't gotten their bodies crossed. That might be more than even I could undo. And I just know Mr. Gotho won't help me out of this pickle."

She brightened as she remembered the jar of bread and butter pickles in her refrigerator. Perhaps she would eat first. She worked so much better on a full stomach. Why, if she hadn't been flattened and starved, surely this mix-up never would have happened!

"What do you mean, you don't know where she is?" Senior partner Hubert H. Klees towered over Jewel, beetling his brows and wringing his hands.

"She . . . uh, had to take care of some business outside of the office today, but I'm not sure where she is right at this moment." There, Jewel thought, that bluff should do the trick. She was far too loyal an assistant to say she'd not heard from Penelope all day, that no one had answered the phone the twenty times she'd rung her apartment, and that she, Jewel, was starting to worry and about to call her brother the cop to ask for advice.

"Well, you tell her the minute you hear from her that I want her in my office ASAP." Hubert glared and strode off, trying to look like a man in control. Jewel had seen Mr. Fitzsimmons stroll into the office in his quiet yet commanding way half an hour ago, so she knew why Hubert was sweating it.

He wanted Penelope to appear and charm the guy again. Or maybe he wanted her to solve his tax problems. Jewel glanced down at the memo Penelope had left her to type, a memo that detailed quite a brilliant solution to Fitzsimmons's dilemma.

She could have offered it to Hubert, but she'd worked in the legal world far too long to have done anything so naive. With Penelope missing from the office, Hubert quite likely would have taken the credit and felt quite justified in doing so. No, if Penelope didn't appear soon, Jewel would find a way of getting the memo to Fitzsimmons. Under Penelope's signature, of course.

Chapter 22

It was all too weird, Penelope thought, watching the sidewalk bob from her vantage point inside the ear of a fat and rather cantankerous yellow cat, a cat she'd be willing to bet belonged to Mrs. Merlin.

Trust the mistress of magickal mishaps to own a cat with an attitude.

Penelope figured she must have lost hours in some magickal time warp, because the afternoon sun beat down bright and hot on the sidewalk in front of the shotgun house where the cat had paused.

When she'd last been herself, the clock had been sweeping past midnight. Penelope shook her head and clung to the inside of the yellow cat's ear. Honestly, to have been reduced to the size of a flea was more of an insult to her ego than she could handle!

But even as that thought crossed her mind, she banished it. Thinking of Mr. Gotho and whatever lesson he'd been trying to impress upon her, she somehow knew this was not the right moment to be demanding of the universe a different set of circumstances for something so minor as her ego.

No, right now she needed her wits about her, sans any distractions of pride, hubris, or whatever the bearded magician might have termed it.

She hoped she hadn't imagined seeing Tony only a few minutes earlier walk out onto the porch of the house the cat had chosen to visit. She hoped she hadn't merely fallen into one of her fantasies. But from her perspective, obscured as it was by the wavy hairs lining the cat's ear, she couldn't be sure.

Or could she?

Penelope sighed. She knew in her heart she'd recognize the man with bedroom eyes even if she were blindfolded. And hadn't Mrs. Merlin insisted there were no coincidences in candle magick? As surely as Penelope had been thrust loose from her usual realm, she had in a miraculous fashion landed close to help.

In a cat's ear, she reminded herself, feeling another sweeping wave of indignation. All she'd tried to do was help Mrs. Merlin back to normal, and look what she'd gotten for her troubles!

The cat must have turned its head rapidly, because Penelope felt herself tipping and sliding in a way that totally disoriented her. Then she experienced hurtling through a vast darkness, exactly the way she had last night during the candle spell.

The sensation lasted only a few moments, but whatever event had occurred, when things settled once again, she could now see the man on the porch ever so clearly. No more peering around fuzzy hairs inside a cat's ear.

She caught her breath at the sight of him.

The wiry legs, muscle and sinew, were all Tony. He wore shorts, his usual uniform, it seemed, but these were much briefer than those she'd seen him wear before, treating Penelope to a mouthwatering view of sculpted, muscular thighs disappearing from her appreciative view under flimsy nylon shorts.

"Go on up to the porch," she urged the cat. She didn't know how she would accomplish it, but she knew she had to have Tony's help to undo Mrs. Merlin's spurious spell.

The cat didn't budge.

She'd spoken to it earlier and it had in some way acknowledged her, either through gesture or kitty language. But now the cat stood on all fours, for all intents and purposes, frozen.

Penelope looked upward. Tony lowered his body to the top step of the porch. Funny how she could see so clearly now, as if she were looking straight at him from her own eyes. . . .

The thought she'd been about to think lodged in her mind. No longer was she looking through the fine hairs inside the cat's ear. It's only a test, she told herself, willing her mind to command one of the cat's front paws to move.

Even as she directed the paw, she glanced down and saw that the cat's foot was indeed moving forward. Now the right one, she said, and watched as she moved closer to the porch.

"Wingtips and whiskers," she breathed.

She'd become the cat!

Across town, in the heart of the French Quarter, the telephone rang in the back section of the Bayou Magick Shoppe.

About to leave for his daily workout at the New Orleans Athletic Club, Alistair Gotho glanced toward the front of the shop to see whether his assistant would reach for the phone. Three customers crowded the counter; the phone continued to peal. Without setting down his gym bag, he reached for the phone to put the caller on hold for his helper.

As he did, he noticed the light flashing on the second line, indicating whoever was calling had dialed his unlisted number.

With a sigh, he lifted the receiver. "Gotho speaking."

"Now, I know you told me you were washing your hands of me, but it really, really would be unfair to Penelope to write me off just now, so don't hang up. Please. I knew Mr. M was somehow crossed with Penelope and I was only trying to straighten things out, but I have a terrible feeling I've really made things worse now!" Mrs. Merlin's voice rushed over the phone line, sweeping into his ears and taking over like an unwanted relative come to stay for an extended visit.

"Ah, Mrs. Merlin, how are you?"

"How can you ask such a question? After what I've just told you! Could things be any worse?"

Alistair dropped his gym bag on the floor, settled into the chair behind the counter, and lifted a hand exerciser he kept for moments like these. Knowing Mrs. Merlin, that would be the extent of his day's workout.

"Perhaps, perhaps not," he said. "For instance, are you back to your usual size?"

"Thank the stars, yes."

"You're welcome," Alistair murmured, thinking of the supplies he'd bundled up to help her out of her miscast spell, but the comment was lost on Mrs. Merlin. "So am I to understand that you have not stuck to your word to practice only the simplest of candle magick's applications?" He didn't know why he wasted his breath asking that question; clearly she had called for yet another rescue operation.

"Well . . ."

"Yes?" He tried to sound stern, but pulling that trick with someone the same age as his own grandmother was pretty hard for him to do.

"Not exactly. But I meant well."

Alistair swapped hands with the phone and the exerciser. "Let's try to get to the point, then, hmmm?"

She laughed, a nervous sound that hummed along the phone line like a rattler gathering itself to strike. "If only I could! But I don't even know what's happened to Penelope. She helped me get back to myself, and then, well, Mr. Gotho, you may find this hard to believe—"

"Try me." From Mrs. Merlin, he'd believe almost anything.

"Hold your horses. I'm telling this story. As I was saying, you may find this hard to believe, but once I was back home safe and sound and back to size, and shape, thank you very much, my cat had disappeared."

Alistair nodded. The cat easily could have run off. He glanced longingly at his gym bag, only to be snapped back to attention when Mrs. Merlin spoke again.

"Yet his collar was wrapped around the candle on my altar."

"Any idea where he might be?"

"None. But I must find him."

"Anything else?" He asked, to give himself time to think as much as out of curiosity.

"Well, there is one more little problem."

He should have known. He waited for her to make a clean breast of the mix-up.

"Penelope's shoes are here, too, next to the collar."

"The ones she wore when she assisted you with your return-to-body spell?"

Silence answered him. He waited, then finally repeated his question.

"What's-a-matter? Couldn't you see me nodding?"

Alistair shook his head. "Can you see that?"

"Of course not, but you have powers I can't begin to imagine ever possessing."

"And you'll never even come close if you keep confusing the heavens and clouding your karma." That time he did manage a tone of severity. "You know you've endangered an innocent woman and an innocent feline by your hurly-scurly rush into spells you've no business attempting."

"Oh, I know, Mr. Gotho!" Her voice wailed at him over the line. "And I promise, if you help me correct this one, I'll never ever do it again."

He didn't even ask her to swear to that promise on the nose of the goddess. He'd only be wasting his breath.

He was about to speak when she came out

with, "There is one other little detail I'd be remiss not to clarify."

"Remiss?" Alistair wondered where this
grandmother from Gentilly had acquired her vo-
cabulary. Better not to ask, though. "And what
is that?"

"I didn't just try once to unmix things—"

"You didn't perform two spells!" Alistair
slapped his forehead. Mrs. Merlin had really
done it this time.

"I do remember you said that once a spell
goes awry, it's best not to tinker with it, but I
did think surely I could get Mr. M back."

"I think," Alistair said, trying not to grind his
teeth, "I'd better come straight over."

"Oh, would you do that?" Mrs. Merlin's voice
perked right up. "I'll set out some bread pud-
ding I just happen to have in the freezer and put
on a pot of coffee."

Alistair shook his head, then said, "Why don't
you do that?" Anything to keep the woman from
lighting another candle. "I'll be right over."

Tony figured he must have passed the cat's
safety inspection, because suddenly the large
orange feline quit hanging back and walked
straight toward the porch. Tony had always
liked cats, but since his old tom Bruno died last
year, and Kathy had moved out with the two
kittens, he hadn't adopted another one.

"You lost or just new to the neighborhood?"
Tony asked in a low voice, gently reaching a
hand out to the cat. "Hey, you look just like
Bruno."

The cat halted on the step beside his feet, then lifted its head up.

Tony stared at the cat's eyes. They were the most amazing blue, deep and glowing. The cat meowed and Tony stroked it lightly on the top of its head. It seemed to like that as it moved closer and rubbed against his leg.

He'd never seen eyes that color on a cat. The cobalt blue was the same shade as Penelope's eyes, and they were unusually rare and beautiful even in a human. Stroking the cat's head and back gently, he propped his chin on the other hand and wondered what she was doing.

Probably at work, too busy to think of Tony Olano, the man who'd stolen her virginity and then pushed her away. He'd been on his way back to the corner basketball court to work out his frustrations.

To his surprise, the cat hopped onto his lap.

"Friendly, aren't you?" Smoothing his hand over the cat's silky fur, Tony couldn't help but think of Penelope's satiny skin, and of the way she'd purred under his touch when they'd made love.

He'd seen the hint of fire in her eyes, sensed that under her starchy exterior lay a woman of passion, and yesterday's lovemaking had only confirmed that. How she had remained a virgin as long as she had, he couldn't understand. Were the other men she'd met blind?

"Meowwwwww." The cat cried plaintively and butted its head against his hand.

Tony realized his hand had stopped. "Greedy little thing, aren't you?" His hand went back to petting the cat, his mind to picturing Penelope.

Trouble was, the more he thought of her, the more excited he got. He found it hard to believe he'd actually mustered the will to stop that night at the cottage. And to have been so cruel to her yesterday.

The cat had started purring and kneading its paws just above Tony's knees. Fortunately the cat didn't have front claws.

Tony ran one finger under the cat's jaw, scratching the narrow edge of its chin, remembering Hinson saying that Penelope was to be his wife. Did she intend to marry Hinson? His hand stilled as an alarming idea came to him. Had Penelope lied? Was she playing some game with him and Hinson, the way she played at shoplifting?

The cat stopped its paw massage and turned its head to look at him.

Staring into those blue eyes, eyes so weirdly similar to Penelope's, Tony almost felt like the cat was trying to answer his question.

"So she's innocent? That's your vote?"

The cat meowed and ran its tongue over his finger. The soft, sandpapery effect tickled slightly and made Tony wish he was holding Penelope on his lap and lapping at her body in exactly the same way.

He'd start with her ear, circling the incredibly soft skin of her lobe, then dart in with his tongue, just enough to tease her into one of those gaspy moans she'd made so often yesterday.

The cat settled onto his lap, purring loudly. At least someone was getting some satisfaction, he thought, shifting his position on the porch, aching to feel Penelope beneath him.

Stroking under its chin, he realized that buried in the fuzzy fur was a delicate silver chain circling the cat's neck. Gently, he worked it around to see if it held an identification tag. As tame and friendly as the cat was to Tony, a complete stranger, this animal surely belonged to someone and had merely strayed from home.

"Not that I wouldn't mind keeping you, kitty," Tony murmured, as he turned over a miniature silver oval.

Fine prickles ran up the back of his neck as he stared at the engraved P on the silver pendant, a pendant exactly like the one Penelope wore.

"I hope you realize how terribly complicated it is to undo things when you've created this degree of transmutation," Alistair Gotho said in a stern voice as he held open the door to the Vieux Carré District police station for Mrs. Merlin.

"There's no need to lecture," Mrs. Merlin replied, pausing to close the purple umbrella she carried as a sunshade.

"No, I suppose not," he murmured, knowing full well that even though she claimed to listen to his advice, she always acted on the impulse of the moment.

A group of tourists in shorts and T-shirts emblazoned with French Quarter motifs trundled out the open door of the station, which also served as a clearinghouse for tourist information.

By the time they passed, Mrs. Merlin had her umbrella under control and the two of them entered, Mrs. Merlin muttering under her breath what sounded like, "We've got to hurry."

She'd insisted they go straight to the police station nearby on Royal Street to locate Tony Olano, saying she felt it in her bones that it was the thing to do. Find this man Tony and we'll find Mr. M and Penelope, Mrs. Merlin had informed him, pretty much all in one breath.

Alistair favored a more studied approach to the issue. He failed to see why the confusions in Mrs. Merlin's spell should necessarily involve Olano. But, despite Mrs. Merlin's habit of getting herself into magickal jams, she had an unerring sixth sense about certain essences.

So he'd followed along; once they had the necessary data, someone had to perform the spell of retroactivity.

Someone who was qualified.

Out of a well-developed instinct to expect the unexpected where Mrs. Merlin was concerned, before he'd left his shop, Alistair had grabbed his portable magick kit that he kept packed for emergencies.

"What do you mean you've never heard of Anthony Olano?" Mrs. Merlin was waving her folded umbrella like a baton at the potbellied officer kicked back behind the reception desk.

The man hooked his thumbs in his gun belt. "He used to be a cop."

"Aha!" She stabbed the air. "And you said you'd never heard of him. Caught you on that one. Now, be a good boy and tell me how to find him. It's a matter of life and death."

He lifted his eyebrows. Clearly he thought Mrs. Merlin another variation on Ruthie the

Duck Lady, a Quarter eccentric who locals routinely made excuses for and tourists fed quarters to.

"Don't make me call a lawyer. The only one I know is . . ." she stumbled, then came up with, "Hinson. And you don't want him after you."

The officer eyed her sourly, not reacting either to the name or the threat. "If you're looking for someone, why not try the phone book?"

Alistair's thoughts exactly. He stepped forward. "Thank you, officer," he said, then placed a hand lightly on Mrs. Merlin's elbow. "Why don't we—"

She smacked him across the knuckles, thankfully with her hand and not with the umbrella. Glaring up at him, she said in the same voice his grandmother used to use when she caught him scraping pralines off the waxed paper before they were set, "Don't be impertinent. When I've gotten what I've come for, then I'll leave."

Alistair dropped his hand. The officer grinned, then wiped that grin from his face as she turned back to him.

Just then, another officer, half the age and a third of the girth of the guy behind the desk, approached from the back of the room. Ignoring the potbellied officer, he said, "Let me get this straight. The two of you are looking for Olano *and* Hinson?"

Something in the way the officer combined the two names set Alistair on alert, though he had no idea what role Hinson played in Mrs. Merlin's mix-up, if any.

Mrs. Merlin stared at the officer and nodded. "That's close enough," she said.

The officer opened the wooden half-door leading to the back of the station. "I think you should come in the back with me. I'll see what I can find out for you."

"Well, thank the stars!" Mrs. Merlin peered at the man's name tag. "Steve, is it?" She swept past the potbellied man, pausing only long enough to show him her nose in the air.

The guy didn't look too impressed. He did scratch his head and point to the sign that said AUTHORIZED PERSONNEL OR PRISONERS ONLY BEYOND THIS POINT, and stared oddly at Steve, which added to Alistair's impression that Mrs. Merlin might have thanked the stars prematurely.

Chapter 23

Penelope had followed Tony into his house and now sat on all fours, watching with interest as he started pulling pots and pans from the cupboard and various items from the refrigerator.

The way he collected things on the counter, then studied them, reminded her of her own cooking style. Finding this compatible trait in the man with bedroom eyes pleased her enormously.

Discovering that he knew his way around a kitchen had been her first pleasant surprise. The room was small, of less size than her apartment's kitchen, but cheery. Penelope swiveled her head around, taking in the white walls, green and white curtains, the white eat-in table with two chairs, both covered in cushions that matched the window coverings.

To get to the kitchen, she'd followed Tony down a narrow hallway to the back of the house. Along the way, she'd gotten the tiniest peek into the rooms leading off the hallway. Living room, bedroom, and bath, she'd decided. Small but cozy.

Penelope longed to explore each room. Watching Tony chopping Roma tomatoes, she wondered if her curiosity had increased since she'd taken on the shape and substance of a cat, or whether her curiosity arose from being secretly in Tony's home, free to explore whatever her heart desired.

What a way to get to know a man, Penelope mused, licking one front paw and considering the possibilities. Perhaps Mrs. Merlin had been trying to help her and had whipped up this spell on purpose.

No, that reasoning didn't fly. Penelope shook her head. But as long as she was here, she might as well make the most of it. Adventure, here I come, she thought, and crossed the floor to Tony.

Butting her chin gently against his muscular leg, she instinctively left her scent on him.

Tony lay down his knife. "Trying to tell me you're hungry?"

Penelope blinked. Much more interested in Tony, she hadn't considered food. But now that he mentioned it . . . she meowed politely.

He leaned down and stroked the top of her head with the back of his hand.

Beginning to purr, Penelope wound between his legs, loving the feel of his touch against her body.

"I don't have any cat food, but maybe some shrimp will do."

Thank goodness for small favors, Penelope thought, sitting back on her haunches and watching Tony dig in the refrigerator again. Cat food! She sure hoped Mrs. Merlin rescued her before Tony thought to run to the corner market and pick up a can of 9 Lives.

She laughed as she thought of Mrs. Merlin complaining about having to eat oatmeal. The noise came out sounding like a hiccupy meow.

"Okay, okay," Tony said. "Demanding little pussy, aren't you?"

What had he said? Penelope's eyes widened, then she reminded herself Tony was talking to a feline.

He cleaned and chopped several shrimp and placed them on a saucer for her. He put it down on the floor and Penelope stared at it, perplexed. No way could she eat standing up, with the saucer at floor level.

She meowed, plaintively this time, and Tony turned back from his chopping. Penelope jumped to one of the chairs at the white table and waited, one paw pointing to a placemat.

"Are you nuts?" Tony shook his head.

She waited.

"You're one spoiled cat," he said, lifting the saucer from the floor and depositing it on the table. "But you are kind of cute."

She thanked him with a meow and nibbled at the shrimp. It tasted like sushi without the rice. She wouldn't have minded some light soy sauce, but as she couldn't think of any way to communicate that preference, she ate the shrimp plain.

One thing was certain, Penelope thought after she'd finished her meal and had sat back on the chair to wash her face with a front paw: She appreciated a cat's point of view much more than she ever had. After she got out of this Mrs.

Merlin–inspired mishap, she might just adopt a cat.

Tony had moved to stewing the tomatoes along with fresh garlic, bell pepper, and onions. Penelope sniffed the air appreciatively. An image of the two of them, happily cooking side by side, entered her mind and she swabbed her face even faster.

He stirred the mixture, then walked over to the chair. "So you want to stay here with me?"

Penelope slowed her ablutions, then lowered her paw. Fixing her eyes on his face, she lifted her body so that her front paws rested on his chest.

With a smile, he picked her up and scratched her under the chin. "I think I'll call you Penny," he said. "In honor of the sweetest and sexiest woman I've ever known."

Penelope purred, even more loudly than before.

"So you're an old friend of Olano's?" Steve asked, scribbling on a notepad.

"Oh, I've known him for ages," Mrs. Merlin said, fluttering her hand. "But I've lost his address, you see, and my memory not being what it used to be, well . . ."

"Of course. And you, Mr. . . . ?"

"Never met the man," Alistair said, unable to understand why the officer appeared to have settled in for a lengthy discussion with them, and even less sure why Mrs. Merlin seemed so rattled. Did she also distrust the way the officer had taken charge when he'd heard who they were seeking? Of course, it was hard to know with Mrs. Merlin. It would be just like her to have left out a few pertinent details when she explained matters to him.

Just then the door opened and another officer peered in. "What's happening, Steve?" he asked, barely covering a yawn.

Steve shrugged. "Performing a little community service."

The newcomer raised his brows. "Is that so?" He leaned against the doorframe, crossed his arms over his chest, and said, "Maybe I'll help and earn some points with the chief, too."

Steve looked as if he were going to object, but Mrs. Merlin piped in with, "Oh, thank you, Officer. Two heads are always better than one. Well, depending on which two, of course. All we're trying to do is find Tony Olano."

"Is that so?" The man glanced from them to Steve, apparently about as interested in Olano as the man in the moon.

"We want to know about Tony, but he wants to know about Hinson."

The second officer studied his fingernails. "Well, don't let me stop you."

Beginning to look annoyed at the interruptions, Steve said, "And you were telling me you're also acquainted with David Hinson?" The officer twirled his pen in his hands.

"Well, sort of," Mrs. Merlin said, beginning to fiddle with the umbrella she held across her lap.

The man threw his pen down, suddenly not nearly so friendly. "Unless I know you're telling me the truth, I'm not going to tell you how to find Olano."

Mrs. Merlin jumped. "My, my, no need to get testy."

"So prove to me you know Hinson."

Alistair held his breath, wondering whether the endearing but ditsy woman had picked the name off the top of her head. To him it sounded vaguely familiar, but he didn't know why. Waiting for her response along with the officer, Alistair thought longingly of the workout and massage he was missing at the club. Why was it anything Mrs. Merlin got involved in always seem to get overly complicated and confused?

A crafty look came into her eyes. "How would I know he's asked someone to marry him if I didn't know him?"

The officer sat up straighter, retrieved his pen. "Prove that."

"Well, he gave a friend of mine a rock to die for. One of those big stones with pointy ends. Only the other night, too."

The officer in the doorway, looking bored, wagged a hand at Steve. "Looks like you've got this under control. Catch you later."

"Sure, Roy."

When he strolled off, the officer left the door wide open.

Alistair realized Mrs. Merlin's story about the fiancée must refer to Penelope, the woman caught in Mrs. Merlin's miscast spell. Her boyfriend must be going nuts worrying about her.

"So you know Hinson's girlfriend." He appeared to chew over that matter.

"Oh, I wouldn't call her his girlfriend," Mrs. Merlin said, making a face of distaste. "She's got far too much good sense to accept the ring. Why,

I know for a fact—well, maybe not a fact exactly, but I feel it in my bones, which is as good as a fact—that she's in love with someone else."

"Mrs. Merlin," Alistair interrupted, "I don't think this officer wants to know any more."

"I'll be the judge of that." He chewed on the end of the pen, an expression creeping into his eyes that set Alistair's nerves on edge. "As a matter of fact, I'd love to know who the lucky guy is who's cutting out Hinson." He winked, suddenly all good-old-boy again. "He's a buddy of mine, and I'd like to rib him over it, you understand."

"That's not my idea of any way to treat your friend," Mrs. Merlin said severely. "I'm not sure I should tell you."

Alistair wasn't sure she should, either. He lifted the duffel bag of magick supplies he'd set on the floor. He wasn't getting any sense of it being safe to trust this guy, plus he wanted out of there.

The officer shrugged. "Have it your way," he said, rising from his chair and heading for the door.

Mrs. Merlin stood, too. "But you haven't told me how to find Tony!"

The policeman shrugged. "Tit for tat," he said, "or not at all."

She pushed her glasses down on her nose and glared at him above the rims. "Any three-year-old could have figured it out from this discussion, but if you must have the answer, I'll tell you."

And suddenly Alistair realized what she was about to say, should have seen it coming.

"It's Tony, of course," she said. "Why would someone take up with a man like Hinson when she can have the man with bedroom eyes?"

"Wait right here," the officer said, and walked rapidly from the room.

To Alistair's amazement, the door slammed shut and he heard the lock click into place behind the cop named Steve.

Tony had just dumped the spaghetti into boiling water when a knock sounded at the door. Since he'd been at home during the day for much of the past several months, his neighbors had taken to asking the mailman to leave packages with him. As it was about time for the mail, Tony stirred his noodles, then headed quickly for the front of the house.

The cat had settled for a nap on the sofa, but when he walked past the living room it lifted its head, fixing those eyes, so eerily like Penelope's, on Tony. She stretched, leaped down from the couch, and padded after Tony.

Out of habit, Tony glanced through the security peephole and stepped to the side.

No friendly postal worker faced him from the other side of his door; rather, one of Rolo Polo's flunkies stood there, trimming a thumbnail with a pocketknife.

Tony grimaced. Just when a man had dinner ready, duty called.

He cracked open the door and slouched against it, looking his inquiry at his caller.

"Boss says he wants to talk to you." The man slipped his knife into the pocket of a pair of baggy silk trousers.

Tony took in the guy's outfit, from the trousers to the floppy silk shirt, lizardskin shoes and Ray-Ban sunglasses. "You been watching those *Miami Vice* reruns?"

"What's it to you?" He jerked his head toward the long black car parked at the curb. "Rolo Polo's waiting."

And so was Tony's boiling pasta.

Leaving the door open behind him, Tony strolled out onto his porch. He had a reputation as a troublemaker and if he acted any differently with his new employer it would only cause suspicion.

He'd been informed via a phone call from the department earlier that morning that he'd been recommended for a reinstatement hearing, which had been set for next week.

So he guessed the organization wanted to test him out, see whether they'd be getting their money's worth.

The overdressed henchman went through his gate first, approached the car, and tapped on the driver's window. It powered smoothly down to reveal Rolo Polo chewing on yet another unlit cigar.

"Rolo, where y'at?" Tony said, making a point of leaning on the car, leaving a nice array of fingerprints.

The fat man lowered his cigar and patted his gut. "Could be worse." He winked. "Found me a new woman who made me feel like I ain't never felt before. Cost me a fortune, but worth it. Yeah, it's the life, all right."

"Yeah, how much did she charge you for

those ten minutes?" Tony laughed at his own joke, and Rolo joined in.

The skinny guy guffawed and slapped his leg. Rolo quit laughing. So did his flunky.

"The old man wants to see you." Rolo Polo planted his cigar back between his teeth and gave Tony a challenging look. "Hinson'll be there, too."

"Any time in particular?"

"Tonight. Eight o'clock." He added the street address of the Mid-City grocery, talking around his cigar.

Tony nodded. "So you want me to drive my broken-down Plymouth or you gonna send a car for me?" He figured he'd show he was a team player, trusting them completely with his safety. They'd pat him down, of course, whether he drove there himself or traveled in style.

Rolo grinned. "You got a lotta nerve. But I think I'm going to like working with you, Tony-O. Yeah, I'll send a car. Maybe I'll send Pretty-Boy for you." He jerked a thumb at the skinny guy.

Tony gave him a thumbs-up and stepped back from the car window. "Keep visiting me here, Rolo Polo, and my neighbors are gonna start thinking I'm a drug dealer."

"Nah. Not once you're a cop again." Then Rolo Polo winked and laughed, a lot longer and harder than Tony liked. God, he hated these creeps and couldn't wait to take them down. For now, he winked back at the fat guy and said, "Gotta run. I'm cooking spaghetti."

Rolo Polo shook his head. "You oughta get a wife." Then he jerked his head at his flunky.

"Come on, Pretty-Boy, let's leave Tony to his supper."

Tony turned and walked slowly up his sidewalk. The orange cat had followed him outside and sat on the porch, its head tilted to one side, giving every appearance of being deep in thought.

He didn't know what cats thought about, but he knew what was uppermost on his mind.

Going undercover into this organization meant he'd have to wait a hell of a long time before he could see Penelope again. Even if Hinson hadn't been pursuing her, he'd have had to be careful not to expose any woman he cared about to the dangers of retribution should something go wrong with the undercover sting operation.

But with Hinson planning to wed Penelope, God only knew what would have to happen before he could claim the time with her he knew he had to have. If she'd have him, after the way he'd pushed her away.

The cat meowed softly and he leaned to scratch her on the head. "Well, in the meantime, I've got you, right, Penny?"

She rubbed against his leg and followed him back inside.

Just thinking about how he couldn't see Penelope made him want to hear her voice. Pausing in his living room, he grabbed his portable phone, then sprinted for the kitchen as he suddenly remembered his pasta.

Foamy water spewed over the edges, sizzling onto the stove. Tony flicked off the burner, snatched two pot holders, and dumped the pot in the sink. Rolo Polo had ruined both Tony's appetite and his dinner.

But not his appetite for Penelope. He punched in the number for her office, picturing her behind a big desk, head bent over books and papers, worrying her lip slightly as she wrote some brilliant legal argument. Overlaying that picture came the image of her in bed with him yesterday, open and loving and completely trusting him with her body and her emotions.

When the receptionist answered, he asked for Penelope and gave his last name when asked, all the while picturing Penelope smiling when she heard his voice.

But the next voice on the line wasn't Penelope's.

"I'm sorry, Ms. Fields isn't in. May I help you?" The woman sounded helpful enough, but Tony wanted Penelope. He'd never thought that she might be unavailable, or worse, might not take his call.

"It's important I speak with her." He put on his most businesslike voice. "This is *Dr*. Olano."

"Oh, well, Doctor, why didn't you say so?" The woman stressed the title in an impertinent way Tony had to admire. "But I'm afraid it doesn't matter whether it's a matter of life and death or merely a hangnail, you can't speak to her because she's not here."

"What do you mean, she's not there?" Tony glanced at his clock; it was still ten minutes shy of five o'clock quitting time.

"Is this really her doctor?" Suspicion sounded in the woman's voice.

"No, it's her lover." He couldn't help himself, the words just rolled off his tongue.

The cat had padded into the room and sat watching him.

"The one who sent the roses?" Some inflection in her voice clued him in. Roses sounded like Hinson; he smiled grimly, hoping Penelope had tossed them into the trash.

"Do I sound like a guy who sends roses?"

"No, you don't." She caught her breath, then said, "Are you Mr. Can't Do Dinner?"

"Guilty. So now may I talk to her?"

"When is the last time you saw Ms. Fields?"

Tony gripped the phone. "Are you telling me she didn't come in today?"

"Not here, not at home."

Tony's knuckles went white. "I'll find her," he said.

"When you do, please tell her to call Jewel right away, no matter what time it is."

"Sure, and if you hear from her, you tell her Tony's looking for her."

"Tony Olano?" He heard the recognition in her voice.

"Yeah."

"Don't break her heart or you'll have me to answer to," the woman said, then hung up.

Tony stood staring at the telephone, wondering whether Hinson had kidnapped her. The snake hated to be thwarted, but surely he couldn't think to get away with forcing her to marry him.

He tossed the phone onto the kitchen table, made sure the burners on the stove were off, dashed for the front door, and slammed it behind him.

He heard the cat meowing loudly, obviously protesting its imprisonment on the other side of the door, but he didn't turn back to let her outside. He had to be ready to meet Pretty-Boy by at least seven-thirty; in the meantime, he was going straight to Penelope's apartment. If there was one sign that Hinson had played his hand, he was going straight to the top.

Even if it blew the entire investigation.

Penelope didn't waste her breath crying for long. She'd been a cat long enough now to have learned that whatever humans were going to do, they were going to do.

Funny, though, she'd probably known that before becoming a cat; maybe it only seemed different because as a person, one had more options for responses.

She sprang onto the sofa under the living room window that overlooked the front of the house. Tail twitching, she considered the conversation she'd overheard between Tony and the unknown person in the Lincoln.

Something was rotten in Riverbend, Penelope told herself, sniffing the air. She mulled over what Jewel had told her about Hinson and his bad-guy associates. Had Tony fallen in with them? He'd raced off the other evening saying duty called.

Hmmm. Penelope licked one paw, wiping it meditatively over her face. Jewel had warned her off Tony, but not because he walked the wrong side of the law. Her assistant never hesitated to speak her mind; surely she would have lumped him in with Hinson, had that been the case.

Another idea occurred to her, one she liked much, much better, and she quit cleaning abruptly. She slowed the swishing of her tail and considered the possibility that Tony wasn't an ex-cop, but an officer in good standing, assigned to a sting operation against Hinson and his cronies.

Forgetting that she'd ever been taken in by the smooth-talking attorney, Penelope practically started to purr, so pleased was she by her conclusion.

Of course, she had no confirmation, but her solution was one of the best fantasies she'd ever concocted. Until proven otherwise, she decided to embrace it.

The telephone rang and Penelope leaped off the sofa, chasing the sound. Out the room, down the hall, into the kitchen at the back of the house she sprinted. She made it to the kitchen, the phone still ringing, then froze in her tracks.

Silly cat, she said, you can't answer the phone.

But she could listen to any answering machine. The phone in the kitchen was a portable one; she turned tail and raced into the bedroom.

There, next to the bed, sat another phone and an answering machine. She was just in time to hear Mrs. Merlin's voice come on.

"Penelope, my dear friend, I am so sorry about landing you smack in the middle of this particular pickle! I'm okay now, but there's been a teeny-weeny—"

A man's voice came on, one that sounded familiar. "This is Mr. Gotho, Penelope. We think you're with Tony, but we can't be sure, and unfortunately—" a dry cough sounded, "we're unable to leave where we are at the moment."

"And you thought *I* was long-winded!"

Penelope smiled a kitty smile as Mrs. Merlin obviously took the phone back. "Just stay where you are no matter what happens. We're setting up the spell of retroactivity and you'll soon be back in your own body."

"What do you mean, *we*?" Mr. Gotho said in the background.

The end-of-tape beep sounded on the answering machine, cutting them off.

At least Mrs. Merlin was trying to come to her rescue. Thankful to put that worry at rest, Penelope looked around Tony's bedroom. Despite the proverbial curiosity of a cat, she hadn't yet padded into this room to explore.

She liked what she saw.

The bed was a four-poster, covered in an old-fashioned Bates George Washington spread. On one bedside table sat the answering machine, phone, remote control, and a large framed photograph of a group of thirty or so people, all of whom looked a lot like Tony.

Penelope walked up to the photograph, studying the smiling faces. How wonderful to have such a large family. She rubbed her chin against the edge of the frame, imprinting it with her scent, asking to be invited in.

The table on the other side of the bed held an array of candles. Penelope's eyes widened when she saw them. Mrs. Merlin always said there were no coincidences in candle magick.

Tony didn't seem like the kind of guy to go for the romanticism of candles. But then, she reminded herself, she hadn't suspected he made his own marinara sauce from scratch, either.

She walked among the candles, sniffing each one, deciding she preferred the squat, nectarine-scented one that seemed to chase away any worries and create what was awfully close to a feeling of euphoria.

When she got back to being a human, she was definitely going candle shopping.

She'd just jumped onto the bed, intending to sniff Tony's pillow, when the phone rang again.

This time she was near enough to hear the greeting, which consisted of, "Hi, this is Tony. Leave a message." There was nothing special about the words, except that they were spoken by Tony.

She began kneading her front paws on the bedspread while she waited for the caller to speak.

"Tony, Roy. Called to tell you there are twelve men on the field and all plays are off."

Click.

The machine whirred as it reset.

Penelope stopped purring and scratched her ear. That sure sounded like a warning. And there was nothing she could do!

Oh, Mrs. Merlin, hurry up!

Chapter 24

It was all Mrs. Merlin could do to keep her tongue still and her lips clamped shut as Mr. Gotho pulled one item at a time from his duffel bag.

After they'd been locked in the policeman's office, it hadn't taken the two of them long to agree they needed to act quickly. Mr. Gotho had located a phone book; Mrs. Merlin called the first listing under Olano and chatted up the woman who answered the phone, thus obtaining Tony's home number.

Mrs. Merlin had insisted on leaving a message at Penelope's office and at her apartment, too, just in case she was wrong about what had gone wrong with the spell and Penelope strolled in very much in human, not feline, form.

If only they'd thought of calling the Olanos sooner, Mrs. Merlin fretted. All her sensors told her danger hovered on the horizon. And if something happened to Penelope and Mr. M— why, she'd be so shattered she'd probably not be able to practice candle magick ever again!

And that was unthinkable.

"While I'm preparing myself," Mr. Gotho

said, "will you please go sit or stand with your back to the door? If someone comes, tell them I'm deep in prayer, facing Mecca, and I'm not to be disturbed."

"I didn't know you were a Moslem," Mrs. Merlin said, following his instructions, dragging the heavy desk chair along with her.

"I'm not," Mr. Gotho said dryly, "just trying to help you out with an excuse."

"Oh, well"—Mrs. Merlin brightened—"I never need much help in that category."

"And I don't need any assistance with this most difficult spell." His tone warned her that what he really meant was he didn't need her interfering.

Mrs. Merlin closed her eyes, deciding the best thing to do was visit her place of peace. She'd at least help put the room in harmony for the spell of retroactivity.

About thirty seconds later, she peeked from under her right eyelid. Mr. Gotho stood in front of the desk, gazing at a spot he had cleared. So far he had only the mirror and sand arranged.

Just knowing she was about to interfere, Mrs. Merlin squeezed her eyes shut tight and prepared to wait, for a longer time than she could ever remember waiting.

Tony barreled up his sidewalk, cursing himself and every fool he'd ever known as he played back in his mind his visit to Penelope's apartment.

The guy he had tailing Penelope swore up and down she hadn't left the building all day. Even threatened with the loss of his job, his manhood, and his precious four-wheel drive, the man stuck to his story.

Getting inside her building had been child's play. The lock on her apartment door had given him a much harder time, he was happy to say. If he had trouble, so would anyone else.

He'd made it inside, though, to find absolutely no sign of Penelope, but also no signs of an intruder before him or a hasty departure.

An odd assortment of bric-a-brac and two candles sat atop sand and glass on her dining table, which suggested to Tony that he hadn't been far off the mark in thinking when he'd seen the odd doll under her bed that Penelope dabbled in the otherworldly arts.

Still, a few things bothered him.

For one, the stereo had been left on. The compact disc in the unit was some sort of relaxation music, which went along with the candles, he assumed.

When he looked more closely at the table, he saw scattered ashes. Shaking his head, unable to figure it out, Tony moved into the bedroom.

A large orange cat, exactly like the one now occupying his house, sat on the bed.

Unmoving, not even blinking.

Tony approached it, then stopped abruptly. Jeez! Penelope had mentioned her cat dying, but having it stuffed and used as a pillow was too far out for his taste. Tony gave the bed wide berth and headed for the bathroom.

Something about the cat niggled at the back of his mind, but he couldn't quite place what bothered him about the plump, stuffed feline. Mrs. Mer, Penelope had called her cat.

No signs of makeup, hair spray, or electric curlers showed in the bathroom. Amazingly neat, Tony observed, appreciative of the fact. His sisters had been bathroom hogs and his ex-wife, as practical as she'd been in most things, used to barricade herself in their only bathroom for an hour at a time, only to appear looking exactly as she had upon entering.

Back in her bedroom, Tony walked to the doorway leading to the front hall, then turned, viewing the room with a fresh eye, the eye of a man in love with the occupant.

At the sight of her worn slippers peeking out from under the bed, he smiled. She'd had them on the first day he'd come to her apartment, an endearing contrast to her proper slacks and blouse.

A bottle of Opium perfume sat on the dresser next to a pair of silver hairbrushes. He noted the perfume, then tiptoed over to the brushes. Lifting one, he rolled the rich brown hairs that clung to the bristles between his fingers. He smiled and returned the brush to the tray. One day soon, he promised himself, he'd brush her hair.

Long, soothing strokes, interspersed with kisses.

"Stop, Olano, you're getting worked up," he said aloud, and took one more look around, noting that while most of her bedroom was as orderly as a barracks room, one exception stood out.

All three shelves, plus the surface of the table next to Penelope's bed, were piled with books. He moved over and checked a few titles. Several cookbooks, a biography of Sandra Day O'Connor, three books on the latest tax law changes, and, stuffed behind these, a paperback romance with a half-naked couple on the cover.

Tony grinned.

He bet he knew which one she read first when she crawled under the covers. "Oh, Raoul," he said aloud, promising himself that as soon as he could, he'd make sure she'd forget all about that imaginary clod.

Looking again at the stacks of books, Tony thought maybe he'd take up reading. Thinking of the two of them curled up together in bed, books in hand, he could see for the first time in his life that reading truly could be a pleasurable pastime.

Not, he amended, that they'd read for long. The phone rang, interrupting the image forming in his mind.

Penelope's proper voice sounded, asking callers to leave a message.

Starchy even on the answering machine. Tony smiled at the sound of her voice, then tensed, waiting to see who was calling.

"Penelope, it's Mrs. Merlin, and in case you're there, I wanted to let you know we're working on setting things right. I don't think it will be long now. If only Mr. Gotho would hurry a bit!"

The phone slammed down.

Tony furrowed his brows. Who in the hell was that?

Something strange was going on, Tony thought as he made his way out of the apartment, then raced back to his place. He'd spent longer than he should have interrogating his man outside the building, then mooning over Penelope's personal effects.

He jerked his car to a halt in front of his house, jumped out, and was walking up the sidewalk when his memory cleared.

He remembered, very clearly, Penelope explaining that Mrs. Mer had been flattened.

If that was the case, what was up with the stuffed cat on her bed—a cat identical to the blue-eyed one who had appeared on his doorstep only hours earlier? The cat wearing a necklace exactly like Penelope's?

His skin prickled and Tony told himself not to be ridiculous. He might have grown up accepting a certain amount of mysticism that attached itself to a city like New Orleans, a city as wed to the traditions of the Caribbean and the African as it was to the order-driven Americans who arrived late on the scene, but he'd learned to deal squarely in all that was rational.

He unlocked his front door and strode inside, headed for his bedroom to change for his meeting with Hinson and the old man.

At the doorway to his bedroom, he stopped. Curled up on the pillow he slept on every night was the blue-eyed cat. Curious, Tony tiptoed to the bed. Stroking the cat under the chin, he murmured, "Is there some secret you'd like to tell me, my lucky Penny?"

The cat stretched its front paws out, eyes still closed, and snuggled deeper against the pillow.

Tony moved away, stripping off his basketball shoes, shorts, and T-shirt as he walked out of the room headed for the bathroom.

When he stepped out of the shower a few

minutes later, the cat sat on the floor of the bathroom, staring at him with wide eyes. For some odd reason, Tony grabbed a towel and covered himself. The cat retreated to the doorway, walked a foot or so into the hall, then returned.

The forward and backward dance reminded Tony of the old Lassie reruns where the collie was trying to tell Timmy someone was in trouble.

Wrapping the towel around his waist, he followed the cat back to his bedroom, where she leaped gracefully to the bedside table, nose pointing to the blinking light on the answering machine.

"Prettier *and* smarter than Lassie," Tony said, hitting the play button, then petting the cat while he waited for the messages to play back.

The first message brought out prickles on the back of his neck. He heard once more the voice of the woman on Penelope's machine, accompanied by the deep voice of a man, again speaking of trying to fix things.

The second message, though, was far more critical.

Twelve men on the field was code for trouble—specifically, that someone had sold out to Hinson's side. And if Roy was leaving the message, only Roy could be presumed to still be trustworthy.

Or was he playing both sides against the middle?

Tony mulled over that possibility as he threw on a pair of jeans and a short-sleeved cotton shirt. If the old man expected him to wear a suit for this meeting, he should have requested black tie, Tony thought, wondering whether they'd expect him to be packing his gun or be trusting enough to leave it at home.

What the hell. Better to be perceived as tough, he thought, and poked it in the waistband of his pants before shrugging into the one lightweight sports jacket he owned.

The cat had settled back onto the bed, where it kept watch on him. He thought if the animal's eyes grew any bigger they would fall out of its head. Funny, but the cat reminded him of Penelope the other night when they'd been at Chris's camp. She'd looked at him with the same wide-eyed wonder when he'd eagerly cast off his shorts.

Only to have to retrieve them a few minutes later.

Don't think about Penelope now, he told himself. Do your job.

Trying to assure himself that, based on the phone messages he'd heard, she had other friends looking for her, Tony headed toward the front of the house.

The phone rang.

"Nuts," he said. Where had he left the portable? He remembered the mess in the kitchen and traced his earlier path to the back of the house. The machine came on; the caller hung up.

With a shrug, Tony collected the phone anyway. He usually left it near the front of his house, in case he got a call while porch sitting, something he liked to do after the temperature finally cooled enough and the early evening mosquitoes gave up their search for fresh blood.

He'd made it almost to the front room when

the phone rang again. The cat, following him, arched her back at the sound, then continued on.

At the same time, a knock sounded at the door.

He pressed the talk button on the phone, glanced outside, identified Pretty-Boy as he expected, then said, "Olano," into the phone at the same time he opened the door, stepping slightly to the side, a habit hard to ignore after his years on the force.

"Don't go—" said the voice on the phone.

The cat hissed and leaped straight at Pretty-Boy's face.

A blast of gunfire slammed into the room.

Tony yanked the gun from the waistband of his pants and fired point-blank at Hinson's underling. At the same moment, the cat dashed between his legs and Tony tripped and crashed to the floor, blood seeping from his left arm.

The last thing he saw before he passed out was the orange cat standing over him, licking him on the face. Then, as pain overtook him, he imagined he saw not the cat, but Penelope leaning over him, kissing him, and saying in the fiercest voice he'd ever heard, "Don't you dare die, Tony Olano, or I'll be mad at you forever."

Alistair had used one of his most powerful candles for the spell of retroactivity.

The spell was never performed except in the most extreme circumstances, such as undoing spells gone awry or to counter evil too strong to be handled through more routine channels.

The flame of the purple, black, and white candle continued to burn. He'd finished the secret ritual, barely whispering the words. He certainly didn't want Mrs. Merlin imitating this spell and getting it wrong!

Bent slightly toward the altar, Alistair continued to gaze into the flame, watching for any indication of success or hint of failure.

Suddenly the healthy blue-white center sputtered and, to his dismay, glowed blood-red.

Beads of sweat broke out on his forehead.

From the doorway, Mrs. Merlin finally found her tongue. "Something's wrong, isn't it? I can just feel it—"

He nodded. Since he figured she'd stayed silent far longer than she ever had in her life, he didn't object to her joining in.

The candle began to smoke.

Alistair tugged on his ponytail and considered the situation.

Mrs. Merlin tugged at his elbow. Her carroty hair stood at all angles, as if she'd been running her hands through it over and over. Concern showed in her eyes and Mr. Gotho felt genuine sorrow for her as she worried over her friends stuck in altered bodies.

Thanks to her messing with magick beyond her power, he reminded himself, suddenly not so sympathetic.

The candle continued to smoke.

A siren sounded.

Both Alistair and Mrs. Merlin jumped.

The noise came from over their heads.

Glancing up, he spotted the smoke detector ringing lustily.

The door burst open and the potbellied officer stuck his head in. "Are you two still in here?"

Then he must have spotted the candle because he said, "And causing more trouble, are you? I've a good mind to arrest the both of you. Where's Steve?"

Mrs. Merlin started to answer, from the looks of her about to launch into a tirade, so Alistair said, "Steve locked us in. No one came to our rescue, so we used the items we had at our disposal to get someone's attention."

The officer gave him a sour glance and popped an antacid tablet into his mouth. "Ever heard of the intercom?"

"Oh, silly me," Alistair said, leaning over and snuffing out the flame, offering, as he did so, a quick prayer to the stars for the safe return of Penelope and Mr. M.

"Well, if Steve locked you in here, he must have had a reason, so I guess you have to stay here or in a cell." He crossed his arms over his gut. "Which one'll it be?"

"I think," Alistair said, beginning to pack his materials back into the duffel bag, careful not to spill any wax, "you ought to be asking yourself why a fellow policeman was so foolish as to detain two citizens without probable cause or even the courtesy of an explanation."

The officer scratched his head, turned, and headed down the hall. No doubt in search of someone to tell him what to do.

"After you, Mrs. Merlin," Alistair said, holding open the door.

The emergency medical techs had Tony on a stretcher, preparing to strap him in for a ride to the hospital when he came to.

He jerked upright, wincing at the pain in his arm and the back of his head.

"Easy there," the EMT, a pretty redhead, said.

"Forget easy," Tony muttered. He looked around, piecing together what had happened. Officers swarmed his living room; he heard more people outside, including the voice of his next door neighbor. Mrs. Sanderson rattled on about how she'd called 9-1-1 and how she'd suspected something bad was going down when she'd seen that fancy car coming around the neighborhood.

Fancy cars, Mrs. Sanderson explained, meant only one thing—drug dealers.

And drugs meant violence.

Tony pretty much agreed with Mrs. Sanderson's logic. And he figured from the way the officers milling around his house avoided his gaze they assumed he'd gone all the way over to the other side.

Then Roy appeared in the doorway.

"Tony!" He rushed to his side. "Shit, man, you don't listen. There I am on the phone trying to warn you and you walk right into a bullet." To the EMT he said, "He's probably not going to want to go with you right away."

"Not exactly your model patient," she said. "But a lucky one. A bullet nicked his arm and he suffered a blow to the back of his head."

"Yeah, I fell," Tony said, embarrassed at his lack of grace under fire. Then he remembered the cat, picturing it going for the assailant's eyes and most probably saving Tony's life. "Hey, anybody seen my cat?"

Mrs. Sanderson stuck her head in the door.

"Your cat died last year, Tony. And if you tell me you're in with those drug dealers, why, I don't think I could stand to believe such a thing of you."

Tony shook his head and smiled at her. "Don't worry. But I do have a cat. It showed up here today. Orange, with blue eyes."

"He must have hit his head harder than he knows, poor boy," Mrs. Sanderson said as a uniformed officer led her away from the door.

Roy waved the EMT away, following her retreat with an appreciative glance. "Yeah, you must have taken quite a conk. I don't think you even noticed the beauty working on you."

Tony shrugged, then he remembered his vision of Penelope leaning over him. She was the only beauty he was interested in. "What went down?" he said to Roy in a low voice.

"Two characters came into the Eighth District station looking for you—"

"What kind of characters?" Tony pressed his hand against his arm, checking the bandage.

"At first I took them for some of the Quarter loonies, but when the woman mentioned you and Hinson in the same breath, clearly something more than met the eye was going on."

"From that, Pretty-Boy decides to take me out?" Tony shook his head.

"Oh, there's more, and it's not pretty at all." Roy made a face of disgust. "Steve sold out."

"What?" Tony shot forward, groaning as he jerked his arm.

"Yep, and if I hadn't overheard him with my own ears, I never would've believed him capable of such a thing."

"Why did he do it?" Tony knew there could be only one answer to that. "Or should I ask what was his price?"

Roy grimaced. "Plenty. Not that he'll get to spend any of it now. I followed him after he questioned this old woman and the guy with her. He called Hinson at the restaurant. That much is on tape. He met him outside, but I was on him like a flea on a dog. Seems he planned to tip Hinson all along, but waited until you were going under with them."

"So why kill me? Why not just feed me bad info and use me?"

"No doubt that's what the old man would have done," Roy said. "But Steve told Hinson that his fiancée was in love with you. The guy went nuts." Roy chuckled. "The best part was, he waited till he got back to the restaurant, argued with the old man, then ordered the hit himself."

"So we've got him on tape?" Tony forgot about the pain in his arm and the throbbing in the back of his head.

"Yep." Roy looked supremely satisfied.

"What happened to Steve?"

"I tackled him, got him handcuffed inside my car, then tried to call you."

"Thanks," Tony said, mulling over what Roy had said. "Hinson's ego finally found him out, didn't it?" One thing the old man had never done was order a hit in anger. His rules might be odd ones, but he'd followed them for years.

Feeling sick, and not from his wound, Tony put his head in his hands for a moment, then said, "So the operation's over before it starts?"

"Oh, but that's not a bad thing, buddy," Roy said, rubbing his hands together. "Your cover's blown, so that puts an end to your vacation, but we might get the old man as an accessory to this one, and to the attack on Squeek, too, plus I have a feeling Hinson will sing to try to save himself."

"Yeah, the pretty ones usually do," Tony said, struggling to his feet. "And some vacation, having my friends and family think I'm nothing but a bum who took a bribe."

Roy chucked him on the shoulder. "You held up okay, Olano, and I think the department should be proud."

"Thanks," Tony said, testing his balance, knowing nothing would keep him from searching for Penelope.

"Where do you think you're going?" The EMT rushed up to him.

"To find the woman I love," he said. "So don't try to stop me."

She grinned and threw him a flirtatious look. "Ah, a romantic. Too bad I didn't arrive on the scene earlier."

"I've got a pain," Roy quipped, eyeing the woman.

"Call a doctor," she said, and started packing up.

"Oh, my, just look at all those police cars," Mrs. Merlin said. "You were right for us to come straight here to check on the outcome of the spell."

Mr. Gotho swung the car to a halt in the middle of the street behind a row of cruisers, all of them with blue and red lights flashing. He nodded, his face grim.

They made their way to the front gate of the address the same helpful relative had given them for Tony Olano, only to be blocked by a patrolman who refused to let them pass.

"But it's a matter of life and death," Mrs. Merlin said, knowing in her bones that it was, even though she sensed the danger had passed over like a thundercloud that scurried by without dumping its burden of moisture.

The patrolman shook his head.

"Oh, that's him," Mrs. Merlin said, spotting the man with bedroom eyes walking toward them on the sidewalk, accompanied by a man in blue jeans and T-shirt. "The one—oh, my, the one with blood on his shirt, that's Tony Olano."

Mr. Gotho nodded. "That explains the blood-red flame," he said, half to himself.

"Oh!" Mrs. Merlin clasped her hand over her mouth. "For a moment there I was glad it was his blood and not Penelope's or my dear cat's. That was selfish, in quite the wrong way."

Mr. Gotho smiled. "I'm sure Olano would have stood in the way of any bullet rather than have one hit Penelope."

"What sense tells you that?"

"Sense? That's just from listening to you talk about the two of them."

Tony had reached the gate.

"Mr. Olano," Mrs. Merlin said, "we need to speak with you."

"I told you to leave," the patrolman said.

"It's okay," Tony said. He glanced at them, an expression almost like recognition on his face. "Mrs. Merlin and Mr. Gotho, I presume?"

Mrs. Merlin clapped her hands together. "No wonder Penelope likes you. You're so smart! Now, where is she? And where's my cat?"

Mr. Gotho stood watching Tony with an assessing look. Mrs. Merlin realized her mentor was probably reading Tony's aura, trying to determine whether any damage had been done to him by the spell. He seemed to find none, because his face relaxed and he nodded pleasantly to Tony, then said to them, "I think we should go to Penelope's home."

"My thoughts exactly," Tony said. "Hold down the fort, Roy, till I get back. Hey, first give me your shirt."

"What?"

"Come on, this one's a bloody mess. I can't go looking for my girl like this. You can grab another one from my house, but we've got to leave now."

The other man nodded, though he grumbled as he unbuttoned his shirt.

Mr. Gotho looked at the bandage swathing Tony's arm. "Why don't I drive?"

Chapter 25

Penelope woke up unsure of where she was. She blinked her eyes. The altar on the table came into focus. Home, on her own sofa. She patted her arms, marveling that she'd fallen asleep in her suit, still wearing those silly high heels.

She kicked them off, straightened her skirt, and yawned. Pushing her disheveled hair from her face, she rose from the couch and stretched, arms high above her head. She felt as if she'd slept around the clock.

And such dreams she'd had!

Then, as her memory flooded back, she stared suspiciously at the candle altar. "Mrs. Merlin," she said aloud, "if you're here, come on out and tell me if what I think happened really happened."

"Meow-ow-ow!"

The demanding, almost grouchy cry sounded from behind Penelope. She jumped and turned. A large orange cat stood staring at her.

"You're not Mrs. Merlin." Feeling more empathetic toward this cat than she'd ever felt toward a feline, Penelope knelt and held out a hand. The cat sniffed the air, then approached with caution.

She stroked him behind his ears, just where she knew it would feel good, then looked at the tag hanging from his purple velvet collar. "Return to Mrs. Merlin," she read, smiling. Next best thing to finding the mishap-making magician; she had a feeling Mrs. Merlin would soon come looking for her cat.

Remembering the shrimp Tony had given her in the dream in which she had been a cat, Penelope crossed to the kitchen in search of a kitty treat. The cat followed at a safe distance.

The intercom buzzer rang as Penelope dumped some albacore tuna onto a saucer. She carried the saucer to the table, then answered the ring.

Several voices sounded at once, but the only one she heard clearly was Tony's. With a cry of delight, she pressed the button to let them in.

She'd had the worst dream that someone had shot Tony. Penelope glanced at the cat, happily licking the tuna. But if she hadn't dreamed transmuting into a cat, then she hadn't dreamed the gunfire, either!

Penelope opened her door and Mrs. Merlin and Mr. Gotho spilled in. But she had eyes only for the man who walked slowly behind them.

He gave her a crooked smile, one side of his mouth curving slightly higher than the other, and gazed at her with fire in his dark eyes.

She stood gazing at him, suddenly shyer than she'd ever been.

"Penelope, what a beautiful sight," Tony said, and opened his arms.

Glancing down at her wrinkled suit and her stocking-covered feet, and fingering her messy hair, she wondered how he could describe her as beautiful, but she didn't quibble.

Instead, she moved into his embrace, as easily as she had when she'd been a cat on four legs, and snuggled against him. Then she realized he wore a bandage around one upper arm. "I didn't dream that gunfire!"

"Mr. M!" Mrs. Merlin advanced on the orange cat, now sitting next to the altar washing its face. "My baby!" She lifted the cat and cradled it in her arms.

Mr. Gotho walked to the table and examined the altar. Shaking his head, he set about dismantling it.

Penelope led Tony to the couch, insisting he sit down, but not letting go of him. "Now, will someone tell me what happened?"

Mrs. Merlin glanced at her, guilt in her eyes. "Oh, I'm afraid I caused another pickle. And when I tried to fix things, somehow they only got worse." Her face brightened. "You might say they went from a sweet pickle to a sour one! But Mr. Gotho came to our rescue." She ruffled her cat's hair. "Didn't he, Mr. M? Even though I think he was fairly well put out with me."

Mr. Gotho piled the pieces from the altar in the duffel bag he'd brought with him. "No problem, Mrs. Merlin," he said. Smiling at Tony and Penelope, he said, "All's well that ends well."

"And was I really a cat?" Penelope knew, even as she asked the question, that she had indeed inhabited that furry orange body.

Tony whispered in her ear, "And what a cat! I loved petting you."

She blushed.

Mr. Gotho lifted his bag. "Mrs. Merlin, I think we can leave these two alone to finish the explanations."

"Oh, yes, I can see they're no longer in need of my help," she said, throwing a wink at Penelope. As she headed for the door, she said, "Remember, my dear, it's all right to be selfish." And to Tony, she said, "Call me when you want that special spell for your friend Squeek."

He nodded and Mr. Gotho shook his head, apparently in despair at ever changing Mrs. Merlin.

And then the door shut behind them.

Tony shifted so he could look directly into Penelope's dark blue eyes. He toyed with the silver pendant around her neck, running his finger over the engraved P.

"Come here, kitten," he said. "Time to make you purr."

Penelope found it almost easier to believe she'd inhabited a cat's body than it was to believe the man with bedroom eyes was saying those words to her, desire lighting his face. When she hesitated, though, he pulled her to him and feathered a kiss over her lips. Then he raised his head. "But first we have to talk."

Penelope, lips parted and eyes slightly unfocused, played with the top button of Tony's shirt. "Talk?" She pouted. "Now?"

He nodded.

"Why is it you're always doing the right thing by me?"

"Because you're so important to me," he said softly. He clasped her hand and stroked her palm. "So, first things first."

She nodded, running the words "so important" over and over again in her mind. They weren't "I love you," but they were certainly significant.

Tony watched her mulling over his words, loving the way she analyzed every word, every gesture. He'd never met a woman like Penelope. Nestled close to him, eyes so alive, face aglow with awakening passion, she smiled up at him and he almost lost his determination to talk first and make love second.

He'd hoped she would say something similar when he'd told her she was important to him, hoped she would somehow reassure him that he wasn't pursuing her in vain. Because if she didn't want him as badly as he wanted her, he'd be suffering a worse punishment than a bullet wound.

"You're looking very serious," she murmured, tracing a finger over his brow.

He cleared his throat. "That's because this time I'm going to tell you the truth about me, not a bunch of made-up stories."

"Like you did in the bookstore?" She trailed her fingertips down his cheek, a feather-light touch that sent hunger for her arcing through his body.

He nodded.

"I bet I know what you're going to tell me," she whispered.

"Yeah?" Her touch was driving him nuts.

Gazing into his eyes, she said, "That you're not an ex-cop."

His surprise must have shown because she

said, "Bingo." She fingered his earlobe, drawing soft circles. "You're too honorable."

He kissed her. "Thank you for your belief in me. I've been part of an undercover operation for more than a year, a scheme blown wide open tonight."

"I knew it!" She jostled his arm, and he grimaced.

"Oh, I've hurt you." Then her eyes gleamed in a way that chased the pain from his body. "Maybe I should kiss it and make you feel all better."

"Getting braver, or just more used to me?" Tony murmured his question, sighing in pleasure as she did indeed apply the lightest of kisses, starting at his neck and circling his shoulder above the bandage.

Penelope lifted her head. "Mrs. Merlin accused me of having no sense of adventure, so I've been working on it ever since she dropped into my life."

"And coming along nicely, too," Tony said, stroking her hair and little by little guiding the path of her kisses from his arm to his chest.

She paused. "Did Mrs. Merlin tell you who and what she is?"

He nodded, not wanting her to stop her kisses. Then he reminded himself he was the one who'd first suggested they talk. Wow, this woman really had his world turned upside down. "I saw you put her in your purse in Pottery DeLite and thought you got your jollies shoplifting."

"Oh!" She paused; she had been blowing breathy kisses between the buttonholes of his, or rather Roy's, shirt. "I'm surprised you didn't arrest me."

"I wanted to"—he grinned and ruffled her hair—"so I could strip-search you." He unfastened the top button of her jacket. "Nice and slow, just the two of us locked in a cell together."

"That would have been very improper and terribly illegal," she said in a prim voice, but her eyes shone naughtily, as if she found the idea exciting. "And I want you to know I'm glad you're a policeman. It fits you and I know you'd never do anything illegal."

"Thank you for that." He kissed her, then undid the second button. "Didn't Raoul ever do anything improper?"

"Raoul?" Her eyes widened. "You're not making fun of me, are you?"

"Never," he said, slipping the third and last button free, revealing the smooth skin and lacy bra.

"As long as we're sharing secrets," Penelope said, "there's something you ought to know about me."

He smoothed a tendril of hair from her cheeks. "And what's that, kitten?"

"Well, I . . . um, suffer from a tendency to fall into fantasy spells."

He grinned. "We can probably use that talent to our advantage."

Coloring slightly, she said, "And I'm not quite as serious as I appear. For instance . . ." she paused and looked almost defiant, "I might not practice law all my life. I've always wanted to become a chef and I'm also writing a cookbook."

Again he kissed her. "The family will love another chef. You'll fit right in."

"Oh, Tony," she hugged him, and he was grateful she avoided his wound. "You make me feel like everything is possible."

"Good. You met my Aunt Tootie; she's nuts for cookbooks."

"Oh, well, the one I'm trying to write is a little different."

Tony cupped one of her breasts and teased her nipple through the fabric of her bra. He'd talked about as long as he could stand right now—not that he wasn't interested, but his body had other thoughts. "How different?"

She started to unbutton his shirt. "It's called *Love Bites*."

"Yum." He nibbled on her neck. "Is there anything else you want to tell me that you think will scare me off?"

"I'm an orphan." She spoke so softly he almost missed her words.

Tony stilled his hand, facing his conscience. He knew who her father was. Should he tell her—burden her with the knowledge that her father walked the wrong side of the law and never intended to claim her? Or should he let sleeping dogs lie? He wished for wisdom he didn't possess.

Perhaps he'd leave the decision to the fates, and he was glad he did when she said, "And that's okay with me, but if I ever marry, I want to have lots and lots of children."

"What do you mean, *if*?" Tony eased her down to his side, and they stretched full-length on the sofa.

She looked at him, uncertainty in her eyes.

"Penelope, my flirting days are over. I want you. I need you." He took a deep breath, risking the biggest rejection of them all. "Some people would say I'm nuts for saying this when I've only just met you, but I love you."

"Oh, Tony," she whispered. "I love you, too. You're my fantasies come to life."

"If there's one thing I plan to show you," he said, pausing to tickle the sensitive lobe of one ear that sent her to trembling and giggling, "it's just how superior reality can be to fantasy."

"Mmm," Penelope murmured, believing that with Tony Olano, such a feat might be possible.

He took her hand and lifted it to his lips. He kissed the back of it, then slowly put one of her fingers, then a second, into his mouth, wrapping his tongue around them and at the same time easing them in and out between his lips. His eyes danced suggestively and the combination left her strangely excited.

When he stopped, she wanted him to do it again. "Wow, that was . . ." she searched for the right word and came up with, "yummy."

He grinned. "Now, did Raoul ever do that?"

Her eyes widened. She shook her head slowly.

By the way he smiled down at her while he tried to work his shirt off, Penelope knew he planned to show her even more delight. She helped him with the shirt, then placed her hand on his belt buckle, knowing she probably looked as shy as she felt.

"Penelope, we don't have to do anything you don't want to," he said softly. "We'll stop right now if you say so."

"Are you nuts? I didn't back off yesterday and there's no way you're stopping me today." She smiled. "Along with challenging my sense of adventure, Mrs. Merlin taught me it's okay to be selfish."

She tugged off his shoes and freed him from his jeans. Pulling her down by his side, he said, "I think I'm liking Mrs. Merlin more every minute." He slipped her bra off, then inched his way down the couch, trailing kisses on her body as he went. He paused as his lips reached her satin panties.

Penelope caught her breath. He kissed the inside of one thigh, then the other, feathery kisses that teased and warmed and made her insides feel like melted butter. She sighed and murmured in a most satisfied voice, "Lollipops and lilacs."

Then he eased her panties from her legs, his eyes dark and more intense than she'd ever seen them. She lay with her head back on her couch cushions, gazing at him.

Then, with a rather wicked grin on his lips, he lowered his head, his tongue exploring her much more intimately than the innocent kisses he'd trailed across her thighs.

She gasped, then moaned in a breathy way she hardly recognized as her own voice.

"Ah," Tony said, "I guess Raoul never did this."

"Oh, no," she murmured, giving herself up to the most exquisite sensations rocking her body. Between gasps of pleasure, she managed to say,

"I think Mr. Gotho was right when he said, 'All's well that ends well.' "

Tony lifted his head slightly and gazed up at her with his bedroom eyes. "Penelope, my kitten, we've only just begun."

Dear Reader,

One of the reasons I love to read romances is that they reaffirm by belief that wishes really can come true. And in next month's Avon Romantic Treasure WHEN DREAMS COME TRUE by Cathy Maxwell, a lonely English lord gets his wish for a bride, when a beautiful, mysterious maiden enters his life. Cathy's love stories are a delight, and this one is especially charming. Don't miss it!

I can't resist a strong hero—he might be infuriating, but you always know he's a man who'll love and protect you. In Alina Adams' contemporary romance, ANNIE'S WILD RIDE, you'll meet Paul, an unforgettable, exasperating man whose love for Annie is so strong he'll do anything for her— even risk his own life.

Of course, I want heroines who know their own mind...just like Aleene in Malia Martin's HER NORMAN CONQUEROR. Aleene must marry to save her beloved castle, but she's reluctant to wed at all...until she meets a virile stranger she is powerless to resist.

And there's nothing more satisfying than a man and woman destined to be together, just like Raimond LeVeq and Sable Fontaine in Beverly Jenkins' THROUGH THE STORM. Raimond believes that Sable has betrayed him, but then fate reunites this pair in an unforgettable romance.

Enjoy!

Lucia Macro

Lucia Macro
Senior Editor

AEL 0798